To Terri —
Hope you enjoy
Hugs,
Kathryn
LeVeque

SERPENT

A Medieval Romance

Sequel to THE WOLFE

By Kathryn Le Veque

Printed by Kathryn Le Veque Novels in the United States of America

Text copyright 2014 by Kathryn Le Veque
Cover copyright 2014 by Kathryn Le Veque
Illustration copyright 2014 by Ellen Tribble

Library of Congress Control Number 2014-010
ISBN 1497336643

Other Novels by Kathryn Le Veque

Medieval Romance:

The Wolfe * Serpent
*
The White Lord of Wellesbourne* The Dark One: Dark Knight
*
While Angels Slept* Rise of the Defender* Spectre of the Sword* Unending Love* Archangel* Lord of the Shadows
*
Great Protector* To the Lady Born
*
The Falls of Erith* Lord of War: Black Angel
*
The Darkland* Black Sword
*
Unrelated characters or family groups:
The Whispering Night * The Dark Lord* The Gorgon* The Warrior Poet* Guardian of Darkness (related to The Fallen One)* Tender is the Knight* The Legend* Lespada* Lord of Light

The Dragonblade Trilogy:
Dragonblade* Island of Glass* The Savage Curtain
-also-
The Fallen One (related)* Fragments of Grace (related prequel)
*
Novella, Time Travel Romance:
Echoes of Ancient Dreams
*
Time Travel Romance:
The Crusader*Kingdom Come

Contemporary Romance:

Kathlyn Trent/Marcus Burton Series:
Valley of the Shadow* The Eden Factor* Canyon of the Sphinx

The American Heroes Series:
Resurrection* Fires of Autumn* Evenshade* Sea of Dreams* Purgatory

Other Contemporary Romance:
Lady of Heaven* Darkling, I Listen

<u>Note:</u> All Kathryn's novels are designed to be read as stand-alones, although many have cross-over characters or cross-over family groups. Novels that are grouped together have related characters or family groups. Series are clearly marked. All series contain the same characters or family groups except the American Heroes Series, which is an anthology with unrelated characters. There is NO particular chronological order for any of the novels because they can all be read as stand-alones, even the series.

Contents

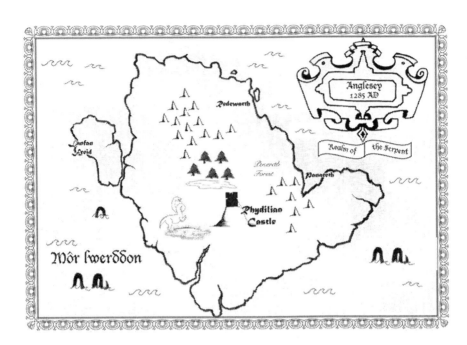

Anglesey, 1293 A.D.

Family Trees for the de Wolfe, Hage, and de Norville Families
The next generation Wolfe Pack

<u>**William and Jordan Scott de Wolfe**</u>

Scott b.1241 (married to Lady Athena de Norville, has issue*)

Troy b.1241 (married to Lady Helene de Norville, has issue)

Patrick b.1243 (married to Lady Brighton de Favereux, has issue)

James b.1245 – Killed in Wales June 1282 (married to Lady Rose Hage, has issue)

Katheryn b.1245 (James' twin) Married Sir Alec Hage, has issue

Evelyn b.1248 (married Sir Hector de Norville, has issue)

Baby de Wolfe b. 1250, died same day. Christened Madeleine.

Edward b.1252 (married to Lady Cassiopeia de Norville, has issue)

Thomas b.1255

Penelope b. 1263 (married Bhrodi de Shera, hereditary King of Anglesey and Earl of Coventry, has issue)

<u>**Kieran and Jemma Scott Hage**</u>

Mary Alys b. circa 1238 (adopted) married, with issue

Baby Hage, b. 1241, died same day. Christened Bridget.

Alec b.1243 (married to Lady Katheryn de Wolfe, has issue)

Christian b. 1248 (died Holy Land 1269 A.D.) no issue

Moira b. 1251 (married to Sir Apollo de Norville, has issue)

Kevin b.1255

Rose b.1258 (widow of Sir James de Wolfe, has issue)

Nathaniel b.1260

<u>**Paris and Caladora Scott de Norville**</u>

Hector b.1245 (married to Lady Evelyn de Wolfe, has issue)

Apollo b. 1248 (married to Lady Moira Hage, has issue)

Helene b.1250 (married to Sir Troy de Wolfe, has issue)

Athena b.1253 (married to Sir Scott de Wolfe, has issue)

Adonis b.1255

Cassiopeia b.1257 (married to Sir Edward de Wolfe, has issue)

Collective grandchildren for the de Wolfe/Hage/de Norville Clan: 19 and counting

Issue means children

PROLOGUE

Present day, May
Pendraeth Forest, Anglesey, Wales
Archaeological Dig for the University of California at San Marcos in
conjunction with the University of Aberystwyth

The forest was thick with foliage, moist in the mid-summer heat. Even this far north, the weather could grow very warm and the humidity could get nasty.

The Pendraeth Forest was one of the dwindling sections of heavily forested land in the United Kingdom. Most of the great forests were gone due to a myriad of reasons; pollution, human encroachment, and other factors had shrunk even the greatest of forests. The most legendary forest of all, Sherwood, was nothing more than a grove of trees these days. Certainly it was no place for great outlaws to hide out in. Times had changed, indeed.

On this bright day in mid-August, a group of students from the University of California at San Marcos was working on a dig deep in the forest near Llyn Llwydiarth, or Lake Llwydiarth. There used to be a great marsh surrounding it but it had been drained around the turn of the last century to produce rich farmlands. However, a section of it closer to the lake had remained undisturbed until last spring when the farmer who owned the land drained it off to expand his grass crop for hay. However, when the water was drained off and the man began to prepare the section, he'd come across something that had put an immediate stop to his agricultural plans. He'd discovered human bones.

The farmer had called the police who had shown up and determined that the bones were very old; in fact, they suspected they were Dark Age burials and called upon the University of Aberystwyth because they had an ancient studies department. The university had sent people to check it out and after some carbon dating samples, determined that it was, in fact, a Medieval burial site. Archaeologists were called in and the farmer lost a good portion of his agricultural site to the scholars.

Dr. Bud Becker, the senior field archaeologist in Medieval Studies at the University of California at San Marcos had been on-site since June, when he had been called in by a colleague at Aberystwyth. Everyone in the field of archaeology knew Dr. Becker's reputation, as the foremost expert in Medieval field archaeology, so the University of Aberystwyth was very glad to have him.

Dr. Becker had brought in twenty-one archaeology students for a summer session along with him so they had plenty of help as they excavated the farmer's field. But more and more as of late, Dr. Becker was convinced this wasn't a burial. Bodies were in pieces, missing heads, missing limbs, and generally scattered all over about a quarter of a mile radius. It didn't look like any battle he'd ever seen; it looked like a massacre. He had been genuinely baffled until they had come across bones that didn't match anything he'd ever seen before. Buried deep in the muck of the field, in the low-acidic soil, had been pieces of a skeleton that wasn't man or animal. He didn't know what it was, which is why Aberystwyth had brought in a paleontologist, also from the University of California at San Marcos. They had no idea what they had, and the mystery deepened.

The paleontologist had created her own sub-dig within Dr. Becker's dig. Dr. Cynthia Paz was a pretty woman with deep blue eyes, small and quick, and very diligent about her work. There were times during the dig when they had to literally pull her out of her hole so they could shut down for the night. The woman put in eighteen hour days and had for about three weeks, ever since they had called her in. The very first thing she had done upon her first inspection of the bones was send samples to a lab in London for analysis. Whatever she was dealing with, it wasn't petrified as a dinosaur skeleton would have been, and it didn't look like anything from the early age of man. The low acidic soil had preserved the bones so much that they were nearly pliable. Brand-new as far as old skeletons went. She was as confused as anyone else.

10

So, she continued her dig while Becker worked around her. There was quite a killing field surrounding whatever the massive skeleton was, and the age of the human bones had already come back from the lab circa 1200 A.D. to 1338 A.D. was the closest the carbon dating could come up with, which clearly made them Medieval. Therefore, Becker and his crew continued to excavate the human remains and, as of this morning, had uncovered five hundred and eleven pieces of bodies. There wasn't one complete corpse in the entire group. Becker, having just finished exposing a skull that had been smashed to bits, took a brief break and headed over to the tent where they had water and other consumables. He was in the process of downing a bottle of Gatorade when Dr. Paz came up behind him.

"Hey, Bud," she said, pulling off her baseball cap and wiping the sweat off her forehead. "Anything exciting today?"

Becker swallowed the last gulp of orange sports drink. "More crushed bones," he said. "I swear, I have never seen anything like this in all my years of archaeology. It's almost like this was a dumping ground for dismembered bodies."

"Sounds like quite a mess."

"You'd better believe it," Becker concurred. "And it doesn't look like ritualistic killing, either. It's too disorganized, which makes me go back to the body dumping grounds theory. Have you ever heard of such a thing?"

Dr. Paz shook her head but the entire time she was eyeing a long table that had a variety of excavated human bones on it. Students were cleaning and cataloging them. She seemed rather ill at ease, edgy even, but Becker hadn't noticed. He was too busy contemplating the dismembered body burial ground.

"No," Dr. Paz said, clearing her throat softly. "But, then again, this kind of thing isn't my area of expertise. In fact, I have to tell you that... uh, can we go somewhere private and talk?"

Becker nodded, following her out of the tent and out into the trees. When Dr. Paz thought they were isolated enough, she dug into her pocket and produced a piece of paper.

"I received this email this morning from the lab in London," she said quietly. "You know that I sent some bone samples from that skeleton you found down there. I also sent them samples of the dirt surrounding the bones just in case anything organic remained. God, I don't even know where to begin with this."

Bud was all ears; he could see that she was acting nervously. It concerned him. "Why?" he asked. "What did the lab say?"

Dr. Paz looked at the paper in her hand. Then, she sighed heavily. "The results from the carbon dating test puts the skeleton between 1248 A.D. to 1300 A.D.," she said. "They're clearly Medieval. The lab also found DNA in the soil surrounding the bones from organic decomposition, but more than that, they were able to extract DNA from the bones themselves. This is what they came back with as to the origins of the skeleton."

She handed the paper over to Bud, who read it closely. When he came to the bottom portion of the results where the lab determined the DNA makeup, his eyes widened.

"What in the hell?" he breathed, reading the results over again. "A... a...?"

"Sauropod," Dr. Paz said quietly. "They've classified it as a Sauropod."

Becker looked at her, confusion rampant in his expression. "What does that mean?"

Dr. Paz sighed heavily. "It means that they've classified it as a dinosaur, but that doesn't make any sense since the bones themselves have been carbon dated to the High Middle Ages." She shook her head, obviously baffled. "What the lab is basically telling us is that there was a dinosaur living as late as the Medieval period. I've never seen anything like this in my entire life."

Becker's jaw was hanging open. "A dinosaur?" he repeated. "In Medieval Wales?"

Dr. Paz lifted her shoulders. "Stranger things have happened," she said. "Maybe it was a mutated creature that had somehow survived into modern times. You know, legends like dragons and sea serpents have existed for thousands of years and who's to say there isn't any real basis for that? It's quite possible a lone branch of the sauropod family somehow survived into the High Middle Ages but eventually died off. Maybe nature decided it had no place in the modern world; who knows? There are always the legends like the Loch Ness Monster and other lake beasts. You hear that kind of thing all the time."

Becker wasn't convinced; he was stricken with the information in his hand and lifted the paper up as if to emphasize his point. "The Loch Ness Monster is bullshit and everyone knows it," he said. "But right here – in this paper- an independent lab is telling us that we've got some kind of... Medieval *dinosaur* right here in Wales!"

Dr. Paz nodded her head in resignation. "I know," she said. "My main goal now is to uncover that entire skeleton and reconstruct it. I really want to see what that thing looks like."

Becker lowered the paper in his hand, struggling to collect his wits. He was genuinely blown away by the information. "Me, too," he agreed, taking a deep breath as he labored for calm. His gaze moved to the tent where the students were diligently working. "But this really puts an entirely new spin to evolution if this information is accurate."

Dr. Paz was thoughtful, trying to be clinical about such outlandish news. "There are lots of descendants of dinosaurs that have lived into modern times, so this isn't completely crazy," she said. "Alligators, for instance. They have dinosaur ancestors. So do birds. Remember the movie 'Jurassic Park'? There are lots of creatures that survived the Jurassic and Triassic periods, evolving into creatures we know today."

Becker knew that and he, too, was trying to be clinical about the information. He was a scientist, after all, so in his mind there had to be a logical explanation. "So something like this really isn't out of the realm of possibility?"

Dr. Paz nodded seriously. "It's entirely possible, as strange as it sounds."

Becker pondered that for a moment. "I've got some students researching local legends simply because I'm trying to get to the bottom of all of these bodies," he said. "I'll see if they can find something about monsters or beasts roaming around out here. There has got to be some kind of local legend. A creature like this wouldn't have gone unseen."

"My thoughts exactly," Dr. Paz said. "You'll let me know if they find anything?"

"Of course," Becker said as he handed the paper back to her. "We keep this between us for now, okay? I don't want this news getting out, at least not yet. We're going to have a hell of a time defending this."

Dr. Paz agreed. "I know," she said, her gaze moving to the tent where Becker's students were working. "But I think I have a theory about your human remains."

Becker looked at her curiously. "What's that?"

Dr. Paz reached into her pocked and pulled out a long, slender piece of bone. Upon closer inspection, Becker could see that it was a fang or

13

sharp tooth. Silently, Dr. Paz motioned for Becker to follow her back over to the tent where she went to one of the tables and lifted up a femur bone. She looked at Becker.

"Do you remember telling me that it looked as if these bodies had been hacked apart or dismembered by knives or chisels because of the hack marks in the bone?" she asked.

Becker nodded. "Yes," he said, looking at the bones spread over the table. "All of the bones have those marks."

Dr. Paz shook her head. "Watch this," she said. Then she took the long tooth and held it up to one of the hack marks in the femur bone. It fit the shape perfectly. When Becker saw that, his eyes threatened to burst from his skull.

"No...," he gasped.

Dr. Paz nodded as she looked at the tooth, fitting into the hack mark like the last piece of a perfect puzzle.

"Yes," she whispered in return. "This is a tooth from that skeleton. These are teeth marks in the bone, not hack marks. Your bodies weren't in a big battle, Bud. They were eaten by that beast out there."

Becker didn't think he could be more astonished than he already was. He took the femur from her, and the tooth, and fitted the two together perfectly.

"Holy crap," he gasped in astonishment. "So there were human sacrifices to it?"

"That's as good an explanation as any," Dr. Paz replied.

As Dr. Becker's overwhelmed mind was trying to digest the information, one of Dr. Paz's students came rushing into the tent.

"Dr. Paz," the girl called breathlessly. "Dr. Becker, you both need to come."

Dr. Paz was already on the move with Becker right behind her. "Why?" she asked. "What's wrong?"

The student shook her head. "Nothing's wrong," she said. "But we were moving away some earth just like you instructed and we came across something."

"What?"

The student looked between Dr. Paz and Dr. Becker, excitement in her face. "We thought it was a piece of wood or a log, but it wasn't," she said. "We came across a broadsword buried in the earth."

Dr. Becker stepped forward. "A broadsword?" he repeated. "Are you sure?"

The girl nodded firmly. "The steel of the blade is black from the acidic soil that it's been in, but the hilt is still there." A grin spread across her face. "It's gold, Dr. Becker. It's a big, beautiful Medieval hilt and it looks like there are stones in it. It's absolutely gorgeous."

Becker was really curious now. "Let's go take a look."

The girl nodded and rushed off with Dr. Becker and Dr. Paz hot on her heels. The mystery in the marsh was deepening.

⌘

A knight, he traveled, lone and weary,
Upon a road so nigh.
Upon this road, a wraith came leery,
And moved the knight to by.
"Behold," said he, "I clearly see,
Your heart is not content."
"Be wise," it replied, "and know, forsooth,
That all is not as it seems.
Your road is long, and your path is wrong,
For you have entered the realm of the Serpent."
~ 17th Century Welsh Chronicler

CHAPTER ONE

Year of Our Lord 1283 A.D., the Month of April
Reign of Edward I
Castle Questing, Northumberland, England

"She did not simply disappear, but I would wager to say she is holed up somewhere in the castle. Woe betide the man who finds her for she shall not make capture easy."

The grim prediction came from an elderly man, big and dark and battle-scarred, and a patch over his missing left eye. He was old, that was true, but the gleam in his one good eye was as youthful and strong as it had ever been. The Wolfe of the North, Sir William de Wolfe, gazed at the men surrounding him, his expression wrought with tension. There was battle in the air.

16

"We checked all of the usual places, Father," a big, brawny man with blond hair and hazel-gold eyes informed him. "She is nowhere to be found."

"She *is* somewhere," William repeated steadily. "I would suggest you are fully armed as you search. If I know my youngest daughter, and I believe I do, she is armed and lying in wait for one of you hapless souls to come across her. She does not wish to be captured so heed my advice; she has a tendency to go for the neck so if I were you, I would take all steps to protect myself should you happen to find her. She will fight like a caged beast."

The brawny blond man grunted, perhaps in disapproval, and glanced at the men around him; four of them were his brothers, including his twin, and they all had the very same thought when it came to their youngest sister, the Lady Penelope Adalira de Wolfe. *Mayhap you should not have raised her as a knight, Father. She can best every one of us if she puts her mind to it.* They were all thinking the same thing but no one had the courage to speak it.

No one dared lecture The Wolfe; to do so was a sign of disrespect and all of them had the very greatest esteem for their father. But even infallible men sometimes had a weakness; in William's case, it happened to be his youngest child. A surprise baby that was born when both of her parents were well past their prime, she had been doted on and spoiled ridiculously, and when she had shown interest in doing what her older brothers were doing, William had not the heart to tell his cherubic little Penelope that she could not do what the boys did. He let her do it. The older she grew, the more strong-willed she had become and now he was facing the results of his lack of parental control. It was about to bite him in the arse.

"'Tis yer own fault, English," came the softly uttered voice of their mother, her words infused with a heavy Scots accent. "Ye taught Penelope well and now ye must pay for yer sins. She has yer cunning and she willna be snared. If she truly wishes tae hide from ye, then ye've taught her enough that she can stay away quite adequately."

William glanced at his wife as she stood in the doorway of his massive solar. Illuminated by the soft light, she looked far younger than her sixty-odd years. "So you have come to scold me?" he asked, somewhat defensively.

"I have come tae warn ye. She'll not be taken easily."

William already knew that. He tried to keep his patience with his wife but he couldn't stomach the "I told you so" attitude. "Then what do you suggest?" he nearly demanded.

The Lady Jordan Scott de Wolfe gazed steadily at her husband of nearly forty years. She knew what he was thinking, just as he knew what she was thinking. There wasn't much they thought differently on, although Penelope had been one of those things. William had indulged the girl's interest in knights and weapons whereas Jordan had tried to dissuade her, knowing how difficult it would be for her once she grew older. She would be an oddity in a man's world. It would seem that Jordan had been increasingly correct, as the current situation now exemplified. They were in for trouble.

Stepping into the solar, Jordan glanced at the rich and comfortable surroundings. Planted in the heart of Castle Questing, a massive fortress that crouched upon the lines of the Scottish border like a lion waiting to feed upon the unwitting souls of the Scots, the solar was a room that had seen more of its share of triumph and tragedy. The cold stone walls themselves reeked of power and warfare, as the lair of The Wolfe weaved its own web of intrigue and mystery.

"Dunna search for her," Jordan said quietly, pulling her wrap more tightly around her slender shoulders against the chill of the room. "She is smart enough tae hide from ye. A trap is the best thing for Penelope."

William was intrigued. "A trap?"

Jordan nodded her head, gazing at the knights in the room; a few were her sons, a few were sons of other elderly knights that had been with her husband since he had been a young warrior. She gazed at the handsome faces of her sons; Scott, blond and brawny, and his twin Troy, who was dark like his father. Her gaze fell upon Patrick, her third son and the biggest and most powerful of them all, and then to Edward and Thomas, strapping men who were seasoned even at their young age. Five sons of the mighty Wolfe, all of them distinguished warriors in their own right, but the sixth son was missing. James had been killed in Wales the year before and the agony was still very fresh when she gazed at her boys. She imagined the missing one who had been tall and blond with an impish grin. Struggling against the familiar grief, her gaze returned to her husband.

"Aye," she said finally. "Ye must lure her out if ye have any chance of capturing her."

"How shall we lure her?"

Jordan shrugged, a twinkle in her soft green eyes. "'Tis ye who are the military genius, English," she said. "I shall leave that up tae ye."

William twisted his lips irritably at her but the truth was that he was trying not to grin. "You are no help at all, woman," he growled.

"Ye didna marry me tae help ye. Ye married me tae breed a host of strong sons and tell ye when ye are wrong."

William's smile broke through. "I shall beat you severely for being so insolent."

Jordan snorted, glancing at her boys, who were also grinning. As she turned for the door, the panel to the chamber suddenly slammed shut hard enough to rattle the expensive plate armor that was stacked up over the massive hearth. The very shelves shook. They all heard something slam up against the door, a second blow, and William, puzzled, made his way to the door and lifted the old iron latch. It was jammed. Curious, he shook the door as if attempting to open it.

"Who shut this door?" he yelled, pounding a fist against it. "Who is there?"

There was a brief pause. "I shall not let you out until we come to an agreement, Father!"

It was a decidedly feminine voice and they all recognized it in an instant. Frustrated, though not surprised, William looked at his wife.

"Penelope," he hissed. "Did you put her up to this?"

Jordan's expression was innocent. "Now, why would I do that?"

He pointed a finger at her. "Because you have been against my decision from the beginning," he accused. "You've not supported me one bit!"

Jordan was trying not to crack a smile. "Yer mad, English," she dismissed him. "Ye know she's a clever lass. Mayhap ye shouldna have piled most of yer knights intae one room. Now she has ye trapped, all of ye."

William scowled at her; he wasn't the scowling type but his wife had pushed his hand. He snapped his big fingers at the eleven knights in the room. "Edward, Thomas," he hissed at the younger, thinner, and more agile sons. "Climb out through the window and get around to the corridor where she is. Do not let her get away from you, do you understand?"

The young knights were nodding even as they swiftly moved for the long lancet windows that overlooked the bailey. The other knights followed them and began helping them strip off the heavy armor so they could move more freely.

"'Tis a two-story drop to the bailey, Father," Scott reminded his father.

William waived him off tersely. "Then use the tapestry near the hearth as a rope," he said. "If the rest of you can fit through the windows, then go with them."

The knights were on the move as William returned his attention to the door. "Penelope?" he called sweetly, hoping she hadn't heard the commands being issued inside the room. "Penelope, my love? Please open the door. I promise we shall speak with reason and wisdom on the matter. Penelope, do you hear me?"

"Father!" Edward called; his body was halfway out of the window but he refused to go any further. He was pointing down into the darkened bailey. "Father, Penelope is down there with a broadsword!"

William and Jordan rushed to the windows, as did the other knights. They could see the young woman down in the darkness of the bailey, dressed in mail and pieces of armor that had been custom-fitted to her body. In her hand was a very sharp broadsword. When she saw all of the faces looking down at her, she assumed a defensive stance.

"Come down here, all of you," she challenged. "You shall be very sorry."

William sighed heavily and looked at his wife. "Now what?" he asked. He threw a hand in the direction of the solar door. "She has us trapped in here."

"That is because ye made it easy for her," Jordan scolded softly. "Did ye not think she would take advantage of it?"

"She would with her mother advising her."

"Then that would make me a better military commander than ye."

William couldn't decide whether to laugh or spank her. "You're so smart," he said sarcastically. "Now what do we do?"

Jordan couldn't help but grin; a small but scrappy woman had twelve very big men trapped in a little room and was holding them hostage. It was a fairly comical situation and very damaging to the male pride. Jordan was very proud of her little girl.

"Mayhap ye should tell her that she doesna have tae marry the warlord ye've pledged her tae," she said casually. "Mayhap then she shall let ye out. She doesna want tae marry the man and unless ye wish tae remain her hostage the rest of yer life, then I would suggest yet negotiate with her."

William's frustration was mounting at his taunting wife. With an angry sigh, he pushed Troy out of the way so he could get closer to the lancet window.

"Penelope?" he called down to her. "Penelope, my sweet, I want you to listen to me very carefully. Will you do this, please?"

Penelope had not moved from her defensive stance. "I *have* already heard you, Father. You know my thoughts on the matter. I will not let you out of that room until you promise me I do not have to go to Wales."

By now, most of Castle Questing was alerted to what was going on; there was too much shouting on the east side of the keep to maintain the secrecy of the situation. The Lady Penelope had her father and most of his senior knights trapped in her father's solar and a shouting match was going on; Penelope in the bailey and her father with his head out of the window two stories above. Men were starting to come around to see what all of the yelling was about, including William's second in command, Sir Kieran Hage.

Kieran, as old as he was, still drew the night watch every night. The massive knight with the piercing brown eyes still guarded the dark. He was on the wall, watching the happening and coming to see what had occurred; in fact, his own three sons were in that solar; Alec, Kevin, and Christian. He knew this was a particularly painful moment for Kevin, in fact, being in love with Penelope as he was. He knew the man was in the solar, cheering her on. *Resist, Penelope! Resist with all your might!*

But that didn't erase the fact that there was a stand-off going on. As Kieran swiftly made his way off the wall, William proceeded to reason with a very angry young lady.

"Penelope," he began, "you understand a knight's heart. You understand what it is to fight and die for what you believe in. You understand what makes England what it is and how important loyalty and allegiance are to the king. You also understand that peace is made in many ways and the least violent method is through negotiations and treaties and contracts. That being said, I know you understand how much of an honor it is that King Edward has asked that you become his emissary for peace."

Even in the darkness, they could see Penelope's scowl, which was an unfortunate expression on her exquisite face.

"I am *not* to be an emissary for peace," she countered firmly. "The king has had a time of it in Wales and he seeks to make me a sacrifice to the biggest Welsh warlord of all by marrying me to the man."

"He is trying to make an alliance."

"He is trying to make me the sacrificial lamb!"

William was struggling to remain calm. "I know you are not that dense," he said. "You know who Bhrodi de Shera is; the man still holds the hereditary title of King of Anglesey, for Christ's sake. He descends from Welsh royalty on his mother's side and on his father's side, he holds the title of Earl of Coventry. He is both Welsh and English, my love, but Edward wishes to appeal to his English blood by marrying the daughter of a great English warlord to him. It will ally our two families, Penelope, and it will guarantee Edward control of Northern Wales. After that disastrous defeat at Llandeilo last year when we lost your brother and then the terrible defeat at Moel-y-don a few months ago, the king is tired of losing so many men. He is hoping you can save lives by marrying the man who holds most of Northern Wales in his grasp. Can you not understand this?"

By now, Penelope had calmed somewhat but she was still clearly unhappy. "You put too much of a burden upon me, Father," she said. "You make it seem as if I do not marry the man, then I will be responsible for all of the English deaths that will result in continued warfare. *I* am not to blame; it is the king. His greed kills men."

"Silence," William hissed at her. "You cannot judge the fortunes of the king. It is his right to expand his holdings and you are, by law, sworn to do his bidding. What is the difference if he sends you to Wales to fight or to marry a warlord to secure peace? Either way, you are doing his bidding. If you are a knight, as you have so often sworn you are, then you have no choice. You must do as you are told."

Penelope was losing ground. "I would rather fight than marry a man I would be bound to for life."

William went for the kill. "Fine," he said as if agreeing to her terms. "Then the next time there are battles in Wales, your brothers will go and fight. We've already lost James, but mayhap that will just be the beginning. It would be a true tragedy to see more of your brothers die in a battle you could have just as easily prevented. They will do their duty and fight for the king; will you do your duty and marry for peace so they will not have to die?"

Penelope held his gaze a moment longer before hanging her head. But as she did so, she caught movement out of the corner of her eye. As quick as a cat, she jumped back and lifted her broadsword but she wasn't fast enough; Kieran had come up behind her and now held her in a great bear hug from behind. Her arms were pinned by his iron grip and she could hardly move.

"Uncle Kieran!" she grunted, struggling against him. "Let me *go!*"

Kieran had her tightly; he was concerned what would happen to him should he lose his grip. Penelope could fight as well as any man.

"In time," he said calmly. "Drop the sword."

"Nay!"

"Drop it or you will be very sorry."

Penelope began to kick and twist, but Kieran was so big that she truly didn't have a chance against him. Suddenly, she began to twitch and spasm. Her howls filled the air.

"Nay!" she screamed. "Don't you dare do that!"

Kieran was laughing low in his throat; the fingers of his right hand just happened to be along the left side of her torso, in a seam where the mail gapped, and he tickled her mercilessly as she screamed. The broadsword hit the ground and she began to beg for mercy as up in the keep, the servants had managed to straighten out the damaged door latch that was keeping William and his knights barricaded inside the solar.

When the door opened, the knights all spilled out except for William. He remained by the window with his wife, watching Kieran tickle Penelope until she was gasping for air. She was captured, that was certain, but he knew it wouldn't be the last of her rebellion. She was too stubborn for that. He knew the best course of action would be to get her to Wales as soon as possible. There, she would marry the Welsh warlord that was the most powerful man in all of Wales, if not all of England. The man had lands and wealth beyond the wildest dreams. He also had the reputation of the Devil.

William had known many powerful warlords in his life. He was, in fact, one of the more powerful ones in the north of England; The Wolfe was legendary. But Sir Bhrodi ap Gaerwen de Shera went beyond William's status. The man had Welsh royalty on his mother's side and English nobility on his father's; he fought for the Welsh when it suited him and the English when he felt like it. His loyalty was to himself and no one else.

It was King Edward's hope that marrying him to the daughter of a legendary English warlord would secure de Shera's loyalty to England permanently. Securing the loyalty of the man known throughout the realm as The Serpent, and for very good reason.

His strike was deadly.

⌘

CHAPTER TWO

Rhydilian Castle, the Month of May
Isle of Anglesey, Wales

"They are on their way." A big knight with shaggy black hair entered the great hall with his grand announcement. "In fact, they are already in Wales."

His statement didn't seem to have much impact to the occupants. Four pairs of eyes looked up at him from various positions around the great open pit in the center of the hall. The smoke from the fire in the pit was creating a fog of sorts, mostly because of the storm outside. Winds were preventing the smoke from escaping through holes in the thatched roof. Rain trickled down through the roof, hitting the glowing embers with a sharp hiss.

The mood of the room was dark and somber, as was usual. There hadn't been any levity in the room in well over two years, ever since "she" had died. No one was allowed to speak her name so she was only referred to as "she". That was as far as it went, memories of "she" having long since been forced into the shadows. That was how their liege wanted it.

As the announced words faded into the smoky blackness of the hall, a man seated near the fire with a sword in his hand, carefully sharpening it with a pumice stone, finally responded.

"How do you know this?" he asked, his voice deep and melodic as he continued to run the stone over the edge of the blade. "Have we received word?"

The knight with the shaggy hair nodded. "Indeed, my lord," he replied. "Word has come. De Wolfe has accepted Edward's proposal and is on his way with your bride."

The man sharpening the sword came to an unsteady halt. His eyes, the color of emeralds, seemed to flicker, to shift, before returning them to the blade. He resumed sharpening.

"Why would he come?" he asked calmly. "I have not yet accepted Edward's proposal. Do they think to force me to marry an English woman, then?"

The shaggy knight eyed the lowered head of his liege; Sir Bhrodi ap Gaerwen de Shera was a cool man in most situations, cooler still when the circumstances grew harried and violent. But the man had been known to have a temper, legendary outbursts that were far and few between yet had been known to have dire if not deadly results. It took a great deal to provoke the man known as The Serpent, but when The Serpent struck, he laid waste to all he touched. Even the men around the fire were watching de Shera, waiting. It was a tense moment as the realization of the words settled.

"De Wolfe's messenger is in the bailey," Ivor ap Bando replied steadily. "I made him wait whilst I informed you of the information he bore. Would you hear him now, my lord?"

Bhrodi continued to rub the stone on the edge of the blade, coolly, but his brilliant mind was working steadily. *They are on their way.* He was mildly annoyed, that was true, but there was also curiosity in the mix. A daughter of the legendary Wolfe would soon be upon his doorstep. If he was to ever consider an English bride, it would only be from a family of a great warrior. Edward had known him well; the man was well aware of his enemy's requirements. He understood his adversary and had acted accordingly. No woman but one from legendary warrior blood would be acceptable. Now, The Wolfe had come to Wales.

Straight into The Serpent's lair.

Bhrodi continued sharpening the blade. "It is a dangerous time to make the journey," he said, eyeing the razor-sharp steel. "By the full of the moon is not the best time to come to these parts."

Ivor nodded. "I realize that, my lord," he said. "The messenger says they should be here on the morrow. Mayhap you should...."

He was cut off by the slam of a door. It was a loud crack, a brutal sound in the depths of the darkened hall, but no one seemed

26

particularly startled by it. It was merely a familiar interruption, one that occurred several times a night. But they all paused, glancing towards a large wardrobe that had been a permanent part of the great hall for longer than any of them could remember. It had been part of a cache of booty from raids along the coast of Eire decades ago and had once contained great and expensive things. But that had been years ago. Now, it contained something different altogether. By the time Bhrodi glanced over his shoulder to look at the wardrobe, something thin and wrath-like burst forth from the cabinet.

A figure danced about in the shadows, shuffling and leaping. There was a good deal of grunting going on as the figure moved about, flickering through the streams of light that reached out from the hearth like fingers into the dim recesses of the room, recesses obscured by the darkness that cloaked the chamber like the dank depths of a polluted soul. They could all hear the hunting and grunting before the figure finally came closer, into the edge of the light, where they could see a little man dressed in filthy rags, with stringy white hair, waving his hand about in front of him as if extending an imaginary sword.

It was evident the man was doing battle with unseen forces, and it was a fierce battle indeed. He thrust, he parried, and he charged forward when he thought he had the advantage. He even shrieked when the invisible weapons aiming for him came too close. It was a macabre dance of a clear madman, though one who was determined to protect himself and the occupants of the room from unseen demons.

As Bhrodi and the others watched, the tiny man with the wild hair moved with leaps and bounds back towards his cabinet. Then, as quickly as the show began, it was summarily finished as he sheathed his imaginary sword and bowed swiftly to his ghostly opponent. And with that, he jumped back into his cabinet and closed the door.

It was over as quickly as it had begun, but no one commented on it. They'd seen it before, many times, and they returned to what they had been doing as if nothing was amiss. Ivor, who had been speaking when the little man had emerged, continued on as if nothing strange had just occurred. It was all quite normal in their world.

"Would you speak with the messenger, my lord?" he asked. "I have kept him in the gatehouse. If he is de Wolfe's messenger, we do not want to show him any disrespect and have The Wolfe down around our ears. It would be wise for you to see him."

Bhrodi inhaled slowly, thoughtfully, and stopped sharpening his sword. "Show him in," he said, his voice a low rumble. "I would like to know what the man has to say about a marriage contract I've not yet agreed to."

Ivor didn't want to debate it with him; any talk of marriage, or women in general, were not healthy subjects to broach with his liege and he was eager for it to be someone else's problem. Swiftly, he turned on his heal and headed back the way he had come.

Ivor's bootfalls faded as Bhrodi continued to sit, inactive, a pumice stone in one hand and his sword in the other, pondering the arrival of the Wolfe Pack. That was what everyone in military circles referred to them as; William de Wolfe and his stable of powerful and legendary fighting men were known as the Wolfe Pack. Bhrodi had been raised on stories of de Wolfe's valor and wasn't hard pressed to admit he admired the man greatly. Tales of de Wolfe's exploits along the Scots border were almost mythical in proportion. Bhrodi wondered if de Wolfe himself would be accompanying his daughter; suspicion told him the man, no matter his advanced age, would come. This was too important a meeting to leave to lesser knights.

So he continued to sharpen his blade, contemplating, as the men around him whispered among themselves. Usually, he ignored it but tonight he wasn't apt to. He spit on his pumice stone to wet it as he sharpened.

"Ianto," he said to the man sitting off to his right. "You will make sure we have accommodations for de Wolfe and his men. The bulk of the men can sleep in the hall but de Wolfe will have his own chamber. See to it."

Sir Ianto ap Huw, a big man from a fine and noble family, looked up from the cup of ale in his hand. "We can put him in the top of the keep," he said. "There are two rooms there. It is big enough."

"See to it."

"Aye, *fy arglwydd*," he said quietly. *Aye, my lord.* "But what of the woman he brings? This is no place for a woman."

Bhrodi stopped sharpening and turned to look at the group. "So that is what all of you are hissing about?" he asked. "The fact that Rhydilian is no place for women? You forget there was a woman here, once, and there is a woman here now."

"But she is kept to her chamber, *fy arglwydd*, and does not wander," a round man with a receding hairline responded softly. "Rhydilian is

28

not a friendly place. The walls of this hall have not seen any woman in over two years."

Bhrodi's piercing green eyes fixed on him. "Two years, seven months, and eighteen days," he said, his tone low and nearly threatening. "And so this hall will see a woman now, Gwyllim. Prepare the chamber next to mine for her."

"That is a small chamber," Sir Gwyllim ap Evan replied again with his soft but firm tone. He was a man of great reason and often tried to counsel Bhrodi when the man was open to such things. "The chamber on the top floor is much larger and would be more comfortable for her. It is a woman's chamber, after all."

Bhrodi shook his head brusquely, as they knew he would. No one spoke of the chamber on the top floor, a chamber that had been sealed up for two years, seven months, and eighteen days, ever since the day Bhrodi's beloved Sian had died giving birth to a son. Since that day, no one had dared to venture into the room which was exactly how it was the moment Sian's body had been removed. Bhrodi wouldn't let anyone in to even clean it up. Stale, with still-bloodied linens and old ashes in the hearth, the chamber sat cold and dark and unloved. Gwyllim had taken his life in his hands by as much as suggesting they disturb what had become a shrine to grief.

"Nay," Bhrodi barked, his mood turning from calm to annoyed in a split second. "Put the woman next to me and that will be the end of it."

Gwyllim glanced at Ianto and another man seated around the fire, noting their various expressions of uncertainty; whereas Ianto tended to be the most outspoken of the group, the man next to him, Yestin ap Bran, would side with Bhrodi until the end. What Bhrodi said was good enough for him, no matter what it was.

Bhrodi had put an end to the discussion of the chamber next to the hall, as they all knew he would. There was no more discussing it and no one would try. As Gwyllim rose wearily to his feet to carry out Bhrodi's command, the keep entry door swung open. They could hear it snap back on the old iron hinges. Gwyllim paused, as did everyone else, their attention turning to the hall entry as Ivor entered the chamber with a knight on his heels.

Immediately, the ambiance of the room changed. This was no ordinary knight; the stench of the *Saesneg* was upon them, an English knight of the highest and most professional order. The extremely tall man clad in expensive and well-used armor entered the hall, his mail jingling as he walked and his big boots thumping purposefully against the wooden floor. As he approached the fire pit where the men were gathered, Bhrodi's men rose to their feet but Bhrodi did not. He was not apt to show any respect or curiosity to a mere English knight.

He did, however, eye the man carefully; he was a big man with big hands and a crown of reddish-gold hair. As the knight and Bhrodi stared each other down, Ivor spoke.

"You are in the presence of the King of Anglesey, Prince of Cefni, Lord of the Green Isle, and the Earl of Coventry," he said in a formal tone. "You will show your respect to him, *Saesneg.*"

The knight didn't hesitate; he folded his long body over, bowing respectfully. "My lord," the knight said in a deep and charismatic voice. "Mae'n anrhydedd yn eich presenoldeb." *I am honored in your presence.*

Bhrodi was studying the man intently, still seated upon a chair with a sword in his hand. It was a most disinterested stance, and meant to be that way. There was no shortage of arrogance in Bhrodi's manner.

"You will speak English in my presence," he finally said. "I will not have the Welsh language sullied upon your tongue."

The knight nodded politely. "As you wish, my lord."

"What is your name?"

"Sir Apollo de Norville, my lord," he replied respectfully. "I serve Sir William de Wolfe."

"Where is The Wolfe?"

"He is camped about six or seven miles to the east, my lord, on the other side of the lake which is at the base of your mountain," he replied. "He thought it best to seek shelter and rest for the night and then present himself to you in the morning."

Something changed in Bhrodi's eyes at that moment; an ominous flicker in the deep green depths. In fact, his entire expression seemed to tighten and he rose to his feet.

"*Where*, exactly, did he camp?" he asked, an odd sense of urgency in his tone.

Apollo tried to be more specific. "There is a clearing to the south, near a copse of trees," he said. "A brook runs next to it and there are some rock formations to the north, although it was difficult to make them out, exactly."

"There is a smaller lake and a marsh next to this clearing."

"Aye, my lord."

Bhrodi's gaze lingered on the knight for a moment before passing a glance at Ivor. "That is not a safe place," he told him. "Get a party together. We must ride for them."

Apollo was confused. "I do not understand, my lord," he said. "Are we not on your lands? Did we mistakenly venture into enemy territory?"

Bhrodi could only shake his head as his men ran past him, calling for soldiers and mounts. Men began shouting and they could hear the calls out in the bailey. Apollo was genuinely puzzled as Bhrodi collected the sheath for his sword and moved past the knight.

"Come along, *Saesneg*," he said. "Let us see if we can save The Wolfe from the demon that lurks in the night."

Apollo followed, growing increasingly concerned. "Demon, my lord?" he repeated. "What demon?"

Bhrodi cast the man a long glance as they headed out of the hall and into the full moon in the bailey beyond.

"Let us hope you do not find out."

⌘

"She is standing watch," Jordan's voice was soft. "She is tending tae her duties as always. Did ye think this journey would be any different than the others?"

William sighed faintly. Bundled up against the cold night, he faced his wife in the well-appointed tent the family shared when they traveled. He had come looking for his daughter but found his wife alone before the brazier. Wrapped in furs, she was small and pale against the glowing embers, but her expression upon him was serious and all-knowing.

"Nay," he replied honestly. "I would expect her to behave as she always has."

"She will not shirk her duties."

William simply nodded, reflecting on his daughter and their journey from England. It had been almost three long weeks of travel, of contemplating Penelope's future. There had been a lot of time to think. He sighed again.

"I would not expect her to, as she is very dutiful," he replied. "In fact, she has settled down remarkably since that scene back at Questing when she locked us all in the solar and attempted to challenge my

31

decision. I have watched her for almost three weeks now and she has not said another word about her impending future. Has she said anything to you?"

Jordan shrugged faintly. "Not in so many words," she said softly. "She has mentioned how she will miss England but nothing more than that. But her expression at times... ye can see she has great longing. And great fear. Yet, she is a daughter of de Wolfe. She has accepted her duty."

"Do you really believe that?"

"I do."

"She will not try to escape this marriage before it can be completed?"

"I dunna believe so. Tae do that would bring ye shame, and Penny wouldna knowingly bring ye shame."

William accepted that. His daughter was honorable above all else. But she was also stubborn and disobedient, as the current situation displayed.

"She should be here, with you," he said, some displeasure in his tone. "I told her to retire early because tomorrow we meet her future husband."

Jordan was aware of the directive. "English," she said, somewhat admonishingly, "ye have raised her with yer own sense of duty. She is a young and beautiful woman, that is true, but inside that lovely façade beats her father's heart. She is the daughter of The Wolfe and ye canna deny her what comes naturally. I told ye she wouldna shirk her duties; therefore, she has taken the night watch. If ye want her tae come tae bed, then ye must go out and bring her in."

William knew that but it did not nothing to ease his mounting frustration. With a growl, he raked his fingers through his graying dark hair, a gesture of aggravation.

"Why is it that all of the women in my family seem intent to disobey me?" he asked. "Nothing on this journey is going as I had planned. I did not want you to come, yet you are here. Because Kieran and his sons came, Jemma had to come. Now I have womenfolk tagging along where there should be none."

Jordan's voice was soft. "Jemma is here tae ease Kevin."

William frowned. "Kevin is a grown man," he said. "He must come to accept that the woman he wants is meant for another and nothing his mother can do will change it. You know I have nothing but respect for

Kevin and his abilities as both man and knight, but Penelope is not meant for him. He will have to find a wife elsewhere."

Jordan sighed faintly, lowering her gaze and looking at the smoldering fire. She felt very sorry for her cousin's son; Jemma was her closest kin, more of a sister to her than a cousin. They had grown up together and had married Englishmen who had served together. Therefore, she was particularly sympathetic to Jemma's son's sorrow.

"He has been in love with her since she was a bairn," she murmured. "Ye canna change how the man feels."

William's frown deepened. "And you do not approve of my offering Penny in marriage to another?" he asked, his jaw ticking. "Is that why you have truly come? To make sure I know of your disapproval with this match?"

Jordan's eyes moved to him again. "There is no disapproval to be had," she said. "I support whatever decision ye make and well ye know it. But Jemma is here tae comfort Kevin, who also happens to be riding escort intae Wales tae deliver the woman he loves tae another man, and I am here tae make sure Penelope behaves herself. Do ye disagree with my logic?"

He calmed somewhat, though it was reluctant. "Nay," he grumbled, turning away. "You are the only one who has any chance of controlling her. I never could."

"That is because ye spoiled her, English," Jordan said softly. "Ye love her too much. I know this marriage was a difficult decision for ye. I know ye dunna want tae let her go."

He was less agitated now, now leaning towards depression. "She is my baby," he murmured. "Of course I do not want to let her go yet I know I must. This marital contract... she is worthy of it. I would not have pledged her had I not thought so."

Jordan rose from her stool and went to him, putting her arms around her big, strong husband who, with the years, had seen his emotions run rampant with his children. He was such a good father, doting and wise and kind, but he was deep and irrevocably emotionally invested in all of his children. The mighty Wolf of the Border had one weakness and one weakness only; his outlook on life was directly related to his children, and mostly to his wife. He couldn't do without any of them, yet it was inevitable that he had to. Children grew up, and parents grew old. He hated that fact of life.

"I know," Jordan said softly. "Now, go out and find her and bring her back. She must sleep for a time. She will meet her future husband tomorrow and must look her best."

"She will hate you for saying so."

Jordan grinned, giving him a hug before letting him go. "Find her, English. Be swift about it."

"Why?"

"Because there is every chance that Kevin is with her, trying to talk her into running off with him."

William rolled his eyes as he dutifully quit the tent. He knew his wife wasn't far wrong with what she had said and he couldn't help the sense of urgency that suddenly gripped him.

Kevin Hage was much like his wise and powerful father; if he wanted something, he would not give up.

⌘

"The moonlight is so bright that it is nearly day."

Penelope was gazing up at the moon, listening to the knight beside her speak of it. It was white and brilliant against the dark expanse of sky, and she nodded at his assessment.

"It nearly hurts my eyes to look at it," she said. Then, she looked at the landscape surrounding them, the silver-cast fields and distant trees. "It makes everything ghostly and glowing. This whole land seems very surreal. Can you feel it?"

Sir Kevin Hage wasn't looking at the landscape; he was looking at Penelope. She was all he ever looked at, and had since he had been a youth and had spent hours upon hours with Penelope as she had trained alongside the young men of Castle Questing.

Even at a young age she had been smart, determined, and tough, and as William and Kieran and Paris' sons had fostered together, Penelope, the youngest of William's nine children, had been allowed to tag along. Kevin, only eight years older than she was, found himself taking her under his wing. He and Penelope had been through a lot together, suffering both hardship and triumph, and over the years Kevin's sense of brotherly protectiveness turned into something else.

Now, he couldn't remember when he hadn't loved her and this journey into Wales was difficult for him. He tried not to think about what lay at the end of the voyage but now, as it would end tomorrow when Penelope was presented to the Welsh prince known as The Serpent, he realized this would be his last night alone with her. It tore at him like nothing he had ever known and he wanted to make this a night they would both remember forever; he simply wasn't sure how to do it without crossing lines and violating trust. There were things he wanted to say and things he wanted to do, now eight years in the making. Trouble was, he didn't want to get slugged for either effort, so he struggled to focus on a benign and meaningless conversation instead.

"Aye," he said, tearing his gaze away from her and looking out over the glistening gray land. "I feel it. It is Wales, a place wrought of demons and wild men."

Penelope looked at him; Kevin was an enormous man, like his father, with broad shoulders and big arms, but he had his mother's coloring in his green eyes and dark hair. He was quite handsome, and he most definitely had his father's temperament, rather calm and sedate.

"I have never heard of demons in Wales," she said. "But I have heard of mysterious creatures and of strange magic. Uncle Paris once told me that the Northmen brought their magic with them and left it here long ago. He told me a story once about a Welsh enchantress who could change form at will."

Kevin snorted. "Uncle Paris likes to tell stories."

"You do not believe in magic, Kevin?"

Kevin fought off a grin as he looked at her. He didn't want to seem condescending. "I believe in what I can see or taste or feel. If there is magic in this world, I have yet to truly see it."

Penelope clawed a hand at him. "Be still, else I will turn you into a fish and throw you into the marsh over near those trees."

His grin broke through. "So you think yourself a witch, do you?"

Penelope lowered the hand and giggled. "Nay, I am not a witch," she said, her smile fading as she gazed upon the silvery landscape of the unfamiliar country. "If I was, then I would cast a spell so that I would not have to marry The Serpent. Why is he called The Serpent, anyway? Can no one tell me this?"

It was difficult for Kevin to bite his tongue. "He is said to be a great warrior and a great commander," he said, feeling his heart tug with sorrow. "He is called The Serpent because his strike is deadly. He was at Llandeilo in the battle where we lost your brother, James. We were told he masterminded the battle. It was a vicious fight, to be sure."

Penelope looked at him, sadness in her expression as she remembered that terrible time. "James died in Papa's arms," she murmured. "Papa has not yet recovered from it."

Kevin nodded faintly. "Nor I," he said. "James was a good friend. I miss him every day."

Penelope thought on her tall, blond brother a moment. "That is why Papa has brokered this marriage," she said, sounding as if she were trying to talk herself into the favor of the situation. "He does not want to lose another son in battle against the Welsh. I understand his logic although it does not make me happy to be the peace offering. Why could he not offer your sister, Rose? Why must it be me?"

Kevin had asked himself that same question a dozen times although he knew the answer. "Because you are the daughter of The Wolfe," he said simply. "Rose is the daughter of a mere knight. It would not have the same impact."

Penelope knew that. She grunted unhappily. "But Rose wants to remarry after James died last year," she said. "She would make a much more willing bride than I do."

Kevin was silent, his gaze moving out over the marsh to the north. "Do you not want children and a family of your own someday?"

He should not have asked it because the answer, either way, would hurt him. Still, he had foolishly asked. Penelope's lips twisted wryly.

"I would not know how to be a good wife," she said. "I have never had an interest in such things. Katheryn and Evelyn did, but not me. Never me."

Kevin glanced at her, studying her glorious beauty in the moonlight and thinking of William and Jordan's two other daughters. Katheryn, the eldest, was in Jordan's image, blond and lovely, while Evelyn, the second daughter, took after the Scots side of the family with her pale skin and red hair. Penelope, however, was all William; she had his dark brown hair and hazel-gold eyes, giving her a most striking countenance.

It was widely accepted that Penelope was the most beautiful out of all of The Wolfe's daughters except for the unfortunate habit she had of dressing, and generally acting, like a knight. It was that lifestyle that her mother had been fearful of, but one Kevin understood completely. He wondered if The Serpent would understand, too. After a moment's reflection of a marriage to the woman he loved that would never be, he sighed sadly and looked away.

"Your marriage will be more prestigious than your sisters'," he said, trying to sound positive when all he really wanted to do was beg her not to do it. "Katheryn married my older brother and Evelyn married Hector, but neither one of them will marry a warlord with such great stature. It is something you should be proud of."

Penelope opened her mouth to speak but something in the distance caught her attention. There seemed to be something moving in the shadows of the marsh, something she couldn't quite make out. It seemed to flicker and roll, and just as she narrowed her eyes to get a better look at it, it quickly vanished. Thinking it was a trick of the moonlight, she returned her attention to Kevin only to see her father strolling up in the darkness.

"Greetings, Papa," she said as William approached. "All is well."

William came upon the pair, glancing at Kevin to see if he could determine the course of the conversation and the mood in the air, but Kevin met his gaze steadily. There was nothing in his expression suggesting anything other than a normal situation and William was relieved.

"That is good to know," he said, pausing as his gaze moved out over the ghostly landscape. It was indeed still and quiet. After a moment, he looked at his daughter. "Leave the night watch to Kevin. You must get some sleep. You have an important day ahead of you."

Penelope frowned. "I will retire soon," she said, trying to ignore her father now that she knew why he had come. "A few more hours and I will come to bed."

"Nay," William said, more firmly. "You will come now. Kevin can handle the north perimeter. Scott and Troy are off to the west while the rest of the knights are spread out. You are not needed."

Penelope's frown deepened. "Papa, truly, I am not tired in the least," she insisted. "I do not want...."

She was cut off by an unearthly howl that came from the direction of the marsh. It was so loud that it literally reverberated off of the trees, tents, or anything else that happened to provide a measure of sound resistance. Penelope whirled in the direction of the marsh, as did Kevin and William. Penelope was armed, as was Kevin, and the broadswords came out.

It had been a terrible and shattering sound, one that sent hearts to racing with apprehension. In this vast and unfamiliar land, it was an unwelcome and unsettling noise. They stood there, watching and waiting, as the entire camp began to stir.

"What *was* that?" Penelope asked, rather breathlessly.

William was characteristically calm, his one good eye scrutinizing the moonlit lands. He slowly shook his head.

"I do not know," he said. "A creature of some kind, I suppose. Hopefully the fires will keep it away."

Penelope looked at her father with some fear in her expression. "A creature?" she repeated. "I have never heard any creature make that kind of noise."

William wasn't inclined to get worked up about it; the man was not easily spooked. He had learned long ago not to get agitated over things he could not control.

"If it shows itself, then we shall know what it is," he said, his gaze lingering on the marshy area a moment longer before returning to his daughter. "Meanwhile, you will come with me and get some sleep. If you resist me, know that I will carry you over my shoulder."

Penelope still had her sword up in front of her, defensively. The otherworldly howl still had the hair on the back of her neck on end. Before she could respond to her father, she could see a pair of men making their way towards them from the darkness of the camp. The first face she could make out was Kieran, looking as if he had just awoken from a deep sleep. He slept heavily and long these days, an old man whose health had seen better times. Next to him came another familiar face, a big and handsome man with graying blond hair. Penelope fixed on him.

"Did you hear that noise, Uncle Paris?" she asked eagerly. "Could that be the creatures you have told me lurk in these lands? The ones that followed the Northmen here those centuries ago?"

Sir Paris de Norville scratched his head as he glanced at William; William and Paris had been the best of friends since their days as squires, having served in the north and fought against the Scots side by side for more years than they cared to remember. Closer than brothers, they could generally read each other's minds. At the moment, Paris was fairly certain that William was unhappy with him for filling Penelope's head with wild tales of Wales. He tried not to look too guilty.

"It was an interesting sound, to be sure," Paris said, avoiding her question. "We thought we heard it come from this direction."

William nodded. "I believe so."

"You did not see anything?"

"Nay."

All eyes were trained on the marsh beneath the full moon. Paris pointed in the direction of the swampy and dark lands. "I saw a small lake to the north of the marsh when we rode in," he said. "There is not much land in that direction. It all seems to be water."

Kieran came to stand next to his son as Paris and William tried to calm Penelope. She had been trained as a knight, that was true, but she tended to get excited due to her young and passionate nature. As Kieran and Kevin scanned the silvery landscape for any hint of what might have made such a terrible sound, it was Kevin who finally spotted the source. He pointed a big finger towards the north.

"Father?" he said to Kieran, struggling to maintain a calm demeanor. "Do you see that?"

Kieran, old as he was, still had sharp eyesight. He was starting to see what his son was pointing at and he didn't like it one bit. At first, he wasn't sure he was seeing clearly but as the thing began to move and its form became clearer in the moonlight, Kieran fought down a sense of shock. He could hardly believe his eyes.

"Aye," he muttered. "What in the hell *is* it?"

"I do not know."

Kieran gazed at the sight a moment longer before turning to William, his expression grim. "How far is Rhydilian Castle from here?"

By now, William, Paris, and Penelope were also straining to catch a glimpse of what had Kieran and Kevin's attention. They all saw it at nearly the same time, a very large and horrific vision that seemed to displace entire mounds of earth and swamp as it moved. Water sloshed and trees were uprooted in its path. It was, in truth, a terrifying and startling sight, and quite difficult to comprehend.

"*Too* far," William growled. Still, he was on the move. "Too far but we have no choice. Rouse the camp and tell them to take only what they can carry on horseback. Leave everything else behind. Knights will hang back and form a line to give the others time to reach the castle. Kieran, Kevin; *move*."

He didn't even wait for the men to swing into action, knowing that they would without question. As Penelope stood there, eyes wide and mouth agape, William grabbed her and pulled her away with him.

The last thing Penelope heard as her father hurried her across the camp was another horrifying, unearthly howl, this one closer than the last. It was coming for them, this nightmare from the mysterious lands of the Welsh, looming closer and closer, perhaps attracted by the smell of human flesh. It was difficult to know why it came, only that it had, and all Penelope could think about was reaching her mother. She couldn't even think about herself; all she knew was that she had to get her mother to safety.

Death approached.

⌘

CHAPTER THREE

By the time William and Penelope reached their tent, they could hear the sentries on the south side of the camp take up a common cry. It was enough to give William pause as, suddenly, men on horseback were charging through his encampment. Shoving Penelope into the tent, he went for his broadsword. Now, he was in battle mode and The Wolfe would spare no one. With his family at stake, especially his wife and daughter, he was in full warrior form. Old as he was, it was still an impressive sight to behold.

"Stay with your mother," he commanded Penelope. "You will protect her, do you hear? Stay here."

Penelope didn't argue; she was in mail, with her broadsword in hand, and she pushed her startled mother to the ground near the brazier. There were a few other candles in the tent, giving off light, and she quickly doused them so they would not throw shadows against the hide walls of the shelter. If the enemy was upon them, she didn't want them to be seen.

There was a good deal of shouting going on in the darkness and she could hear the clash of swords. Most definitely she heard weapons being produced. She could also hear the thunder of horses and the roar of the approaching horror. Men were shouting and she could hear lines being formed. Suddenly, another woman appeared in their tent. She was small and rather round, but she was feisty and quick. Wrapped in a heavy cloak, with her dark hair escaping its net, the Lady Jemma Scott Hage was making an appearance.

"What in the bloody hell is that noise out there?" she demanded, but kept speaking before Penelope could answer her. "Alec tossed me in here and told me to stay with ye. Me own son tossed me about like an ale-house wench! Now, what *is* all of the madness about?"

Penelope grasped her Aunt Jemma and pulled the woman over to the brazier, which she then toppled onto its side to douse the embers. Jordan saw what her daughter was doing and quickly pushed dirt upon the coals to quench them. Even Jemma kicked at the dark, moist earth as they hurriedly buried the coals, but she was more interested in what was happening.

"Penny?" she urged. "What has happened?"

"I am not sure, Aunty," Penelope said honestly "I was on watch at the north perimeter of the encampment when something roared. Did you hear it? And then it seemed as if the entire marsh came to life because the water was churning and this... this *head* came out of the water."

Jordan and Jemma looked at Penelope as if the woman had gone mad. "Head?" Jordan repeated, incredulous and apprehensive. "What kind of head?"

Penelope thought back to that terrifying moment; in truth, she was frightened, perhaps more frightened than she had ever been in her life. She struggled against that fear, an unfamiliar sensation.

"I do not know," she said, listening to the shouting about camp grow closer. Horses seemed to be all around them. "It was big and... and silver, I think. It looked like the head of a horse. Or a snake. Oh, I do not know *what* it looked like, exactly. It was difficult to tell in the moonlight."

The thunder of hooves was right outside the tent now and the side of the tent suddenly caved in. Penelope pulled her mother and aunt out of the way of the folding fabric and then leapt in front of the pair, broadsword lifted, as a man burst into the collapsing tent. She thrust violently at the figure only to be met with a block of greater power. It was dark so it was difficult to see who she was engaging, but after a short and panic-filled moment, Penelope realized she was looking at her brother, Thomas.

"'Tis me!" Thomas hissed, shoving her broadsword aside. Another dark de Wolfe son only a few years older than Penelope, he reached down for his mother. "We must get to the horses."

Penelope grasped her Aunt Jemma and followed her brother from the partially-collapsed tent. "What is happening, Thomas?" she demanded.

There were horses all around and men shouting as they exited into the cold and bright night. Several soldiers ran past them, nearly knocking Jemma over, and the woman cursed loudly. Penelope was trying to help the woman along, glancing over her shoulder towards the northern perimeter as they fled. She could see a line of men, and knights on horseback, and as she watched, a very large creature with a long neck and a snake-like head reared up and roared into the night. She could see the silver moonlight reflecting off of long and terrifying fangs. It was too astonishing to believe.

There was tangible terror in the air as the four of them raced to several horses that were tethered near a small copse of trees. The ground was heavy with moist earth and wet grass, making it difficult to move quickly and not slip. By the time they reached the horses, more men were rushing in from the road to the south astride steeds that were fast and lightly armored. Penelope watched the men rush past them, trying not to feel an inordinate amount of confusion. For a knight, confusion could be deadly.

"Thomas," she called to her brother as the man moved to help his mother mount a skittish horse. "Who are these men?"

Thomas launched his mother onto the back of the horse. His gaze moved to the group of men who were fending off whatever hellish creature was upon them, helping The Wolfe's men in their fight. He shook his head, genuinely puzzled, but nonetheless focused on what he must do. Like his father and brothers, he was a competent and powerful knight.

"I do not know," he said, moving to his Aunt Jemma. "They came in from the road to the west and headed straight into the fight. They are Welsh, that is certain, but we do not know who they are. All that matters at the moment is that they are with us, not against us."

Penelope helped her brother get Jemma to a horse and assisted her in mounting. The horses were agitated and Thomas grabbed his sister.

"Get mounted," he told her. "Father wants you to take Mother and Aunt Jemma and ride for Rhydilian Castle."

Penelope tried not to be startled by yet another horrific roar as the creature was fended off by a host of well-armed men. But as she mounted the nearest steed, which happened to be Thomas' horse, the lure proved to be too great and she turned to watch as men began lighting arrows and shooting flaming projectiles from their crossbows. The light of fiery arrows began to fill the night sky as they shot overhead, illuminating the terrible beast at the edge of the marsh. In fact, there seemed to be a good deal of flame happening on the northern perimeter, so much so that the creature, whatever it was, began to shrink back, clearly turned away by the men with flame.

"Thomas, *look*," Penelope pointed to the battle in the distance. "It is moving away!"

Thomas was preparing to send his mother and aunt off into the night but he paused at his sister's insistence. His hazel eyes watched the scene, carefully gauging the degree of battle and of danger as the flame arrows continued to fly and the creature turned back for the marsh. With the bright moon and flaming projectiles, it was easy to see what was going on. He had to admit that his sister's assessment seemed to be correct; the creature seemed to be returning to whatever hellish cave it crawled out of.

But for Penelope, it was not enough. She had to see for herself, attracted as she was to the heart of any conflict. It was the de Wolfe in her, the traits passed down by her father. As Thomas yelled after her, she spurred the black charger towards the gathering of men, most of whom seemed to be backing away, in a line, just as the creature was moving away from them. She could see de Wolfe men poised for battle, and knights she had known all her life who were watching the retreat with concern; her father, Paris, Kieran, her brothers Scott and Troy and Patrick, Kieran's sons Kevin, Alec, and Christian, and Paris' sons Hector and Adonis and Apollo.

... Apollo?

Penelope could see the tall, red-haired knight standing next to Alec Hage. The last she had seen of Apollo, he had ridden on to Rhydilian Castle to announce the arrival of the party from Castle Questing. Logic would dictate, then, that the men who had ridden to their aid must have been from Rhydilian Castle if Apollo was with them. Further logic would dictate that The Serpent must be among them; it must have been the man himself who had ridden to their aid. There was no other clear alternative.

Penelope didn't like that thought at all. She didn't know why she was suddenly apprehensive, but she was. To know that the man she was pledged to was somewhere in her midst unnerved her. When she heard someone give the retreat cover command, she drove her heels into the sides of the horse and charged after the men on horseback that were pursuing the beast. As she raced towards the marsh, unknown to her father or the rest of his knights, the de Wolfe encampment began to hastily pack up and prepare to move out.

It hadn't been a particularly wise move on her part, she thought in hindsight, going in pursuit of a dangerous beast, but she found that she had to get away. She had to do what came naturally, to fight and defend, and then perhaps it would help her clear her mind and not feel such apprehension. She didn't like the feeling. But the truth was that she didn't know this land and in the bright moonlight, it made movement more difficult. Everything was gray or shadowed, making it difficult to focus on the details of her surroundings. She knew she had put herself in some danger by bolting off but she wouldn't dwell on it. She was riding at the tail end of the group of men going after the beast until abruptly, they split up and went different directions. The swiftness of the movement caught Penelope off guard and she was unable to pull her horse up before the animal slipped headlong into the marsh.

Panicked, she spurred the animal out of the water and back onto firm land. She could see men off to her right in the distance, skirting the edge of the marsh, and she thought to go in their direction until the water in front of her suddenly exploded up into the air like a great silver fount. The charger startled and reared, dumping Penelope off onto the soft and wet ground. Falling on the hilt of her broadsword, she grunted in pain as she rolled to her knees. She tried to grab the horse but he was too spooked and bolted off. As she struggled to regain her footing, a familiar and terrible roar burst out next to her.

The creature was suddenly there, emerging from the marsh in a great eruption of water and mud. Penelope, stunned and horrified, watched the beast rear its neck out of the water, no more than a dozen feet away from her. It spied her instantly as she knelt on the ground, halfway to her feet, and the big mouth gaped open, roaring again. It was an utterly terrifying sound.

Penelope could see that it was looking at her and at that moment, she could have done one of two things; she could have surrendered to the inevitable, knowing it meant to kill her, or she could do what her character dictated - she could fight it. She was a de Wolfe, born and bred for battle, and whatever this creature was, it would not be the end of her. She would not allow it. She had to kill it, or injure it, before it did the same to her. The crossroads of life and death were staring her in the face and she was not about to back down. She was not going to concede defeat.

Quick as a flash, Penelope unsheathed her broadsword, the one she had fallen on when the horse had dumped her. There was nowhere to run or hide as the enormous head of the beast began to reach for her; if she turned her back on it to run away, it would surely kill her, and she couldn't run fast enough to get out of the reach of its very long neck. Therefore, she stood her ground as a trained warrior would, watching the thing come down on her and waiting until the last second to roll away, away from the momentum of the lurching head. As it slammed to the ground beside her, she lifted her sword and jammed the blade straight into the baleful right eye.

The creature screamed, a howl that was so loud it nearly ruptured her eardrums, and her broadsword remained stuck in the beast's eye as it reared up and screamed in pain. Terrified, Penelope scrambled to her feet and began to run, running so hard and so fast that she dare not look behind her. As she ran for the safety of the nearby trees, men on horseback raced past her, heading for the animal. All except one; he pulled his horse up as she ran past him and bailed off of the animal, grabbing her on the arm.

Her momentum sent them both to the ground. Penelope was in a flurry of panic, beating at the man who held her, struggling to get away from his grip. But his embrace was like iron; he was a very big man and extraordinarily strong.

"Let me go!" she howled. "We must run from this place! It will come back!"

The knight held on tightly. "Easy," he said, laboring to calm her. "You'll not run that way. There is only more swamp and many ways to drown."

Penelope had stopped fighting him but she was still struggling. "Please," she begged. "We must get away from here. That beast will surely return."

The man sat up, pulling her with him. His dark green eyes were on the scene in the distance; the creature with a broadsword in its eye had quickly submerged and his men were standing on the edge of the marsh, waiting and watching for the beast's return. But his attention was more on the knight he had grabbed than the beast; he had no idea it was a woman until she spoke and now, his curiosity had the better of him.

He studied her intently in the silver moonlight; her dark hair was pulled back against her skull, braided and pinned behind her head. He hadn't noticed her hair until now; she must have had a lot of it because the bun and the braid were very thick. At close range, he could see her exquisite features with a pert nose and seductive, long-lashed eyes. She was a remarkable beauty, even in the dark, but she was also wearing heavy mail, portions of plate armor that was custom –fitted to her body, and a scabbard for the sword she had just launched into the beast's eye. His curiosity turned to confusion.

"You... you are not a knight," he stated the obvious. "Who are you?"

Penelope looked at the man, hearing the disapproval and hazard in his tone. She resumed her attempts to pull away from him. "I am with William de Wolfe," she said, avoiding giving him an answer for the most part. "Who are *you?*"

Bhrodi wasn't going to tell her; at this point, he really didn't want anyone to know. He still wasn't sure he wanted de Wolfe here and certainly didn't want to meet the man on a level playing field, here out in the middle of the marsh as they fought off The Serpent. He wanted to meet the man in his great hall where he had the upper hand and the perception of being in control in his own castle.

"A man who has saved your life," he said, eyeing the mail hood about her shoulders. "What are you doing dressed as a knight? Where is your husband that he would let you dress like this?"

Penelope could see he was more interested in *what* she was than *who* she was. Still, she didn't like the questions. She didn't like his tone. But there was something in the depths of his dark green eyes that smoldered at her, like the glowing embers of a raging fire that were waiting to be rekindled. There was something very unsettling and powerful about the man, something that was starting to shake her.

"What was that... that *creature?*" she asked, instinctively shrinking away from him.

He sat next to her, watching her pull away. His grip tightened. He didn't want her going anywhere. After a moment, he stood up and pulled her up next to him. "Where is de Wolfe?" he asked, ignoring the question. He could hear the shouts of men in the distance. "I want to know why this man lets you fight for him. Are the English so desperate for knights that they are now recruiting women?"

Penelope had enough of his condescending attitude. She tried to yank her hand away but he held fast. "He lets me fight for him because I am a warrior," she said snappishly. "Let me go immediately or you will not like my reaction."

Bhrodi looked at her, his eyes glimmering with amusement. "Is that so?" he said. "I would like to see your reaction, in fact."

"Nay, you would not."

"I think I would."

Those eyes were pulling at her again, stronger than before. There was something in the glimmer that made her heart skip a beat. But she was also incredibly frustrated, fearful and angry to boot, so she lashed out a fist and nearly caught him in the neck. Bhrodi was too fast for her, however, and managed to move out of the line of fire just in time. Penelope's momentum took her forward and he got in behind her, wrapping her up in a bear hug. Infuriated, Penelope threw her head backwards, right into his face, and hit him squarely in the nose. Stars danced before Bhrodi's eyes but he didn't release her. Something about the tussle excited him. Something about her intrigued him.

I can feel her heat through the mail, he thought even as his nose throbbed with the blow. He could feel the blood begin to trickle. Trapped against him, Penelope stomped on his foot, hard enough to cause him to flinch and loosen his grip. As she threw herself forward to get away, Bhrodi reached out and snatched her by the hair, pulling loose the bun and sending the iron pins flying.

Penelope was furious to realize he had her by her long, thick braid, now like a leash in his hand. Turning around, she flew at him with hands and feet, ably landing some blows because he was handicapped with only one free hand. Still, he was able to very adequately defend himself and he never made any attempt to strike her in return; he simply prevented her from doing any further damage to him. When she came too close, he managed to block a series of strikes and spin her around, trapping her yet again. This time, he had her hair wound around one of his big fists and her head was against his chest. He wasn't about to put himself in a position where she could head-butt him again.

"That was a good reaction," he admitted. "Had you caught me off guard, you might have done real damage. You are skilled for a woman."

Angry, insulted, Penelope struggled against his iron grip. "I am skilled for *any*one, man or woman," she said. "Let me go, do you hear?"

"Not until you tell me your name."

"I will *not* tell you my name."

"Then we will be here for a very long time. I will not release you until you tell me who you are and why you fight for de Wolfe."

"I'll not tell you anything!"

He didn't reply for a moment and Penelope knew that was not a good sign. So far, he had proved to be cunning and powerful, and she knew he was about to turn those attributes against her. Unfortunately, she was correct; abruptly, the knight picked her up and, still clutched against his torso, began to walk towards the marsh.

"Tell me or I'll throw you to the beast," he said.

Penelope could see the ghostly silver expanse of marsh drawing closer and her heart began to race with fear. "Never!"

"Then the beast will enjoy your tasty flesh."

With a furious and frightened shriek, Penelope went mad, kicking at his legs savagely until she made contact with his knees. It was enough of a blow to cause him to lose his balance and together, they fell into the soft, marshy earth. Penelope fell beneath him and Bhrodi's entire body weight came crashing down upon her. Even though she had on mail and pieces of armor, it hadn't prevented the full impact of his substantial weight. Momentarily stunned and unable to breathe, she lay there gasping.

The humor was out of his expression when he realized how hard he had fallen on her. Releasing her hair, he pushed himself up and looked at her with worry.

"Are you well?" he asked, concerned in spite of himself. "Did you hurt yourself?"

Penelope didn't respond; she continued to gasp for air, but after the first few moments, it was all an act. He had released her and she wasn't about to let down her guard. She wanted to get away from him. Peering through slitted eyes, she saw that he was rather close to her, his brow slightly furrowed upon his darkly handsome face. When he opened his mouth to ask her again, she reared up and hit him squarely in the throat.

Bhrodi fell onto his back, gasping savagely for air as Penelope bolted to her feet and raced off into the darkness. He continued to lay there, struggling to breathe, until his men came around and found him there some time later.

They had no idea why Bhrodi was on the ground, laughing.

⌘

CHAPTER FOUR

"It has guarded the pass through Pendraeth Forest since ages past and it always emerges on the full moon to feed. Your party was in the wrong place at the wrong time and it is fortunate there were not any deaths as a result."

In the great hall of Rhydilian Castle that smelled heavily of smoke and dogs, William and his knights stood just inside the doorway as a man standing near the enormous hearth lectured them. They had just arrived at Rhydilian as a result of their flight from the marsh and William was in no mood for foolery. The entire night had been unnerving and exhausting, and his usually calm temper was in danger of flaring because it was clear that Bhrodi de Shera was not happy to see the English upon his doorstep. Instead of polite Welsh hospitality, they were receiving a lashing.

"I will not speak another word until I know who it is I am addressing," William said, his tone a growl. "Although I am deeply appreciative of your protection for my people this night, your behavior since I have walked within these walls has been rude and arrogant. I am a lord with titles and honor and will not tolerate your discourteous behavior any longer. Either you bring me de Shera or I will turn and ride from here. I do not speak with hired men on a matter of such importance."

Bhrodi was standing near the flames with Ivor, Ianto, Yestin, and Gwyllim. Since the moment they had returned from the marshes near Llyn Llwydiarth, he had purposely kept the English waiting and when he did speak to de Wolfe, it was without introduction. He was making his displeasure at their uninvited appearance known but he wasn't willing to push it too far; there was a part of him that wanted peace, an alliance, although it was difficult to admit it. Only since he had aided the English in chasing off the beast from the marsh had he really given it serious thought.

Oddly, it had felt empowering fighting with The Wolfe and not against him. He rather liked the feeling when he should not have. There was a sense of unity and strength, something he'd never known with the *Saesneg*. Indeed, perhaps he needed to give the marriage proposal more consideration. Perhaps it was time to ease his rough stance and show the English a measure of welcome.

With a faint sigh, Bhrodi moved away from the flames and in William's direction. His gaze was intense upon the enormous man with the eye patch. He knew he was looking at a legend; the entire room filled with the presence of de Wolfe the moment the man passed through the doors. There was no mistaking such power.

"I am de Shera," he finally said, "and you, my lord, are William de Wolfe. I was raised on stories of your valor. Even Welshmen respect you."

William eyed the very big, and very muscular, young lord. He was dark, like the Welsh, but he had eyes the color of emeralds that looked strangely bright on his shadowed face. The most predominant feature about the man that struck William was the size of de Shera's shoulders; the man was tall, although he'd seen taller, but the pure muscular width of his shoulders and chest was truly something to behold. The only men he'd ever seen close to that kind of power were Kieran and Kieran's son, Kevin. De Shera radiated nothing but pure, unadulterated power. So many master races culminated in de Shera; English, Welsh, Norse, and Irish. The powerful qualities of each race filled him. The man was bred to kill.

But he also radiated a sense of entitlement and arrogance; William could see it in his face. De Shera spoke with a deep, succinct voice, as if there was no room for discussion or debate because he knew better than everyone else. Therefore, William had suspected the man's identity all along but he wanted a formal introduction. He didn't like being treated like a lesser class because he was English; it was simply good manners.

"If that is true, then why have you treated me so poorly since my arrival?" he asked after a moment. "You show your respect in strange ways."

Bhrodi smiled wryly. "And you appear in places you have not yet been invited to."

William wouldn't back down, especially not to a Welshman regardless of his titles. "I am here on the directive of my king. If you have issues with whether or not I was invited, then I suggest you take it up with Edward."

Bhrodi's smile turned real. "I intend to," he said. "And I will thank him for sending The Wolfe to my doorstep. In spite of the circumstances, I would say that it is an honor for us both."

William couldn't help it; the man's arrogance was astounding and he cocked an eyebrow at the comment. "How kind," he said, although he didn't mean it and they all knew it. "Now, let us return to the subject at hand when I had entered the hall; what was that... that *beast* that attacked us? I have never heard of such a thing in all of my travels."

Bhrodi didn't seem too concerned about it; he lifted those enormous shoulders in response. "As I said, it has guarded the pass through Pendraeth Forest for as long as anyone can recall," he said. "My grandfather used to tell me the Northmen brought it with them hundreds of years ago, a serpent that had followed them from their land who then took up residency in the marshes. It remains in the marshes, and in the lake at the base of the mountain, and it feeds when the moon is full although it has been known to expose itself in the daylight. Surely you've heard of The Serpent in these parts."

"I thought that was you."

Bhrodi's intense eyes focused on him. "It *is* me," he said. "Some say my family draws strength from the serpent of the lake; therefore, I am also called The Serpent. The beast and the lake and I are one and the same. We are both deadly."

It was a hugely egotistical statement and William resisted the urge to roll his eye. Paris, however, was not so discreet; he clearly rolled his eyes, glancing to Kieran as he did so. The two old men looked at each other, displaying expressions that suggested they'd had enough conceit for one day. William caught sight of Paris' antics and hastened to keep Bhrodi's attention away from it. He didn't want the man becoming angry with the posturing of the elderly English knights.

"As your reputation would suggest and I will not dispute," he said, moving closer to the man and stepping on Paris' foot in the process. It was a hard pinch, one that suggested the man keep his opinions off his face. He could hear Paris grunt in pain. "But surely that creature has not lived for hundreds of years. Nothing can live that long. It is quite clearly a living, breathing animal and not one of magic."

If Bhrodi had noticed the elderly knights and their impatience with him, he didn't acknowledge it. Evidently, only The Wolfe was worthy of his attention.

"Nay, it is not magic," he agreed, his voice quieting. "Truthfully, my grandfather has spoken of it and he said his father before him did as well, but that is as far back as the legend goes. Mayhap it did not come with the Northmen hundreds of years ago as my grandfather said; in fact, the Northmen still come to these parts on occasion, although they have not attacked in recent memory. Have you seen their long ships? Often they have serpent's heads carved upon the bow to break the waves. That is why my grandfather believes the Northmen brought that serpent with them and left it here to terrorize us."

William still wasn't convinced, of anything. "And that is all you know about it?"

"That is all I will tell you."

It was an evasive answer but William didn't pursue it. Whatever the creature was, either de Shera wouldn't tell him all of it, or couldn't tell him all of it. What mattered now was that they had survived the attack and were now in Rhydilian's great hall, facing a man with more royal and noble blood in him than most. William tried to keep that in perspective because he wasn't at all sure he liked or even respected the man for the way they had all been treated.

"Then I will again thank you for riding to our aid," he finally said. "We had no idea such things even existed and surely no ideas on how to fight it off."

"Fire is the only thing that works."

"I deduced that."

Bhrodi held the man's gaze for a moment, sensing something edgy in the old, one-eyed knight. He had no doubt that, if challenged, de Wolfe could quite easily put a blade in his belly. Men like de Wolfe had lived to a ripe old age for good reason. Perhaps now it was time to ease the standoffishness and create a more sociable atmosphere. This was a gathering of peace, after all. It was time to be hospitable.

"I suppose we should discuss the reasons for your visit," he said, turning his back and motioning to Ianto, who disappeared into the shadows. "Please be seated and be comfortable. I will have food and drink brought to you."

It was the first real show of hospitality and William motioned to his men; Kieran, Paris, Kevin, Scott, Troy, Patrick, and Paris' son, Apollo, cautiously moved towards the feasting table in the middle of the room, chipped and worn with age, and began to sit. They, like William, were perturbed by de Shera's attitude and slightly hostile as a result. The younger knights eyed de Shera's men as they claimed their seats, feeling the uncertain mood settle. They were in enemy lands in an enemy castle. Anything could happen, and they would not be caught off guard.

Accordingly, they all leapt to their feet when the big wardrobe in the shadows rattled and the door suddenly popped open. Kevin went so far as to unsheathe his broadsword when a tiny little man with stringy white hair burst out of the wardrobe, but William held out a calming hand to prevent his knights from doing anything drastic. He kept his eye trained on the small figure who shuffled around back in the shadows. Like his men, he would not be caught off guard.

Bhrodi could see what had the attention of his English visitors and he realized they were startled by something that was an everyday occurrence to him. He put up his hands as if to force them to relax.

"Have no fear," he said. "'Tis only my elderly uncle, and he is quite mad. He lives in the wardrobe and only emerges to fight unseen enemies or steal food. He is harmless, I assure you. When I was a child, however, I use to think he was a ghost. Most frightening."

William cast him a long glance. "A ghost?"

Bhrodi nodded, turning to look at the tiny man as he battled against unseen forces. "He is my mother's uncle and he has been mad as long as I can recall," he said. "He has lived in that wardrobe for at least thirty years, mayhap more. When I was small, I was terrified of the man who lived in the wardrobe and only came out at night."

"But a ghost?"

Bhrodi shrugged. "If you were five years of age and you saw such madness in the dead of night, what would you think?"

William conceded the point. "That he was a ghost, I suppose," he replied. Then, he eyed the man. "Are there any other ghosts or creatures we should know about so that my men are not startled by such things? Startled knights tend to react with deadly consequences, as they are trained."

Bhrodi shook his head. "Nay, no more oddities that I am aware of," he said. "But be mindful that my uncle may come into the hall in his quest to vanquish his invisible enemy. He will not harm anyone but do not try to stop him; he must run his course. Just stay out of his way."

"What happens if someone interferes?"

Bhrodi lifted his eyebrows. "Then my uncle might do some genuine harm," he said. "He becomes even more insane if another human being touches him. Therefore, it is best to simply stay out of his way."

An interesting statement in an evening that had been full of them. *This is a very odd place*, William thought as he glanced over at Paris and Kieran. He knew they were thinking the same thing. Without further delay or questions, but keeping an eye on the strange old man as he battled ghosts, William took a seat at the big feasting table just as Ianto emerged from the shadows with kitchen servants in tow. The servants were weighed down with food and drink, and soon the big and worn table began to fill with warm edibles and cold alcohol.

Bhrodi took a seat across from William where he could better see the man. Ivor and Gwyllim sat on either side of him, and he was eventually joined by Ianto and Yestin as more food was set upon the table. William and his knights didn't touch the food until his host did, an example of good English manners, but once Bhrodi reached for a knuckle of beef, it was as if the dam had burst and many English hands were reaching for the presented fare.

In the wake of the feeding frenzy, mutton was torn apart and all that remained of the beef was a few scraps. There was quite a bit of fish on the table, or at least they thought so, until the English discovered it was eel and they passed on it. No one particularly liked it. There were also bowls of beans and fat green peas, and great loaves of cream-colored bread.

It was a surprisingly lavish feast, but not completely unexpected considering Bhrodi's station. The man had access to much and a fortune behind the de Shera name. As the English and Welsh ate silently, eyeing each other across the big table, Bhrodi finally broke the silence.

"I would assume by your presence, my lord, that you have brought me my bride," he said, mouth full of beef. "Tell me who you have selected for this auspicious position."

More arrogance. William heard Paris grunt unhappily beside him and he elbowed the man to keep him silent.

"I have only three daughters, two of which are already married to fine knights," he said. "Therefore, I have pledged my youngest daughter as your bride."

Bhrodi didn't seemed pleased by the statement; in fact, he appeared suspicious. "Youngest?" he repeated. "*How* young?"

"Penelope has seen twenty years of age."

Bhrodi's eyebrows lifted in disbelief. "*Twenty* years of age?" he repeated, nearly outraged. "She is not young in the least; she is an old maid at that age. Why is she so old? Could you not find her a suitable husband before now? I will take no cast-offs, de Wolfe."

William gazed at the man a moment before setting his cup of nearly-finished wine down and rising to his feet. When he stood up, his entire stable of knights stood up with him and when he spoke, it was with the greatest restraint. The man had finally reached his limit; words were about to be exchanged, and not pleasant ones.

"I came to Wales with the greatest of intentions of securing a peace between your loyalists and mine," he said through clenched teeth. "I came to Rhydilian with the respect for your station that your bloodlines warranted, but what I found when I got here was a man of such conceit that he vomits it out of every pore of his body, forcing the rest of us to choke on it. Tell your men to remove their hands from the hilts of their weapons or I will tell my men to charge and we will have a bloodbath. Are we clear? Thank you. As I was saying, I came here with purely noble intentions but I draw the line at you insulting my daughter. Let me make this very clear so there is no mistake; it is *you* who are unworthy of her and unless something drastic changes my mind, I will return to England on the morrow and take her with me. I would rather see her a spinster or a nun than marry a lord so arrogant that he truly believes all of Wales and England is at his beck and call. You have much to learn about graciousness and tact, de Shera, but it would be beneath me to teach it to you. And with that, I will thank you for the meal, and for your assistance earlier, and bid you a good eve."

William swept from the table with his knights in tow, each one of them eyeing Bhrodi and his men as they followed their liege from the hall. They were hostile glares and perhaps gloating ones. De Wolfe had said everything they wanted to say but were in no position to say it. The victory, for the evening, had gone to the English, and everyone knew it.

Bhrodi's men were not so accepting of it, however; Bhrodi practically had to sit on Ivor to keep him quiet and Ianto had Gwyllim by the neck to keep him from charging. They were clearly outnumbered against the English so to provoke a fight would have more than likely ended badly for them.

Only when the English had cleared the hall did Ianto let go of Gwyllim and return to his food as if nothing unusual had happened. Truth was, he was very curious to see how Bhrodi would react considering no one had ever said such things to him. Not that it hadn't been a long time in coming, but no one had ever had the nerve.

Therefore, Ianto sat and waited, watching as Gwyllim began drinking heavily because he was so frustrated. Ivor had lost his appetite and Yestin seemed to be the only one actively eating and drinking, waiting and watching, as Ianto was, for Bhrodi's response. It was a tense wait.

Bhrodi, however, had no immediate reaction. He simply gazed at the doorway where the English had disappeared, a cup of wine in his hand. If he was embarrassed, he gave no indication. If he was furious, no one would have known. His features were utterly devoid of emotion.

Without another word, he set his cup down and quit the hall.

⌘

"Was it *that* bad, English?"

Jordan's question was soft but William, animated when in the presence of his family, looked at her as if she had just grievously insulted him.

"Of course it was that bad," he said. "I would not lie to you."

Jordan looked at Paris, who was standing just inside the doorway of the tent they had pitched against the walls of Rhydilian's bailey. In fact, there were several tents pitched in the enormous bailey because Rhydilian didn't have accommodations for visitors. They had a great hall, a massive D-shaped keep, and outbuildings. The complex was rather spartan and obviously not meant to house guests.

In fact, the de Wolfe party was stuffing the entire east side of the bailey with their men and tents and wagons. The covered traveling wagon that carried the de Wolfe women on long journeys was positioned next to the big family tent. It was long, a fortified box on wheels, and had several shuttered windows that could be propped open to allow for ventilation. It also had two long and cushioned couches in it, one on each side of the wagon, that were also used as beds. On this trip, Penelope had slept in the wagon while her mother had slept with her father in the big tent. Even now, Penelope was in the wagon, busying herself with repairing some damaged mail as her mother and father discussed the first meeting with Bhrodi de Shera in the big tent.

It was a meeting that had evidently not gone well. Jordan's gaze lingered on Paris for the man to either confirm or deny William's version of the meeting.

"Was that how it happened?" she asked Paris. "'Tis hard tae know considering de Shera is tae be Penny's groom. I doubt Christ himself would be good enough."

But Paris nodded his head in full support of William. "Pompous oaf," he muttered. "From the moment we entered the hall, 'twas as if we were no more than insects beneath his feet. The great and mighty Bhrodi de Shera was very clear in that respect and your husband was handling himself quite well until de Shera insulted Penelope."

The doubtful expression vanished from Jordan's face and she bolted to her feet. "He *insulted* my daughter?" she demanded. "An madra ideal! Beidh mé buille air soundly más rud é go bhfuil an fhírinne!" *The foolish dog! I will beat him soundly if that is the truth!*

Jordan lapsing into Gaelic was never a good thing. William could see that there would be more trouble if he didn't calm his wife; his anger was one thing, but Jordan's was entirely another. If she was mad enough, she'd go after the man with a dirk. He'd seen it before.

"He seemed to think that twenty years of age was quite old," he replied steadily, hoping to calm her. "He thought that mayhap there was a reason why she was so old and still unmarried. It was not a horrific reaction, but one that had my initial ire."

That didn't soothe Jordan in the least. "So he thinks we would provide him with a hag of a wife?" she said, outraged. "Penelope can have her pick of any man in England!"

William went to her, putting his big hands on her shoulders to calm her. "I know, love," he said soothingly. "Do not upset yourself so."

"She is far too good for the likes of him!"

"I know, love."

Jordan wouldn't be eased. "What are ye going tae tell him?" she wanted to know. "I dunna want me daughter marrying such an arrogant lout as that. He isna worthy of her!"

"I know."

"Then ye tell him or I will!"

As William grunted softly, with regret that his wife was so angry, the flap to the tent was pulled back and Jemma entered bearing a tray of cups. Something was steaming from them as she approached William and Jordan.

"Warmed wine," she told them. "Drink it while it's hot. There's some food for ye, too, if ye are hungry."

Jordan turned to her cousin, furiously. "Do ye know what Bhrodi de Shera said about Penelope?" she said. "He said she was too old for a bride! He thinks we would give him a relic of a wife!"

Jemma, who possessed the legendary fire of a Scots more than anyone alive, scowled at her cousin. "That is ridiculous," she said, glaring at William. "Did ye tell him so?"

William knew he had his hands full with two very angry Scotswomen. One did not insult a member of their family and get away with it; he'd seen their retribution towards someone who did and had no desire to beat them off of de Shera. With a grunt of impatience, he held up his hands.

"Do you think I would let the man insult my youngest, my baby girl?" he said, more forcefully to gain the upper hand with them. "Of course I put him in his place and I do not need anger from either one of you at this moment. I have a bigger problem on my hands."

"Bigger than an insult tae yer daughter?" Jordan asked, incredulous. "What could that be?"

William looked at her with exasperation. "I have already pledged Penelope to him and if I withdraw that pledge, then that will be very serious, indeed," he replied. "At this moment, I am not at all certain I want to leave her here with him. With his arrogance and her temper, they'd be at each other's throats in a matter of minutes."

Jemma made a face. "Well and good," she said. "Mayhap Penny will kill him and our problems will be solved."

William just rolled his eye, shaking his head and turning away from the pair. Jemma, still riled, turned to see Paris standing back in the shadows. The man had historically been her nemesis, since the very day they had met, but there was also a very strong loyalty and camaraderie between them. Paris was Jemma's biggest antagonist but he was also, behind her husband, her biggest supporter. It was a true love-hate relationship in every sense of the word.

"Were ye there when the arrogant Welshman insulted Penny?" Jemma asked him. "Well?"

Paris nodded patiently. "Ease yourself, banshee," he said, using his familiar nickname for her. He was the only one who could call her that and get away with it because between the two of them, it was a term of affection. "It was not as bad as what you might think. Twenty years of age *is* rather old to be married. The man's reaction was understandable, although the words of insult dealt after that were not."

Jemma flared. "So ye admit he did insult Penny!"

Paris actually took a step back as Jemma and Jordan both approached him; though they were elderly women, there was nothing elderly in their expressions. It was all fire.

"You'll not harm me, do you hear?" he said, moving away from them as they followed. "I do not like women following me about in rabid packs. I shall tell my wife and then you'll both have trouble!"

Jemma and Jordan slowed but they didn't stop completely. Paris' wife was also their cousin, a tall and sweet woman whose health had been terrible over the past few months. It was why she had not come to Wales; the physics said it was a cancer, something that sickened and saddened all of them deeply. Paris, in fact, couldn't deal with it at all; the man was an excellent healer and understood well how the body functioned, but when it came to his wife, he couldn't face the reality of it. It was something they didn't speak of in front of him for that reason. The end of Paris' world was approaching and the man couldn't accept the fact.

"Caladora is too fine a lady," Jemma said after a moment, her expression softening somewhat. "Nay, Callie wouldna give us trouble. She'd applaud us for telling ye to stand up for Penny!"

William watched the pair go after Paris, daring him to tell them something they did not want to hear. He had to step in.

"Leave him alone," he said. "In fact, I would have both of you put this out of your mind. My dealings with de Shera are my own and I do not need or want your interference. Is that clear?"

Jemma was still going after Paris but Jordan stopped. "She's me daughter, too, English," she said. "I am very concerned by what ye have told me. De Shera needs tae be put in his place."

"And I shall."

"When?"

"Let me sleep on it, at least. I will deal with him tomorrow."

"May I come?"

"You may not."

That started the riot all over again.

CHAPTER FIVE

Two hours of mail repair and Penelope was bored out of her mind. The squires usually did this kind of thing but her father's squire was occupied with a charger that had a swollen fetlock, so she had been relegated to repairing her own armor.

She could hear her parents arguing in the great tent but she couldn't hear what they were saying. Every once in a while there would be a raised voice, or she would hear her father's scolding tone, but she couldn't hear what was being said. She gathered that the first meeting with de Shera hadn't gone well. Truth be told, she wasn't particularly surprised. Her father had a way of not getting along with men when the subject was her.

It was a cold and damp night, and the mist from the marsh was settling heavily over the castle. What had once been a bright moonscape was now covered up by the advancing fog from the nearby bay, giving the grounds a spooky and edgy feel. Torches were upon the battlements, giving off spots of light in the gray mist, and all was very quiet for the most part.

After the battle with the beast of the lake, it seemed that everyone had settled down, but there was a feeling that perhaps they were waiting for something more to happen. Perhaps the violence of the night was not over yet.

Penelope could feel the uneasiness, too, even though she was safe and sound in the protected wagon. The wagon actually had armored sides so she was perhaps the best protected out of anyone in the entire party. It was a very cozy wagon, like her own private chamber, and she felt very safe. But she was also very bored and very curious as to what her parents were arguing about.

Finally, her curiosity got the better of her and she put the mail down. It was mostly repaired, anyway. She had changed clothes after the battle at the marsh because she had been covered in mud, and had washed down as well. Lavender water provided by her mother had washed the mud off her neck and hands and face, and she had dressed in a heavy linen shift, snug leather hose, and a heavy leather and fur robe that went all the way to the ground. The sleeves were snug, and the wrists and neck lined with fur so that it was very warm. The long, dark hair that fell past her buttocks was re-braided and pinned with great iron pins into a bun at the nape of her neck. Penelope didn't like to wear her hair free as a maiden would have; she found it got in the way of what she was doing, so it was always neatly braided and pinned. It also fit better under her helm that way.

She was well protected against the chill as she wrapped herself up in a big shawl that belonged to her mother. It smelled like Jordan and Penelope took great comfort from it. Swaddled in the shawl and her leather and fur robe, she was insulated against the cold as she opened the wagon door and took the five wooden steps down into the bailey. The mist, growing thicker by the moment, cloaked her as she made her way to the tent where her parents were still bickering.

Penelope lingered outside the tent flap for a moment, listening to her mother scold her father about something. Most of it was in Gaelic, which Penelope understood somewhat, and from what she could tell, her mother wanted her father to fight someone. Probably de Shera from the way they were talking; something about the meeting hadn't gone well at all.

Penelope didn't want to get in the middle of it, mostly because she knew she would only exacerbate the problem, so it would be best to stay clear of her mother and father until they decided what to do about it. They both knew her position on it so one more opinion to the situation wouldn't help. When she heard her Aunt Jemma pipe up, she moved swiftly away from the tent. With Aunt Jemma in any argument, things were likely to get lively and she didn't want to get caught in the crossfire. She wondered if she should go for her Uncle Kieran; he was usually the only one who could calm Jemma. But her better sense told her to just stay away.

So, she did. Penelope rounded the tent and moved through the very tight collection of shelters that dotted the eastern portion of Rhydilian's bailey. She passed by her brothers' tent, hearing them muttering inside and moved past the tent belonging to her Uncle Paris. Just as she passed by, Apollo emerged.

"You, there," he called softly. "Where do you think you are going? You are not running away, are you?"

Apollo had his father's sense of humor and his mother's red-headed looks. He was one of her favorite cousins with his ready smile and gentle manner.

"And if I am?" she retorted.

He made a wry face. "I will be forced to stop you."

"You can try."

She was grinning as she said it and he shook his head. "Nay," he said, putting up his hands in surrender. "You take too much pleasure fighting with me. Where are you going, anyway?"

Penelope shrugged. "I thought to search for the privy," she said. "I am going to assume it is near or in the great hall over there."

Apollo glanced in the direction of the big stone hall with the sharply angled thatched roof, now shrouded in mist. "Mayhap," he said. "Shall I escort you?"

Penelope shook her head. "Nay," she replied. "I do not need you."

Apollo grinned. "You have never needed of us, Penny. You are too independent for your own good."

"Will you be sorry to see me go, Apollo?"

He shook his head firmly. "I will wish the man the best of luck. He will need it."

Penelope grinned and balled her fist at him, but she continued on. The mist seemed to be heavier now as she wandered across the bailey, glancing up at the sentries on the walls with their torches and knowing that Apollo was watching her from afar. The boys were always watching her from afar to make sure she didn't come to any harm. It used to annoy her badly and it still did, so she ducked behind the D-shaped keep in order to break the man's line of sight. When she was sure he couldn't see her anymore, she moved into the shadows of the great stone wall, moist with the mist and slick with moss, and headed in the direction of the cold and dark hall.

As she had hoped, there was indeed a garderobe in the great hall; there were two, in fact, built into the thickness of the wall with chutes that emptied out into a great hole to the north side of the structure. When Penelope emerged from the hall, she could see that the entire north side of the hall was perched on what seemed to be a precipice; the bailey angled very sharply down the rocky slope and the walls were built to accommodate not only the drop, but the rocks, and the river of muck from the garderobe ran down the hill and collected far away. It was a very odd portion of the bailey and she stood a moment, studying the drop and the rocky terrain, as the mist settled down upon it. It was becoming very thick now. Pulling the shawl more tightly around her neck and shoulders, Penelope turned around and plowed directly into a big, warm body.

Startled, Penelope gasped and instinctively jumped back, grabbing for the dirk she always kept strapped to her upper left arm, just above the elbow. The dirk came out in a flash but a massive armored arm blocked it, knocking it from her grip. Penelope was about to launch into full battle mode until she saw the face of her accoster. She stilled her fighting inclination but she made sure to back away from him at the same time. She put obvious distance between them.

"*You* again?" she asked, sounding displeased. "What are you doing here?"

Bhrodi gazed back at her, his emerald eyes glimmering. "I live here," he said, a hint of humor in his tone. "What are *you* doing here?"

Penelope eyed the man; he was certainly enormous and strong, and his reflexes were cat-like and swift. He was also rather handsome if she allowed herself to think on it, but that thought disturbed her greatly so she pushed it aside. She didn't want to think the man handsome. He was annoying and she didn't like the way he looked at her; there was something rather lusty reflected in the dark green depths. It unnerved her and intrigued her at the same time.

"Looking," she said simply. "I am leaving now. Good eve to you."

She pushed past him and Bhrodi watched her go. "I surely have that effect on you," he said. "The last time we met, you ran off, too."

Penelope paused to look at the man. "You gave me little choice," she pointed out. "I asked you to release me and you did not. Therefore, I was forced to break free."

Bhrodi cocked his head, perhaps in agreement. "I am sorry that you find me so terrible and disgusting that you would bolt from my arms," he said. "Most women do not think so."

It was a horribly arrogant statement but one that brought a twitch of a smile to Penelope's lips; with six older brothers, she had heard her share of conceit. It was always great fun to cut them down to size.

"I am not most women," she said, her gaze moving over his enormously broad shoulders. They weren't unappealing, in fact. "Good eve to you, my lord."

"Wait," Bhrodi took a step after her as she tried to walk away again. When she paused to look at him, he offered a weak smile as if he really didn't have much more to say but didn't want her leaving just yet. "Won't you tell me your name?"

"No."

"What can I do to wrest it from you? Jewels? Money? A promise of servitude?"

He was being funny and she struggled not to smile. "There is nothing you can do," she said. "I am afraid you will have to go the rest of your life wondering who I am."

"Can I guess?"

"No."

"Why not? Surely there is no harm in guessing."

There was a game afoot and even though Penelope knew she should return to the safety of her encampment, she found herself staying, if only to shoot arrows into the man's overinflated ego. She could tell he was very sure of himself. It made him rather attractive, actually. There was something impish in his expression.

"You could never guess in a thousand years," she said. "You will embarrass yourself trying."

Bhrodi cocked an eyebrow. "Is that so?" he said, pondering. "That is a bold statement."

"Mayhap."

His grin broke through, a beautiful smile that revealed a row of straight, white teeth. Penelope felt her heart race at the sight, just a little.

"You are obviously English," he said. "Did I get that much correct?"

"You did."

"Since you do not know who I am, do you want to guess, too?"

"Nay."

"Why not?"

"Because I do not care."

He burst out laughing, putting a hand over his chest as if she had mortally wounded him. "Ouch," he gasped, pretending he was having difficulty breathing. He began to go through exaggerated death throes. "Cannot... speak... the wound... it is great."

Penelope bit her lip to keep from smiling. "You will survive," she said confidently. "Do you have any other silly questions for me?"

He put out a hand, either to stop her from speaking or to beg a pause. His other hand was still over his heart and he continued to wince dramatically.

"I am not finished with my pains yet," he grunted. "Your aim is sound."

"Of course it is."

He grunted and groaned. "Why would you say that?"

She was enjoying his performance, and the game in general, so much so that she wasn't as cognizant of her answers as she should have been. "Because I am a knight from a long line of great knights," she said. "My aim is always true."

He stopped posturing and looked at her. "A knight from a long line of great knights," he repeated. "The greatest English knight at Rhydilian is de Wolfe. Are you related to him, perchance?"

Penelope's smile fled and her cheeks flushed. *He'd nearly caught her, damn him!* She pulled the shawl more tightly about her and began to turn away, hunting for the dirk he had knocked from her hand.

"I will not tell you," she said. "It is cold and I must return. Good eve to you."

Bhrodi took three enormous strides and was right behind her. "Please," he begged softly, fearful of grasping her should she respond by trying to stab him again. "Do not go. I did not mean to be so forward. I simply want to know who you are."

When Penelope realized he was right behind her, she snatched her dirk off of the ground and whirled on him, pointing the dirk at his chest.

"You are bold to be so close to an armed woman," she said, the humor gone from her tone. "I will ask you to please leave me alone."

Bhrodi came to a halt, watching her as she backed away from him. He was genuinely sorry, and rather ashamed, that he hadn't warmed her to him. He'd felt sure he could accomplish it and it was a significant blow to his male pride to realize she had not instantly fallen for him.

"I cannot," he said simply.

Penelope was still backing away. "You'd better," she said. "My father will not like it if...."

She stopped herself from continuing, furious that she had let it slip about her father. Ever the shrewd tactician, Bhrodi pounced on the information. Like a good warrior, he took advantage of his adversary's weakness and Penelope knew she had given him more fuel for the information he sought.

"Your father is here?" he asked, sounding rather eager. "Who is he that I may speak to him?"

She scowled as she continued to move away. "Speak to him about what?"

Bhrodi followed at a safe distance. "About you, of course."

"What *about* me?"

Bhrodi came to a halt. "I find you astonishingly beautiful and very intelligent," he said. "Mayhap your father will sell you to me."

Penelope came to a halt, outraged. "*Sell* me?" she repeated. "Sirrah, you overstep yourself. I am not a slave to be bartered!"

Bhrodi gazed at her, a faint smile on his lips. "Nay," he said softly, "but mayhap you are a bride to be negotiated. You have his eyes, you know."

Off-balance, Penelope wasn't sure what to say. "Who?"

"De Wolfe's."

Penelope came to a halt. So he knew; well, she'd as much as told him with her foolish answers to his questions. She'd tried to be clever but he, in fact, was cleverer. He had played her soundly and gained the upper hand. There was nothing left to do now but surrender. She sighed heavily and put the dirk down.

"What do you know of him?" she asked.

Bhrodi shrugged faintly. "I know he has come to Rhydilian with a bride for de Shera."

"And what do you know of de Shera?" she wanted to know, sounding exasperated. "Does he spread his business around so that everyone knows why we are here?"

Bhrodi shook his head, the smile still on his lips. "He does not," he said. "But I am sure if he knew it was you he would be receiving as a bride, he would be most receptive."

Penelope eyed him. "Why do you say that?"

Bhrodi's grin broadened. "Because I have never seen such a magnificent woman," he said simply. "Does your father truly allow you to fight as a man? I find that utterly astonishing. Did he, in fact, expect it from you because of who he is?"

Penelope didn't know what to say. The heat coming from the man's eyes was unnerving enough, now with the rather gentle voice behind it. Everything about him was unnerving and her heart was thumping loudly against her ribs. She could feel... something from him. Like invisible fingers, she could feel something from the man reaching out to grab her.

"Please," she said softly, quickly sheathing the dirk as she turned away from him. "I really must go or you shall have de Wolfe's entire contingent down around your ears."

"You would not protect me?" he asked softly.

She paused to look at him. "You do not look as if you need protecting."

"But as my wife, it would be expected of you."

Penelope's eyes widened. "Your *wife*?" she spat. "What madness is this?"

He smiled, his expression surprisingly gentle. "No madness, I assure you," he said quietly. "I am de Shera. Now, will you again tell me you are not de Wolfe's daughter and my intended?"

Penelope stared at him, realizing he indeed knew everything. There was no point in being coy any longer; in fact, she wasn't sure she wanted to be. Perhaps she wanted him to know. Perhaps it was all part of this silly but charming game he had been playing with her all along. Softly, she sighed, and stopped trying to run off. She found she was willing to face him.

"I am Penelope de Wolfe," she said softly. "I fight with my father because I have always fought with my father, as the daughter of a great knight. He should not have allowed me to train as a knight but he could not deny me; he has never been able to deny me except one time."

Bhrodi was thoroughly, utterly upswept in her soft voice and the expression on her face. "When was that?"

Her hazel eyes were fixed on him. "When I told him I did not want to marry the Welsh prince."

His gentle expression didn't change. "Do you still object to marrying me?"

Penelope shrugged, a vague gesture. She seemed to be quite caught up in the man and his thoroughly magnetic pull. Those invisible fingers were pulling at her again.

"I do not know," she said honestly. "I would be lying if I did not express some fear at all of this."

His smile was back. "Fear?" he replied. "I do not believe it. You do not seem as if you have ever been fearful of anything in your life. The courage you displayed earlier this evening when you fought the beast was more than I have seen in most men. It was both impressive and astonishing."

Penelope thought back to that terrifying moment and the reflection unsettled her. "You saw that?"

"I saw it all."

Her confidence, so strong during their entire encounter, began to waver. Perhaps it was her guard coming down, just a little.

"What *was* that creature?" she asked, as if he could supply all of the answers,

Bhrodi gestured in the direction of the keep. "It is much warmer inside," he said. "If you will come inside, I should be happy to tell you what I know."

"I do not believe I should."

"Please?"

It was a very polite request, one she could have easily denied. But for some reason, she couldn't bring herself to do it. Something about his expression stilled her tongue. Perhaps she wanted to speak with him, just a little. Perhaps it was nothing more than pure, insatiable curiosity. In any case, she found herself agreeing.

In silence, she followed de Shera into the keep.

⌘

CHAPTER SIX

Penelope and Bhrodi ended up in the small hall of Rhydilian's keep, a half-rounded room that occupied the entire second floor of the structure. At this late hour, it was dark and still, with the fire burning low in the very tall hearth and a haze of smoke from the malfunctioning chimney lingering up near the ceiling. It was very quiet, quiet enough for two people to have an uninterrupted conversation, which Bhrodi very much wanted to have. Penelope, however, was not so sure.

Seated at the small table near the hearth with a few dogs sleeping at their feet, Penelope sat across from Bhrodi because he had tried to sit next to her, twice, but she had moved away both times. Therefore, he was content to gaze at her from across the table. Like a beautiful, skittish mare, she would not let him come any closer. As long as she wasn't running away he was satisfied, but now came the important part; keeping her engaged in the conversation so she wouldn't grow bored and leave. Bhrodi immediately lapsed into tales of the beast from the marsh.

"When I was a child, I was not allowed to go near the marshes at all because of the beast you saw this evening," he said as they settled down in their seats. "My mother would forbid it. Of course, when you are a child and your mother forbids you anything, it is imperative that you disobey her. Am I not correct in that assumption?"

Penelope fought off a smile. "In my house, it was the opposite," she replied. "If we disobeyed my mother, then we were in for a row."

Bhrodi smiled faintly. "And you have a large family?"

She nodded. "There are nine of us," she said. "I am the youngest."

Bhrodi pondered the information. "I would imagine having a large family makes you feel as if you belong to something," he said. "As if you are a part of something big."

Penelope shrugged. "It does, I suppose," she said. "But my siblings were all so much older than I was that sometimes I felt like an only child."

Bhrodi lifted his eyebrows in understanding. "I have no brothers, although I have a younger sister," he said. "Many times I wished for more siblings, but it was not to be."

"Why not?"

He was thoughtful as he stood up, heading for the earthenware pitcher and wooden cups that were down towards the middle of the table. He spoke as he collected them.

"Because my father was a good deal older than my mother," he said, setting the cups down in front of them and beginning to pour the dark red wine. "My father was married before, you see, many years before he met my mother, but his wife bore him only a daughter before she died. My father was friends with my mother's father, my grandfather, and with the promise of the Coventry earldom, he was able to marry my mother, who was very young. I was born a short time later. Then my younger sister came along when I was almost twenty years of age, killing my mother in childbirth. My father passed away of sheer old age shortly thereafter, so there was no opportunity for more siblings."

Penelope listened with some interest, taking the cup he put before her. "Then who raised your sister? It sounds as if she was an infant when both of your parents passed away."

He nodded as he reclaimed his seat and collected his cup. "She was," he said. "I was fostering at the time and, of course, in no position to raise my sister, so she was raised by my mother's father. When she grew older, she went to Coventry to foster and returned to Rhydilian last year to marry."

Penelope pondered the younger sister's situation as she sipped at the tart red wine. "If she was born when you were nearly twenty, then she must be very young indeed."

"She turned thirteen years of age in January," he said. "Her husband was an illegitimate son of Dafydd ap Gruffydd, cousins to the ap Gaerwens and the last Welsh prince, but the lad was killed last November at the battle of Moel-y-don when Edward tried to storm Anglesey. My sister is almost eight months pregnant with their child."

Penelope tried not to show her dismay over a very young pregnant widow; it wasn't a new story in this world of battle and conquest, but thirteen years of age was still very young to have suffered such trauma. She wasn't very good at expressing sympathy, afraid she would say the wrong thing, so she stumbled to find something more to say to all of that.

"Does she live here with you, then?" she asked.

Bhrodi nodded. "She does," he replied. "The child she carries is full blooded Welsh royalty, so she will remain here in my charge. I am sure Edward would love to get his hands on the child so I must keep it under my protection. Mayhap it will be the last child ever born of pure Welsh royalty, because I, too, have attempted to carry on my royal blood but my attempt has failed so far."

Penelope was drawn in by the curious statement. "What do you mean?"

Bhrodi found his thoughts turning to Sian, his dead love, and the child that had died with her. It was the forbidden subject, now raised fairly early in the conversation. He would not speak her name, or clean her chamber, but somehow as he gazed at Penelope, he found the carefully-held control leaving him. Something about the woman softened him and before he could stop himself, the forbidden subject was upon his lips.

"Because I was married but my wife died in childbirth," he said quietly. "I lost my wife and child two years ago."

Penelope was in the uncomfortable waters of death and pity. She didn't know this man but he had thus far disclosed some very personal details to her and she was unsure how to react. Was he trying to gain her sympathy? Was he trying to soften her towards him? She didn't know him at all and, not knowing, she couldn't be at all sure that this wasn't a ploy of some kind. Therefore, her guard was up.

"Then I am sorry for you," she said without too much emotion. "But I can see how it would be important for such bloodlines to continue. Surely there are many fine Welsh noblewomen who would gladly help you."

He nodded, unwilling to further linger on thoughts of Sian and disappointed that Penelope hadn't shown more pity about it. In fact, he was starting to feel embarrassed that he had confided in her. Either she didn't care or she thought he was lying. If the situation was reversed, he would have believed the latter. It had been too soon for him to discuss his loss with her and he knew it. Somehow, he had cheapened it. The anger he felt was purely directed at himself.

"There are," he said, his tone no longer soft and more business-like. "I have had my pick of them, of course, but your king had other ideas. He seems to think that I need an English bride to dilute the Welsh blood. Mayhap he thinks it will make me less resistant to his rule over Wales."

There was something decidedly haughty in his statement and Penelope stiffened. "If you do not want an English bride, that can most definitely be arranged," she said. "Do not believe for one moment that I am eager or happy to be here."

Bhrodi put his hands up to soothe her. "I did not mean to offend you, my lady, truly," he said. "I was simply relaying my opinion on why your king wants this marriage."

Penelope would not be eased. "If you have your pick of Welsh brides, then I suggest you take one and leave me out of it," she told him. "I was quite happy living with my parents and fighting within my father's ranks. I did not ask for a husband nor do I want one, but my father seems to think this will somehow benefit me."

Bhrodi was quickly coming to understand that she was not a willing bride in the least, which he truly should have suspected all along. It was another blow to that enormous ego; didn't all women want to marry the powerful and handsome Bhrodi de Shera? Apparently, one did not. But he also saw something else in Penelope, something beyond the beauty; the woman was inordinately strong and unafraid to speak her mind. She wasn't a cowering female to do a man's whim. He imagined that a marriage to such a woman would be very adventurous.

He began to imagine a life with her, listening to her opinions, perhaps laughing with her, and most definitely loving her. He could only dream of the prospects that await him in the bedchamber where she was concerned and the thought made him smile. But as he thought on that subject, something else occurred to him; sometimes women who behaved as men did it because they did not, in fact, like men as mates. They preferred a woman in their bed instead. He sincerely hoped that was not the case but knew he had to ask.

"May I ask a question, my lady?" he ventured.

Penelope nodded reluctantly. "If you must."

He hesitated. "You do *like* men, don't you? That is to say, you are not opposed to this marriage because you prefer women over men?"

Penelope knew exactly what he meant. Strangely, she wasn't overly offended by the question. She'd been asked the same thing before, given the fact that she had chosen to follow a man's vocation. It was a natural question. She met his gaze steadily for a moment before shaking her head.

"I do not prefer women in my bed," she said. "If I were to choose a mate, it would be a man, even though men believe they know better than I do. Men like to dominate while women do not. At least, most women do not. Still, I am not particularly fond of my sex in general. Women are weak and foolish. I do indeed like men."

It was a relief to hear it, and Bhrodi was furthermore relieved to realize she wasn't grossly insulted by his question.

"I am very happy to hear that," he said. "As for men trying to dominate you, I do not imagine anyone can get the better of you, my lady. You are too strong for that."

It was a genuine compliment. Penelope eyed him with some doubt, trying to gauge what he meant by his comment. Was he trying to manipulate her emotions again? To play on her vanities? Her reply was careful.

"I will stand up for myself if that is what you mean," she said.

He cocked his head as he gazed steadily at her. "Partly," he said. "I can see such strength in you, my lady. You are a worthy de Wolfe daughter, for certain. It is my thought that such a woman should breed because for her to be childless would be an extreme waste of those fine qualities."

Penelope wasn't sure what to say. Their gazes locked over the table top and, after several long moments, she found she had to look away. Those invisible fingers that seemed to sprout from his eyes were grabbing at her again and she was trying to avoid their pull, but it was very difficult. If Bhrodi had been attempting to manipulate her emotions, to endear himself to her, he had done a very good job. The man had an aura about him that was positively magnetic; the more she tried to resist, the more he pulled at her.

"I... I have never thought of it that way," she admitted, looking at her half-empty cup. "It has always been my opinion that there are other women better suited to marriage and childbearing than me."

He scowled, gently done. "You are the one woman on this earth that should breed children," he said. "Your children will be the finest anywhere and your sons... well, they will be the finest knights this land has yet to see. I would like for them to be my sons, too. I am the only one worthy of such a fine bride."

Her head came up, the hazel eyes staring at him and he waited for the explosion. But there was none; she remained seated, staring at him with an element of thoughtfulness in her expression. *At least she isn't glaring*, he thought. *Perhaps there is hope.*

Hope or contempt; it could have been either emotion but Penelope wasn't sure. In fact, she wasn't sure what she felt. She continued to stare at Bhrodi, feeling the pull stronger than before. She found herself studying the shape of his jaw, square and solid, and the size of his neck.

It was very big, just like the rest of him. She'd never seen a man with such an aura of strength about him.

Bhrodi de Shera radiated an abundance of it and being that she had been raised as a knight and with men all about her, she appreciated physical strength. She respected it. The man's ego aside, she respected him for his reputation alone. De Shera was pure power. At that moment, the resistance she'd been harboring since the introduction of the marriage proposal began to falter. What was it that he had said? *I am the only one worthy of such a fine bride.* Perhaps he was the only one worthy of her, too.

"Are you telling me that you are agreeable to this contract that Edward has forced upon you?" she finally asked. "Will you agree to the king's terms?"

Bhrodi's warm expression faded. "If you are the contract, I will agree to it. If it were any other woman, I would not."

He meant it as a compliment and, this time, she took it as one. "He means to subdue you," she said quietly. "Surely you know that. Llewelyn is dead. The only thing that stands between him and complete domination of Wales is Llewelyn's brother, Dafydd, and you."

Bhrodi wasn't stupid; he knew what Edward wanted. In fact, he knew it better than Penelope did. Llewelyn and Dafydd, the great Welsh princes who had been waging war against Edward for over ten years, were weakening. Llewelyn had been killed and Dafydd was on the run, but Bhrodi, secure in Anglesey with a population that deeply supported their hereditary king, was Edward's last obstacle.

Edward had tried to capture the island nearly six months before when one of his commanders actually built a bridge across the Menai Strait that separated Anglesey from the rest of Wales. It had been the Battle of Moel-y-don, a very significant Welsh victory when the English commander had brought a regiment of men over that bridge and had been soundly defeated by Bhrodi and his allies. Now, Anglesey remained firmly in the hands of the Welsh and Bhrodi knew that Edward had great plans for him; the marriage contract was an option Edward hadn't tried before. Bhrodi knew, eventually, Edward would not be satisfied with an alliance. The man would want complete dominion.

But Bhrodi wouldn't let on all he knew about it, and certainly not at this early juncture in his acquaintance with his future wife. Being English, he knew where her loyalties were and she could very well go back and tell her powerful father whatever Bhrodi told her. He didn't know her enough to trust her yet. Therefore, he was ambiguous in his reply.

"He means to secure peace," he said quietly.

Penelope's gaze was intense. "He means to secure *Wales*."

"Mayhap," he replied softly. "Time will tell."

Penelope watched the man, now interested in his thoughts on the matter of an alliance between him and King Edward. She was very, very curious.

"Surely you will not lay down your arms simply because you marry me," she said. "Edward wants Wales under his control. If you marry me, he will expect your loyalty. That is the only reason he has offered a marital contract. The king doesn't simply want peace; he wants *you*."

Bhrodi regarded her carefully. "You speak as if you are attempting to talk me out of the contract."

"I simply want you to understand what is being offered to you. Why do you think he sent the greatest knight in England to secure the deal? He is offering you a bribe for your fealty."

"I like the bribe."

"Then you intend to take it?"

Something in Bhrodi's face changed; his eyes hardened and his expression tightened. Leaning forward on the table, his voice was low and gritty.

"I will do what is best for me, in all things," he said quietly. "If I agree to this marital contract, it is because I want something, too. Do not think your king can outsmart me because he cannot. I have proven that time and time again. If Edward and I strike a bargain, you can be assured that it will be to my advantage."

Penelope could hear the cold steel of his voice, the power she had reflected on just moments before. In that statement, she could see all of the kings of Anglesey speaking out to her. Bhrodi had that kind of strength in him and more. Her respect for the man grew. She backed down in her questioning; at the moment, she felt as if she didn't have the right to question his motives. He was many steps ahead of her, evidently. He had seen far more battle action than she could ever hope to and he knew his enemy well. Bhrodi de Shera already knew his future.

"My father does not want to lose any more sons in Wales," she said after a moment. "That is why he has offered me. I had six older brothers; now I have five. Papa does not want to lose any more children."

Bhrodi held the steely expression a moment longer before relaxing somewhat. He reclaimed his cup.

"Sound reasoning," he said as he poured himself more wine. "But he will lose his daughter to me."

Penelope's eyes glimmered with unexpected humor. "Mayhap he does not see it that way," she said. "Mayhap he sees it as gaining the son he lost."

Bhrodi saw her humor and couldn't help but respond. It was the first time since he met her that he could recall seeing warmth in her face. He grinned, revealing his big white teeth.

"There could be worse things in this world than being the son of The Wolfe," he said. "He and I will make very strong bloodlines. Our children will be more powerful and noble and royal than anyone on earth."

Penelope cocked her head. "They will be *my* children, not my father's," she said, "and that is the second time you have mentioned sons and children. Just how many do you expect to have?"

He could see trepidation in her expression and it amused him. She was fun to taunt; humor, at the moment, was the one thing they had in common between them. It was something they both understood.

"At least a dozen," he said, watching her from the corner of his eye. "I would say the first eight or ten should be boys. We can have a few daughters as well if it pleases you."

Penelope knew he was jesting with her; he had that type of personality. Already she could tell that he liked to provoke a reaction from her.

"I am not entirely sure we can pick the sex of our children," she said. "We may have all girl children. Have you not considered that?"

He scowled fiercely. "You wouldn't dare!"

She bit off a grin. "I might. Just to teach you a lesson in humility."

His scowl turned into an expression of outrage. "Humility?" he repeated, aghast. "I need no such lesson. I am Bhrodi ap Gaerwen de Shera and I will not have a house full of unruly girl children."

"Why not?"

He was back to scowling, realizing she was baiting him. She was quite strong in her resolve not to let him bully her and he liked it more than he thought he would. She wasn't intimidated by him in the least.

After a moment, his scowl eased and he shrugged his big shoulders carelessly.

"Because they are expensive," he said flatly. "Every one of those girls will need a dowry."

"You are wealthy. You can afford it."

He looked at her, a wry expression on his face, but was prevented from replying when Ivor came rushing into the hall. Both Penelope and Bhrodi looked at the man, noting his rather wild-eyed expression. Bhrodi was immediately on his feet.

"What is it?" he demanded.

Ivor went to Bhrodi but he was eyeing Penelope. "De Wolfe is tearing up the compound," he said. "They are missing a daughter."

Penelope was running from the keep before Bhrodi could even turn to her.

⌘

CHAPTER SEVEN

Upon discovering Penelope missing from the armored wagon, William had not been overly concerned and neither had Jordan. Penelope was known to wander and she was further known to prefer the company of her brothers, so they proceeded to the tent that housed the sons of de Wolfe only to find it devoid of their youngest girl child.

This, of course, garnered the concern of Scott and Troy, and most of all Patrick, the most powerful de Wolfe son, and soon they were milling about the tents in the English encampment looking for Penelope. A thorough search turned up nothing and when Apollo mentioned that he had last seen her in her quest to find the privy, all hell broke loose. The Wolfe Pack went into battle mode.

William had unleashed the full brunt of The Wolfe's fury on the unsuspecting occupants of Rhydilian in his quest to locate Penelope. His men tore through the gatehouse, upending beds and roughing up de Shera's men. They rushed the entire wall walk, looking over the sides of the twenty foot walls and hoping they wouldn't see Penelope's crumpled body on the other side. They completely rousted the great hall, inspecting every nook and cranny, and disturbing the servants and soldiers who were sleeping there. All this in the quest for one small female who could possible mean the difference between complete peace and utter chaos.

The keep was the last frontier to search and they tackled it readily. Just as the pack of de Wolfe's men, led by William himself, came charging up the exterior staircase, Penelope bolted from the entry. She collided with her father somewhere at the top of the steps and William had to grab her so they both wouldn't pitch over the side.

"Penny!" he gasped. "What happened? Are you well, lass?"

Penelope had a tight grip on her father, but not because she had nearly fallen over the side of the steps; it was because she was afraid he was going to go rushing into the keep after de Shera. Given the conversation she had just had with the man, she wasn't entirely sure her father, as an elderly knight with age-diminished reflexes, could best him. De Shera was indeed deadly and powerful. What she did was in protection of her father.

"I am very well," she assured him and the host of anxious faces around him. "De Shera and I were simply having a discussion. I am sorry to have frightened you."

William went from being thrilled to see her to exasperated with her explanation as to why, exactly, she had been missing. He scowled.

"What do you mean you were having a discussion with him?" he demanded. "I have yet to introduce you two."

Penelope patted his arm patiently. "We came across each other earlier when I was looking for the privy," she said. "We introduced ourselves and have been having a pleasant conversation."

William was doing a slow burn at that point. He was furious that Penelope had taken it upon herself to seek out her prospective groom and more furious that de Shera had evidently been a party to it. He had seen how conceited and confident the man was; he could only imagine how he had persuaded Penelope into his lair.

"Pleasant conversation?" William repeated, his jaw flexing. "I cannot believe my ears."

"Why not?" Penelope asked innocently.

William opened his mouth to speak but was interrupted when Bhrodi suddenly appeared through the entryway, the expression on his face one of great concern. He saw de Wolfe, and all of the heavily armed men behind him, and began to speak but William cut him off.

"Given the fact that you and my daughter have not yet been formally introduced, when did it occur to you that having a conversation with her without the presence of chaperones would be a good idea?" he asked with thinly restrained rage. "Mayhap this is the way they do things in Wales, allowing unprotected women to be in the company of strange men, but in England we do things a little differently. We have care for our women's safety and for their reputations."

Bhrodi could see that he was in a very bad position; de Wolfe was furious that Penelope had been alone with her prospective groom and had every right to be. Bhrodi wasn't foolish; he had been taking a chance when speaking alone with the woman but he had considered it worth the risk. It was still well worth the risk because he had briefly come to know a woman of astonishing beauty and intelligence. However, protocols dictated chaperones and escorts upon such a meeting. Therefore, he was in a weak position to defend himself and struggled not to sound as if he was at de Wolfe's mercy.

"My lord, I assure you that nothing improper took place," he said evenly. "I found the lady wandering in the bailey and we introduced ourselves. We were simply speaking on the current situation and on the future in general. I was preparing to escort her back to your encampment quite soon."

A small lie, but de Wolfe didn't have to know that. Already the man was about to explode. Bhrodi could read the distrust and disgust in the man's expression. But William was prevented from replying when Penelope stepped in.

"Papa, nothing unseemly happened in the least," she said, sounding irritated, as if her father had no basis for his anger. "Do you really think I would let it? Do you trust me so little that you would think I would allow a man I just met to take advantage of me?"

William tore his gaze away from Bhrodi, looking at his small and agitated daughter. "You know better than to allow yourself alone with a man," he rumbled, avoiding her questions and grasping her by the arm. "Come, now. We are returning to England on the morrow."

"Wait," Bhrodi stepped forward, his expression one of concern. "What do you mean by that? You came here for a reason, de Wolfe. You came all the way to Wales to offer your daughter to me in marriage to cement an alliance. I will gladly accept your contract."

William was simmering with fury as he looked at Bhrodi. "I withdraw the offer," he grumbled. "You are not worthy of my daughter, a man who would undermine propriety simply to gain his wants. You are a spoiled and insufficient man, de Shera. Edward will have to find you another bride if he wants an alliance."

He spelled out his intentions, leaving no doubt that the arrogant Welsh lord was an unsuitable match for Penelope. The decision had been made. But along with that declaration came the obvious; if they were not here on a peace mission, then they were in enemy territory. Tension filled the air as the de Wolfe knights began to form a protective barrier around William and his daughter. Without another word, the English contingent headed down the stairs except for Penelope; she dug her heels in, preventing her father from dragging her down the steps.

"Papa, *wait*," she insisted, forcing the man to come to a halt. "I agree that we should not have been alone in conversation, but I am glad that Lord de Shera and I were able to speak without you or Mamma hanging over us. There was much less pressure and it was an honest conversation. You know I was opposed to this marriage contract but after speaking with him, I... I do believe it might be an amiable agreement, after all."

William just looked at her and shook his head. He tugged on her arm, forcing her to take the top step. "Not now," he grumbled. "Come with me."

Penelope grabbed the hand that was holding onto her and began to peel the fingers away. "Papa, *stop*," she commanded, holding firm on the top stair. "I am not going anywhere until you listen to what I have to say."

William's fury was gaining steam. "This is *my* decision, not yours," he hissed. "It has been my decision from the beginning. You must trust that I know what is best for you and you will cease to shame me in front of everyone with your arguing."

Penelope jerked his hand free of her wrist and jumped back, out of his reach. "You are embarrassing *me*," she snapped softly. "You are so stubborn, Papa. You did not listen to me when I told you I did not want to come here, so I came. Now that I am here, I believe you were correct in wanting to broker this marriage and I am willing to stay. Will you listen to me on something that will affect me for the rest of my life or will you ignore me as you have always done? You do not always know what is best for me, Papa. Sometimes, I can be correct, too. I am not an idiot."

William forced himself to draw in a deep, calming breath; he had to or else he would be putting her over his knee. Penelope was very much his daughter, clever and unafraid to speak her mind. He had raised her to think for herself. He had to keep reminding himself of that as his intense gaze fixed on her.

"I know you are not an idiot," he said. "But you are young. You do not understand fully what is in men's hearts or who they truly are. De Shera used coercion to bring you inside where he could be alone with you; do you not understand that? He broke propriety for his selfish wants. If he wanted to speak with you, he should have waited until the time was right. I cannot abide by a man who will circumvent me to get at you."

Penelope lifted her eyebrows. "Just as you circumvented my mother's intended husband those years ago so you could get at her?"

It was a low stab, directly to William's honor. Everyone in the north of England knew how The Wolfe had once been the captain of Lady Jordan's intended husband those years ago. He carried on an affair with her until he was finally able to marry her. It was the legend of The Wolfe, long romanticized until reality and fiction blended. The truth was that William, long ago, had used subversion to be with the woman he loved. But the situation back then had been markedly different; he wouldn't allow Penelope to use that circumstance as a parallel comparison. There was no comparison at all.

"I loved your mother," he muttered. "Where love is concerned, anything can and will happen. But de Shera does not love you, Penny; he simply wanted to be alone with you and to compromise your reputation. God only knows what he would have done had your clandestine meeting with him been allowed to continue."

Her expression was serious. "Then you do not trust me?" she asked, hurt. "Do you truly think I would have allowed the man any liberties at all?"

William sighed faintly, glancing at Paris and Kieran as he did so. "I trust you, love," he said. "It is de Shera I have issue with."

"My lord, I swear to you I would not have molested her," Bhrodi spoke up in his own defense; he had to. The fact that Penelope was defending him filled his heart with a joy he hadn't felt in over two years. She was stirring something inside of him that he thought was long buried. "I will again reiterate the circumstances; Lady Penelope was standing alone in the bailey and we spoke. Because it was cold and misty, I invited her into the keep to offer some shelter. She sat on one side of the table and I sat on the other. I did indeed invite a beautiful woman into my keep, alone, but it was not for the reasons you think; it was because I very much wanted to speak to her, this woman whom you intend for me. I have not touched her, nor will I, until she is properly mine. This I swear on my oath as a knight, and on my ancestors as the kings of Anglesey. If you still do not believe me, then I suppose there is nothing left to discuss. But I will say one last thing; you insult me by believing I have only ill intent where it pertains to your daughter. If the situation was reversed and based upon your reputation alone, I would not have thought the same thing of you. I would have assumed you were honorable until proven otherwise."

They were prudent words, ones that William could not readily reject. De Shera made perfect sense and he could feel himself waver. *Honorable until proven otherwise.* In fact, the man had him dead to rights. Perhaps William was the one who was wrong in all of this. He had instantly assumed the worst, about everything. It was the zealous father in him, protecting his daughter against all harm regardless of the facts. Protecting her against an arrogant young lord who, if he was honest with himself, reminded him a good deal of himself when he was younger. Perhaps that was the problem all along; Bhrodi was much as he had been, once.

William glanced at Penelope; she was looking at de Shera with a hint of respect in her expression. Coming from Penelope, that was like moving the Walls of Jericho; earning the woman's respect was nearly impossible. William's stance began to waver a little more and he sighed heavily, looking at all of the knights on the steps below him, men who rushed to do his bidding without question.

His gaze traveled over Scott, big and brawny, and Troy, dark and tall, and to Patrick, who was an enormous mountain of man, and finally to Edward and Thomas, his youngest sons. Both of them were broad and dark, like their father. Sons he adored more than he could express, but then he looked at Penelope... God, could he really let her go? Was this something he was ready to do? He simply wasn't sure. Perhaps he was looking for excuses not to let her out of his sight. Perhaps that was really what this was all about.

"Very well," he finally said, turning to look at Bhrodi. "Mayhap you are correct; mayhap I should have given you the benefit of the doubt. But if your daughter disappeared under similar circumstances, what would you think?"

Bhrodi lifted his eyebrows. "What you thought," he said honestly. "But I swear to you, once again, that nothing improper occurred. We were simply talking."

William gave up the fight; too much in him was uncertain right now. "I will believe you," he said. "But I am taking Penelope to bed now. I am sure you understand."

Bhrodi nodded, taking a step or two towards William and Penelope, his gaze moving between the two of them. "Then may we discuss the contract on the morrow?" he asked hopefully. "I would very much like to."

William looked at his daughter; for once, he would give her the final word. It was her future, after all. Perhaps she needed to make the ultimate decision.

Penelope met her father's gaze, seeing sadness and hope and sorrow and adoration in it. She knew what he was feeling; it was written all over his face. *Perhaps I do not want you to go, after all.* But Penelope wasn't of that mindset; the conversation with de Shera had opened her eyes to a great many things. He was arrogant, that was true, but he was also humorous and protective and loyal. She liked those qualities. She could envision herself tolerating such a husband and perhaps more; perhaps she would even be fond of him someday. Nay, she wasn't opposed to the marriage contract in the least.

"We will discuss it," she said to her father, then looked at Bhrodi. "I must take my father to bed now. He has had a very eventful night and needs his rest."

Bhrodi grinned, noticing that a few of the English knights were grinning, too, but they quickly sobered when they realized de Shera was looking at them. Silently, the English wandered down the steps of the keep, leaving Bhrodi standing on the entry landing, watching about twenty Saesneg knights filter back towards their encampment.

His gaze never left the small woman in the center of the pack as she clung to her father; the affection between them was obvious. Seeing that she was capable of such affection gave him hope that someday, perhaps he would know such warmth from her. Perhaps he would know happiness again.

It had been a very eventful night, indeed.

⌘

CHAPTER EIGHT

Penelope was squirming so much that her mother jabbed her with an iron pin for the tenth time that morning. This time, it was in the thigh and Penelope howled.

"Mamma!" she cried, rubbing her stung leg. "You keep spearing me!"

Jordan was at the end of her patience with her wriggly daughter. "If ye stood still, I wouldna stick ye," she scolded. "For the love of God, Penny, stand still or we shall never be done with this!"

In one of the two top floor chambers of Rhydilian's keep, Jordan, Jemma, and Penelope were spread out all over the room. Trunks had been brought up from the tents and the chamber, once cold and dusty, had been cleaned and swept by Welsh servants to provide a suitable living space for the family of de Shera's betrothed.

A fire burned in the hearth and there were comfortable furnishings. It was a cozy chamber indeed, although the second chamber on the same floor was still one that had gone undisturbed. It still held bloodied linens and things from two years ago, not touched since then. Although Bhrodi had been willing to put Penelope on the top floor, he was still unwilling to disturb the indisturbable chamber. It sat, cold and silent still.

The past two days had seen some progress, however, on the marital front. After forty-eight hours of negotiations, of William laying down his boundaries for Penelope's dowry and of Bhrodi declaring he wasn't so interested in her money as he was in additional manpower as part of the bargain, it had been two solid days and nights of bartering until both parties were satisfied with the outcome. It was then, and only then, that Bhrodi opened up the entire upper floor of the keep for his future wife and her kin. Now, the real preparations began in earnest and messengers were sent out with invitations and announcements to local chieftains.

While William, Paris, Scott, and Troy slept off the effects of the marathon bargaining session they had all participated in to varying degrees, the rest of the English camp was preparing for a wedding. Bhrodi, after about an hour's worth of sleep, took several of his men and three of Penelope's brothers on a hunting expedition to provide meat for the wedding feast while others in the English contingent polished armor and made other preparations. Bhrodi's men, for the most part, went about their usual duties while servants made ready the hall for the festivities. The priest was expected on the morrow and a great wedding would take place. Rhydilian had not seen so much activity in years. The old fortress in the heart of the Pendraeth Forest was alive once again. There was hope in the air.

But Penelope wasn't happy with the dress her mother had brought for her, one that was too small in the bust line and too narrow in the hips. It had been Jordan's wedding dress, in fact, a beautiful garment of pale ivory silk embroidered with gold thread around the cuff of the sleeves, the hem of the full skirt, and around the neckline. Jordan and Jemma had been trying to fit it to Penelope's curvy figure but Penelope had no patience for such things. She hated surcoats, shifts, corsets, delicate shoes, and anything else feminine, so it was a struggle for her to be patient through all of it.

When Jordan finally finished pinning and peeled the garment from Penelope's body, the girl, clad only in a shift and hose, threw herself onto the nearest bed while Jordan and Jemma sat down next to one another and continued working on the alterations together. Penelope was fidgety and bored, a bad combination.

"I wanted to go hunting," she said wistfully, her gaze moving to the lancet window and the bright blue sky beyond. It was a cool day with puffy clouds scattered across the sky. "Do you suppose they have gone anywhere near that marsh?"

Jordan shuddered. "I hope not," she said. "Yer da said that de Shera told him the beastie had been there for many generations, brought by the Northmen when they sailed these shores."

"I seem to recall hearing a similar tale of a beastie far to the north of Scotland," Jemma said, concentrating on the stitches she was making. "I seem to remember me da telling me stories of it. Do ye remember, Jordie? It was a tale of St. Columba and how he vanquished a beastie from the River Ness. Do ye think the beastie came down here to Wales, then? Mayhap he found another home."

Jordan shrugged as she fixed the stitching on one of the sleeves. "A Scots beastie would never come tae Wales," she declared. "The animal has too much taste. He would stay in Scotland."

Jemma giggled and even Penelope smiled as she looked over at her mother and aunt. Even at their advanced age, they gossiped and teased as if they were young girls again. She would miss them very much when they returned home and left her here, alone, to face a new future. She tried not to think of the moment when her entire family would leave her.

"Whatever it is, and *wherever* it is, my sword is still lodged in its eye," she said, her smile fading. "I want my sword back."

Jemma's head snapped up. "Dunna go back to the swamp to get it," she warned. "Have de Shera make another one for ye. I wouldna risk me life trying to retrieve something that can be just as easily replaced."

Penelope sighed, sorrowful at the loss of the sword her father had given her, and returned her attention to the window. She could hear seagulls crying, having come over the mountain from the bay on the other side. They were riding the drafts and swooping down on potential food in the bailey. As she rolled over onto her belly, there was a knock at the chamber door and she leapt up, moving to open it. It was nearing the nooning hour so she was hoping it was food. Lifting the iron latch, she opened the heavy oak door.

The small corridor outside was dim but her focus immediately found a small, dark-haired girl standing well back from the doorway. Looking at the girl, Penelope immediately realized two things; that there was no food in the girl's hands and that she had an obviously pregnant belly. She was dressed in simple clothing, leading Penelope to believe it was a servant.

"What is it?" she asked.

The girl blinked as if startled by the question. She took a step back as if fearful of Penelope, but then suddenly lifted her hand and thrust a bundle of pale fabric in her direction.

"I... I thought you would like this," she said, her voice quivering with fright. "M-my brother said you were getting married and... and... this was my mother's."

Penelope was confused. "Your brother?"

The girl nodded unsteadily. "He said you were his bride."

Penelope peered more closely at the girl; she was very small and very pregnant, and it began to occur to her who it might be; *my sister is eight months pregnant with her first child.* Realization dawned and, with a start, Penelope came away from the door, turning to her mother.

"Mamma!" she hissed. "Come quickly!"

Jordan was off her chair, scurrying to the door. Penelope, her eyes wide, gestured towards the girl in the corridor. Jordan looked at the young woman curiously and then to Penelope as if expecting more of an explanation as to why she had been called over. Penelope's gaze lingered on her mother a moment, hesitantly, before returning her attention to the girl.

"Are you Lord de Shera's sister, then?" she asked timidly. Since she was so terrible with tact or gentleness, she had called to her mother. She needed help in the face of the nervous and terrified young girl. "He... he told me you that you were here at Rhydilian."

The girl had backed away nearly to the stairs, looking fearfully between Jordan and Penelope. The ball of fabric in her hand was still extended.

"Aye," she whispered. "I have come to... to bring you this. It belonged to my mother."

Jordan, seeing a child who was very pregnant, tried not to gasp at the sight. She was shocked by it. Being gentle and sweet and motherly by nature, she carefully moved towards the skittish young girl.

"Why, what is it that ye've brought us, child?" she asked, her manner kind and soothing. "What is yer name, lass?"

The young girl wanted to back away but the steps were behind her so, for the moment, she held her ground as Jordan came close.

"Tacey," she murmured, her voice quaking pitifully. "My name is Tacey. This was my mother's wedding cap. My brother said I should bring it to you."

Jordan smiled encouragingly as she reached out, very carefully, and took it from her. She unfurled the wad of silk and pearls. "'Tis beautiful, it is," she said gently, holding it up to get a look at it. "Have ye been keeping it safe all these years?"

The Lady Tacey de Shera ap Gruffydd nodded, her dark hair flapping down over her dark eyes, but she remained silent and nervous. A tiny woman with bird-like arms and quick movements, Jordan smiled sweetly at her.

"Yer mother would have been very touched tae see ye take such good care of it," she said kindly. "Would ye like tae come in and visit with us, lass? Come along, now. Since ye are tae be kin, we would like tae come tae know ye."

Jordan was able to reach out and grasp the girl gently by her very slender arm. Tacey, torn between her innate fear of people and the lure of a kind, motherly voice, allowed herself to be directed towards the chamber. She was dragging her feet, however, very timid and nervous. She spent so much of her time alone that being around people terrified her, and being around strangers made her want to faint.

But she permitted Jordan to carefully pull her into the chamber, her eyes darting about fearfully. When she saw Jemma, she nearly bolted but Jordan held her firm. In fact, she pulled her towards the hearth where they were sewing on the big silk dress.

"We were just sewing Penny's wedding dress," she said. "This is me cousin, Lady Jemma. Do ye sew, lass?"

Tacey didn't even know what to say; she was being pushed around by a well-meaning woman with a heavy Scots accent. Jordan gently sat the girl down in a chair that Penelope had pulled up and Jemma was already bending over her, handing her needle and thread.

"Ye can sew the sleeve," Jemma said in a gentle tone that was much different from her usually-aggressive manner. She was very good with babies and children. "See how the gold thread has come unwound? Just follow the pattern around the sleeve and re-stitch it. It will be simple."

Tacey took the needle, dumbly, looking at the sleeve in front of her as Jemma pointed out the repair work. All the while, she was quivering in fright but there was something about these women that instinctively put her at ease. They were very kind and very gentle with her, something that had been missing for most of her life and especially as of late. She'd hardly seen a soul in over a year other than her brother and her brother's knights. Now, here she was in the midst of strange women and hardly knew how to behave.

So, very hesitantly, she lifted the needle, peering at the sleeve and really having no idea what to do. When she looked up at Jordan and Jemma, they were smiling encouragingly at her. She swallowed hard.

"I… I have not sewn much," she said. "I am afraid I might make a terrible mistake."

Her voice was so small and young-sounding, and she seemed so very lost and bewildered. Jordan's heart ached for the girl as she sat down beside her.

"Nonsense," Jordan said firmly. "Ye canna make a mistake. All ye need tae do is stitch in and out, in and out, and follow the pattern. Here, I will show ye."

Carefully, she took the needle and fabric from Tacey and began to carefully stitch as an example to Tacey. Tacey watched with a mixture of apprehension and curiosity, glancing up at Jemma and Penelope and noting the kind expressions on their faces. She was coming to realize these women were trying very hard to be kind to her. When Jordan handed the material and thread back to her, she took it timidly.

"Are you sure you want me to help you?" she asked, looking at the women around her. "I would feel terrible if I damaged the dress. I would never forgive myself."

She sounded so very beaten and sad. Penelope sat on the floor next to her, gazing up into the small, fine-featured face.

"Of course I want you to help," she said. "You are Bhrodi's sister, are you not? Think what it would mean to me to wear a dress you helped to sew. It would make you part of the wedding ceremony, would it not? That makes it special."

Tacey gazed down into Penelope's lovely face, studying it closely for the first time. When Bhrodi had come to her last evening and informed her that she would soon have a sister, Tacey was understandably surprised. And she was understandably anxious. But within the first few moments of knowing Penelope and her mother and aunt, she was coming to see that they were all very lovely and kind women. Her fear of the new situation, and of these unfamiliar women, was subsiding somewhat. She swallowed hard, struggling to summon her courage.

"I... I have not sewed in a few years," she admitted. "I was never very good at it."

Penelope was inspecting the sleeve in Tacey's hand. "Nor am I," she said. "That is why my mother and aunt are doing the sewing. Surely you must be good at other things?"

Tacey could feel herself warming to the conversation although it was difficult; she'd spent so much of her life in isolation because of her rare royal status that she'd hardly had the practice in social situations. She was a young woman literally locked in a tower for her own safety.

"I do like to draw," she said hesitantly. "And I speak four languages. I also play the harp and sing, but it is difficult to play these days because... because...."

She was indicating her big belly and Penelope smiled, trying desperately to put the frightened girl at ease. "You must be very excited about the baby," she said. "When is he due to arrive?"

The faint glimmer of warmth in Tacey's eyes faded and she averted her eyes, looking at her lap. "I... I am not entirely certain."

Jordan and Jemma, who had birthed sixteen children between them, were listening carefully. "What do ye mean ye are'na certain?" Jordan wanted to know. "What does the physic say?"

Tacey seemed to shrink, her eyes riveted to her belly. "There was a physic at first and he thought mayhap in early summer," she said, her voice barely above a whisper. "But he was not certain."

Jordan and Jemma passed concerned glances. "What do ye mean?" Jordan continued, trying to be gentle but genuinely concerned. "Do ye not recall when ye had yer last menses? The physic would know based upon that."

Tacey was still staring at her lap. Then, she lifted a boney hand to flick away a tear that had made its way onto her cheek.

"My... my menses... they do not come anymore," she said, confused by the question and trying very hard not to weep. "When I married my husband last year, he only... he was only fifteen years of age, you see, and... and he was killed and... I have been here ever since."

Jordan, Jemma, and Penelope were all looking at each other with various stages of unease. Penelope was simply confused and concerned over the girl in general but Jordan and Jemma, as the older women, could see much more than that. Tacey ap Gruffydd seemed very lost and forlorn, and incredibly neglected. Moreover, it seemed that she really didn't know anything about her pregnancy, or even how it physiologically happened. Was it possible she didn't even know the reality of how a woman became pregnant? Based upon those observations, Jordan could feel the rage building in her heart. Who could have done such a terrible thing to this tiny little woman? The mothering instinct began to run wild.

"Has no one tended ye, lass?" Jordan asked softly, daring to put a hand on Tacey's dark head. "Has no one bothered tae talk tae ye about this?"

Tacey appeared confused. "I... I do not know," she said. "The physic told me I was pregnant and he told me I would soon have a son."

Jordan was stumped. "But no one else?" she asked. "Has no one taken care of ye?"

Tacey nodded firmly, wiping away the tears on her cheeks. "My brother has provided very well for me," she insisted, trying to sound as if she wasn't totally alone and discarded. "I have a comfortable chamber and good food. And he comes to talk to me every day so I am not lonely."

That wasn't enough for Jordan; the entire situation was unacceptable. She stroked the girl's dark hair to give her some measure of comfort that had evidently been sorely lacking. She couldn't help herself.

"But has anyone *tended* ye?" she wanted to know. "Has anyone looked at the babe tae see if he thrives? Has anyone checked on ye tae make sure *ye* thrive?"

Tacey shook her head, daring to look up at the host of concerned faces around her. "Nay," she said. "But I am well and the babe moves around. He is well, too."

"But who will come when it is time to deliver the babe?"

Tacey looked completely bewildered by the question. "My brother has a surgeon for his men," she said. "He will be here."

Jordan was outraged. "To deliver a baby?"

Tacey nodded hesitantly and with that, Jordan looked at Jemma, biting off words of anger. She did, however, throw up her hands in exasperation. And then she could remain silent no longer.

"I canna believe what I am hearing," she said to Jemma. "Did ye hear the lass?"

Jemma was as disgusted as her cousin. "She is no more than a bairn herself," she said. "She needs someone to look after her. Who would leave this child to fend for herself? And who wants a smelly old barber delivering the babe?"

"Outrageous!"

"Terrible!"

Penelope watched her mother and aunt go into a private huddle. They were speaking in Gaelic, obviously about Tacey, hissing and whispering, and casting long glances at the young woman. Tacey watched them with great concern, fearful that she had said or done something wrong. When Penelope glanced at Tacey and saw the expression on her face, she hastened to reassure her.

"They are always like this," she said, grinning to ease the girl's anxiety. "They have sixteen children between them and they think they know everything about babies. I suppose they do."

Tacey was eased, somewhat. Penelope's manner soothed her a bit. "I would like to know something," she said timidly. "I would like to know how to tend him when he is born."

Penelope's smile faded. "Has no one told you anything?"

Tacey shook her head. "There are only men around me," she said. "What do they know?"

"No female servants?"

"My brother does not like them at Rhydilian. He says they are disruptive."

Now it was Penelope's turn to be surprised and mildly outraged. She turned to her mother and aunt.

"Did you hear what she said?" she asked. "She said there are no womenfolk here at the castle at all. No one to help her or tell her how to tend the child."

That was it for Jordan and Jemma. The older women set down all of their sewing implements and grabbed for their cloaks. Penelope and Tacey watched them mutter and grumble to each other as they donned capes. It was clear that they had a mission to attend to; what it could possibly be was anyone's guess. But Penelope thought she might have an inkling.

"We shall return," Jordan said, forcing a smile at Tacey because she looked so pale and frightened. "Take heart, lass. We shall make sure ye are well tended and that the babe is well tended when he comes."

Tacey was nearly beside herself with anxiety. "But... but I do not want to be any trouble," she said. "Please do not bother my brother with anything. I do not want him to think I have done something wrong."

Jordan patted the young girl on the head. "Ye haven't done anything wrong, lass," she said. "And we will make sure to take care of yer brother."

The last words were spoken rather ominously.

⌘

Bhrodi had no idea what he was returning to when the hunting party returned from their very successful jaunt. It was close to sunset and although the meat his men carried on their steeds would not be for this meal, it would make fine provisions for the feast on the morrow.

As the sons of de Wolfe returned to their encampment and Bhrodi's men disbursed, Bhrodi headed into the keep. He found that he was very eager to see Penelope. She was all he had thought of most of the day, an unusual occurrence. Usually, his mind was on his tasks or other important items. To have his attention garnered by a woman was something that hadn't happened in two years. He'd missed it.

Penelope's brothers, Patrick and Edward and Thomas, had accompanied him on the wedding hunt. They seemed like decent men, but of course it was hard to tell considering they looked at Bhrodi as if he was a thief to steal their sister. Patrick, an enormous knight with pale green eyes, seemed to be the most amiable, but frankly, Bhrodi was a little intimidated by him. The man's size alone had him leery, and his fists were as big as a man's head, so Bhrodi kept a civil conversation with him and tried not to get within arm's length should Patrick have an ulterior motive with his sister's intended.

It was an odd sensation, really, for Bhrodi had never been intimidated by any man, ever. Even now, as he walked towards the keep, he found himself chuckling about his fear of Sir Patrick. The Wolfe certainly had produced sons worthy of his legend. Bhrodi hoped he would do the same someday.

But the smile faded from his lips quickly enough. Upon entering the keep, the first thing Bhrodi saw was a female serving woman in the smaller feasting hall. The woman was scrubbing the worn, chipped table that was the centerpiece of the hall. Confused, Bhrodi took a few steps into the hall itself to realize there were two more women inside; one was on her hands and knees, washing the floor corner where the dogs liked to sleep and the other one was cleaning out the hearth itself. There were clouds of ashes coming forth.

Bewildered, Bhrodi looked around to make sure he was even in the right castle. It looked like his but it certainly didn't smell like it. The dog and feces smell had nearly been erased. With a furrowed brow, he backed out of the hall and took the spiral steps to the next level where there were two chambers; his and his sister's. He peered inside his sister's chamber only to see that it was completely empty. Tacey wasn't anywhere to be found, and he quickly realized the entire third floor was empty.

Now he was truly puzzled as well as concerned. He took the steps two at a time as he made his way to the top floor where he had given his bride and her family free reign. The moment he hit the upper landing, he could hear the voices of women – heavy Scots accents mostly. He knew it was Penelope's mother and aunt; he'd come to know them briefly over the past two days and had seen that they were very practical, mothering women. But cursory observations were as close as he had gotten with them. When he finally poked his head inside of the chamber where Penelope had been sleeping, he was hit by an astonishing sight.

Instead of one bed there were now two. The second bed had been stripped down and there were two more strange serving women pulling off linens and fluffing up the re-stuffed mattress. On the bed against the eastern wall that was covered with hides and linens, he could see Tacey sitting there, propped up with pillows as Penelope's aunt fed her something out of a bowl. Penelope herself was standing on a stool while her mother fussed with a beautiful ivory gown that was draped over her body.

Bhrodi's confusion took a dousing as his gaze beheld Penelope in the ivory garment; her hair, which he had only seen braided and bound to her head, was free and unbridled, tumbling in a great wavy mass down to her knees as she stood upon the stool with her back to him. He'd never seen such glorious hair. Penelope's mother, a very lovely and young-looking woman for her advanced years, was focused on a sleeve but glanced up when she caught movement in the doorway. The woman's pale green eyes immediately zeroed in on Bhrodi.

"Ah!" she called, turning to snap her fingers at her cousin as the woman spooned something into Tacey's mouth. "The laird has returned, Jemma. Come, now. We must tend tae him."

The entire room began to move with a purpose before Bhrodi could say a word. It seemed that women were coming at him from all directions, as if he were a magnet pulling them into his orbit. Jemma set the bowl down quickly and bade Tacey to lie down while Jordan put aside her pins. The two older women moved quickly towards Bhrodi as Penelope, realizing he was in the room, turned to catch a glimpse of him. But a glimpse was all she was able to catch as Jordan and Jemma surrounded him and whisked him away to the chamber across the corridor.

The door slammed shut and Penelope might have even heard them lock it. Having listened to her mother and Jemma most of the afternoon discuss the changes for Rhydilian, she knew Bhrodi was in for a serious conversation. She had wanted to be a part of the discussion but her mother had denied her. This was something Jordan felt strongly she needed to do alone as the mother of the young woman who would soon be living here. Now, all Penelope could do was wait and hope her future husband would still want to marry her after her mother was finished with him. She wouldn't have been surprised if he called the whole thing off when all was said and done.

As for Bhrodi, he was still mightily confused, wondering what it was all about; strange servants, bustling activity, and now two serious women who seemed to be closing in on him. The door to the chamber he had been herded into wasn't locked but it might as well have been; The Wolfe's wife and her cousin were standing in front of it as if daring him to try and escape. Never mind the fact that this was the indisturbable chamber; Bhrodi sensed this wasn't going to be a pleasant conversation if their expressions were any indication. He smiled weakly.

"You will forgive me for accidentally seeing my intended in her wedding gown," he said, thinking perhaps they might be angry with him for that reason. "I simply came to see if...."

Jordan cut him off. "Not tae worry, m'laird," she said. "The gown 'tisn't finished yet. However, there is much tae speak tae ye about, if ye please. Ye must understand that we mean no disrespect, but there have been some... changes."

Bhrodi lifted his eyebrows. "What changes?"

Jemma stepped forward; she was much more blunt than her cousin and in this case, since it wasn't her daughter marrying the man, she could afford to be. She fixed him in the eye.

"*Many* changes," she said frankly. "Let us begin with yer sister. Is it true ye keep the girl locked up with no one for company but yerself?"

Bhrodi had a feeling this might be part of their issues. When he found his sister's chamber empty, he could only guess what had happened in his absence. To an outsider, he realized how the situation with Tacey might appear. After a moment, he nodded.

"It is for her own protection, I assure you," he said quietly. "She carries a child of full-blooded Welsh royalty. Your king would love to get his hands on such a child. What I do, I do to keep her safe."

"Bah," Jemma spat. "She's a child and ye've left her completely alone in a time when she needs womenfolk about her. Do ye know she doesna even realize how she became pregnant? No one ever explained to her the ways of men and women. And this boy who was her husband – he was brutal to her. Did ye know that? The lad kept her abed day and night since the moment they were married because it was put into his head that he had to beget her with child. Do ye know how frightened and hurt she was by that?"

Bhrodi was mildly taken aback, struggling not to feel guilt or confusion. "She is of royal blood and so was her husband," he said as if he wasn't sure what her problem was. "It was their duty to reproduce. Thanks to God she is pregnant now that he is dead. She alone is carrying on valuable royal lines."

"And that's another thing!" Jordan said, wagging a finger at him. "Ye keep her locked up because ye say ye're protecting her, but that's rubbish. Ye're keeping her locked up tae preserve the pure bloodlines of the Welsh and I tell ye now that it's disgraceful what ye've done. That poor lass in there is a babe herself with the expectations of all of Wales upon her. Ye've treated her with less compassion than ye would a dog. She's a child, for God's sake, not a brood mare. I'll not stand for it, do ye hear? If ye expect tae marry me daughter, then there will be some changes around here that are fit for womenfolk or, by God, I swear I'll pack me daughter up and take her back with me tae England. Are we clear on this?"

Bhrodi was in no position to do anything other than agree. Like most men, an angry woman, especially an angry woman who was to become his mother and kin, struck fear into him. He understood some of their concern, but for the most part, he honestly had no idea what had them so angry.

"What changes to you mean?" he asked seriously. "This is a military installation and I will not have you turn it into swamp of feminine finery and foolishness."

Jemma growled but Jordan held her hand out to the woman to silence her. "Firstly, there will be women about this place. Ye need them. Therefore, while ye were out hunting, I asked one of yer soldiers tae take me tae the nearest town, which is the village on the other side of this mountain. I was able tae secure eleven women who were willing tae come and work here. One of them will be yer chatelaine because, God knows, me daughter knows nothing about that. Even now, the women are working on cleaning the keep and the hall. We must make this place livable for me daughter."

Bhrodi's eyebrows lifted. "So *you* engaged the women?" he said, incredulous. "Did you not stop to think that there was a reason I did not employ women at Rhydilian?"

Jordan waved him off. "Whatever yer reason 'tis ridiculous, I say," she snapped. "This entire place stinks of men and foulness, and if me daughter is tae live here, then it will be made acceptable. As for the women, if yer soldiers canna keep their hands off them, then that is something ye must deal with. A strong commander would not have issue with his men's behavior. He would control it."

Bhrodi's incredulity cooled into great displeasure. Now she was offending his senses as a military commander and he was close to letting loose on her regardless of the fact that she was The Wolfe's wife. If the woman wanted an argument, he would certainly give her one.

"Madam," he said slowly, "say what you will about my keep and the way I run it, but when you question my ability to control my men, you have gone too far."

"Not far enough," Jemma piped up. She had never been afraid of confrontation and, quite frankly, she was furious. On behalf of the neglected young woman she had spent the day with, she had to right the wrongs with the ignorant brother. "I will indeed question yer very ability to show mercy or compassion. Judging from the way you have kept yer sister shut up, ye have no sense of mercy at 'tall. Is that what kind of husband ye'll be also? If yer wife doesna please ye, then ye intend to lock her up, too?"

Bhrodi looked between the two angry women; at the moment, he had quite enough anger of his own and he put his hands up to stop the accusations.

"Listen to me," he boomed, stopping the angry chatter. When two sets of startled eyes focused on him, he continued. "My sister has been confined to her room to keep her safe. I do not want her out and about where men can molest her, or where she can fall down steps and harm both her and the child. What I did, I did to protect her and if it is wrong, then I do not know what to say to all of that. Given the circumstances and my knowledge of such things, I did the best that I could. The last pregnant woman that was here did not fare very well and I sought to ensure that my sister fared better."

Like water on a fire, that statement seemed to extinguish the angry Scots down considerably. At least they were no longer yelling at him. In fact, they looked at each other with a mild dose of confusion and perhaps a pinch of regret. It was evident that they were rethinking their strategy; perhaps they had acted with some haste in the matter, judging Bhrodi before they knew all of the facts. Jordan was the first one to speak, more calmly this time.

"Who was the last pregnant woman within these walls?" she asked softly.

For the second time since the arrival of Penelope and her family, Bhrodi found himself on the verge of speaking on the forbidden subject. He could feel the mood of the room around him, the old linens and old memories, as they clutched at him, begging him to free them of their cold and lonely prison. It occurred to him that, somehow, the subject of his wife was easier to discuss with women. They understood more, especially about the mysteries of childbearing. He thought that perhaps they understood death better, too.

Gazing into Jordan's eyes, the shape of Penelope's, he realized he was about to speak of the most painful moment of his life once again but perhaps this time, the reaction would be better. Perhaps these women wouldn't think he was trying to earn their sympathy. Perhaps they would believe him.

"My wife," he said, his voice hoarse and soft. "Her name was Sian and we had been married for seven years before she fell pregnant. She was from the House of Gwenwynwyn, a very old and royal Welsh family, so our child, much like my sister's, was very much anticipated. Sian's health had never been very good and the pregnancy was difficult. She was a very active woman so it was impossible to make her rest; she was always moving, always overseeing the keep, always doing something. When her time came, she labored to deliver our son for nearly three days and in the end, her body wasn't strong enough to expel the very large infant. When she died, the physic took a dirk and cut the child out of her belly but it was too late; he was dead as well. Look around you; this was her chamber. This was where she bore my son and where she died. I shut this room off the day she perished and I have not returned since."

Jordan and Jemma were looking at him with various degrees of sorrow. Jemma sighed sadly and lowered her gaze, realizing they'd been quite harsh with the man without discovering his reasons first. Given the circumstances, however, there had been few other conclusions they could come to. As Jemma shook her head with regret, Jordan put her hand on his big forearm.

"I am so sorry for ye," she murmured. "I know what it is like tae lose a child. I lost one meself. Her name was Madeleine and she was born dead. Jemma lost a daughter, too, many years ago so, ye see, we both understand yer grief in losing a child. They say it is God's Will but I will admit I have questioned the wisdom of such a thing. I canna see God killing a child for a greater good."

Bhrodi shook his head, glancing from side to side, at an old chair and the old wardrobe that used to belong to Sian. "Nor I," he murmured. "After she died, I banished all women from Rhydilian. I didn't want to see them here. Physics were banished as well. They are worthless old fools. And then my sister came and when she became pregnant, I locked her in her chamber to force her to rest in the hopes that her child would be born healthy. I could not do that with my wife but I would do it with my sister. Now you know, so if my sense of mercy is ever in question again, mayhap now you will understand why I do what I do. I will not make the same mistake twice."

Jordan nodded patiently. "And so ye willna," she assured him softly. "Ye went through a difficult time but ye survived it. The death of a loved one tears yer heart out and nearly destroys yer soul, but ye dinna let it defeat ye. Ye're stronger now than ye were before."

Bhrodi gazed at the woman, feeling an odd connection with her. The Wolfe's wife was the first woman he had ever met who had suffered the loss of a child and he found his guard going down even more. Finally, someone who could perhaps understand the anguish he had gone through. The arrogant de Shera persona was giving way to the vulnerable man beneath as he spoke to her.

"Mayhap," he said softly. "But you must understand that I am doing what I can to help my sister. I am not trying to keep her from the world; I am trying to keep the world from *her*. I only want to keep her and the child safe."

Jordan patted his hand in complete and utter understanding. No longer was she an enraged mother; now, she was coming to understand things just a bit more. She could see that Bhrodi, in his capacity as a warrior, was doing the only thing he could to protect his sister. Jordan was coming to see that The Serpent was just the least bit human, with human frailties. It gave her hope, for Penelope's sake.

"Not tae worry, now," she said confidently. "Jemma and I will help ye take care of yer sister and yer keep, but ye must trust us. Can ye do that? We only want what is best for ye and for Penny and for yer sister, I swear it."

Bhrodi could see that she meant it. Beneath all of the Scots fire, he could sense that she was a loving and compassionate woman. He'd had little doubt of that even if she had overstepped her bounds in the process, which he was coming to see was for altruistic intentions. The woman meant well. Therefore, he was willing to give her a free hand in things she knew more about than he did. As the mother of his future wife, he was willing to trust her but as a practical man, he suspected he had little choice. If he wanted to marry the woman's daughter, then he would have to bow to her wishes for the time being.

"No one has taken care of this keep for more than two years," he muttered. "It may prove to be a difficult task."

"I think we can manage. "

He had little doubt of that. After a moment, he shrugged. "Very well," he said. "But I will admit, I still do not want womenfolk here."

Jordan patted his arm again. "I realize that, but it will only serve to help ye," she said. "I wouldna say so if it wasna true. Women are good for things other than childbearing."

She said it with some humor and he smiled weakly. "And what are Scots good for?"

"Beating down the Welsh."

"You did a good job of it."

Jordan laughed softly. Then, her gaze moved over the dusty chamber and a measure of regret filled her features. "I must confess something tae ye," she said quietly. "We dinna know this was yer wife's room so we removed the bed and put it in the other chamber so that yer sister could share the chamber with Penelope for the time being. I have women washing the bed linens. I truly dinna know this was a chamber of sorrow. We thought it was simply unused."

Bhrodi hadn't noticed the missing bed when he had entered the chamber and felt a flash of anger at the confession but it was just as quickly doused. It was indeed an unused chamber, this indisturbable room, but perhaps two years was long enough to leave it as a shrine to loss. He was coming to think that perhaps it was a good thing Lady Jordan had taken charge of the room because he certainly was unable to do it. Perhaps it was better left to another, someone who would tend it and clean it the way Sian had. Nay, he realized that he wasn't angry about it in the least. There was a part of him that was relieved.

"It *was* unused," he murmured. "You… you have my permission to clean it. It was a warm and tidy chamber, once."

Jordan was glad he wasn't angry about it; now that she knew the history of the room, he would have had every right to be furious. But he seemed rather accepting of what she had done.

"And it shall be again," she assured him. "We will see tae it."

It had taken a strange woman to accomplish in one day what close friends and servants had been unable to accomplish in two years. Bhrodi could feel the tension and uncertainty of the situation lift. When he had entered the room, he had felt their hostility but now he could feel their optimism. He was satisfied with it, he realized, and much more at peace than he had been in a very long while. The situation was changing at Rhydilian after two years of darkness and Bhrodi sensed that light was once again returning. For the first time in a years, he had some hope for the future. Aye, things were changing and he was receptive for the most part.

Without another word, they began to move out of the chamber, heading for tasks that required their attention. There was a wedding on the morrow and they all had preparations to make.

It was going to be a very big day for them all.

⌘

Castell Meurig
The village of Llangefni, seven miles south of Pendraeth

They had all received the missive from Rhydilian Castle the same way – one of Bhrodi de Shera's *teulu*, or personal guard, had brought the news of de Shera's impending wedding. It was something that under normal circumstances would have been cause for great celebration, but the *teulu* who had delivered the missive to Lon ap Ganol of Castell Llandegfan had mentioned that de Shera's bride was not Welsh. She was the daughter of a great English warrior sent by

King Edward and even now, Rhydilian was filled with English who had practically taken over the castle.

The *teulu* was showing disloyalty to de Shera by divulging the information but ap Ganol was glad that he had. He was, after all, a staunch Welshman, proud of his heritage he was. What de Shera was doing was nothing short of treason.

Therefore, ap Ganol had immediately sent word to Tudur ap Gwyfn of Llangefni and also to several other Anglesey warlords. Since distances were not as great as they were in other parts of the country, it was in little time that several major warlords in Anglesey received the news of de Shera's intentions and within hours, men were moving to gather at Castell Meurig, the largest fortress in Anglesey aside from Rhydilian. It was a gathering of houses to discuss de Shera's latest news and it was an angry mob that collected in Meurig's hall.

"The wedding is on the morrow," ap Ganol said to the group. "Though I respect de Shera for his hereditary titles and his abilities as a warrior, I do not respect him for his intentions. Why would he take an English bride when there are plenty of good Welsh women about?"

The gathering rumbled ominously. The great hall of Meurig was more of a round house, built upon the foundations of a Norse structure that had been round in shape. The walls were waddle and daub and the roof thatched with heavy sod. Smoke from a great pit in the middle of the room clogged up against the ceiling in great gray clouds. Men inside inhaled as much smoke as they did air, and now with all of the bodies present, it was a stuffy and polluted place.

"I do not think to question de Shera," another man said. Bron Llwyd was a childhood friend of Bhrodi's. "The man is our king. He is our greatest warrior. I was at Moel-y-don last November when the English built a bridge over the waters and marched upon Anglesey. De Shera was the first man they came across and he crushed them. He hates the English as we do, so if he takes an English bride then he must have an excellent reason."

The group roared and argued, shouting their disagreement across the room at Bron, who jumped up on a feasting table to be better heard. The crowd was growing restless, angry with de Shera's intentions. He knew what this group was capable of.

"So what is it that thee wishes?" Bron yelled at the crowd. "Do you wish to destroy de Shera? You cannot and you know it. He is too powerful!"

"Too powerful, aye, but he borders on betrayal with this marriage," ap Ganol pointed out and the crowd roared its approval. "Never forget that the man's father is English; therefore, de Shera is half-Saesneg and he has been a known ally with them in the past. He fights against the English, or with them, depending on what's in it for him. The last time he fought with the English, he gained more English lands that just Coventry. Have you forgotten?"

The gathering was thoroughly upset by now and Bron put up his hands to quell the anger. "De Shera is all Welsh, with a Welshman's heart and soul," he pointed out. "Through his mother, he is our king. He would not betray us."

That didn't seem to help. Men were arguing, shoving each other around, uneasy and angry. As Bron began shouting at those who were beginning to fight, another man leapt onto the feasting table.

Tudur ap Gwyfn was an older man from a very ancient and distinguished family and this was his castle. Men listened to Tudur, including Bhrodi. He respected the man for his wisdom and insight. Therefore, before the situation grew out of control, Tudur would speak his mind. He held up his hands to silence the crowd.

"De Shera is not a traitor," he said flatly. "What he does, I suspect, is for peace with the English king. De Shera is a shrewd man and he is not foolish; if he is marrying an Englishwoman, then there must be a good reason. You will not question him on his motives."

The group of men didn't particularly like that statement but the rumbles weren't as angry as they had been; Tudur had that effect on the crowd. The old Welshman continued.

"However, I will say this; I do not approve of this marriage," he said. "It reeks of another English attempt at conquest. Therefore, if it is English blood you want, then there will be plenty of it at the wedding. De Shera wants an English bride; then he can have her. But the English attending the wedding are under no such protection. They are the enemy in our lands and it would send a message to Edward if we were to massacre his retainers."

Bron had been listening to the speech calmly until the last sentence. That wasn't what he had expected. He moved in Tudur's direction.

"Do you not think Bhrodi will have something to say about that?" he asked. "The English are there as his guests."

Tudur turned to him. "But they are not *our* guests," he replied. "I will not sit in the same hall peacefully with English who have killed all three of my sons. I do not want an English foothold in Anglesey with de Shera's marriage."

Bron cocked an eyebrow. "You just said that de Shera had his reasons for marrying an Englishwoman."

"Mayhap he has his reasons, but they are not *my* reasons. His alliance is not mine."

Bron sighed heavily. "You are a vassal of de Shera," he reminded him. "His alliance is your alliance."

Tudur shook his head. "Mayhap the man needs to be reminded that we, as a group, are his true strength," he said "He did not consult us on this marriage and he should have. Therefore, the English at Rhydilian belong to us. We will kill them and send a message to Edward, and the message is that we will not tolerate the English in Anglesey. Edward tried to gain foothold here last November and we destroyed him. Now he tries to do it with a marriage to de Shera. We will fight him off once again by destroying the English contingent at Rhydilian."

Bron didn't like that suggestion at all but he knew he couldn't stop it. He was a lesser warlord with only one hundred men sworn to him and if the group turned against him, he knew they would destroy him. He wasn't strong enough to fight them off. Therefore, he did the only thing he could for self-preservation; he backed down on his argument lest they think he was a traitor, too. He looked at Tudur.

"Then what do you intend to do?" he asked. "Do you not think that there will be armed English at the wedding?"

Tudor glanced at Lon, who was very much in approval of the plan. "It will be better to strike at the wedding feast when the English have too much drink in them," he said. "We will attend the wedding and the feast, as de Shera has requested, and when the English are too drunk to fight back, we will strike. In fact, de Shera will not even have to know our true motives. Fights break out at weddings all of the time and no one ever seems to know what started them. It will be the same at de Shera's wedding; no one will ever know what started the battle, but they will know that we were victorious in the end. The Englishmen will die."

Bron shook his head with regret. "Bhrodi will know your motives," he said. "If you do this, you are defying him and his intention to create an alliance with the English. How do you think he will react?"

Tudur knew that The Serpent could be deadly when provoked but he would not back down. "If the situation was different and it was one of us marrying the English to create an alliance, I would suspect de Shera would not approve of it," he said. "He would be here right now plotting with us and declaring Welsh sovereignty. In time, he will understand our motives and he will agree. We are not meant to ally with the English."

"The Serpent will strike you down, ap Gwyfn," Bron said softly. "You will not survive his anger if you do this."

Tudur could see that Bron was not entirely convinced. He was afraid that the man might even warn de Shera of their plans. Therefore, he muttered something to Lon, who in turn whispered something to two of his men. Soon, several men were moving for Bron, who was pulled off the table and dragged from the hall.

Bron ended up in a dank, moldy cell as the Welsh warlords of Anglesey continued to plan their attack well into the night.

⌘

CHAPTER NINE

The great hall of Rhydilian was alive with the glow from hundreds of candles, expensive tallow tapers that had been brought out of storage and ignited in celebration of the lord's marriage. The dogs had been cleared out and the entire room smelled of roasting meat and fresh rushes. Knights were dressed in their finest and ladies were clad in beautiful garments. On the event of The Wolfe's daughter's wedding to the hereditary king of Anglesey, it was indeed an occasion to celebrate.

As Penelope sat next to Bhrodi at the head table, she was rather taken aback by the spectacle on a rather grand scale. Four massive feasting tables were weighed down with more food than most people saw in a lifetime and a group of six minstrels from the village of Menai played enthusiastically near the hall entry, filling the room with the sounds of harps and mandolins. One of Bhrodi's *teulu* commanders, also a musician, played along with his citole.

Penelope smiled as she watched her Uncle Kieran and Aunt Jemma dance their way by the head table; she'd never seen her Uncle Kieran dance before and surprisingly enough, for such a large man he was rather light on his feet. She could hear Jemma laughing all the way across the room.

As the feasting and gaiety went on long into the night, Penelope remained seated and wouldn't dance, not even when her father begged her to. She was embarrassed to be in a dress even though she looked spectacular in it; the ivory silk clung to her delicious body, something that had not gone unnoticed by Kevin Hage or Bhrodi's men, and she had been completely mortified to stand up in front of a roomful of people in the dress to say her vows. She was dying to change into clothing she was comfortable with but her mother had flatly denied her; she was the bride, Jordan had scolded, and it was time she acted like one. Brides did not dress in breeches and tunics, Jordan told her, and Penelope had been crestfallen.

In fact, her mother had spent a good deal of time lecturing Penelope on how she was to behave now that she was to be a married woman. No more breeches, no more mail. She would dress and behave like a woman from now on because that is what Bhrodi de Shera deserved. He needed a wife, not another knight, and Penelope had been grossly unhappy with her mother's directions even though she knew, deep down, that the woman was correct. That being the case, she was somewhat resigned when Jordan had dragged out her trousseau the morning of the ceremony, filled with lady-like things and more items to furnish a new household.

There were chests filled with surcoats, shifts, undergarments, hose, and shoes. There were other chests filled with plate armor and other valuables as part of her dowry. There were no chests filled with mail or swords or armor, and Penelope had actually gone to her father and cried for an hour about it while William had listened patiently. Then he told her that she was to be a married woman now and things would have to change. Unhappy, she had pouted considerably after that but it didn't change things. She was to be a wife and not a warrior. God, she hated the sound of that.

Therefore, at sunset on a dreary and misty day, Penelope Adalira de Wolfe had become the Lady Penelope de Wolfe de Shera in front of a hall that was full of both English and Welsh. In addition to the family members who had accompanied her to Wales, Bhrodi's guests included several local chieftains, which made the atmosphere very strange considering they were in the same room with English warriors and not fighting them.

There was a minute amount of tension but not enough to concern William or the other Englishmen. It was a wedding, after all, and even as the wedding feast went deep into the night, the English and Welsh were actually getting along. Some of them were playing dice in one corner of the hall while others scattered about were drinking and laughing, or just drinking. It had been a remarkable show of unity, one that the older English knights including William found quite astonishing. Had they only known it was all an act by the Welsh, they would have been on their guard. As it was, they were enjoying the celebration just as the Welsh seemed to be, festive under a false sense of security.

Bhrodi didn't suspect any of what his vassals had in mind. They seemed to be having a good time and that was all he could sense. He hadn't left Penelope's side all evening even though she had been too nervous to carry on a lengthy conversation with him, but he remained with her, trying to engage her in small talk. He could see that she was uncomfortable in a crowd, more of a private person than someone who enjoyed attention, so he didn't press her to dance. He was content just to sit with her.

He did, however, want to speak with her; since their long discussion in the keep four days earlier, he'd hardly had time to talk to her and he was very anxious to continue coming to know her. More than that, he was quite anxious to consummate their marriage and had been since he first saw her in the body-skimming ivory dress. For a man who'd not had sexual relations in well over two years, the mere sight had been enough to arouse him. Now he found he could think of nothing else and the alcohol he had been drinking only magnified those thoughts. As the gaiety and music went on around them, he leaned into her ear.

"Would you like to retire now?" he asked quietly.

Penelope looked at him as if he had just suggested something very shocking. She had a wide-eyed look but quickly settled down when she realized he had every right to make the request. He was now her husband although it would take some getting used to. She was torn between resisting him and simply getting it over with.

"If... if that is your wish," she said, then looked around the hall. "I would like to bid my parents a good eve, if I may."

Bhrodi nodded graciously, following Penelope's gaze to the dance floor where William was now escorting the very small and very pregnant form of Tacey to the center of the hall. Tacey had been in the company of Jordan and Jemma all evening, each woman paying particularly close attention to the girl, but as William carefully pulled her out to where others were dancing, Bhrodi's brow furrowed.

"What is your father doing?" he asked, trying not to sound too worried. "He cannot think to dance with her, can he?"

Penelope grinned at her father, who was being very gentle with the timid young girl as he explained the dance steps. "Why not?" she asked. "I think it is very sweet. Besides, do you really think my mother would allow her to dance if she did not believe it to be perfectly safe?"

Bhrodi had to admit she had a point but he was still uncomfortable. "He is a very big man," he said, watching as William led Tacey about in her first few steps. "God's Blood, he's going to step on her."

Penelope began to giggle. "He will *not* step on her," she said, turning to look at him. "He has eight granddaughters. He knows how to handle young women."

Just as she said that, Tacey went one way and William went the other and they ended up crashing into one another. Tacey actually laughed as William set her on the right course. Bhrodi winced.

"He will crush her," he said. "I am not entirely sure I can watch this."

Penelope's laughter grew. "Are you always so worrisome?"

He gave her a look that rather suggested he wasn't about to admit anything to her. "Your father is three times, nay, *four* times Tacey's size. It is well within my right to worry."

"And I suppose you will not allow him to dance with our daughters, then?"

He scowled. "What daughters?" he said. "I told you we were to have all sons."

"And I told you all daughters."

He could see she was jesting, thrilled that her nervous manner was loosening and she was starting to enjoy herself. It was the same woman he'd seen those days ago when they'd had their most wonderful private conversation. It was the woman he could see himself growing fond of. At least, he hoped so. Eager to maintain the light mood in a more secluded setting, he shook his head at her.

"We will continue this conversation in private because I am sure that if I spanked you in public, your father might have something to say about it," he said, rising on his big legs. "Shall we retire to our chamber, Lady de Shera?"

Our chamber. Penelope's smile faded and her nervousness returned although she fought it. He was her husband now, as alien as that thought was. She didn't even really know the man at all, but she was about to come to know him better than she'd ever known any man in her life. It was inevitable.

Taking a deep breath to summon her courage, she stood up and Bhrodi politely grasped the long silk train that was wound up around her chair. He picked it up and followed her as she made her way over to her parents and family, who had an entire table all to themselves.

Jordan, who had been watching William and little Tacey, caught sight of her glorious daughter approaching and she immediately went to her.

"Are ye having a good time, sweetheart?" she put her hands on Penelope's face and kissed her cheek. Then she looked at Bhrodi. "A fine feast, m'laird."

He dipped his head graciously. "My thanks, Lady de Wolfe," he said, "but I did not have a great deal to do with it. You organized the majority of it."

Jordan smiled. "'Twas those women I brought from the village," she said. "As I told ye, women are very useful. I think ye'll come tae appreciate it."

"Mayhap I will."

Jordan nodded her head, catching a glimpse of her husband and Tacey as they moved across the hard-packed floor. "Speaking of women," she said, "yer sister seems tae be enjoying herself a great deal."

Bhrodi turned to watch William and Tacey, now dancing in sync. "I am glad," he said. "Thank you for what you have done for her, Lady de Wolfe. She seems very happy."

Jordan beamed. "She is a sweet lass," she said. "She has taken a liking tae me husband, as ye can see."

Penelope smiled as she watched her father whirl the young woman around. "Papa likes to dance," she said. "It looks as if he has found a willing partner."

"Penny, lass," Jemma, a cup of wine in hand, came up behind Jordan. "Why have ye not danced yet?"

Penelope could feel her cheeks grow hot with embarrassment. "I am not much good at dancing, auntie," she said. "Mamma tried to teach me but I never really learned."

"But it is yer wedding, lass," Jemma persisted. "I never had a decent wedding and neither did yer mother. The least ye could do is let us see ye dance and enjoy yerself."

Penelope was mortified as she looked to her mother for help. Jordan took pity on her. "The lass has no aptitude for dancing," she told her cousin. "She would trip and kill herself and ye know it. Leave the dancing to those who know how."

Jemma shrugged and drank deeply from her cup before setting it down and pulling Kevin out onto the floor. Kevin, so much in looks and manner as Kieran had been at that age, gladly took his mother for a dance. He wouldn't even look at Penelope as he moved past her; he couldn't. He hadn't said a word to her all night and as Penelope watched him dance with his mother, she knew why. She felt a great deal of sorrow in her heart because of it. It would seem all of them were growing up one way or the other, being forced to deal with situations that made them unhappy or uncomfortable. She knew she would sorely miss Kevin in the coming years and she genuinely wished him happiness. Her gaze lingered on Kevin a moment before returning to her mother.

"We are going to retire for the evening, Mamma," she said. "I wanted to bid you a good eve before I went."

Jordan's face washed with a gentle expression; it would be such a momentous night for her daughter and her heart naturally ached for her. It was a bittersweet moment. Forcing a smile, she grasped her daughter's cheeks again and kissed her by the ear.

"Be patient and kind," she whispered. "Obey yer husband in all things, lass. I can tell ye no more except I love ye."

Penelope could feel the sting of tears as her mother released her and turned to Bhrodi. The man accepted a kiss on the cheek from Lady de Wolfe also, as he was developing a genuine fondness for the woman who had virtually taken over his keep. More than that, she had helped him straighten out some things in his own life desperately in need of straightening. Sian's clean chamber was one of them. From yesterday to today, everything was in order and he'd never seen the place run more smoothly. Lady Jordan and the women she had hired had the household running as well as any he had ever seen. This feast was a direct result of that efficiency and he was grateful. Now, all he had to worry over was his new wife and, at the moment, she was clearly occupying all of his attention.

"My thanks to you, Lady de Wolfe," he said. "Your visit to Rhydilian has been an agreeable one."

Jordan smiled. "I am pleased," she said, her gaze moving between the pair. "We will see ye both on the morrow whereupon me husband will pay the balance of the dowry. I am sure he has discussed all of this with ye already."

Bhrodi's gaze lingered on the woman. "He has," he replied. "The majority of the gifts were presented after the ceremony today and I do believe there is very little left."

"But there is some left."

"Has he actually discussed this with you?"

Jordan's brow furrowed. "Of course he has," she said. "Who do ye think gave him the terms of the marriage before he went tae negotiate with ye?"

Bhrodi cocked an eyebrow, shaking his head with mild disbelief. "I am certainly not surprised," he said. "You are a formidable woman, Lady de Wolfe."

Jordan was back to grinning. "So is me daughter," she said, touching Penelope's cheek affectionately. "Ye will find that out for yerself. Go, now; sleep well and we shall see ye on the morrow."

Bhrodi didn't have to be told twice. He'd just been given permission to be alone with his new wife and he intended to do it, and do it fast before something else prevented them from leaving the hall. He knew Penelope was reluctant but he wouldn't acknowledge it, nor would he give in to it. She was his now and he intended to do with her just as he pleased. He moved to take Penelope's elbow to lead her out of the hall but she balked.

"I want to bid my father a good evening," she told him.

Jordan interrupted. "I will tell him for ye," she said. "Ye and yer husband retire for the night. It is been a very big day for ye both."

"But...."

"*Go* now, lass."

It wasn't a request; it was a command. Penelope reached out to grasp her mother's hand, one last effort to stay with her, terrified to let her go. This was such a pivotal moment in her life and she found that she wasn't at all as prepared for it as she would have liked to have been. She wanted to be back in England in simpler times, not in Wales set to embark on a new life. All of this flashed through her mind and it was a struggle to push it away.

"You and Papa will not leave tomorrow until I have had the chance to say my farewells to you?" she asked.

Jordan patted her hand and removed it from her arm. "Of course not," she assured her daughter. "Go with yer husband, now. Sleep well."

Penelope nodded with a mixture of sadness and forced courage. She was trying hard to be brave. With a lingering glance at her mother, and a meaningful one, she let Bhrodi lead her out of the hall to a chorus of well-wishes. The newly married couple was retiring for the evening and everyone seemed to have advice, bawdy or otherwise.

Ivor, Ianto, Gwyllim and Yestin, who had been huddled at a table with several local chieftains, began to follow the couple from the hall but Bhrodi called them off with a balled fist. They received the message loud and clear, backing off as their lord and his new wife retired for the evening.

Thrilled that they were nearly clear of the hall, Bhrodi couldn't help but notice that his uncle's wardrobe, the one the old man slept and lived in, was chained shut. He also couldn't help but notice that the door was rattling steadily. He wasn't sure who had chained the doors but whoever it was had more than likely done the right thing. He had no idea what would have happened had his mad uncle been allowed to follow his usual routine this night. At the moment, he didn't want to have to worry about it.

Unfortunately, Penelope noticed the rattling wardrobe just as they were about to quit the hall completely. She even pointed at it.

"What is happening there?" she asked him. "Is someone locked up in the wardrobe?"

Rather than explain everything, Bhrodi continued walking and took her right past it. "Something like that," he said vaguely. "We can discuss it on the morrow."

Penelope looked at him queerly but he simply smiled. Now they were in the darkened foyer with two big torches burning hot and sooty in iron wall sconces. There were at least six of Bhrodi's men guarding the door and even more outside that she could hear but couldn't see. All of the men were wearing red tunics that were simple and unadorned, and as the couple quit the great hall and headed towards the keep, led through the night by a soldier with a brightly burning torch, Penelope turned to Bhrodi.

"I have noticed that your soldiers do not wear armor, not even mail," she said. "Even those men at the door do not wear it. What happens if they must engage in a fight in order to protect the door? Would it not be to their advantage to wear mail?"

Bhrodi was helping her with the train of her gown, collecting it in his arms as they crossed the bailey so it would not become soiled. "Nay," he said. "Those men are my *teulu* and they do not wear armor. It is not their way."

Penelope cocked her head curiously. "Teulu?"

He nodded. "My personal guard," he said. "Most Welshmen of rank have them, although some have more than others."

117

"Why do they not wear armor?"

They had reached the entry to the keep and took the stairs up to the second floor entry. "Because the *teulu* must move swiftly and they cannot do that with armor," he said. "There are many things about the Welsh that you will come to learn, but I will be honest when I say that I do not wish to speak of such things on my wedding night."

He was grinning, which made her grin in return. "Why not?" she demanded, though it was lightly done. "If I am to be the wife of a great Welsh warlord, then I must know everything."

He shook his head at her, laughing softly, as they mounted the narrow spiral steps to the third level. The master's chamber was immediately to the left when they reached the landing and Bhrodi lifted the latch.

"You shall know everything," he said, "but can we have at least one night when I am not teaching you the ways of my people? Mayhap there are a few other things I should like to discuss."

"Like what?"

He threw open the door for her. "Like getting to know my new wife. I have one, you know. I hardly know her."

Penelope opened her mouth to reply but was cut short when her gaze fell on the master's chamber. Startled by the scene spread out before her, she looked around the room with some awe.

The room was aglow with dozens of tallow tapers, bathing the room in golden light. A fire burned brightly in the hearth, offering warmth, and the floor was covered with sheep hides. It looked like a sea of cream-colored fluff. There were two big chairs near the hearth with a table between them and upon the table sat a fine pitcher made from cut rose quartz and two matching cups. Fruit and cheese and bread was spread out over the table, creating a fine place to sit and talk and eat before retiring.

"I gave your aunt free reign in the chamber," Bhrodi said, watching her face as she inspected the room. "I told her to make it warm and wonderful. Did she accomplish that?"

Penelope grinned as she took a few steps into the room, noting the giant bed. It had a massive canopy with curtains around it and the bed itself was covered in hides and linens. It was very inviting.

"She did," she responded. "I am surprised she is not in here still, making sure our every need is fulfilled."

Bhrodi began to loosen his tunic; he was dressed in his finest, mail and leather breeches and the traditional red and silver ap Gaerwen standard.

"You come from a family of aggressive women," he commented as he pulled the tunic over his head. "They certainly saw no issue with taking over my keep and household."

Penelope turned to look at him as he lay the tunic over a chair. "You could have told them not to."

He looked at her as if shocked by the suggestion. "And risk their wrath?" he shook his head. "My one consolation is that they will be leaving on the morrow and all will return to normal."

Penelope giggled. "Except that you now have a new wife," she said. "And if you think my mother will stay away indefinitely, think again. She will come back to visit us every year, I promise."

Bhrodi was grinning because she was. "God help us."

"Do you not like my mother?"

"She is a fine woman."

Penelope saw the humor in his statement. "You have to say that now," she said. "If you say one bad word about her, I shall run and tell her."

He was still grinning as he sat in one of the chairs. "I will never say anything negative about her, I swear," he replied. "At least, not to you."

Penelope's smile held as her gaze lingered on him; he had looked particularly handsome today with his shaved face and freshly cut hair. He even smelled good, like pine and rosemary. Standing next to the man as they said their vows had made her heart race. Every time she looked at him, her breathing seemed to quicken.

Aye, he was a handsome man and her unfamiliar reaction to him was both confusing and exciting. No man she had ever met had elicited such a reaction from her, something giddy and warm. She hardly knew him and had hardly spent time with him but already he was able to make her feel like a silly young girl simply with his presence. She thought that it was a good thing and bespoke of the natural attraction between them. Holding up her train, she went to take a seat in the chair opposite him.

For a moment, they simply looked at each other. The fire was casting a good deal of warmth into the room, making everything seem rather seductive and liquid. It was an odd and fluid sensation and one that made Penelope's heart race just a little more. Those invisible fingers that came from Bhrodi's eyes had her within their grasp and this time, she gave in to the sensation. It was difficult to resist.

"Now," she said softly. "You wanted to come to know me better. What is it you wish to know?"

He laughed softly and her heart leapt at the sight of his magnificent smile; she was coming to appreciate it very much.

"I am not entirely sure where to start," he said. "I believe our last conversation involved bloodlines, how many children we are to have, and the significance of our marriage and how it relates to the English crown. I suppose what I would really like to know is more about you, personally."

"What do you mean?"

He cocked his head thoughtfully. "Well," he began, "what do you like to do? Do you like to sing? Or play an instrument?"

Penelope burst out laughing. "Never in my life have I done those things," she declared. "I like to hunt and I like to ride. Whenever my father purchases new chargers, I have the honor of riding them first and training them. I am very good at training horses."

Bhrodi wasn't surprised; his expression said as much. "So my new wife likes to hunt and fight," he said. "I knew from the onset that you chose, shall we say, male activities, but I thought that you might have feminine pursuits, also."

Penelope shook her head. "Not one," she said. "I have never liked anything that girls did. I always wanted to do what the boys did because it seemed much more fun. How much enjoyment can you get out of sticking a needle into cloth hour after hour? I would be so bored I would want to scream. It is much better to handle a skittish horse or take down a wild boar. I am excellent with a bow and arrow."

As Bhrodi listened to her, more prevalent thoughts came to mind. He tried to be careful in the way he communicated them, as he did not wish to offend her.

"I am sure you are," he said. "But I should like my wife to have some feminine accomplishments. Would that be so difficult?"

Penelope looked at him dubiously. "Like what?"

"Like... like the ability to adequately run a household. Do you not have skills such as that?"

Penelope was coming to suspect he wasn't thrilled with her male-associated skills. *Your husband wants a wife, not another knight,* her mother had said. Perhaps the woman had been more than correct in that statement because her new husband seemed to reflect the same sentiment. The smile faded from Penelope's face as she sat back and crossed her arms.

"I have been educated in mathematics, languages, and history," she said. "While growing up, I schooled with the young squires in such things. I understand the basic premise of running a household but I would be bored to death doing it."

"Why?"

"Because I am a kn-," she cut herself off, suspecting that wasn't the answer he wanted. After a moment, she hung her head and sighed heavily. "I realize that I am now Lady de Shera and there are certain expectations that go with that. However, you must understand that my entire life up until the last few months have revolved around my duties for my father. Never once did I have household duties. But if that is what you want from me, I... I suppose I will have to learn."

Bhrodi was watching her face carefully, seeing the sadness and resignation in it. "What do *you* want to do?"

Penelope's head came up and she cast him a side-long gaze. "I am afraid I will not give you the answers you seek."

"I am not expecting any particular answer. I am asking you an honest question. Will you give me an honest reply?"

Penelope thought seriously on the question. "I told you once that I never saw myself marrying," she said. "I thought my life would be filled with service to my father and nothing more. I suppose it would be too much to ask to serve my husband as a knight, would it?"

Bhrodi cleared his throat softly as he pondered his answer. "Wives do not usually serve their husbands on the field of battle," he said. "When I look at you, I see such a gloriously beautiful creature. I knew it the first time I laid eyes on you. It would make me enormously proud to have a wife who could efficiently run my household and tend my children. I would be the envy of every man in Wales to have such a beautiful and talented wife."

Somehow, Penelope knew that would be his answer and she hung her head again. "You would be ashamed to have one who could fight with a broadsword and ride headlong into battle, then."

He shook his head. "Nay," he murmured. "I would be proud of those qualities, too, but you will admit that most men would not understand such a thing. I do not want to see you ridiculed and I do not want to be ridiculed. I am sure you must understand that. Men in Wales are different from the *Saesneg*... they are defined by the women they marry in many ways, and also by the character of those women. I will be judged by your actions."

Her head came up, the hazel eyes narrowing. "And you do not wish for me to embarrass you?"

"As an ap Gaerwen and a de Shera, I have a reputation to uphold."

It was an arrogant statement and she wasn't surprised by it. Bhrodi was a very prideful man, although he was also one of great understanding. Still, she wanted to argue the point; God's Blood, she wanted to very much, but she knew in her heart that she could not. Her mother had told her to be a wife and not a knight. Penelope knew that times were changing for her; it was time for her to outgrow the knighthood and become a woman. It was so very sad for her to realize that.

"As you wish," she muttered.

Bhrodi could see how sorrowful she was. He couldn't honestly believe that she would have expected him to let her continue in her knightly ways, but evidently she had hoped for it. Leaning forward, he uncapped the cut quartz pitcher and poured her a measure of the rich red wine inside.

"You are now the Lady Penelope de Wolfe ap Gaerwen de Shera, hereditary Queen of Anglesey, Lady of Ynes Mon, and Countess of Coventry," he said softly. "Have you ever heard of a queen riding to battle?"

Penelope knew he was trying to comfort her in his own way. It was a kind thing to do when he really didn't have to. She accepted the cup.

"Papa told me once of an ancient queen named Boudicca that led her troops to battle," she said.

Bhrodi made a face. "She was a barbarian," he sniffed. "Her chariot was pulled by slaves and she drank the blood of her enemies. Surely you do not wish to be compared to that dirty witch."

Penelope fought off a grin because he had a very humorous way of speaking when things did not suit his tastes or he was expressing his disapproval. She had seen it before; the man might have been an arrogant and powerful warlord, but he had a comical streak in him that bordered on the dramatic. It was a surprising trait.

"I did not say I wished to be compared to her," she clarified. "You asked me if I had ever heard of a queen riding to battle and I told you that I had."

He poured himself a cup of wine and drained the entire thing in one swallow. "Hmpf," he grunted. "No more talk of barbarians in my presence and especially not on the eve of my wedding."

"It is my wedding, too."

He poured himself more wine. "That is true," he agreed, downing the second cup. "Therefore, I suppose I should clarify my wishes as we have discussed them. It would make me very happy and proud to have a wife who is an accomplished chatelaine, a wife that would make me the envy of all men. Would you be willing to learn these things, my lady?"

It was an honest request. After a moment's hesitation, Penelope nodded. "I will try," she said. "But on one condition."

"What is that?"

"That you take me hunting sometimes when it is not too much trouble."

He smiled faintly. "I would like to do that."

"And I would still like to ride and train horses."

He thought on that, eventually nodding. "If that would make you happy, I am sure we can come to terms. However, I do not want you training chargers any longer. That is a man's job."

Her face fell somewhat but she agreed. "Very well."

He was still smiling faintly as he watched her expression. "May I ask something else?"

She nodded, staring at her hands. "Of course."

"Would it be acceptable for me to kiss my bride on the event of our wedding?"

Penelope's head shot up, her eyes wide on him. But, quickly enough, she stilled herself. She knew this time would come, physical contact between the two of them. She hadn't allowed herself to think much about it because it made her sick to her stomach. She had no idea what to do or how to behave even though her mother had explained the ways of men and women to her. Still, it was a terrifying mystery and not one she wished to explore, but she had no choice. She now belonged to a stranger, a man she barely knew, and he had every right to her body. Nervousness began to overtake her.

"I... I have a confession," she said.

"What is that?"

"I have never...," she struggled to find the correct words, "that is to say, I have never even... other than my father, I have never had any manner of contact with a man. Ever."

She said it haltingly and Bhrodi struggled to suppress a smile. "I understand," he said. "But you realize that I have been married before, of course."

"Of course," she repeated nervously.

He bit his lip to keep from grinning. "Being married, I have indeed kissed a woman before. And more."

Penelope's cheeks flamed a bright red and she lowered her gaze so he wouldn't see her dull red face. "That... that is to be expected."

"I would be honored if you would allow me to lead you through this," he said as carefully as he could. "I promise I will be very gentle."

Penelope truly thought she was going to burst into flames from embarrassment. Her cheeks had never felt so hot. With quaking knees, she stood up and immediately began fumbling for the stays on her gown. Bhrodi stood up and went to her.

"Here," he put his hands over hers, stilling her fingers. "You do not have to do that right now. Come sit with me on the bed."

Big dress and all, Penelope allowed him to lead her over to the bed that was covered with mounds of furs and linens. He pushed her gently to sit and sat down beside her. Reaching over, he took one of her hands in his big, calloused mitt. It was very warm and soft and he inspected it, turning it over and running a finger over the callous on the palm. Penelope watched him, feeling the newness of his touch with the most electrifying of reactions. She could hardly breathe as he touched her and her mouth ran dry. It was both frightening and exciting.

"This is something all newly married couples must contend with," he said softly, studying the shape of her slender fingers. "My mother and father, in fact, met for the first time on their wedding day. At least you and I have had a few days to come to know one another."

Penelope nodded nervously. "We were introduced by the beast."

Bhrodi laughed softly as he lifted her hand and kissed it. Penelope jumped, feeling as if he had just branded her with his warm lips. But when she settled down, she realized that it had been a tender gesture. He had been very soft and gentle about it; it was her nerves that had caused her to bolt and certainly nothing he had done. Her heart thumped loudly against her ribs and she resisted the urge to ask him to do it again.

"Ah, yes, the beast," he murmured. "The serpent that lives in the marsh. It did indeed introduce us and chase your entire family to my doorstep. How fortunate for me."

He lifted her hand and kissed it again before releasing it. As Penelope watched, quivering with excitement and trepidation, he reached out and grasped her by the shoulders.

"Turn around," he murmured. "Face the fire. That's a good lass."

Penelope did as she was told, facing the fire while he moved up behind her. She could feel his enormous body, the heat reaching out to scald her. It was the most exquisite sensation she had ever experienced, having this man whom she was so tremendously attracted to so close yet not touching her. She hardly knew how to react and her unsteady breathing filled the air. Surely Bhrodi could hear it. She could feel his gentle breath on her shoulder as he began to unfasten the stays of the dress, one at a time.

"I realize that this is all quite new to you," he murmured, kissing the flesh of her back as the dress began to peel away, "but I sincerely hope it is something you enjoy. There is no great mystery about it; God created a man and a woman for this purpose."

Penelope swallowed hard, trying to bring some moisture back into her dry mouth, as he continued to undo the stays. Her entire body was quivering and the further the dress unfastened, the more she trembled. His kisses against her back were incredibly arousing; with each successive kiss, her heart beat louder. She could hear it in her ears. Coupled with the heavy breathing, she was positive she was going to faint.

Very carefully, Bhrodi peeled the silk dress away from her body and had her lie back on the bed while he pulled it free of her feet. Clad in only her silk shift and hose, she watched as he draped the big dress over one of the chairs and returned to the bed. When he saw the rather wide-eyed expression on her face, he smiled.

"No need to be nervous, *caria*," he whispered. "I will be as gentle as possible, I swear it."

Penelope realized she must look like a scared rabbit so she struggled for some composure. She didn't like to show weakness but was aware she had conveyed little else since entering the chamber. Therefore, she squared her shoulders with false bravery.

"I am not nervous," she lied. "And why did you call me *caria*? That is not my name."

He sat next to her on the bed again. "It means 'love' in Welsh," he said. "If you do not like it, I will not call you that. What should I call you?"

"My friends and family call me Penny," she said. "I give you permission to call me that if you wish."

"You do not like *caria?*"

She smiled with some embarrassment. "It is pretty," she said. "My mother calls me her love all of the time."

"I would like to call you mine as well. You are my wife, after all, and I am already fond of you."

Penelope looked at him with surprise. "You *are?*" she asked. "How do you know?"

He grinned and reached out, putting his big, muscular arms around her and pulling her against him. She was stiff, startled by the move, and he could see the anxiety in her eyes. Without another word, his lips descended gently on hers.

"I cannot tell you how I know," he murmured against her lips. "But I can show you."

Within the first few heated and tender moments of his kiss, Penelope knew she liked it. Already, she liked it and as his kiss grew in intensity, she liked it even more. Wrapped up in his enormous arms, deep within the folds of the first real embrace she had ever shared with any man, she was coming to see very quickly what all of the fuss was about. She was coming to understand why her mother and father embraced frequently, or why her brother and their wives were so affectionate with one another. There was indeed something to be said for such an exquisitely wonderful moment, something that made her heart light with joy.

As the fire in the hearth snapped and crackled, Bhrodi continued to kiss his new wife, acquainting her with the feel and taste of him. Penelope didn't even realize that her arms had found their way around his neck; she clung to him as his mouth left hers, kissing a scorching trail across her jaw and down her neck. The sensations were so new and exciting that all she could do was hold on to him as he took the lead, kissing her in places and ways that she had never been kissed. All of it was so fresh and overwhelming, so much so that Penelope began to audibly gasp.

As Bhrodi's mouth moved down her arm and began to suckle on her fingers, she couldn't grasp a coherent thought. Her body was limp and pliable, so much so that he was able to lay her on her back without any resistance whatsoever. He suckled her fingers, her skin, and as she panted and gasped beneath him, he snaked his hands underneath her silk shift and very quickly pulled it over her head.

Naked. That thought briefly flashed through Penelope's mind as she lay nude beneath him but for the hose and ribbons still upon her legs. She had always imagined this moment would come with such embarrassment but Bhrodi's touch had been so exquisitely distracting that Penelope felt no embarrassment at all. He was warm and big and muscular, and he suckled the fingers of her other hand as he yanked off his tunic and breeches. Penelope could really only see his silhouette with the firelight behind him, but when he lay on top of her once more, their flesh against flesh was a searing experience.

Bhrodi's lips were on her neck once more and he stroked her arms, moving out until he reached her wrists. Using both of his hands, he grasped her wrists and brought her arms up above her head. Penelope was so wrapped up in the heated sensations he was creating within her body that she was aware he had bound her wrists to the bed well after the fact. Opening her eyes, she looked up and saw that he had tied her hands together and secured them to the woodened post of the headboard.

Eyes wide with surprise, perhaps a bit of fear, she looked at him only to see him grinning quite lustily back at her.

"Do not worry," he murmured. "You will enjoy this, I promise."

"But why did you bind me?"

Carefully, he pulled her legs apart and settled his big body between them. Then, he lowered himself down onto her torso.

"So that I could do this," he whispered.

His hot, wet mouth came to bear on a tender nipple, suckling firmly, and Penelope let out a groan of both shock and ecstasy. Something was unleashed in Bhrodi now; his movements were firmer, quicker, and his hands fondled her full breasts as he suckled her nipples into taut pellets. When his hands weren't on her breasts, they were moving over her body, feeling her silken skin and arousing her in the process.

Overwhelmed, Penelope bucked and groaned beneath him as he worked her breasts, feeding from one to the other. She had such beautiful breasts, and an exquisitely beautiful body, and when his right hand moved to the fluff of dark curls between her legs, some primal impulse in Penelope told her to open her legs wide to him. She did out of sheer instinct and he stroked her gently at first, realizing that she was already quite prepared for his body to enter hers. To make it easier on her, he inserted a finger into her.

Penelope gasped at the sensual intrusion, drawing her knees up as he thrust first one and then two fingers into her, mimicking the lovemaking they would soon be doing. It was an introduction of sorts, a promise of things to come, and Penelope wasn't afraid. She liked it very much, her body responding in ways she could have never imagined. When Bhrodi finally withdrew his fingers and placed his big, throbbing manhood at her threshold, Penelope didn't react other than to open her legs wider. It seemed like the right thing to do and she was no longer afraid of what was to come. So far, she liked it very much. She wanted more.

Bhrodi gave her more as he thrust into her, seating himself fully upon entry because she was so wet and relaxed. It was as if her body was made for him, accommodating him, and he realized without a doubt that this was the most exquisite coupling he'd ever known. There was something magnetic and beauteous and exciting about Penelope. The past few days had seen such a remarkable change in his outlook on life and in how he viewed her, his new wife. At first, he hadn't even wanted her but now, she belonged to him completely and he would mark her, a more delicious chore he could not imagine.

Penelope gasped as Bhrodi thrust into her and for a moment, there was a brief flash of pain as her body became accustomed to the intrusion. But the discomfort was quickly gone as he began to move within her, thrusting steadily in and out of her body as his mouth suckled her breasts and his hands fondled her buttocks. Her entire body was experiencing a delight of sensations as his thrusts began to build a sensitive friction between her legs. She could feel it low in her belly, blossoming, reacting every time he moved within her.

The harder and faster he thrust, the greater the sensation until it suddenly exploded and ripples of bliss cascaded throughout her body. At the same time, she felt Bhrodi give one final great thrust and he grunted, whispering *"caria"* upon his groans of pleasure. Her body, reacting to his, exploded again in a lesser burst of bliss, but still one that sent her limbs to quivering. When his grunting subsided, he untied the bindings on her wrists and let her arms fall. Carefully, he gathered her up against him, his lips against her forehead.

"Are you well?" he whispered. "I did not hurt you, did I?"

Penelope was fairly certain she had swooned because he had to ask her twice before she was able to give him a coherent reply.

"I am well," she murmured.

"I am glad to know that," he said, kissing her forehead. "Was I gentle enough?"

"I believe so."

"If I ever do anything that does not bring you pleasure, you will let me know."

"I am sure you will know before I even have to tell you. I have a habit of reacting before speaking."

"I might find a fist in my nose?"

"That is possible."

He snorted softly. Reaching a long arm to the end of the bed, he pulled up a coverlet that had been carefully folded and tucked it in around them both. He still held Penelope tightly in his arms and was quite sure that he would never let her go. The woman had him completely enchanted and he felt such peace at the moment, more than he had felt in over two years. He wasn't sure he'd ever feel this way again, but somehow, it was different with her. It was more intense, a deeper edge of peace. That was the best way he could describe it. He didn't see an English bride; he hadn't in quite a while. All he saw was a woman who clearly overwhelmed him. As he pondered that thought, someone pounded very loudly on the chamber door.

"Bhrodi!"

Startled right off the bed, Bhrodi was up before he could draw another breath, moving for the door.

"Who comes?" he demanded.

"Gwyl!" It was Gwyllim, yelling at the top of his lungs. "You must come!"

Bhrodi's brow furrowed and he looked at Penelope, puzzled. She had the exact same expression he did; no fear, merely concern.

"Why?" Bhrodi hollered, hunting for his breeches. "What has happened?"

"An attack!" Gwyllim cried. "The English are under attack!"

Bhrodi had never moved so fast in his entire life. Penelope moved faster.

⌘

CHAPTER TEN

By the time Bhrodi and Penelope entered the great hall, it was utter bedlam. Bhrodi had tried to keep Penelope in the chamber but, being a trained knight, she wouldn't remain behind, and most especially if her family was threatened. She threw on her shift and ran out before he could stop her, so he followed her out of the keep, watching her run in front of him with her careful hairstyle unraveling.

By the time they reached the great hall, it was a shocking sight; swords were out, daggers were flashing, and the entire room was in upheaval. There was blood on the floors. Bhrodi turned to Penelope, putting his big hands on her arms in order to prevent her from charging into the room.

"Do not enter," he commanded. "I do not want you injured. I want you to return to the keep, do you understand?"

Penelope was stricken. "But...!"

He gave her a brief shake, as if to emphasize his point. "Go back to the keep," he told her. "I will not say this again. Go *back*."

With that, Bhrodi charged in and started yelling, bellowing something in Welsh. Penelope had no idea what he was saying but whatever it was, it didn't seem to be helping. Men were still fighting with swords, daggers, chairs, and anything else they could get their hands on. As she stood and watched, aghast, an entire bank of tallow candles went flying across the room and crashed into a group of men, spraying hot fat everywhere. Penelope could see her father at the far end of the hall, engaging in a sword fight with a broadsword that was not his own. Since it was a wedding feast, none of the English had been wearing armor or broadswords. They were therefore unarmed as the room was torn apart.

As much as Penelope wanted to charge in and join the fight, she knew she was in no condition to do so. She was unarmed and it would be a stupid move. Therefore, in complete disobedience of her husband's wishes, she turned on her heel and ran out into the bailey, heading for the English encampment against the northern wall and noting, as she drew closer, that her father's foot soldiers were also in some kind of skirmish.

Something had happened, something serious enough so that the English were engaged on all fronts, and all Penelope could think was that it had been an ambush. The English had been invited to a wedding under the guise of peace when, in fact, the Welsh had been planning to attack them all along. That was her warrior's instinct talking. Surely there was no other alternative.

Furious and frightened, she knew she had to make it to the fortified wagon where her possessions were, including her mail and her array of weapons. She didn't have her broadsword but she had a myriad of other blades. Moreover, her father's blade was more than likely in his tent, which had been guarded by her father's personal guard, but there was no one near the tent at the moment and she ran into it, spying her father's weaponry still in its frame. She rushed forward and grabbed the broadsword, yanking it from the frame as she bolted from the tent.

The fighting was over near the northern edge of the encampment and her wagon seemed to be in the clear. She ran to it, throwing open the heavy fortified door and climbing inside. When she shut the door, she made sure to bolt it. She didn't want to fall victim to a Welsh surprise.

It took her a little more than a minute to throw on a pair of leather breeches, a snug undergarment that helped support her full breasts, and a heavier leather tunic. There was no time to don the heavy and cumbersome mail. The clothing she wore was part of the clothing stash her mother had denied her to wear now that she was married, carefully tucked away in the wagon. There were no available shoes for her but there was plenty of weaponry; opening up a compartment beneath one of the wagon benches, she pulled forth two daggers and a very sharp sword she had used before she had gotten her big broadsword. Collecting the weaponry, she grabbed her father's broadsword and leapt from the wagon.

The chaos in the bailey had grown. She ran through groups of men, dodging through them with a big dagger in her hand. One man made a swipe at her and she planted her blade into his hand, listening to him howl. By the time she reached the great hall, there was a fire in one of the corners, creeping up the waddle and daub wall. Penelope looked at it with some horror; she knew that once it reached the thatched roof, it would spread very quickly. Therefore, her mission was to find her parents and get them out of the hall. Dagger in hand, she plunged into the fight.

Penelope engaged more men than she had expected to as she pushed through the room. One man received a slash to his face while the other received a stab to his arm. She could hear her father bellowing and she found him over near the feasting tables where all of the English had been sitting. Food was on the floor, drinks were spilled, and it was a general mess. William still had the unfamiliar broadsword and she raced in his direction.

"Papa!" she yelled. "Papa, your sword!"

William heard Penelope's voice and, distracted, his gaze searched her out as she pushed through the battle. She was slashing and kicking all the way, a very tough young woman who was unafraid of a fight. He called to Jordan and Jemma, who were underneath the table with Tacey. The pregnant young woman was weeping hysterically as the turmoil went on around her.

"Penny is here!" he bellowed. "Jordan, go with her! Let her take you out of here!"

Penelope arrived and leapt onto the table, handing her father his beloved broadsword. Now, fully armed with his familiar weapon, William could do serious damage. He yelled to Paris, who was several feet away and doing battle with the only thing he had on him, a dirk. When Paris took his eyes off his opponent to look at William, the man tossed the confiscated broadsword to him. Now Paris was properly armed and his opponent went down quickly.

"Penny!" William commanded. "Remove your mother and aunt out of here!"

Penelope was battling with a soldier who had come at her. She sliced him in the chest with her dagger and kicked him in the face to send him to the ground.

"I cannot!" she said, kicking another man who came at her. "There are too many of them to fight off between here and the entry!"

William had to admit she might be correct; there was a sea of battling men and, for the moment, the women were safe underneath the table. But *only* for the moment; he could see Paris and Kieran fighting for their lives while Scott, Troy, and Patrick were beating down several Welshmen. He knew it would only be a matter of time before the table was compromised as well. His sons Thomas and Edward were also in mortal combat while Kevin and Apollo seemed to have their men under control. At least, that was what William thought until he saw Kevin gored through the torso by a Welshman who came up behind him. As he watched, Kevin fell to his knees and Patrick, close by, rushed to assist him. The situation was going from bad to worse.

"Where is your husband?" William bellowed.

Penelope looked around the room but couldn't see Bhrodi through the chaos. "I do not know!" she called back. "He was here a moment ago!"

As William and Penelope stood on the table and fought off the onslaught, Paris and Scott leapt onto the table as well. It was high ground and easier to fight from there. Meanwhile, Patrick was dragging Kevin across the floor towards them, fighting off a huge offensive of Welsh until Troy and Thomas and Edward rushed to help him. Penelope hadn't seen Kevin fall and by the time he was dragged over and shoved under the table where his mother and aunt were hiding, she was horrified. The man had left a trail of blood behind him. Furious, she went mad and began chopping and stabbing at anything that moved. *Damn the Welsh!*

William knew they were outnumbered and he, too, believed what his daughter did, that this was an ambush orchestrated by de Shera. He was sickened by it, having led his entire family into a trap. As Troy leapt up beside him to aid his father in fighting away the rabble, Bhrodi suddenly appeared in the hall entry with a gang of men behind him. He was seriously armed for battle and William thought that lives would soon be over. He was sure the man was coming for them. However, Bhrodi did something unexpected; rushing in to the burning room, he and his men began beating down the Welsh contingent.

William saw what was happening; it was clear that de Shera was trying to protect the English, or at least trying to help them. He and his men were tossing people aside and killing others, and they carved through the chaos of the room as they headed for the English now largely isolated on top of a big feasting table. As Bhrodi drew near, he began waving at them.

"Come on!" he bellowed. "You must get out of here! The place will burn down around you!"

William didn't need to be told twice; he had no choice but to trust de Shera as he leapt off the table and reached underneath to grab his wife, who in turn grabbed Tacey. Paris and Kieran were moving also, dragging Jemma and the wounded Kevin from beneath the table. Between Kieran and Patrick, they managed to carry Kevin out of the hall and, along with the rest of the English, found their way to the keep under Bhrodi's protection.

There was a sense of panic as they fled the hall. Bhrodi and his *teulu* herded the Saesnegs into the massive D-shaped keep of Rhydilian, away from the pandemonium that was growing worse. When the Welsh attempted to follow, Bhrodi's men beat them back, allowing the English time to escape. The keep loomed ahead through the misty night, promising safety. The English fled up the stairs into the second floor entry and the last people up the stairs were Penelope and her father, followed by Bhrodi and several of his men. As the English rushed into the smaller hall directly across from the entry, Bhrodi slammed the massive entry door and bolted it.

The sudden silence and stillness of the keep was somewhat overwhelming. From the midst of such bedlam and into the heart of silence caused them all to pause a moment to regroup. No one could really believe what had happened. Breathing heavily, Bhrodi leaned against the door, looking to his men surrounding him; Ivor, Ianto, Gwyllim, and Yestin were all panting with exertion. It was clear that they, too, were startled at what had gone on. They all looked at each other with varied degrees of astonishment and anger.

"What in the hell happened?" Bhrodi demanded. "When I left, everything was peaceful. What went on?"

Ianto, with a cut on his chin, sighed heavily as he tried to catch his breath. "I do not know for certain," he said. "One moment, we were speaking with Tudur and in the next, Lon ap Ganol gave a cry and his men produced weapons. They went after de Wolfe and his men."

Bhrodi could hardly believe what he was hearing. "Tudur and Lon attacked them?" he hissed. "Are you sure?"

Ianto nodded, wiping at the blood on his chin. "That is when I sent Gwyllim for you," he said. "I knew something terrible was happening."

Terrible, indeed. The rest of the *teulu*, at least the ones Bhrodi could gather for his rescue mission into the great hall, were spread out around the entry. Some had filtered into the solar, and nearly all of them had cuts and bruises of some kind. It had been a terrible night for them all. Now that he had some information as to what had happened, Bhrodi pushed himself off of the door and headed into the hall to see how badly the English had fared. He didn't relish facing them.

It didn't look good; one of the English knights was lying on the floor while Lady Jemma and another knight worked on him, trying to stop the bleeding in his gut. The rest of the group had cuts or were generally roughed up; one of de Wolfe's younger sons was sporting a great wound to the arm.

As Bhrodi walked into the room to see what assistance he could offer, Penelope was suddenly in front of him. She threw a punch which, had it made contact, would have probably knocked out a tooth. As it was, Bhrodi grabbed her by the wrist, that tender and sweet wrist he had kissed so sweetly not an hour before. Looking into her angry face, it was like seeing an entirely different woman.

"You bastard," she hissed. "Is this what you planned all along? An ambush?"

William was beside her, trying to pull her away from her husband. "Calm yourself, Pen," he said quietly, but when he turned to Bhrodi, his expression was anything but quiet. There was mortal fury behind it. "I will give you the opportunity to explain yourself."

Bhrodi knew how bad this all looked and struggled not to sound as if he was pleading. "I had no knowledge of this, I swear it," he said to both William and Penelope. "Do you seriously believe I would have planned this attack? If I'd wanted to kill you, I would not have saved you from the beast of the marsh. I would have let it destroy you. Whatever happened in the hall was not of my doing but I vow upon my honor that I will find out who is behind it."

William believed him for two reasons; he did indeed save them from the marsh beast and he had rushed them to safety from the chaotic hall. A man trying to kill them would not have done those things. But before he could reply, Kieran came up beside him and punched Bhrodi in the jaw so hard that the man went stumbling. William grabbed hold of Kieran to prevent him from going in for the kill, but Kieran, the usually cool and consummate knight, was uncharacteristically out of control. He was wild with grief.

"I should kill you," Kieran growled. "Look what your wedding has done to my son. Look at him!"

Bhrodi was still on his feet but his head was spinning; the old knight had delivered a devastating blow. Hand to his jaw, he looked to the knight on the ground as Jemma cradled his head and wept, and Paris worked furiously to save him. He went to them.

"What do you need?" he asked Paris. "I have a surgeon. I will send for him immediately."

Paris had the blood flow stopped but Kevin was in a bad way. He had been gored just underneath his ribcage on the left side of his body and had lost a lot of blood. Paris, an excellent healer, glanced up at Bhrodi. His expression was serious.

"Send for him," he said. "I need gut to sew this wound with. I also need medicaments that your surgeon should have. Send him to me now."

Bhrodi nodded, snapping orders to Yestin, who went on the run. Since the entry door was bolted, he and Ianto went to a smaller trap door in the corner of the hall that led to the storage level below. That level also had a well-fortified door that led to the bailey on the west side. As his men left the room, Bhrodi returned his attention to the thrashed English.

"I can do nothing more than apologize for what has happened but please know that I had no hand in it," he said so that everyone could hear him. "My intention since the moment you arrived has been that of an alliance, but it is clear some of my vassals do not share that opinion."

William was still holding on to Kieran. "We will be leaving here on the morrow and I do not wish to fight my way out of Wales," he said. "Moreover, it looks as if I will be traveling with wounded. I will make a prime target."

Bhrodi shook his head. "I will send an escort with you to see you safely out of Wales," he said. "You needn't worry over you safety. No one would dare attack a convoy under my protection."

William's brow furrowed. "We were attacked in your hall," he pointed out. "Clearly, there are those who would attack us regardless of whether or not we are under your protection."

He was correct and Bhrodi was starting to fume; not only had his vassals attacked the English that were here peacefully, but they had betrayed him as well. He could not have men under his command who would act with such treachery. Men like that would do it again given the opportunity. He had been shamed in front of men he was attempting to seal a treaty with but more than that, he had been shamed in front of his new wife, a woman he truly hoped to cement an amiable relationship with. There was much at stake at the moment, more than simply an attack against the English. The fury within him, The Serpent of legend, was beginning to rise.

"Those who are responsible for this will pay," he said, his tone low and threatening. "You will remain here for the night; you are welcome to sleep in the upper chambers, for I will not be retiring. At the moment, mayhap Lady de Wolfe will be kind enough to take my sister to bed. She should rest."

Jordan, pale and shaken, was holding Tacey's hand. She had been ever since they made their mad dash from the hall. When Bhrodi made his polite request, Jordan nodded unsteadily and led the girl away. Bhrodi watched them go, thankful that his sister was unharmed and thankful for Jordan's mothering. He'd never seen his sister so happy as he had tonight. In fact, they had all been happy and, God only knew, it had been a very long time since they had all known such joy. For it to end so terribly filled him with a deep and burning rage.

Penelope, standing next to her father, deliberately turned away when Bhrodi finally turned to look at her. She was too angry and confused and terrified to meet his gaze at the moment. Bhrodi, sensing she wanted nothing to do with him, would not give in to her displeasure. He had to take control if there was any hope of salvaging the relationship. She was a strong woman, and a wise one, but he was stronger and wiser. He had to show her that. Moving to her, he took her by the arm.

"I would speak with you for a moment," he said quietly.

But Penelope wanted no part of him. She yanked her arm away savagely but he grabbed her again, this time throwing her over one broad shoulder. She squirmed and beat on him as he carried her away, going so far as to try and hit him on the head. Bhrodi, with his twisting and fighting wife slung over his shoulder, smacked her hard on the bottom to still her. Penelope screeched and stopped fighting purely out of shock. When she started up again, he smacked her once more and she stopped completely because his big hand stung. Her arse was already sore. When he took her into a small alcove near the door that led down into the storage area, he put her on her feet.

Penelope was in no mood to listen but Bhrodi blocked her when she tried to get away. In fact, he threw his arms around her and trapped her against his enormous chest. Frustrated, pinned, Penelope refused to look him in the eye. She could feel his hot breath on the side of her face as he looked down at her.

"I know you are irate and bewildered," he murmured. "In truth, I am also. But I swear to you that I knew nothing about this and I apologize profusely for the occurrence. I want you to know that I will discover the truth behind this event. This I vow."

Penelope was still looking away from him. After his explanation to her father, she was coming to see that he was as shocked by the happening as she was. He seemed truly distressed over it. Moreover, he was right; if he had been behind the attack as she had first suspected, he would not have come to their aid. Perhaps she should not have so rashly judged him before she had all of the facts. She could feel her guard slipping, just a little.

"My parents could have been killed," she hissed. "We *all* could have been killed. Kevin is lying out there terribly wounded and my brother Thomas has an awful gash to his arm. Do you have so little control over your vassals that they would violate the peaceful nature of a wedding?"

He sighed faintly. "Will you look at me, please?"

She held out for a few seconds before, very slowly, turning to him. Her hazel eyes met with his deep green and those invisible fingers she was becoming so familiar with were reaching out to her once again, caressing her, reminding her of his touch. She vividly recalled his lips on hers, his body against hers, and her cheeks began to flame. So many memories of him tumbled upon her all at once.

Bhrodi gazed into her lovely eyes and he could see the defiance slip away. His grip on her loosened and his hands began to caress her. He simply couldn't help himself.

"The chieftains who came here tonight have betrayed me," he muttered. "For my sake and mine alone, I will deal with them appropriately. Do not think that this will go unpunished. I swear to you that I will do what is necessary to keep firm my command of my men and vassals. Do you believe me?"

She did; there was something in the way he said it that made her believe him completely. Much like her father, Bhrodi had an intensity about him that was undeniable, an intensity that conveyed absolute control.

"What will you do?" she asked.

"It will be sufficient, whatever it is."

It was a kind way of telling her that it was not her business and she didn't press him, although it was difficult. She was naturally curious, and nosy, as her father called her. With a heavy sigh, she simply nodded her head and lowered her gaze, and he released her completely. But his eyes never left her.

"You will retire to our chamber for the night," he told her softly. "I will see you on the morrow."

Her head came up. "Will you be escorting my family out of Wales?"

He nodded. "More than likely."

"Then I want to come. *Please*, my lord."

He cocked an eyebrow. "You will call me Bhrodi in private," he said. "Or Husband. I will answer to whatever you chose."

She nodded unsteadily, as they were somewhat off the subject. A flash of warmth sparked when he said that, something that warmed her heart, and she struggled to ignore it. But she would not let the subject go completely.

"May I please come?" she asked again.

He grasped her gently by the upper arm and planted a kiss right on her forehead. It was a bold move, one that broke protocol even though she was his wife. It was a gesture reserved for those who had feeling between them and it certainly wasn't done in a public place. But Bhrodi couldn't help himself. It seemed like the right thing to do.

"Mayhap," he said as he turned her in the direction of the main portion of the hall where everyone was gathered. "We will discuss it on the morrow."

Penelope knew she would have to be satisfied with that but no matter what he said, she planned to ride escort for her family as they left Anglesey. Bhrodi just didn't know it yet. Obediently, she let him lead her back to her family and leave her in the care of her father. Bhrodi then proceeded out into the entry hall where he collected his vigilant *teulu,* including Ivor and Gwyllim, and pulled them into a huddle. It was clear he was discussing something serious with them. He was planning his retribution.

As Penelope watched with curiosity, William had turned back to his group. They now had Kevin up on the table and were working on him there. Yestin and Ianto eventually returned with a tiny old man carrying a sack, their surgeon they declared, and the old man began to confer with Paris on the extent of Kevin's injury. Just as they began to put bone needles into Kevin to stitch him up, Bhrodi and his *teulu* unbolted the entry door and left the keep. Ianto went with him, leaving Yestin to bolt the door and remain with the English.

After Bhrodi left, Penelope remained pensive and inactive for a very long time. Her mind was awhirl with the events of the day and particularly the events of the night. So much had happened, leaving her disoriented and muddled. More than anything, her thoughts seemed to be lingering on her new husband.

Bhrodi de Shera was a great warlord who seemed to have trouble controlling his vassals. The Welsh were rebels, indeed, and evidently acted without orders and saw nothing wrong with betrayal. She began to wonder what sort of world she was now a part of, fearful of the future she could not fathom. True, she was coming to like Bhrodi and, truth be told, she had very much enjoyed the consummation of their marriage when she surely should not have. Perhaps it made her a hussy; perhaps not. Perhaps it simply meant she enjoyed the pleasures of the flesh with the man she was married to. In all, it was so very confusing. She tried not to feel distress over it.

As the shock of the evening wore down and the English began to feel safe once again, they began to settle in around the hearth and relax as much as they were able. Penelope sat up all night sitting next to Kevin, holding the man's hand as the surgeon and Paris worked to save his life. He had been conscious the entire time, grunting through the pain of the deep sutures put into his body, and Penelope had tried to comfort him. But her mind was with Bhrodi as she wondered what he was doing. He had told her he would punish his vassals and she would trust that he was doing so. She had little choice.

Deep inside the keep, they couldn't hear what was transpiring in the bailey now that the great hall had completely burned to the ground. She couldn't hear the fighting that was still going on and how Bhrodi and his *teulu* sided with de Wolfe's guard, and how the Welsh and English had rounded up the chieftain rebels and had corralled them in the gatehouse. The vault was there, two big cells cut into the bedrock of Rhydilian, and by morning it was full of the Welsh agitators and their followers. Bhrodi's threat to them was the same threat he used for any prisoner facing execution; he would take them to the beast of the marsh who would feast upon their flesh and end their miserable lives. The dark secret of Rhydilian, for four generations, was that they fed their mortal enemies to the beast.

The serpent with a taste for human flesh. It was why Bhrodi had been so eager to save the English on the night of their arrival; the beast from the marsh fed upon mortal man and Bhrodi had worked hard to ensure it did not sink its teeth into English flesh. Now, he would feed the beast those who had betrayed him so that when de Wolfe's party passed through the marsh on their return to England, the beast would be well fed and would leave the English alone. Tudur ap Gwyfn howled all night when he had realized what Bhrodi's intentions were. As a Welshman, and a native of Anglesey, he knew what happened to those who crossed de Shera's path in violence. He just never thought it would happen to him.

Just before dawn, when the mist lay heavy in the swamp and upon the green and lush mountain, Bhrodi and his *teulu* moved seventy-nine Welsh prisoners out to the swamp, all of them tied together with rope and all of them stripped of their clothing so that they were naked and freezing. Reaching the spot in the glade where prisoners were tethered to await their fate, Bhrodi and his men made sure all of the prisoners were tightly bound, awaiting their fate at the fangs of the great beast.

Tudur and Lon begged and pleaded for mercy, but Bhrodi wouldn't hear them. They were traitors and the penalty for treachery, in Bhrodi's world, was death. Standing at the edge of the marsh with the horn that his grandfather's father had used, he blew into the horn, creating a mournful cry that sounded somewhat like the beast itself. It was the call to the beast, the summons for it to come forth, and soon enough they heard the stirrings of the creature. When they began to hear the grunts, Bhrodi and his men mounted their horses and thundered out of range, turning to watch the scene unfold from a distance. It wasn't long in coming.

Bhrodi usually watched these executions to reconcile in his own mind that his enemies were dead. He had to know the threats were gone. This time was no different; he watched as the beast devoured Tudur, and then Lon, and feasted upon the remaining prisoners as they screamed and begged for God's mercy.

In this land of the beast, in the mysterious wilds of Pendraeth, there was only Bhrodi's mercy and he wasn't apt to give it today. As the beast executed Bhrodi's prisoners one by one, it emitted a foul roar that echoed off the mountains. As far as Bhrodi was concerned, it was a roar of victory.

Inside the keep of Rhydilian a few miles away, even the English heard the unsettling roars inside the thick walls.

It was the sound of the serpent's strike.

CHAPTER ELEVEN

William knew this moment was coming and he didn't want to face it. As his party was saddled up, secured, and ready to depart, the most difficult part of all was coming. He had to tell his youngest child farewell and he wasn't at all sure he could accomplish that and not break down like an idiot. In the cold and misty morning following the rather eventful wedding feast, he was dressed in full armor, watching his wife and daughter say their good-byes.

It was a tearful scene. Jordan and Penelope had clung to each other for the past fifteen minutes as Penelope wept softly and Jordan whispered words of strength and encouragement in her ear. William knew that when the time came for him to hug her, it was very possible he would not let her go at all. He was both dreading the moment and anticipating it. He wanted to hug her in the worst way. It was time to leave his baby to her new life and he was having a difficult time facing it.

Given the events of the previous night, Bhrodi had arranged for a one hundred man escort from his personal guard to accompany de Wolfe to the ferry that crossed over to the Welsh mainland. The de Shera *teulu* were dressed in their red de Shera tunics and well-armed with spears and crossbows. None of them carried broadswords, as it was not their way, but they were an extremely efficient fighting squad.

Based on the interrogation of the prisoners the night before and coming to understand that the attack on the English had been an isolated event, Bhrodi had made the decision to send his escort as far as the Menai crossing; he had sent word early that morning on ahead to Caernarfon, a city occupied by the English because they were starting to build a castle there, so that the English would provide additional protection for de Wolfe once the man crossed onto mainland Wales. De Wolfe was his kin, after all, and he wanted to make sure the man had ample protection as he traveled through Wales, even if it meant he had to contact the English in order to accomplish it. He had gone out of his way to make sure de Wolfe had a safe crossing, and William was grateful for it. De Shera was coming to prove himself a man of thoughtfulness and courtesy.

Penelope, however, had been deeply unhappy that she would not be allowed to escort her mother and father back through Wales. Bhrodi had denied her and William had supported that decision, which thoroughly upset her. Jordan even entered the discussion and reminded her daughter that she was a wife now and not a knight, and riding escort did not fall under her scope of duties.

Because Penelope was so unhappy, Bhrodi decided not to ride with his escort, instead choosing to remain behind and comfort his wife. They'd had a very turbulent beginning to their marriage and he thought it best to remain with her during this time of emotional turmoil. Whether or not she would accept his comfort was another thing entirely. Since the battle in the hall, she had been quite distant from him and he didn't like it one bit. He longed for the warmth he had felt from her during the ceremony and at the feast before the chaos; to have such warmth, such feeling, and then to have it ripped away from him had left him feeling hollow and sad. He was anxious to reclaim it.

There were other decisions made as well, decisions that both Bhrodi and William had agreed upon. Kevin Hage was too ill to be moved so it was decided he would remain behind until he was healed, whereupon he could then return to England. Thomas, Penelope's older brother by eight years, would also remain behind for Penelope's comfort. She was in a strange world with strange people and Bhrodi agreed that a brother might be of comfort to her until she felt more confident in her surroundings. Moreover, Thomas had a massive gash in his arm which had rendered it useless so, like Kevin, he needed time to heal. Having both of them remain behind for the time being made Penelope feel as if she wasn't so utterly alone.

But time was passing and the morning was advancing, and the time had come to leave Penelope with her new husband and new life. William broke from his stance near the wagon where he had been watching his wife and daughter say their farewells and made his way over to them.

"Jordan," he said quietly. "We must depart. The day is upon us and we cannot linger."

Jordan knew that although it was still difficult to hear. Squaring her shoulders, she released her daughter from her tight embrace and smiled bravely at her, struggling not to burst into tears.

"Now," she said decisively, "ye'll write tae me next week and tell me how everything is. Make sure ye let me know about Kevin and Thomas, too. I would hear all about everything."

Penelope's eyes were red and watery but she nodded. "Aye, Mamma," she said, sniffling. "Will you come to visit again soon?"

Jordan nodded firmly. "Of course we will," she said, noting William standing next to her. Reluctantly, she stepped aside. "Bid farewell tae yer father, now. He has been waiting patiently tae hug ye."

As she stepped back, William took her place. For a moment, he simply stared at his daughter. The words just wouldn't come. Then, his big hands came up and gently cupped her face; he could see that tiny baby who had surprised them all with her late birth, then the toddler who would only eat bread crusts and follow her brothers around, and finally the young girl who demanded a sword and pony so she could be a knight. He saw all of those things at that moment and it was tearing him apart. Leaning forward, he kissed her on the forehead.

"I will miss you with every breath," he murmured, watching her face crumple in tears, "but I know I leave you in good hands. I believe that de Shera is a man of honor and will treat you well. You must give him that chance, Penny. Will you do that? Give the man a chance to be a good husband to you."

Penelope nodded although she was far gone in tears. "But I do not want you to go, Papa."

He clucked sadly and kissed her on the forehead again, drawing her into a tight embrace. He could feel tears sting his eyes, too, as she sobbed against him.

"I love you, lass," he murmured. "You are my heart. Should you ever need me, I will come."

Penelope sobbed deeply as she held him. "Papa, I miss you already."

William had a lump in his throat as he gave her a squeeze and let her go. "I miss you, too, but I know you will be very happy here," he whispered tightly, forcing a smile when she looked at him. "You are going to have such a grand adventure here. You are the mistress of a great empire and you have a proud and powerful husband. I could wish no more for you, Penny. I am content."

She tried to hug him again but he held her off, grasping her hands and kissing them. He knew if she hugged him again he would not be able to release her. Tears in his eye, he kissed her cheek and forehead once more before letting her go. As Penelope stood there and sobbed, Paris came up and gave her big, gentle hug, wiping his eyes as he released her. Seeing that her Uncle Paris was weeping made Penelope weep harder, especially when her Uncle Kieran hugged her farewell with tears trickling down his cheeks.

"Take care of my son," Kieran whispered. "I leave him in your care."

Penelope nodded as she wiped at her face. "I will take very good care of him," she said, sniffling. "I promise he will be well again."

Kieran nodded sadly, touched her cheek, and walked away. Jemma was next, sobbing loudly as she hugged her niece, which set Penelope off again. In fact, Kieran had to peel Jemma away; she was more distraught about leaving her son behind than she was in leaving Penelope. One by one, the brothers and cousins told Penelope farewell, Patrick lifting her off the ground and gently shaking her as he had always done. Penelope squealed and protested, as she had always done. It was enough to make everyone smile.

Bhrodi, who had been watching everything from a distance, finally came to stand beside Penelope as the English mounted their horses and the great gates of Rhydilian yawned open to reveal the foggy landscape beyond. Penelope wept softly, hand over her mouth, as she watched the party trickle out of the gates. Her father was the last one to go, waving at her as he turned his charger for the gates. When Penelope tried to run after him, Bhrodi grasped her firmly.

"They will be back soon," he assured her. "Or mayhap we will go and visit them. I have never been to the north of England before."

Penelope wept as she watched her father ride off. She felt so very alone, so very sad. William rode straight and proud, his armor gleaming weakly in the mist as the sun struggled to break through it. As Penelope and Bhrodi watched, the mist swallowed him up and the great gates began to close. Penelope hung her head and sobbed.

Bhrodi watched her lowered head, feeling a good deal of sorrow for her. She was very attached to her family, which was something he'd never known. It was an intriguing mystery to him, but one he hoped to know. He hoped that someday she would be as attached to him as she was to her parents. Finally, he reached out and gently took her hand.

"Let us go inside," he murmured. "There is warm food waiting for us and Tacey should be awake. We will also go see to your brother and the English knight. Come along, *caria*."

Surprisingly, Penelope didn't pull away from him as he began to lead her back towards the keep. His big, warm hand gave her some comfort and she was coming to realize that he was her family now. This man she had only known for five days was now her family; it was an odd sensation but not an unpleasant one. It was simply... strange. Together, they headed towards the keep, shrouded in mist, and disappeared into the dark, warm innards.

Thinking that perhaps Penelope would want to see her brother and knight first, Bhrodi took her to the third floor of the keep where the master's chamber and a secondary chamber, once belonging to Tacey, were situated. When Lady Jordan moved Tacey up into the big, roomy chamber on the fourth floor, her former chamber had been transformed into a hospital ward.

When Penelope and Bhrodi entered the chamber, it was dark but for smoldering embers in the hearth giving on an orange glow and it smelled heavily of clove, thought to ward off infection. Thomas was on a bed near the southern wall, lying flat on his back and snoring soundly, while Kevin was on a bigger bed that had been pulled closer to the hearth. As the most gravely injured, the physic wanted to make sure the big knight remained warm.

Penelope walked into the room while Bhrodi lingered near the door. She peered first at Kevin, who was sleeping heavily, and then went over to her brother. Thomas was snoring so loudly she was confused as to how he could actually sleep through such a sound. She even poked him to see if he would awaken but he didn't. Concerned, she went back to her husband.

"Why are they sleeping like the dead?" she whispered loudly. "What did your surgeon do to them that they would sleep like this?"

Bhrodi looked at the two sleeping knights. "He must have given them a sleeping potion," he murmured. "Sleep will heal them. 'Tis best to let them rest as much as they can."

He had a point but Penelope checked on both men one more time before quitting the chamber. Now that she knew the men were faring as well as could be expected, Bhrodi took her up to the top floor where Tacey now had a big and spacious chamber. He knocked softly on the door, only to have it opened by one of the serving women Lady Jordan had hired.

It was a very old women with no teeth and a nearly bald head that she kept covered with an old kerchief. When she saw the lord and his wife, she curtsied unsteadily and bustled from the room. Bhrodi and Penelope could see Tacey over near the hearth, seated in a cushioned chair with a table of food spread out before her. When Tacey caught sight of her brother and Penelope, she struggled to her feet.

"Did they leave yet?" she asked.

Bhrodi entered the room, followed by Penelope. "They did indeed," he said. "Lady Jordan bid you farewell last night, didn't she?"

Tacey nodded, her attention drawn to Penelope. Over the past few days, the very timid and frightened young woman had come out of her shell somewhat. Now, she wasn't nearly as nervous in the presence of others. She smiled hesitantly at Penelope, daughter of the woman who had been more of a mother to her in the few short days that she had known her than her own had been in her entire life.

"Your mother gave me a muff made from fox fur," she said, pointing to the muff as it lay by the pillow her bed. "I slept with it last night."

Penelope couldn't help but smile. "I am glad you like it so much," she said. "My mother is fond of you.

"And I am fond of her," she said quickly, looking to her brother. "When do you think they will come back to visit? Or can we go and visit them? I have never been to England."

Bhrodi patted her shoulder. "We cannot go anywhere until your son is born," he said, watching her face fall. "But perhaps we can go later in the year when the child is older. I am sure my wife would like to see her family soon."

Penelope thought on her family, so recently departed, and tried not to become weepy again so she simply nodded her head. Bhrodi, sensing her sadness, wasn't particular adept at handling female emotion. He sought to change the subject, turning to his sister.

"It looks as if you have already eaten your morning meal," he said. "Penelope and I were going to eat in hall downstairs. Do you wish to come with us?"

Tacey nodded eagerly, thrilled to be included. She rushed at Penelope and latched onto her hand.

"Have you ever been to Scotland?" she asked Penelope as they walked from the chamber. "Your mother told me that the hills are covered with purple flowers. Have you ever seen such a thing?"

Penelope smiled weakly at the young woman, forcing herself from her sorrowful thoughts. "I have," she said. They began to take the stairs down to the lower level. "My grandfather lived in Scotland and we went often to visit him. My mother still has kin there; her father was chief of the Clan Scott."

Tacey was duly impressed. "A chief?" she repeated, awed. "Is that like a king?"

Penelope carefully helped Tacey down the last of the steps because the girl wasn't paying much attention to where she was going; she was more interested in talking.

"It is, in a way," Penelope said as they reached the second floor entry. The feasting hall was off to the left. "A chief is head of a family and often it is hundreds of people."

Bhrodi was listening to the conversation as he followed them. "But if you are Scots, then your king is Alexander from the House of Dunkeld, except that Edward wishes to be king over Scotland, too," he said, winking at Tacey as she turned to look at him. "A country can only have one king."

"But our ancestors were kings," Tacey insisted as they moved into the feasting hall with its malfunctioning hearth spitting ribbons of smoke into the air. "They were the kings of Anglesey."

Bhrodi nodded. "That is true."

"Why were they not king of all of Wales?"

They had reached the feasting table where Ianto, Ivor, Yestin, and Gwyllim were seated, eating their morning meal. The men looked up as Bhrodi and the women approached, moving down the table so that Bhrodi and the ladies could be seated. The serving women hired by Jordan began moving in, setting down cups and pitchers of warmed wine and great loaves of bread.

In fact, it was a bit of a feast and Bhrodi eyed the women strangely simply because he wasn't used to having them around. Mornings meals before their arrival usually consisted of whatever was left on the table from the night before. He felt rather odd, watching as one of the women patted Tacey on the shoulder and told her she would bring her some warmed milk. Seeing his sister's face light up when the woman was kind to her somehow took away the oddness he was feeling. Instead, it was replaced by guilt. Had he really been mistreating her all of these months under the guise of protection? He was pondering that very question when Tacey spoke.

"Well?" she said, tearing into a warm loaf of bread. "Why can't there be one king of all of Wales?"

Bhrodi poured himself some warmed, watered-down wine. He sniffed it; it smelled of spice. "Because," he said, sipping his wine, "Wales has had many separate kingdoms. There was never one man to bring them all together like there was in England or Scotland."

Tacey chewed thoughtfully. "Why aren't you king of Anglesey now? Everyone says it is your hereditary title but I do not understand why. Why aren't you king?"

Bhrodi pulled another loaf of hard-crusted bread apart and handed half to Penelope as she sat silently next to him. "Because our grandfather's grandfather gave up that right to the Kings of Gwynedd," he said. "He was defeated by Owain Gwynedd in battle and was forced to swear fealty to him. We have been loyal to the House of ap Gruffydd ever since."

"But I married into that house."

"I know you did, which is why your son is so important to us."

Tacey chewed on her bread, looking between Penelope and Bhrodi. "What about your children?" she asked. "Will they be very important, too?"

Bhrodi nodded as a serving woman put a big trencher of eggs mixed with cheese in front of him. "They will be the most important of all because they will be my sons," he said, casting Penelope a side-long glance. "All twelve of them."

Penelope, who had so far sat silent and brooding during the conversation, thinking of her departed family, suddenly lifted her head and looked at him. He smiled quite boldly at her, full of mischief, and she couldn't help but grin. She shook her head reproachfully.

"I told you no boys," she said. "Only girls."

Bhrodi made a face at her and Tacey giggled. But Penelope's mood seemed to have lightened a bit and Bhrodi spooned some eggs onto her trencher. Tacey picked up her spoon and dug into the pile of eggs, eating straight off the platter. She was ravenous and Bhrodi watched her shovel eggs into her mouth, thinking it rather amusing. He didn't have the heart to call her off. Next to him, Penelope was forcing food into her mouth although she didn't feel much like eating. Her gaze lingered on the men towards the end of the table.

"These men are always with you," she murmured to Bhrodi. "I have seen them since the day I arrived and they assisted us last night in fighting off the ambush, but you have never introduced me to them. Who are they?"

Bhrodi looked at the group at the end of the table. "Are you for certain you have not met them? I was sure you had."

Penelope shook her head. "With everything that has gone on since my arrival, there has not been the opportunity."

Bhrodi wriggled his eyebrows at his oversight. "Then you will forgive me," he said, reaching out to thump Ianto on the arm. "Ianto, my wife tells me you have not formally met her."

Ianto shook his head, his gaze lingering on Penelope. "Not formally, no, but I certainly know who she is."

Bhrodi frowned. "Then I am a poor husband indeed to allow my wife to mingle with people she has never been introduced to," he said as he began pointing from right to left. "Lady de Shera, this is Ianto ap Huw. He is my older cousin and a wiser man you will never meet. Next to him is Ivor ap Bando, who has been my friend for many years. That boney man with the dark hair is Yestin ap Bran and last but not least is Gwyllim ap Evan. He is my voice of reason in all things. These men are my *teulu*, the commanders of my personal guard, and they will serve you as well. They are here for your protection."

Penelope nodded her head politely at each man in succession but she didn't have much to say to them. She was still lingering in depression over her family's departure so she turned back to her food and pretended to eat it. She was really just playing with it. Bhrodi watched her from the corner of his eye, trying not to stare because he didn't want to offend her. Truthfully, he wasn't sure what more to do in order to cheer her up but he was determined to try. He'd never been in a position like this before, wanting very much to make someone other than himself happy. It was a foreign concept.

It occurred to him as he watched his wife pick through her food that this was the first time he had truly been alone with her. Before, there had always been her family, always someone to intervene, or to interfere. He'd spent time with her, that was true, but her family had always been lingering about. Now, it was just the two of them facing

150

this new life together. He had to take charge of the relationship if there was ever going to be any hope of building a good one. He thought they had a decent foundation but he wanted it to be better. He'd had a good marriage with Sian and had missed it terribly, but Penelope was completely different. He very desperately wanted things to be good between them. He was more than willing to try. He was about to suggest a trip into the village of Pendraeth to visit the merchants there when they all heard a cracking sound in the southeast corner of the hall.

It was darkened in the recesses of the D-shaped room but as Bhrodi turned to see what the commotion was about, he could see his uncle's wardrobe lingering in the shadows. The furniture had been in the great hall but when the hall burned, the *teulu* had dragged it out so it would not burn and kill the little man within it.

Bhrodi had realized his uncle had been pulled to safety early that morning, as the de Wolfe party was assembling, when he had gone over to the hall to survey the damage and had noticed the wardrobe lingering out in the bailey. He'd had his men bring it into the keep. Now, the tiny man inside was beginning to stir.

Penelope, of course, had never seen the uncle nor did she have any knowledge of him. They'd never crossed paths. The moment the wardrobe began to rock and crack, she would have bolted from her seat had Bhrodi not reached out to grab her. He held her fast as the little man burst forth from his wardrobe and began his mad dance in the darkened corners of the hall.

"Not to fear," Bhrodi said quietly as they both watched the figure in the shadows. "That is my uncle. He lives in the wardrobe and emerges now and again to fight an unseen enemy. Can you see him in the darkness with his imaginary sword? He had been doing that for at least thirty years, as long as I can recall. He is quite mad but he will not harm you so long as you do not interfere or try to stop him. He lives in his world and we live in ours, and they do not cross."

Penelope watched, wide-eyed, as the man, no larger than Tacey, leapt and grunted in his battle against his invisible foe.

"Your uncle?" she repeated, glancing at him although her focus was still on the dancing figure. "

He nodded. "My grandfather's brother," he said. "He is extremely old but, as you can see, still quite spry."

As they watched, the old man suddenly fell to the ground as if he had been gored. He rolled around as if in great pain, hand over his shoulder, until eventually dragging himself up from the ground and, as if he were harboring a terrible wound, he stumbled across the floor until he reached his wardrobe. Pulling himself inside, he shut the door softly. Astonished, Penelope turned her full attention to Bhrodi.

"He does this every night?" she asked.

He nodded, resigned. "Every night," he confirmed. "Do you recall when we were leaving the great hall last night? His wardrobe doors were chained and you asked me why."

Penelope remembered clearly. "Because you keep him locked in there?"

He shrugged. "He lives in there and one of my men had the presence of mind to lock the doors so he would not interrupt our wedding feast," he winked at her. "Nothing like a mad uncle to liven up any occasion."

Penelope thought on that a moment. "He *lives* in there?"

"Indeed."

"Mayhap he would have stopped those men from attacking my family had his doors been unlocked."

"Or he would have helped them. With old Evan, there is no knowing what he will do."

Penelope thought the same thing her father had at that moment; *an interesting family*, she reflected. A very interesting place she now found herself mistress over. It would take some getting used to.

Tacey, who was still shoving eggs into her mouth, hadn't paid much attention to the old uncle because she'd seen him before, many times. However, she had been listening to her brother's explanation of the man.

"Have you ever tried to speak to him, Bhrodi?" she asked, mouth full.

He looked at his little sister with egg on her lips. "Nay," he said. "He has been insane since I was a young boy. Mother told me to stay out of his way and I always have."

An oddity, indeed. As Tacey shrugged and went back to her eggs, Penelope's thoughts lingered on the insane uncle and she resumed trying to eat something of her meal but was fairly unsuccessful. She didn't feel like eating at all. She felt like going upstairs and sitting with her brother and Kevin. Disoriented and sad, she felt like going where she knew there were familiar people.

"With your permission, my lord, I should like to go and sit with my brother for a while," she said.

Bhrodi didn't want her to leave. He could feel her slipping away from him and he didn't want her out of his sight. If he had to overwhelm her with his presence in order to warm her to him again, then he would. He knew of no other way. As she moved to stand, he put his hand on her arm.

"Wait," he said. "The surgeon is seeing to your wounded friends and they are well tended. I would like to take you into the village of Pendraeth this morning. It is the biggest village in my realm and I would like for the vassals to see my new wife."

"I would like to go, too!" Tacey exclaimed. "You told me once that there is a vendor there who sells sweets! I would like some!"

Penelope looked between Bhrodi and Tacey, seeing their eager faces and realizing she couldn't refuse. She was a part of their world now and needed to participate. Resigned, she nodded her head.

"Very well," she said. "If that is your wish."

"It is," Bhrodi said, relieved she hadn't refused him. "Will you change into appropriate clothing? I should like my vassals to see you well dressed."

Penelope looked down at what she was wearing; having been up all night with her family, she was still in the leather breeches, the undershirt, and the tunic she had thrown on. The one difference was that she had her boots on. She was comfortable in her usual attire but she knew that Bhrodi wanted her in regal women's clothing. Inwardly, she sighed; she had never been any good at dressing in women's clothing. She had no idea what to wear with what, or what colors matched, or any of the things she should have known. But she knew she had to learn. It was one more thing to make her day unhappy.

"I will go now," she said, standing up. "I... I shall return shortly."

"I will go with you," Tacey announced, standing up as well. "I would like to help you."

Penelope smiled weakly at the girl, knowing she was about to make a fool out of herself in front of her with her ignorant dressing habits. "My thanks," she said, although she didn't mean it. "I would be... honored."

Tacey smiled brightly and grasped her hand, pulling her from the hall. As they went, Tacey called out to the first serving woman she came across, one who was bringing more drink into the hall.

"We are going to dress," she announced to the woman. "Send someone up with warmed water."

The serving wench nodded and went about her business as Tacey practically dragged Penelope up the stairs. The young girl was eager to be of use and Penelope wished she could jump out of the window.

Now she was the wife of a warlord and the time was finally upon her to dress the part. God, she was dreading it. All of it. She missed her family and was unhappy to be in this strange and new world. She had told her father that she had not been opposed to this marriage and she hadn't been in theory, but the reality was something new entirely. Terrible creatures, rebelling chieftains, an insane uncle, and her new role in life were all contributing to great regrets. She didn't belong here. She wanted to go home.

Sneaking away from Rhydilian and running to catch up with her father's party was looking better by the second.

⌘

CHAPTER TWELVE

Pendraeth Village

 There are Welsh everywhere.
 That's what Penelope thought as she rode into the village of Pendraeth in the company of her husband, her sister-in-law, and her husband's *teulu*. Since most of them had ridden out with her father's party, only about forty were available to escort them into town. It was like being in the belly of the enemy, but in this case, they were not the enemy at all. They were her vassals. Bhrodi's *teulu* were dressed in their traditional garments, tunics of red that were plain, no crests as the English wore, and they carried nothing but spears and crossbows with them. It was all quite strange considering when Penelope had ever traveled with her father, they wore mail, plate armor, helmets, shields, and were generally armed to the teeth. The Welsh didn't do that and it was all quite puzzling to her.
 Even more puzzling was the fact that she was not dressed in her usual traveling attire; with Tacey's help, she had donned some of the clothing in her trousseau that her mother and aunts had made for her; she had on a fine, soft shift and over that she wore a gown of lavender wool, snug in the bodice and sleeves, with a full skirt that she had already tripped on twice. Over the lavender gown she wore a coat of pale ivory that was tight at the waist but ended just below her hips. It was lined with white rabbit fur, very elegant and warm. Instead of her usual boots, she wore fine doeskin slippers. For as lovely as she looked, she was absolutely miserable.

But Bhrodi was as proud as a peacock with his lovely new wife as they made their way into the berg. Tacey was on a small and gentle palfrey, being led by Ianto, while Penelope rode at the head of the group with Bhrodi. Although she had a big gray charger she was very fond of, Bhrodi had shown some reluctance at her riding a war horse in such fine attire, so she reluctantly agreed to a gentle white mare. And she was hating every minute of it; she wondered if the torture and humiliation would ever end.

Her unhappiness faded as she became interested in the town around her. Welsh towns didn't seem too different from English towns except they were speaking the very harsh Welsh language, which sounded like gibberish to her. When Bhrodi spoke to his *teulu*, it was in Welsh, and sometimes he spoke to Tacey in it as well. They were heading towards the center of town, near a big well and a stream that ran right through the middle of town, when Penelope finally asked him about his native language.

"Is Welsh your first language?" she asked him.

Bhrodi nodded as he reined his charger near the well where several women were doing their laundry. "Even though my father is English, I learned Welsh first," he said. "I will teach it to you so that you and I may converse in it."

Penelope looked dubious. "It sounds very difficult."

He grinned as he dismounted his steed. "I do not think it is, but it is very different from your language," he said. "For example, *croeso* means 'welcome'. Welcome to Pendraeth."

He was stretching his arm wide to indicate the village as he rounded his horse and moved to help her dismount. But Penelope had already leapt off the little mare, nearly tumbling when she stepped on the skirts she was not used to. Bhrodi grasped her by the elbow to steady her.

"*Croeso*," Penelope repeated. "Welcome. What else?"

He cocked his head thoughtfully, watching Ianto lift Tacey off her horse and set her to her feet very carefully. He pointed to his sister.

"*Chwaer*," he said, "means 'sister'."

"And brother?"

"*Brawd*."

At this point, they were gazing steadily at one another and for the first time all day, Penelope's mood seemed to be lightening considerably. Her personality seemed to be coming back as did the light in her eyes. Bhrodi smiled at her as she mouthed the words he had just taught her, whispering them as she rolled them over her tongue. When she caught his expression, she returned his smile.

"Mayhap I will allow you to teach me your language," she said. "My mother speaks Gaelic constantly but I never learned. I do, however, speak French."

He nodded his head. "As do I," he said. "Often, there are men under my command that speak different languages. I must know them all if I am to tell them what to do."

Penelope nodded, her smile fading. "In speaking of men under your command," she said, "you do not think that my father will run into any trouble as he travels through Wales? That is to say, the trouble from last night will not follow him, will it? The men who are escorting him, your men, will see him through safely?"

He was surprised the question hadn't come up sooner and he nodded as he began to lead her towards a small avenue near the well that seemed to be very busy. There were open merchant stalls, very tiny and crowded stalls, but very busy.

"My men will make sure your father makes it safely out of Anglesey," he said. "English from the garrison at Caernarfon will be waiting to escort them the rest of the way. They should not run into any more trouble."

Penelope could see that he was leading her towards a cluster of merchant stalls. "But what of the men last night who caused all of the trouble?" she asked. "Did you chase them away?"

Bhrodi's smile, and his good mood, faded as he thought on the fate of those he thought were his friends. That ancient and horrible fate. "Nay," he said after a moment. "I did not chase them away."

Penelope took the news with some relief. "Then you imprisoned them," she assumed and he did not correct her. "Excellent. I was fearful they would be lying in wait for my father."

Bhrodi didn't say anymore. He didn't want to tell her what he did with those who had betrayed him, at least not now. It would be too much for her to bear when she was still emotionally fragile in this new world. He was about to change the subject when Tacey rushed up and latched onto Penelope's hand.

"This is so exciting!" she gasped, her young face alight at all of the vendor stalls. "Where is the sweet vendor?"

Bhrodi pointed off into the cluster of stalls. "In there, somewhere," he said. "We shall find him."

Perhaps that was the truth, but Tacey wouldn't wait. She tried to run ahead, pulling Penelope with her, but Bhrodi cautioned her to slow down. Tacey tried, but for a young girl who hadn't been out of Rhydilian in over a year, she was wild with excitement. As they entered the busy avenue, Tacey spied a man with all manner of food about his stall. Letting go of Penelope's hand, she ran towards the stall before her brother could stop her. He did, however, send Ianto after her so she wouldn't get into any trouble. By the time the rest of the group caught up, Tacey already had two sweets in hand.

"This is a fruit pie," Tacey said happily, indicating a big, brown, and fried piece of crust. "It has figs and raisins and apples in it. And this is a custard with rice and almonds. There is honey in it, too!"

She was indicating a small box made from dried grass that was filled with a lumpy white pudding. Bhrodi eyed the treats.

"Is this what you want?" he asked.

Tacey nodded eagerly. "I do!"

Bhrodi shrugged and indicated for Gwyllim, the keeper of the purse, to pay the merchant. As the man counted out the coins, Bhrodi turned to Penelope.

"Would you like sweets also?" he asked.

Penelope watched Tacey, so very happy with her treats. "Nay," she said. "I have never been very fond of them."

Bhrodi cocked an eyebrow as he took her hand and tucked it into the crook of his elbow. "Is that so?" he asked. "What are you fond of?"

Penelope snorted. "Great black ale that comes from Scotland," she said.

He made a face. "Ale? God's Blood, woman, must you be fond of a man's drink?"

Penelope laughed softly as she allowed Bhrodi to lead her down the street. She was feeling better now, her depression lifting, and she was coming to enjoy Bhrodi's company once again. The last time she had enjoyed being with him was last night before the attack in the hall. William had believed in Bhrodi's innocence in the matter and, truth be told, she did, too. She never truly believed he had been behind it although, at the time, she hadn't known what to think.

Now, she was feeling somewhat guilty for thinking the worst of him. He had, in truth, been trying very hard to be kind to her since the

158

moment they met. He was still trying very hard as he helped her come to know her new world and she knew she wasn't making it easy for him. As they passed by a blacksmith's stall, she paused to look at the swords he was working on.

Bhrodi paused as well, watching her face as she watched the blacksmith. When she realized she was being watched, she smiled rather sheepishly at him.

"Sorry," she said. "I have always been interested in metalworking. My father has allowed me to help the blacksmith at Castle Questing. I find the whole process fascinating."

Bhrodi gazed at his beautiful wife, looking so elegant and womanly in her lavender gown. But it was coming to occur to him that it was going to take a lot of work to turn her from a knight into a true lady. He wondered if he would ever truly be able to do it. He wondered if he should even try. She seemed so uncomfortable in her fine clothes even if she looked delicious and he liked to see her in them. To see the woman dressed in tunics and leather was such a waste. Aye, her mother had said it best – he wanted a wife, not a knight, but he knew it would be a difficult transition.

"It is man's work," he finally said, his voice quiet. "I do not think I should like to see my wife in the stalls, banging away on an anvil."

Penelope laughed softly. "I would not do it if you did not give me permission," she said, her gaze finding the half-finished swords again that the smithy was working on. "But... but I did lose my broadsword in the battle against the beast. I was hoping... well, I should like to have another one."

Bhrodi pondered her request. It was the first one she'd truly made of him and he hated to deny her, but he didn't want to encourage her either. He settled for a wink. "Mayhap you will be surprised with one at some point in the future," he said, taking her elbow and pulling her gently along with him. "Come and look over her; there is a merchant who has traveled all over the world and he has some marvelous and mysterious things in his stall."

As he'd hoped, Penelope was interested in the change of subject. "Like what?"

Tacey, full of sweets, was walking on ahead of them and had already reached the stall where the merchant carried all manner of amazing things. Bhrodi watched his sister pick up a beautiful silk veil.

"Anything you can imagine, I am sure," he said as they arrived. "See if there isn't something you would like to have."

Penelope was hesitant but Tacey wasn't; she plunged into the stall with the leaning roof and pulled Penelope in after her. There were so many items for sale that it was all quite crowded; fabric, veils, combs and mirrors, jewelry, and finally perfumes. Tacey, so very eager to shop, picked up a bronze comb and matching mirror. Made of polished bronze, she held it up to Penelope.

"You need this," she declared. "You only have a horsehair brush and you have no mirror at all. You need a mirror."

Penelope gazed into the mirror, seeing her clear reflection for the first time at close range. Certainly, her mother and sisters had mirrors, but she had never paid much attention to them. Now, she found herself gazing back at a beautiful woman with pale skin, a few freckles on her nose, wide hazel eyes, and delicately arched brows.

"You are beautiful," Bhrodi murmured.

He was standing directly behind her, watching her as she inspected her reflection. Embarrassed, she went to set the mirror down but he grasped her wrist and forced her to hold it up in front of her face again. He continued admiring her for a moment, inspecting the face that was unlike any he had ever seen. *My wife.* Even as he thought it, the truth of the situation seemed unreal.

"You, there," he said to the merchant. "Bring me those necklaces over there. Aye; those are the ones. I would try them on my wife."

Penelope shook her head. "Please," she whispered. "I do not want to...."

He cut her off though it was gently done. "Aye, you do," he said softly, his hot breath on her ear creating shivers down her spine. "You wish to make your husband happy, and he is happy when he sees you in beautiful things. Let me do this, Penny. Please."

He had called her Penny, sounding sweet and gentle coming from his lips. She'd never heard her name sound so tender, not even from her parents. With a sigh of resignation, she forced a smile as he had the merchant place necklace after necklace on her slender neck. All of them had precious stones, some were made of gold and some were made of silver. Some were chokers around her neck and some hung low between her breasts. All the while, Tacey was exclaiming how beautiful everything was, which made Penelope take a second look as the jewelry hung around her neck. She really never wore jewelry so she wasn't particularly adept at knowing what was beautiful and what was gaudy. But very quickly she learned that she liked things that were simple in design. When the merchant hung a simple necklace of gold chain and purple stones, she liked it right away.

"That is quite nice," she said, admiring it in the mirror.

"We shall take it," Bhrodi said quickly. "It is the first thing she has liked and I'll be damned if I am going to let it get away. Wrap it up for her."

The merchant nodded, thrilled at the big sale, and went to package up the jewelry. Tacey, meanwhile, had set aside several different things and when she asked her brother if she could have them, a denial was perched on his lips until Penelope cast him a quick glance before inspecting all of the wonderful things.

"I think you deserve all of these," she told Tacey. "The baby deserves some things, too, does he not? Did you pick out anything for him?"

Tacey instinctively put her hand on her big belly. She looked rather confused. "Your mother told me the things I would need," she said. "She told me that babies need swaddling and pillows, and I do have blankets and pillows in my chamber."

"For the baby?"

"They belong to me but I will share with him."

Penelope glanced at Bhrodi with a rather worrisome expression. "The baby needs his *own* things," she said, putting her hand on Tacey's shoulder. "Didn't my mother tell you that?"

Tacey was so young; a child having a child, and it was difficult for her to think of others over herself. The child was in her belly, that was true, but it still wasn't real to her yet. Penelope knew that her mother and aunt had tried to tell Tacey things to expect with the baby, but it was clear the girl hadn't absorbed much. She was only capable of thinking about herself at the moment. She was just too young to truly grasp the concept of what she was in for.

"He will share my things," she said, looking at her brother as if he would confirm her decision. "Can I have these lovely items, please? The silks and the perfumes?"

Bhrodi sighed, looking at Penelope to see if he could read her expression. Penelope, however, didn't give him much encouragement one way or the other; she had simply turned away to set down the mirror she had been holding. Without Penelope's support, he went with his natural instinct.

"Nay," he said. "You have enough fine things and any money I spend from now on will be for your son. He will be here in two months and we must start planning for him."

Tacey's features fell. "Like what?" she demanded. "He is just a baby. What does he need?"

"A bed," Penelope said. "Does he even have one? He cannot sleep with you, you know. He is too tiny. He will need swaddling and blankets and clothing to wear. Does he have any of that?"

Tacey shook her head unsteadily. "Nay," she said reluctantly. "I... I do not suppose he has any of those things."

Penelope looked at Bhrodi. "Then that is what we must buy today," she said. "Material for clothes for the baby and we must find a carpenter who can build him a bed."

She seemed very determined about it, much as her mother had showed such determination in everything she did. But the fact was that Bhrodi couldn't disagree with her; he was the first one to admit that he had been rather lax in taking care of his sister's needs much less the baby's needs. Therefore, he nodded his head.

"Then let us find these things," he said, waving the women onward in the direction of the avenue. "My nephew must have something to wear and a place to sleep."

Tacey was disappointed as she left the shop without any of her precious items, even more disappointed when Bhrodi collected the necklace he had purchased for his wife and handed it over to Gwyllim to keep safe. Tacey wished it was *her* necklace. Now, she wasn't so excited about coming to town as she realized her brother would not be purchasing things for her; he would be purchasing things for the baby. She was jealous. Unhappy, she followed Penelope and Bhrodi down the avenue in their search for baby items.

It didn't take long for them to find fleecy-soft lamb's wool for the baby's clothing and very soft linen for his swaddling. Penelope reckoned that any one of the women her mother had hired could sew, so she wasn't worried about who would make the clothing. Tacey certainly couldn't and even now as they moved down the muddy avenue, she was dragging behind, obviously pouting that she was not getting any pretty things.

Ivor and Yestin had gone off in search of a carpenter and had quickly located one on the next block. When Bhrodi told the man what they needed, the carpenter agreed to make a baby's cradle and have it to Rhydilian Castle within a month. As Bhrodi was giving the man half of his payment, with the promise of the other half when the cradle was delivered, a wretched and low sound filled the air.

It was a startling sound, something between a moan and a hiss. It came from the direction they had just come from, the center of town, and they all turned to see a cluster of women who had come up behind them. The sound was coming from them.

"I heard you were in town, de Shera," a woman wept loudly, pointing fingers at him. She was an older woman, finely dressed, and was surrounded by other ladies who evidently served her. They were all weeping and pointing. When she realized that she had Bhrodi's attention, she screeched. "My husband went to your wedding yesterday and has not returned. I was told you killed everyone who attended! Well? Is this true?"

It was Tudur ap Gwyfn's wife, Lady Ceridwen. Bhrodi knew the woman fairly well; she was from a powerful Welsh family and a woman of breeding, but at the moment, she was howling like a low-born wench. Given the complex circumstances of his wedding, he wasn't about to engage her in a conversation about it much less a shouting match. Without a word, he turned away from her.

"Let us move down the street," he said quietly to Penelope and Tacey.

He began to move with his *teulu* surrounding him, but ap Gwyfn's wife would not be ignored. She followed.

"My servants told me that you had come into town," she said, yelling after him. "I came to find you, de Shera. What have you done to my husband? You have punished him because he opposed your marriage to the Saesneg whore!"

Penelope's knightly training kicked in; she was adept at covering her emotions when faced with a crisis, at least for the most part, but she did glance at Bhrodi to see how he was reacting. His features were tight as he kept walking. Tacey, however, kept turning around to look at the woman who was following them.

"Who *is* that?" she whispered to her brother.

Bhrodi kept his eyes on the avenue straight ahead. "No one," he replied. "Ignore her."

Tacey was frightened by the woman's yelling but she forced herself to face forward just as Penelope and Bhrodi were. Ceridwen, however, would not be discarded so easily; she began to throw great clumps of mud at them, digging them up from the avenue.

"Murderer!" she screamed, throwing mud that hit Ianto in the neck. "You murdered my husband because he came to speak to you of your wedding and of your betrayal to all things Welsh. You have brought English blood into our lands, de Shera! The Devil now walks among us!"

Bhrodi had Penelope in one hand and Tacey in the other. He pretended as if he didn't have a care in the world. "There is a cobbler down here who does excellent work," he told Penelope. "In fact, he has made me several pairs of boots. Sometimes he comes to Rhydilian to work if we have enough tasks for him. He had his own stall at the castle."

Penelope turned to respond to him when a flying wad of mud hit her on the side of the face. As she gasped and wiped it away, Bhrodi turned around and plowed back through his men, emerging from the group to where ap Gwyfn's wife was digging up more dirt out of the avenue. Her ladies screamed as he rushed at her and the woman looked up in time to see de Shera bearing down on her. Startled, she lost her balance and ended up on her bum in the mud. Bhrodi loomed over her, his eyes blazing. *Serpent eyes.*

"You are a foolish and reckless wench if I've ever seen one," he growled. "You know nothing of what you speak. Your husband came to my wedding; indeed, he did. He also led an attack against the English at the feast, who were there under my protection. He betrayed me and my trust, and this I cannot abide. If you do not want to end up as he did, then I suggest you shut your mouth and return home. If I ever see you again, I will make sure you join your husband. Is this in any way unclear?"

By this time, the woman was cowering. Her arm was up over her head as if to prevent him from striking her.

"Where is he?" she cried, her voice considerably weaker. "What did you do to him?"

Bhrodi just looked at her. "You have lived in my realm long enough," he said. "You know what happens to traitors."

The woman's face crumpled and she began to weep. "You killed him!"

Bhrodi shook his head. "I did not kill him," he said. It was technically the truth. "He brought the serpent down upon himself. I had nothing to do with it."

All of the women began to weep and hiss at that point, all of them collapsing beside their stricken mistress. It was a writhing, dirty mass that laid down on the street and wept.

"The beast!" ap Gwyfn's widow cried. "He was fodder for the beast!"

Bhrodi didn't say another word. He turned around and headed back to his group in time to see Penelope wiping the remnants of the mud off her face. She was looking at him, however; she had heard the woman crying about the serpent. She also noticed that everyone around them seemed to be watching what was going on, listening to what should have been a private conversation. She was beginning to feel uneasy.

"Shall we go?" Bhrodi said casually as he walked up. "I fear our business is concluded for the day."

Tacey was anxious to get away from the frightening women and scooted up with Ianto and Yestin to hold their hands as Bhrodi clutched Penelope by the elbow. Bhrodi, knowing what Penelope did, that others had heard the edgy conversation, turned everyone towards an alley that led back in the direction of their horses.

"We will go this way," he said as the group shifted. "It is shorter."

The alley was narrow, smelling heavily of urine, and Penelope picked up her skirts so they wouldn't drag through the rancid mud. They could hear the crying of the women fading but she couldn't help but notice that Bhrodi was moving rather swiftly. All the while, she was reflecting upon what had been said. She was particularly interested in one thing in particular.

"What did she mean that her husband was fodder for the beast?" she asked quietly, turning to look at Bhrodi. "What did you do to those men? I thought you imprisoned them."

He wouldn't meet her eye; they were emerging from the alley and the horses were straight ahead, being tended by several of Bhrodi's men. Bhrodi snapped his fingers at Ianto, pointing at Tacey as he did so and indicating for the man to take charge of his sister. Bhrodi took charge of Penelope and led her straight to the pure white palfrey she had ridden into town.

"I never said I imprisoned them," he said as he grasped her around the waist and lifted her up onto the horse. "*You* said I did."

Penelope was genuinely puzzled. "Then what did you do?"

Bhrodi handed her the reins. "We will speak of it later," he said. "For now, we turn for home."

It was a rather swift party that made its way back to Rhydilian Castle. In fact, Penelope had to shift the way she was riding because of the quick pace; unused to riding side-saddled, as a lady would, she threw her right leg over the saddle and ended riding astride. She was afraid she would fall off if she didn't. Lavender gown trailing out behind the horse, she followed her husband and his men as they made haste back to the dark-stoned castle on the hill.

As they cantered down the road, Penelope couldn't help but reflect on the words of the distraught woman; he was fodder for the beast. Was it possible that she was correct? Was it possible that there was more to that beast than simply a nuisance? She remembered the night she had fought with the beast and how it seemed very determined to kill the men around it. It snapped and hissed, lunging for men with its gnashing jaws as if... as if it wanted to bite them. Or eat them. Aye, there was something more to the beast's actions than simply anger. There was a hunger there that she couldn't begin to describe.

A feeling of fear and trepidation gripped her that only grew in intensity once they reached the castle.

⌘

CHAPTER THIRTEEN

Bron had a devil of a time escaping from ap Gwyfn's prison at Meurig Castle, as he had been blocked off in the buttery with a great bar across the door. It had been very cold and very dark, but after two days he'd managed to work free a slat of wood, which turned into a bigger hole, and eventually he was able to slither out. Now, he was heading for Rhydilian.

Tudur's small castle was on the west side of the village of Pendraeth and it hadn't been difficult to escape from the grounds once he stole a horse from the stables. It was an old horse used for agriculture, but Bron rode the old beast down the road, through the town, and on to Rhydilian Castle. He wanted to make it before nightfall but the horse was exhausted, and he watched the setting sun with some apprehension as he spurred the beast up the hill that led to the castle. Night was falling, as was the mist that usually settled heavily in these parts, and he reached the castle just as they were sealing up the gates for the night. Bron slipped through and they shut the gates behind him.

The first thing he noticed was that the great hall of Rhydilian, the big structure that was such a fixture in the bailey, had been burned to the ground. Nothing remained but the charred bones of the structure. Concerned, he dismounted his frothing horse and headed to the keep.

An old serving woman greeted him at the door and admitted him. Bron walked into the smaller feasting hall of the keep, with one big, rounded wall, and realized he must have walked into a festive gathering. Bhrodi, his *teulu*, and two women were sitting around the table that was strewn with big pitchers of some kind of drink and one of Bhrodi's commanders, Yestin, was seated near the hearth playing his citole. When Bhrodi looked up and saw Bron, he immediately jumped to his feet.

"Come no further," he boomed, holding out a hand to him. "State your business."

Bron had never received such a hostile greeting from Bhrodi and threw up his hands. "I mean you no harm, *fy arglwydd*," he assured him. "I come in with peaceful intentions, I swear it."

Penelope was up, collecting a fire poker from the hearth and wielding it threateningly. "Who are you?" she demanded.

Bhrodi could see she was about to take Bron's head off so he held up a stilling hand to her. "I know him," he told her, but his focus returned to Bron. "But what I want to know is if his intentions are the same as the others who called me their friend yet betrayed my trust."

Bron knew what he was talking about; after Tudor and Lon's meeting, he now knew why the great hall of Rhydilian was burned down. It seemed that they had carried out their threat against de Shera and he truthfully wasn't surprised.

"Bhrodi," he said, soft and pleadingly. "The hall; did Tudor and Lon do that? Did they attack you?"

Bhrodi eyed the man he considered a very good friend but, at the moment, he wasn't sure if he trusted him. Considering what had happened the night before, he didn't trust anyone.

"You knew they would?" he asked, his manner hardening. "Where were you? Why do you come now?"

Bron sighed heavily. "Because Tudor locked me up in his buttery when I did not agree with his plans," he said. "I have only now broken free. I came as soon as I could. What has happened?"

Bhrodi let his guard down a bit; Bron had always been extremely loyal to him and he could feel his resistance slipping. He very much wanted to believe him. He wanted to have at least one loyal vassal in this chaos that surrounded his marriage.

"Lon and Tudor launched an offensive against the English during the wedding feast," he said. "Fortunately, no English were killed but my wife's cousin and brother were wounded."

Bron appeared ill by the news. "Those fools," he hissed. "I knew they were going to do something stupid."

Bhrodi's gaze lingered on the man, studying his expression to see if he could determine just how sincere the man was. "And you?" he asked. "How do you play into this? How did all of this come about?"

Bron caught movement out of the corner of his eye, watching Penelope as she slowly lowered the poker. She was an exquisitely beautiful woman and he could only assume she was Bhrodi's new wife for he'd never before seen her. His gaze moved over her briefly, studying this woman that Bhrodi risked much for, but his focus quickly returned to Bhrodi.

"When you sent messengers with the invitation for your wedding, one of your messengers told Lon that you were marrying a Saesneg," he replied quietly. "Lon called a meeting of the local chieftains and the subject was discussed. They felt that you should have consulted them before agreeing to a Saesneg marriage, Bhrodi. There are many still in these parts who hate the Saesneg and see you as a traitor for marrying one."

Bhrodi understood a good deal in that softly uttered statement. "So they thought to attack my new kin at the wedding to prove a point," he said.

Bron nodded. "A point to you and a point to your English kin," he said. "Where are Lon and Tudor?"

Bhrodi looked at him, his eyes flashing with rage. Like the flicker of lightning, the burst was strong but quickly gone. It was the serpent strike of legend, quickly flaring, quickly gone, leaving only devastation in its path. Bron had seen it many times before and knew what it meant.

"They are dead," Bhrodi said, "as I would kill anyone who would betray me."

Bron knew that. "The beast, then?"

"That is the penalty."

Bron sighed faintly, raking a dirty hand through his equally dirty hair. "They were not alone, Bhrodi," he said. "There are other chieftains who did not attend the wedding in protest. Those men are angry as well and you will find yourself in a serious situation if you do not soothe them."

Bhrodi was well aware of that. He felt quite disillusioned by the presumed loyalty of those who were his vassals. He was disgusted by it even though he understood it all too well. With a sigh, he turned back for the feasting table and motioned for Bron to join him.

"They are fickle children, all of them," he said as he plopped down into his seat. "They do not seem to realize that I am their liege. I do not need their permission or consultation for any decision I make."

"But they are your supporters when you go to war," Bron reminded him as he sat beside him. "When you call for men, they heed your call. Fickle children or not, you need them as they need you."

"So what are you saying?" Bhrodi looked at him. "That I should have asked their permission before taking an English wife?"

Bron shrugged as he poured himself some much-needed wine. "If not permission, then you should have at least discussed your intentions," he said. "You have professed your hatred for the Saesneg time and time again, and now you marry one of their women? It looks as if you are not a man of your word. You have confused them."

"Pah," Bhrodi grunted, bordering on anger. "In this world, their sole purpose is to serve me and I do not have to ask their permission to take a wife. If I took a Saesneg as my wife, then I had very good reason for it."

"Then mayhap you should tell them your reasons."

Bhrodi's brow was furrowed; he didn't like to be answerable to anyone, and especially not his vassals. "Tell them what?" he demanded.

Bron took a long, fortifying drink. "Tell them why you have married a Saesneg," he said, smacking his lips. "If you do not, this will continue to fester and the next time you put out a call for men, your chieftains may not answer. If they band against you, you will have serious trouble, Bhrodi."

He was right although Bhrodi didn't want to admit it. The more he thought on the matter, the angrier he became.

"Damn them," he rumbled. "So I must explain my every move to them?"

Bron reached for the trencher of bread. "Nay," he replied, "but you must tell them why you have married the enemy."

Bhrodi's gaze found Penelope, seated across the table from him. She was listening very carefully to the conversation and Bhrodi almost felt embarrassed by it. She was hearing that his vassals were not as loyal to him as he would have hoped, but she had already figured that out when they had attacked her parents during the wedding feast. He didn't like that his weaknesses were being exposed in front of her. To her, he wanted to be strong and invincible.

"I married a Saesneg to hopefully secure some peace in my lifetime," he said. "Edward wants Wales. Mayhap if I marry a bride of his choosing, he will leave Anglesey alone."

Bron nodded. "Then tell your chieftains your reason," he encouraged him. "If they hear it from you, it should ease them. They all want peace for their families, Bhrodi; deep down, they all want to live in peace. Tell them you are trying to make it so for them and they will believe you."

Bhrodi was chewing on his lip, a nervous habit he had when particularly pensive or angry. He glanced across the table again to see how Penelope was handling all of this and noted that she was nodding her head. He spoke to her.

"What do you think?" he asked quietly. "Surely your father has dealt with situations like this before, unruly vassals. What do *you* think about all of this?"

Penelope was rather surprised he was asking her opinion; usually, the man conveyed the impression that he knew best about everything. The conceit she had seen in him from the first moment they met hadn't faded; it was still there, like a mask. It masked the vulnerable man beneath, the man he really didn't want her to see. Although she hadn't known him that long, even she was coming to see that. Therefore, she took the question seriously.

"I believe what he says is correct," she said, glancing at Bron. "You did not inform your vassals that you were marrying to create a peace alliance. For all they know, you could have been bribed, or worse. They have no idea why you married me. Mayhap… mayhap you should call a meeting and discuss it. Tell everyone why we have wed. That way, there will be no question. What we did, we did for peace, for everyone."

It was well-said. Bhrodi's eyes glimmered with approval. "Wisely spoken, wife," he said, looking at Bron. "You have not yet met my wife, the Lady Penelope de Wolfe de Shera. Penny, this is a very old friend of mine, Bron Llwyd. His family is very, very old in Anglesey. We grew up together."

Penelope nodded her head politely. "My lord," she greeted, but she returned her attention to Bhrodi. "I would call a meeting but I would not have it inside the castle in case your chieftains decide to riot. They will remain outside of the walls while you speak to them from the battlements. I will speak with them also, with your approval. When they see me, and hear me speak, I will cease to become the hated enemy and they will hopefully see me as a woman who wants peace as much as you do."

Bron was watching the woman, seeing that she was very intelligent and well-spoken. She was, in fact, a most impressive match for de Shera. He turned to Bhrodi.

"She speaks wisely," he concurred. "Let them hear you and let them *see* her. Mayhap that will ease them."

Bhrodi pondered the advice. In truth, he hadn't much choice; he knew these chieftains and they were a petty lot. After what happened at his wedding, they were also not to be trusted. Eventually, he nodded.

"Very well," he said. "I will send out messengers tomorrow and invite them to a *cyfarfod*. They will hear what I have to say about my marriage and they will agree with it."

It was a decisive statement. Penelope cocked her head curiously. "What is a *cyfarfod*?" she asked

Bhrodi turned to look at her. "It is a gathering of chieftains," he said, turning his attention back to Bron. "You will say here with me tonight. There is more I wish to discuss with you after my wife retires."

He meant a meeting she was not invited to. Penelope took the hint and, trying to behave like a good wife, stood up and reached out to take Tacey's hand. The young girl had sat through the exchange between the men, not saying a word because she was eating little bread rolls with cheese baked into them that one of the serving wenches had brought to the table. She was more interested in food than talk of rebelling chieftains. Even as Penelope pulled her to stand, she grabbed a couple of the little rolls and chewed on them as Penelope led her out of the hall.

"Good eve to you, my lord," Penelope said politely as she led Tacey from the hall.

Bhrodi's eyes were riveted to her, thinking of finding her in his bed when he retired later on. "Good eve, my lady," he replied, his tone bordering on seductive. "I will join you later."

Penelope merely nodded, lowering her head so he wouldn't catch the blush in her cheeks. She had heard his tone and it sent shivers coursing through her body. After their voyage of discovery last night, she was embarrassed that she was anticipating what might come tonight. The red hue to her cheeks gave her thoughts away.

Bhrodi watched the pair leave, hearing their footfalls fade as they mounted the stairs for the upper floor. As Bhrodi admired his wife as the woman left the room, Bron had tucked into the bread on the table, ravenous after his stay in the buttery with no food or water. He had a full mouth when Bhrodi returned his attention to him.

"Now," he said, his voice low as he motioned Ianto and the others closer. "You will start from the beginning of your meeting with Tudur and Lon, and tell me exactly what was said. I would know what manner of rebellion I am dealing with so I can better deal with the remaining chieftains."

Bron swallowed the bite in his mouth, eyeing Ianto and Ivor as the men sat on either side of Bhrodi. "Did you really feed them to the beast?" he asked quietly.

Bhrodi didn't acknowledge the question, which was an answer in and of itself. When he prompted Bron to tell him of the meeting that led to the wedding feast assault, Bron told him everything he could because perhaps deep down, he was fearful he might end up in the belly of the beast as well. Bhrodi could be unpredictable that way.

When the discussion was finally over and Bron headed home to see his wife and sons, he couldn't help but wonder what the coming days would bring. Bhrodi had made it clear that treachery from his vassals would not go unpunished. He wondered if more chieftains would meet their fate at the fangs of the serpent.

⌘

Kevin wasn't quite sure how long he'd been awake. All he knew was that somewhere over the past few minutes, he realized that he was staring at a ceiling. There was a fire in the room because he could see it dancing off the walls, flickers of orange and yellow against the stone.

It was an odd sensation, really. He had no idea where he was nor could he remember how he got here. The last memory he had was of watching Penelope as she married that arrogant Welshman and then there was something about drinking too much wine. He could hear his mother begging him not to drink anymore. He thought very hard on what he was doing at the time of all the drinking and seemed to recall a wedding feast. Aye, that's what it was – a wedding feast. He had been drinking too much, feeling very bad over Penelope's marriage, and then chaos ensued.

Crashing tables and men with short-blade swords. Welshmen who wanted to kill him. Aye, he remembered that clearly. As he stared at the ceiling and tried to recall how he ended up on his back, he heard the door to the chamber open and soft voices enter. Turning his head slightly, he could see Penelope approaching.

"Kevin," Penelope gasped as she quickly moved to him. "You are awake. How do you feel?"

Kevin gazed up into her lovely face, feeling a good deal of angst but he hid it well. He shifted slightly, trying to get a feel for his level of discomfort.

"Wounded," he grunted as pain shot up his torso, into his chest and down his left arm. "What happened?"

Penelope reached out and grasped his hand. "You do not remember anything?"

Kevin tried to take a deep breath but he ended up hurting himself again. "I... I am not sure," he said, trying to sort through the cobwebs in his brain. "There was a fight at your wedding feast."

Penelope nodded. "Indeed there was," she said. "Local chieftains who did not agree with Bhrodi's decision to take an English bride."

Kevin remembered that much. "My parents? They are well?"

Penelope squeezed his hand. "They are very well," she said. "Only you and Thomas were injured. You must remain here at Rhydilian until you heal."

"Did everyone else leave?"

"This morning. Your mother was very distraught about it but my father thought it best to return to England as soon as possible."

Kevin grunted. "A wise decision," he agreed. Then, he tried to move his stiff neck around as if looking for something. "Where is Thomas?"

"Here," came the muffled reply from the corner. "You snore like an old bull, Hage. I thought you were going to bring the walls down around us."

Penelope grinned and let go of Kevin's hand, moving to where her brother was just rolling over onto his back. His hazel eyes gazed up at his little sister.

"What has happened since I've been trapped in this room with the great rumbling beast?" he asked. "What day is it?"

Penelope giggled as she grasped her brother's hand. "It is the day after my wedding," she replied. "You have been asleep since last night when you were injured. Bhrodi's surgeon gave you both a potion to make you sleep."

Thomas sighed heavily, putting a hand to his head. "No wonder I feel as if I've been hit in the skull with a hammer," he said, looking over at Kevin. "Do you feel that way, too?"

Kevin nodded faintly. "My head feels as if it weighs as much as my horse," he said. "But I will admit that I am thirsty. And hungry."

A roll suddenly appeared in his face. Startled, Kevin pulled back a little to see a very young woman standing next to his bed. She was tiny, dark haired, and very pregnant. He blinked at her, somewhat surprised to see her there.

"Greetings," he said.

Faced with a stranger, Tacey reverted to her stammering shyness. "You... you can have my bread," she said. "You said you were hungry."

Penelope let go of Thomas' hand and came over to Tacey as the young woman stood over Kevin's bed.

"I will go to the kitchens and get him something to eat," she said, taking the girl by the shoulders and turning her for the door. "You go up to your chamber now and prepare for sleep."

Tacey was all but pushed to the door. "Will you come and see me before I go to sleep?"

Penelope nodded. "Aye," she replied. "Go, now. I will see you in a few moments."

Taking a bite of her roll, the one she offered to Kevin, Tacey quit the chamber and headed up to her bower. When she was gone, Penelope turned back to Kevin and Thomas.

"I shall send the surgeon to you both," she said. "I am sure he will want to know that you are awake."

As Kevin nodded weakly, Thomas climbed out of bed with great effort. "I have had to piss badly for the past several hours," he said, grunting with exertion. "I was having dreams of pissing great yellow rivers. It is time I find a garderobe before I burst."

Penelope giggled at her crude brother. "There is one downstairs in the feasting hall."

Thomas staggered past her, holding his tightly wrapped arm and shoulder. "I shall find it."

"Do you need my help walking?"

"Nay."

Penelope followed him to the door anyway, making sure he made it down the stairs without falling. Once she was sure he had made it down unharmed, she returned her attention to Kevin.

"I will send for food for you," she said quietly. "I am sure you will not be able to eat anything substantial for a while, so it may only be broth and gruel. Not very filling."

Kevin's right arm moved to the heavy bandages across his torso. "A chest wound?"

Penelope went back over to his bed, looming over him. "Abdomen," she said. "Right in the middle of your body."

He fingered the bandages, pondering her reply. But as he did so, his thoughts inevitably moved to the feast and the wedding itself. He struggled to shake off the extreme sadness the event provoked but he couldn't help himself from speaking on it.

"You are married now," he said softly.

Penelope nodded, wondering where the conversation was going to lead. She didn't want him upsetting himself over things he could not change.

"Aye," she responded quietly.

"Your husband," he continued, "has he been good to you so far?"

Penelope nodded again. "He has been kind and generous," she said, hoping it would ease Kevin's mind. "I fear he wants me to be a true lady, however. He does not seem to approve of me wearing armor and carrying a broadsword."

She was smiling as she said it, hoping he would see the humor in it, but Kevin's expression remained neutral. "I would have permitted it," he whispered. "I would have let you be what you wanted to be."

Penelope's smile faded. "You know me too well," she said, hoping to avoid the emotion of his statement. "Besides, I can best you in a fight. You would not have had a choice in letting me do what I wanted to do."

He reached out and grasped her hand, unwilling to give in to any humor at the moment. He wanted to be serious and she was jesting.

"I want you to listen to me and listen well," he muttered. "This wound may kill me yet and I want to say all I must say to you in case I die. Will you hear me?"

Penelope's humor vanished and she tried to pull away from him. "Nay," she said. "There is no reason for you to tell me anything, Kevin. What is done, is done. I am a married woman now and nothing you can say will change that."

He wouldn't let her go, showing surprising strength for a man who was gravely injured. "I realize that," he said. "But there is so much I have wanted to say to you for so long but I never did. I want you to know how much I love you, Penny. I will always love you. If anything happens to de Shera, know... know that I will be waiting for you."

There was pain in her expression as she gazed at him. "I do not want you to wait for me," she said softly. "I want you to find a wonderful woman to marry, one who will worship you as you deserve to be worshipped. For you to remain unmarried and without sons to carry on your name is such a tragedy, Kevin. Do not make me the reason for this tragedy."

He sighed faintly. "If my sons cannot have you as their mother, then I see no point," he murmured. "You were always my destiny, Pen. I am sorry I was not yours."

Penelope was having trouble looking him in the eye. "You give me such guilt, Kevin. I wish you would not say such things."

"I do not mean to give you guilt," he said. "This is my burden to bear. But... but if your marriage to de Shera had never happened, would... would you have accepted me as a suitor?"

She looked at him then, a reproachful sort of expression. "I have been of marriageable age for four years," she said. "You had four years to declare your intentions and you never did."

"Because I knew you would have rejected me," he said frankly. "Your mindset was not one of marriage or children and I knew that. I was waiting until you grew up a little but, unfortunately, your father had other plans."

Penelope wasn't sure what to say to that. Kevin was still holding her hand, refusing to let it go, so she squeezed his fingers. "Bhrodi is a good man," she whispered confidently. "He will take great care of me. You do not have to worry."

Kevin didn't say anything to that. Part of him didn't want to hear that de Shera was a good man; he didn't like Penelope speaking fondly of another man. However, his mind was eased to know she was in good hands. It was a strange paradox.

"Please tell me just this once and I shall never ask again," he whispered. "Could you... would you have accepted my suit?"

Penelope looked down at the man she had always been very fond of. She'd known for years he had been in love with her but he had been correct when he said her mindset hadn't been one of marriage and children. She had always taken it for granted that Kevin would always love her and when, or if, she ever decided to marry, he would have been the one. It had been terrible of her to put the man through such grief. After a moment, she nodded.

"Aye," she murmured.

"Could you have loved me?"

She wasn't even sure how to answer that. She wanted to ease him, feeling terribly sorry for him. "Aye," she whispered, barely audible. "I am sure I could have."

Kevin's expression changed at that moment; he grasped her so tightly that he was hurting her hand.

"Then come away with me," he begged softly. "Let us leave Wales and go somewhere together. France, mayhap. They are always looking for skilled knights to fight their wars. We could live as man and wife, and I would love you and only you until the end of my days. Please, Penny; go with me."

Shocked at his suggestion, Penelope tried to be tactful in her reply. "I cannot and you know it," she said. "I am married to Bhrodi, a wedding arranged by my father. How would it reflect on my father if I were to run away with you? Would you bring such shame down upon our families?"

Kevin stared at her as her words sank in. It was the rejection he always knew she would give him and he felt ashamed. He wasn't a weak man by nature but she made him feel weak; so very weak. He was also ill and feeling desperate, a bad combination when it came to his self-control. Closing his eyes against her disapproving face, he looked away.

"Forgive me," he muttered. "I should not have... please forgive me. It will not happen again."

Penelope felt so very sorry for him. She squeezed his hand. "I am sorry, Kevin," she whispered, "so truly sorry. I wish things could have been different for your sake, but my future is already set and I must face it. I pray you find peace in yours."

Leaning over him, she kissed him on the forehead and he reached up his good hand, touching her face in a manner he'd always wanted to touch her. But he just as quickly pulled away and his hand fell to his side. His eyes remained closed and Penelope's gaze lingered on him sadly. Turning for the door, she came to an immediately halt by the sight in the doorway.

Bhrodi was standing there and, from the expression on his

face, she was certain he had heard every word between her and Kevin.

⌘

CHAPTER FOURTEEN

The messengers had gone out to all of the chieftains under Bhrodi's command and the conference to discuss his marriage was set for morning of the next day. Five days after her marriage to the great Welsh warlord and hereditary King of Anglesey, Penelope's life at Rhydilian was starting to setting down and settle in, including the anticipation of facing those who were opposed to the marriage.

Even with the opposition, however, a balance was forming between her and her husband, and it was clear that a strong bond was beginning to be established. It was something that seemed to be forming fairly quickly, as it was coming naturally. There was a pull there, an attraction, that could not be denied, and it was gaining in intensity by the hour. Once Penelope began to warm to him again after the attack on her family, everything became easier.

The night of Kevin's confession, Bhrodi hadn't said a word about it. He'd merely escorted Penelope to their chamber, speaking on his meeting with Bron but little else. Penelope thought perhaps to bring up the subject and discuss it, not to hide it from him, but he glanced over it when she tried to bring it up. After two tries, she gave up. Evidently, he didn't want to discuss it so she let the subject go. They had much more serious things to worry about other than a wounded knight who was in love with Penelope. It had been clear that she hadn't returned that love.

The night before the big conference, Bhrodi seemed to be in a particularly good mood. The serving women, the ones who had disturbed him so at the onset, had indeed proved to be an asset at Rhydilian and the place seemed to be running better than it ever had. The floors were swept, Tacey was tended, fires were kept burning and the kitchens were in order, so much so that Penelope didn't have to do much of anything. It was evident that her mother had conferred with the serving women and told them that her daughter wasn't much of a chatelaine, which didn't bother Penelope because it was the truth. The women were a small army of attendants and Penelope hadn't even learned their names yet.

But it was something she intended to remedy. She was coming to be the least bit bored since she didn't have anything else to occupy her time, so she thought that perhaps she should learn something of running a household. Therefore, on the evening before the great meeting of the chieftains, she wandered down into the kitchens where three of the women were cooking. Bread was in the oven, pots were boiling over the fire, and in the middle of the giant butcher's table in the kitchen was a fully roasted pig. The animal had cooked in the yard all afternoon and had just been brought inside to dismember. It smelled delicious.

Penelope was mostly observing. The three women in the kitchens were all widowed, with children long grown, and were cousins. They had a good camaraderie going and Penelope liked that. It reminded her of her own family and her myriad of female cousins. Dilys, Awen, and Braithe were very friendly and answered all of Penelope's questions, even about the simplest of things. They showed her the ovens, told her what was cooking in the pots, and even showed her how to butcher the cooked pig. Penelope rather liked the look of the big butcher's axe and asked if she could give it a try. They handed it over to her and, with much glee, she ended up hacking apart the entire pig. It was the first time she had held a blade in her hand in almost a week so the thrill of it was almost too much to bear. The roast pig didn't stand a chance.

When the supper hour rolled around, Bhrodi began looking for his wife because she was nowhere to be found. She wasn't in their chamber, or in the stables, or even with the recovering English knights. Bhrodi had politely invited them to sup with him in the great hall if they were able to move, but had left before either one of them could give an answer because he was more concerned with finding Penelope. He eventually did, in the kitchens in the lower level of Rhydilian, and was just in time to see his wife hack the head from the roasted pig in one clean stroke. As a knight, Bhrodi recognized a kill stroke when he saw it, and Penelope had delivered it with a good deal of skill.

"The poor and troubled pig," he said as he came off the narrow staircase that led into the kitchens. "What did he ever do to you that you should sever his head so cleanly?"

Startled at his abrupt appearance, Penelope tried not to look too guilty as she thrust the butcher's axe at Awen. She wanted to get it out of her hands quickly, knowing that Bhrodi wasn't too keen on her continuing her knightly pursuits. She smiled weakly at him as she made her way in his direction.

"I....," she stammered, looking at the women around her and silently begging forgiveness for the lie she was about to tell. "I came down to the kitchens to supervise the meal and... well, as you know, it is a skill I need to learn and... and... they were having difficulty butchering the pig so I offered to... well, I was helping."

She was so nervous that Bhrodi laughed softly and touched her gently on the cheek. "You did a very good job," he said. "Shall we go to the hall and prepare for the meal? I invited your brother and the other English knight to join us if they are able. Mayhap they will."

Penelope was confused at his lack of a scolding. She was fairly certain he didn't believe her about helping but, to his credit, he didn't dispute her. Just as he hadn't when he had overheard Kevin begging her to run away with him. Either Bhrodi didn't like confrontation, he didn't care, or he simply chose his battles wisely. Penelope didn't know him well enough to know which it truly was but she was coming to suspect it was the latter.

All things considered, he had been extremely gracious in two situations where he would have had every right to become cross with her. In fact, he'd never become cross with her at all, not once. That told Penelope that Bhrodi had an exceptionally accepting nature, which was surprising for a warlord with such a terrible reputation. Or perhaps he was only accepting when it came to her. She wondered.

The feasting hall was littered with fresh rushes and a collection of dogs hovered beneath the table, knowing the meal time was approaching. They could smell the food on the floor below. As Bhrodi and Penelope emerged from the narrow stairs that led up from the kitchens, they were just in time to see the old uncle burst from his wardrobe and begin his furious dance about the room.

Oh, but it was a vicious battle this night. The old man was working feverishly against an unseen enemy, cutting and slashing, fighting his ghostly foe. Bhrodi wasn't paying much attention to him, as usual, but Penelope was. She found it rather fascinating that the man had been doing the same thing, like clockwork, for over thirty years. She watched him as he remained in the shadows, in the darkness, barely emerging into the light. In fact, it seemed as if whenever he neared the light, he deliberately veered away.

This night, however, he seemed to be heading towards the darkened foyer of the keep's entry. It was very dark in the entry and the old man danced and shrieked his way towards that small room. At one point, he fell to his knees and grabbed his gut as if he had just been terribly gored. Moaning and groaning, he struggled to his feet just about the time Thomas emerged from the upper floors. The young knight came off the stairs into the darkened hall and came up behind the old man. When the old man, acting out a grievous injury, looked up to see the knight, he screamed like a woman.

Startled, Thomas jumped back, away from the old man who suddenly produced a dirk and slashed at him. Bhrodi was up, running in their direction as Thomas, who truly had no idea who, or what, the old man was, lashed out a big fist and knocked the dirk out of the old man's hand. The elderly man fell to the ground, screaming, as he crawled back towards his wardrobe. Bhrodi put out a hand to Thomas to prevent him from pursuing, putting himself between the English knight and his insane old uncle.

"Hold fast," he told the young knight, watching the old man crawl away. "He cannot help what he has done. He is my grandfather's brother and quite mad."

Thomas was in battle mode, his brow furrowed as he watched the skinny old man drag himself into the wardrobe and close the door. Incredulous, he looked at Bhrodi.

"What is he doing?" he demanded. "He pulled a dirk on me!"

Bhrodi nodded patiently, holding out a hand to indicate the feasting table where Penelope was sitting.

"I know," he said. "Please come in and sit. I will explain everything to you."

Keeping a wary eye on the wardrobe, Thomas came into the hall and sat next to his sister, who looked anxiously upon him.

"Are you unharmed?" she asked, concerned. "He did not catch you with the dirk, did he?"

Thomas shook his head; his left arm was still heavily wrapped and he rubbed his right hand over the bindings.

"Nay," he said. "I doubt anything less than a broadsword would nick me through these wrappings. They would make fine armor."

Bhrodi got his first good look at Penelope's brother; he was a mixture of his parents with his father's dark hair and mother's pale eyes. He was actually quite handsome, rather average in height but with that muscular de Wolfe build that all of the men in the family seemed to have. Moreover, he seemed friendly enough. After the circumstances of his injury, Bhrodi wasn't entirely sure how the man would view him. He seemed rather pleasant, in fact.

"Dwyn was my grandfather's surgeon," Bhrodi said. "He has been a healer for more years than I have been alive. He soaks the linen bandages in vinegar and then once he has wrapped the wound, he puts a mixture of flour and water all over them to harden them on the outside. That is why they are stiff like armor, but the method protects the injury quite well."

Penelope knocked on her brother's wrappings, grinning when she realized they were, indeed, very stiff. "I hadn't looked closely at them," she said, looking at her brother. "Has he taken great care of you?"

Thomas nodded. "He comes every morning when I awaken and also every night before I got to sleep," he said. Then he glanced at Bhrodi. "Does the man speak any English?"

Bhrodi shook his head. "Not a word."

Thomas grunted. "No wonder he would not speak to me," he said. "I thought it was because I was English."

As Bhrodi grinned and began to pour some wine, Tacey entered the hall. She was eating something, which seemed to be usual with her as of late, and she planted herself next to her brother as he poured another cup of wine. Bhrodi was preparing to hand it to Penelope but Tacey snatched it and drank deeply. Bhrodi frowned.

"That was not meant for you," he scolded softly. "Unless it is offered to you, do not take it."

Contrite, Tacey hung her head but she still continued to put bits of cheese in her mouth. Thomas and Penelope looked at the girl, varying degrees of smirks on their faces. Penelope finally spoke, simply to move past the scolding.

"Tacey, have you met my brother?" she asked. "He has been sleeping in your former chamber."

Tacey's head came up, timidly, as Penelope introduced them. "Tacey, this is Sir Thomas de Wolfe," she said. "Thomas, this is Bhrodi's sister, the Lady Tacey de Shera ap Gruffydd. Her husband was a son of Dafydd ap Gruffydd."

Thomas knew that name only too well; every Englishman did. He nodded his head politely. "My lady."

Tacey bobbed her head nervously and looked at her lap again, or what was left of it with her blooming belly. There wasn't much more to say by way of introduction or greeting, so Penelope shifted the subject.

"How is Kevin, Thomas?" she asked. "Is he coming down to eat, also?"

Thomas shook his head. "Nay," he replied. "He seems better but the old surgeon has forbidden him from moving about too much. He says the man must heal."

"And I will only heal if I am allowed to walk and breathe," came a voice from the hall entry. They all turned to see Kevin standing there, dressed in the tunic he was stabbed in and leaning against the door jamb wearily. When he saw that everyone was looking at him, he pushed himself off the wall and continued, very slowly and stiffly, into the hall. "I am tired of lying in bed and being fed mashed-up food. I am going to eat like a man tonight if it kills me."

Penelope was already up, rushing to him to help him walk but he waved her off. She stood there and frowned at him as he plodded, hunched-over, to the table.

"Look at you," she scolded, following him at a distance. "You walk like an old man. You should not be up!"

Kevin was holding his torso with his left arm as he walked. "That may be, but I am nonetheless on my feet," he said, his gaze coming to rest on Bhrodi as the man sat at the table. "My lord, may I join you for sup?"

Bhrodi eyed the very big knight. After what he'd heard the other night when the man had declared his love for Penelope, he wasn't exactly glad to see him but he would not deny him a seat at his table. He had invited him, after all. He gestured to a seat without saying a word and turned back to his wine.

Penelope could see, in that gesture, that what Bhrodi had heard in the darkened chamber between her and Kevin had indeed left a mark. The man had been very polite to Thomas but when Kevin had appeared, his manner cooled considerably. Not that she blamed him. But it was important that she show attention to Bhrodi in Kevin's presence. She thought perhaps it would reassure Bhrodi that whatever the knight had said had no meaning to her. Even if Bhrodi wouldn't discuss what he had heard, Penelope could still show him that her loyalty was with him. She was his wife, after all.

As Kevin gingerly took a seat next to Tacey, Penelope went to Bhrodi and sat next to him. Usually, she sat across from him so he could look into her face. He seemed to like being able to speak with her face to face. But she resumed a seat next to her husband and he looked at her, seemingly pleased, as she claimed a cup of wine and put it to her lips. As she drank, her gaze fixed on his, she couldn't help but notice the warm glimmer in the dark green eyes. Beneath the table, his hand came to rest on her knee and it was enough to make her heart skip a beat. It was the first true display of affection, in a public place no less, that she'd ever received from him. She was thrilled.

As Penelope relished the feel of Bhrodi's warm hand against her leg, the serving wenches began bringing out steaming bowls of food and great, trenchers of bread that sat atop big wooden trays. The pork that Penelope had so gleefully butchered was produced, smothered in a rich gravy that had apples and cloves in it. There was plenty of food to go around and Tacey, in her eagerness, ended up on her knees on the bench, shoving pork into her mouth and reaching across the table to grab at bowls of pears soaked in honey, or carrots with dill and herbs. There was also a big bowl of beans and pieces of pork simmered in a sauce made from onions and garlic.

In all, it was a massive spread, fit for a king, and soon enough the commanders of Bhrodi's *teulu* joined them. Ivor, Gwyllim, and Yestin joined the meal, eating peacefully alongside English knights that had once been considered their enemy. Now, they didn't seem so much like the enemy any more. Because of Penelope, they were now family. Penelope realized she felt comfortable with them for the first time since her arrival. Aye, she was most definitely settling in and they even began to include her in conversation. Soon, the entire table was chatting, even Kevin, and it seemed like a calm and pleasant meal.

The only commander missing was Ianto. That wasn't unusual because the man had command of Rhydilian, setting posts for the night and taking some of the burden of command off of Bhrodi at times. But tonight, there was more to it than that; deep inside the keep with its three-foot thick walls, the feasting inhabitants hadn't heard the cry from the sentries out in the gatehouse, nor had they been aware of the man-door in the massive outer gates opening to admit a lone rider.

Ianto had been there, in his diligence, and he had heard the message that the rider had been ordered to deliver. It was a message for Bhrodi, a most important message, and once Ianto had obtained all the information, he had told the gate sentries to feed the messenger as he ran for the keep.

After tonight, things would never be the same again.

⌘

CHAPTER FIFTEEN

Welsh Marches

"Castell y Bere has fallen to the English," William told his men, gathered in his great tent. They had been on the border of Wales and England, heading home, when they had come into contact with a gaggle of English soldiers on their way out of Wales. That gaggle had brought much news with them. "Dafydd ap Gruffydd has escaped the siege and it is suspected that he is moving north."

Paris and Kieran, as the oldest and most experienced men of the group, cast each other concerned glances. They had been through Henry's wars and now they were going through even worse wars with his son, the very powerful Edward. The man had a blood lust that his father had never had so this was serious news, indeed.

"The Welsh prince has been running from Edward for quite some time now," Paris said quietly. "I was unaware there was a siege at Castell y Bere."

William nodded grimly. "Dafydd started the rebellion in the north last fall and he has been battling Edward ever since," he said. "Why do you think our king was so determined to secure Anglesey? He wants de Shera neutralized but if that is not possible, then he certainly wants the man's allegiance. If Bhrodi de Shera jumps into this fight, then all of northern Wales will be in turmoil because de Shera is nearly unbeatable in the field. But if Dafydd has escaped Edward once again and is moving north...."

"... then he could very well seek refuge and support with de Shera," Kieran finished.

William nodded gravely. It was the logical path of progression in Dafydd's war against Edward. As William drew in a deep breath and pondered the information, Scott spoke.

"We cannot turn back for Rhydilian, Father," he said. "We carry women with us. We are not prepared for battle."

William nodded. "I am well aware of that," he said. "We could, however, send the women and an escort back to Questing while we return to Rhydilian to see if Dafydd shows himself there."

"And then what?" Scott wanted to know. "We would be fourteen knights against Dafydd and his men. Moreover, Bhrodi is now your son. What if he sides with Dafydd? Do we fight against Bhrodi or with him?"

William eyed his eldest son; the man had a point. After a moment, William simply shook his head. "I do not know," he admitted. "The marital contract was for peace so I suppose I could neither fight for him or against him."

"So we would let Dafydd ap Gruffydd do as he pleases and not intervene?" Troy spoke up, incredulous. "Father, we are English and our loyalty is to Edward over all others. We could not side with de Shera."

William knew that; God, he knew that all too well. This was extraordinarily serious news and he was greatly torn by it. He knew what his duty dictated, but he also had a marriage contract to consider with his daughter involved. He was in a terrible position and they all knew it. With a heavy sigh, he turned away from the group, his thoughts pensive and sorrowful. It was several long and painful moments before he spoke again.

"If de Shera decides to support Dafydd, then the marriage contract would be void," he muttered, turning to the group of powerful knights that filled his tent. "If the marriage contract is void, then Penny is in great danger."

"So what do we do?" Troy demanded, but it was without force. "Do we go back to Wales and rescue my sister?"

William lingered on the question. "Nay," he said, although it was killing him to say it. He very much wanted to run back into Wales and get his daughter. "I think we need to find Edward. I must consult with him before we do anything."

"But what about Penny?" Troy wanted to know. "Do we just leave her to the mercy of the enemy?"

189

William shook his head. "De Shera is her husband, not the enemy," he said, "and we do not know for certain if Dafydd has even made it to Rhydilian. It is all speculation at this point. Therefore, it is my inclination to find our king and discuss all of this with him. He will want to know what we know, and I require his counsel on how to proceed. To act foolishly and rashly would not do Penny any good at all. For now, we must trust that de Shera is still our ally."

He was proceeding rationally, which at this point was the best course of action. But Kieran spoke softly.

"Kevin and Thomas are at Rhydilian," he reminded them. "If de Shera decides to support Dafydd, they will more than likely become prisoners."

William shook his head firmly. "Penny would not allow it and you know it," he said. "For now, we must seek Edward. Apollo, Adonis, Alec, and Nathaniel will take the women back to Questing along with half of our men as escort. The rest of us will proceed into Wales to find Edward. The last intelligence I received said he was Corwen Castle, so we will proceed there. I must know what the king says to all of this."

"And if he demands you fight against de Shera?" Scott wanted to know. "What then, Father? Do you fight against Penny?"

William sighed heavily; the mere thought made him ill. After a moment, he shook his head. "I am not for certain," he said. "I must seek counsel from a higher source in that matter."

He went to find Jordan.

⌘

Rhydilian Castle

"Dafydd is at Dolbadarn Castle," Ianto said. "He has requested aid from you. He is facing an English onslaught and he requires your support."

Bhrodi was listening to Ianto's message with both disbelief and indecision. They were standing just outside of the keep and had been ever since Ianto had entered the hall in the midst of a very pleasant meal and requested a private audience with his liege. Bhrodi had complied and had been the recipient of some very serious news; the last Prince of Wales, Dafydd ap Gruffydd, was running from Edward and needed Bhrodi's help. After Ianto delivered the bulk of the information, Bhrodi sighed heavily. There was regret there.

"What about Castell y Bere?" he asked. "Who was in command?"

"Cynfrid ap Madog," Ianto replied quietly. "He surrendered the garrison but did it in a way that allowed Dafydd time to escape with his entire family."

Bhrodi listened closely. "And he went to Dolbadarn?"

"Aye, my lord."

"Who holds that garrison?"

"I am not certain, my lord."

Bhrodi was silent a moment, pondering. His mind worked very quickly and he already had a thousand questions and a thousand solutions. But he needed more information.

"Where is the messenger?" he asked.

"In the gatehouse," Ianto replied.

Bhrodi's gaze moved to the massive gatehouse, silhouetted against the full moon. "Bring him to me," he instructed. "Make sure he speaks to no one else. I will question him personally."

Ianto nodded and went along his way. Bhrodi remained at the top of the keep steps, thinking many things at that moment. He realized his first instinct was to support Dafydd and give the man what he needed, but upon the heels of that thought came another, more prevalent thought – he was now married to an English woman and he had a peace accord with Edward.

But peace went both ways; Edward was obviously continuing his attempts to conquer Wales if Dafydd was now on the run. The situation had been quiet as of late, which had given him hope that perhaps Edward was backing off, but he could see it had been a foolish hope. All of northern Wales was compromised except for Anglesey. Here, there was still some peace, but that wouldn't last long, Bhrodi knew. He knew Edward would eventually come for him, treaty or no. Penelope had known it too, as she had indicated before they were even married. Bhrodi had hoped to have more time before he had to deal with that but it looked as if he had no time at all. Dafydd was about to be crushed and once he was out of the way, Bhrodi would be the next target.

With heavy thoughts of warfare on his mind, Bhrodi met the messenger from Dafydd on the steps of Rhydilian. The messenger was very young and Bhrodi recognized him as one of Dafydd's illegitimate sons. The man had many of them. The lad was still a youth, perhaps not

191

quite twenty years of age, very thin and exhausted. The young man acknowledged Bhrodi respectfully.

"*Fy arglwydd* de Shera," he greeted. "*Rwy'n diolch i Dduw fy mod wedi eich cyrraedd.*"

I thank God I have reached you. Bhrodi spoke Welsh to the lad. "And so you have," he said. "Where is Dafydd?"

"At Dolbadarn, my lord," the lad replied. "Baedden ap Ceron is the garrison commander and is providing for Lord Dafydd, but he is very short on men and requires your assistance. He asks you to send him no less than five thousand men. Can you do this, my lord?"

Bhrodi didn't outwardly react to the enormous amount of men requested, but he was shocked by it. "Why so many men?"

The boy swallowed hard. "Because Edward closes in on him, my lord," he replied. "It is thought that Edward has ten thousand men surging north through Wales, destroying everything to get to Dafydd. They come for him, my lord, and Dafydd has asked for your help."

Ten thousand men. If that was true, then things were worse than Bhrodi could have imagined. All he could feel at the moment was a great sense of foreboding. Once Edward was finished razing Dolbadarn, there would be little between the castle and Anglesey. Edward would soon be on his doorstep.

Bhrodi had two choices; he could fight for Wales and hopefully keep Anglesey free of English rule, or he could refuse to help Dafydd and embrace the English when they came to his lands. But he knew very well he couldn't welcome them; he was Welsh and fighting was in his blood. This was his land, and his people, and so long as Edward left them alone, Bhrodi wasn't going to start any wars. But Edward was acting with great aggression towards the Welsh, trying to force them into submission. That being the case, Bhrodi would defend what was his. He would not go down without a fight.

"When does he need them?" he finally asked the lad.

The boy wiped at his exhausted eyes. "As soon as possible, my lord," he said. "Dafydd had just arrived at Dolbadarn when he sent me to find you, and it took me almost four days. He fears the English are not far off."

"He wants us to go to Dolbadarn?"

"Aye, my lord."

"What of his other strongholds in Snowdonia? We are not to go there?"

"Nay, my lord. He asked for you to go to the castle."

Bhrodi digested the information; he wasn't entirely sure about going to a castle that the English were closing in on because that might leave them vulnerable should they run into the English on open ground. But he agreed.

"Very well," he said. "I have a meeting with my chieftains tomorrow morning and I will consult with them. For tonight, you will rest and eat, and you will tell no one what you told me. Is that clear?"

The boy nodded firmly. "Aye, my lord."

With that, Bhrodi flicked at hand at Ianto, indicating for the man to take the young messenger away. As they headed off back towards the gatehouse, Bhrodi turned for the keep. His mind was on the news he had been given and the situation in general as he entered, hearing the distant voices in the feasting hall, realizing that he was going to have to tell Penelope what had happened. She was a warrior, after all; she would understand the path of their present and the course of the future. She was as involved in it as he was and he came to wonder what her reaction would be. Would she staunchly defend the English? Or would she submit to her husband's will in all things? He wondered.

It would be a pivotal moment for them both.

⌘

Penelope had remained in the hall well after the evening meal was concluded, waiting for Bhrodi to return. She sat in small talk with Thomas and Kevin, and even Tacey when the girl stopped eating long enough to speak. Ivor, Gwyllim, and Yestin also politely conversed with her and even the English knights when the conversation called for it. When the *teulu* commanders did speak, Penelope found herself studying them simply because she was curious about them. They were always nearby, but always silent, like shadows. She didn't know them at all, yet she lived in the same keep with them.

Ivor was a tall, handsome man with dark hair who seemed to do most of the talking for all three. He also had a habit of scratching his face repeatedly, which Penelope thought was rather humorous. Gwyllim was older, quieter, and seem to be watching the situation much as she was. Yestin, oddly enough, came across as very arrogant when he did open his mouth, as if he was bored with the entire conversation. It didn't matter who he was talking to; Welsh, English, man or woman. Everyone seemed to bore him.

As the evening dragged on and the food was cleared away, Tacey somehow convinced Thomas to play a board game with her. She ran all the way up to her chamber to get it, bringing it down and setting it upon the table between them. It was called Fox and Geese, and a hand-painted wooded path encircled the game board with the game pieces being small carved wooden foxes or geese.

The object was to roll three sticks, which had hash marks on the front and back of them, and based upon the number of hash marks that landed face–up, that was the number of spaces on the path a player moved. Tacey wanted to be the fox so Thomas had to be the geese, which amused Kevin to no end. When Tacey's fox beat Thomas' geese, she was the one who dictated the punishment to the loser. Therefore, Thomas had to sit with a kerchief over his head while they played another round.

Tacey was very good at the game; given that she'd spent so much time alone, she'd had little else to do but practice games or other pastimes. Thomas was beaten three times before he turned the game over to Kevin, who was able to beat the unhappy Tacey on the first try. In punishment for losing, he made her hold a spoon between her upper lip and nose, scrunching her face up to keep it there, while they played another round.

Penelope thought it was all great fun and she was pleased to see everyone getting along well enough. Kevin, having three sisters of his own, was rather antagonistic in a brotherly sort of way with Tacey, making her screech and giggle in frustration. It reminded Penelope of her days at Castle Questing when she had a whole host of brothers and cousins to tease her. She tried not to sink into depression again over the thought of her missing family; instead, she just tried to remember the fun of it all. It was a struggle.

Eventually, the three *teulu* commanders bid everyone a good eve and left the hall, and Penelope was growing rather anxious about Bhrodi's absence. When one of the old serving women came to take Tacey to bed, collecting the girl's game and scolding her gently when she resisted, Penelope followed the pair upstairs and ended up in the master's chamber, alone.

A fire was burning in the hearth and the room was warm and fragrant with rushes thanks to the diligent serving women. Penelope went to her trunks, stacked neatly against the eastern wall, and began to remove her clothing. She was trying to dress very simply these days, as complicated fashions intimidated her, so it was a matter of pulling off her gown and shift, and donning a warm sleeping shift. With that, she was finished.

Prepared for bed, she thought perhaps to wait for her husband, realizing she very much wanted to see him before she went to sleep. The nights between them since their wedding had been uneventful for the most part. There had been so much going on that twice already, Bhrodi hadn't come to bed at all and she had slept alone in the big, fluffy bed. On those nights that they had gone to bed at the same time, she was ashamed to admit she'd fallen asleep quickly. Rather than wake her, Bhrodi had let her sleep. He must have realized what a big change all of this was to her and she had been understandably exhausted. He had played the patient bridegroom.

But not tonight; Penelope was determined to stay awake for him. That brief taste of coupling she had received on their wedding night had been enough to stoke her curiosity about it. She could still feel the man's touch and she clearly remembered how he had made her feel. It was all she could think about. She wondered if he had given it as much thought as she had. As she sat on the bed, brushing her hair with the big horsehair brush her mother had given her, the latch on the chamber door shifted and the panel opened quietly.

Bhrodi entered the room, shutting the door softly behind him and bolting it. When he turned to see Penelope sitting on the bed, brushing her luscious dark hair and looking at him rather anxiously, he smiled faintly.

"So you are awake, are you?" he said. "I half-expected to come in here and find you on the floor, having fallen asleep before you were even able to reach the bed. You seem to fall asleep rather swiftly."

Penelope giggled. "I do not usually," she said. "I suppose I have simply been overly weary as of late. Wearing women's clothing and being kept away from my charger has sapped all of my strength."

His grin broadened as he approached the bed and began untying his tunic. "You poor child," he clucked sadly. "Forced away from your beloved armor and snapping destrier. How *will* you survive?"

She lifted her eyebrows optimistically. "I am not entirely sure, but I am hoping my husband might be kind and generous enough to at least let me do a little of what I'd like to do."

He pulled the tunic over his head, revealing his muscular chest. As he tossed the tunic aside, he nodded thoughtfully to her statement. "And what is it you would like to do?"

Penelope was distracted by the sight of all that naked flesh and struggled to stay on subject. "I would like to get my broadsword back from the beast of the marsh," she said. "And I would like to tend my charger and ride him daily. Is that too much to ask?"

He sat down on the edge of the bed, looking at her radiant beauty in the soft firelight. For a moment, he just stared at her, thinking she was the most glorious creature he had ever seen. He'd felt emotion for a woman before, for his first wife, but with Sian the emotions were more like the soft harvest moon. It was radiant and pure and comforting. But with Penelope, he felt such depth of emotion that it was like the blinding sun. It was everywhere, and all about him. He was still trying to grasp it all but wasn't entirely sure he ever really would. At the moment, what he felt for her was purely physical although he was quite fond of the woman he was coming to know. He was positive that once he came to know her better, and more thoroughly, everything he felt about her would consume him and he was glad for it.

"Would that truly make you happy?" he asked softly.

She nodded firmly. "It would," she said, lowering the hair brush. "Bhrodi, I know you want a fine and beautiful wife, and I am more than willing to try, but... but I was happy the way I was, riding chargers and wearing armor. I have been doing it such a long time that, much like you, it is a part of me. Now I find myself being expected to become a fine lady and... and it is just so difficult for me."

He smiled, reaching out to stroke her tender cheek. "I do not want you to be unhappy," he said. "I suppose there are things we could compromise on."

She was seized with hope. "Like what?"

He shrugged. "Like your wearing armor," he said. "No one around here wears armor except me or my *teulu* when we head into battle. It is not such a part of us as it is with the Saesneg warriors. It would make me very unhappy to see my beautiful wife in ugly and manly mail. However, if it makes you happy, you may wear it when you tend or ride your charger, and only if you are not heading into town or going someplace where many people would see you. They simply wouldn't understand, Penny. I hope you can comprehend that."

It was a fair enough compromise and she nodded. "I promise I will not wear it when I am around you, or to meals," she said. "But what about my broadsword?"

He sighed and stood up from the bed, eyeing her as he began to unfasten his breeches. "It really means that much to you?"

She nodded eagerly. "It does."

He looked down at his breeches as he untied them. "Then I will have one commissioned for you," he said. "There is no use in going back to the marshes to look for it. It now belongs to the beast and is long buried in the muck."

Penelope nodded sadly, hanging her head. "My father gave it to me," she said. "It has the de Wolfe name on the hilt and it is set with amethysts because my mother loves the purple color."

Bhrodi glanced at her as he sat back down on the bed, untying his boots so he could slide his breeches and boots off in one smooth motion. Then he stood up, gloriously naked, and moved to the hearth to stoke it. The night promised to grow cold.

"If it pleases you, you may design your sword," he said. "I will take you to Chester to commission your sword because God only knows the Welsh cannot make a proper broadsword. If you want it done correctly, then we will need to go to England to do it."

Penelope's head came up, smiling, until she realized he was without a stitch of clothing on. Startled, she quickly turned away and her cheeks flushed madly. She could hear him poking around by the fire until, satisfied, she heard his joints pop as he rose from his crouched position and moved back to the bed. The bed gave a great deal as he crawled beneath the coverlet and suddenly, a hand was reaching out to grasp her.

Penelope ended up with her head in Bhrodi's lap, gazing up into his handsome face. He smiled gently at her.

"You and I have not had much time together as man and wife," he said. "I plan to remedy that tonight, but first, I must speak with you on matters of importance."

"Of course," Penelope agreed. "What is it?"

Bhrodi gazed down at perfect face with its dusting of freckles across the nose and the big, wide hazel eyes that were so sharp and intelligent. Reaching down, he brushed a stray lock of dark hair off her cheek. All the while, he was formulating his thoughts, thinking on how he would phrase what was to come. Things were changing in their very new world and she needed to know.

"I received a messenger tonight from Dafydd ap Gruffydd," he said quietly. "It would seem that the English have captured Castell y Bere and Dafydd barely escaped with his life. He has asked me to help defend his cause against Edward, who seems to be plowing through the north of Wales in search of the last Welsh prince."

Penelope's gaze was serious. After a moment, she sat up so she could look him in the eye, more on his level. Her features were full of concern.

"Where is Dafydd now?" she asked.

There had been a time, very early in their relationship, when he would not have told her what he knew. But he was coming to trust her and saw no harm in telling her the truth.

"Dolbadarn Castle," he replied. "It is very close to here in mainland Wales. A man on a swift horse can make it there in a couple of hours providing the ferry moves swiftly across the straits."

Penelope thought on that. "And Edward is heading for Dolbadarn?"

Bhrodi reached out and grasped her hand, bringing it to his lips. "We are not for certain of that yet," he said, his lips against her flesh. "But one thing is for certain; the man has staked his claim in Wales. He already has castles in Caernarfon, Rhuddlan, and Conwy. Now he is making a massive push to capture and destroy Dafydd once and for all, and when he is finished with Dafydd, it is my sense he will come for me as the last royal blood in Wales. He never wanted peace with me; he simply wanted my submission. I stand between Edward and complete domination of my country."

Penelope was having a difficult time breathing as his lips gently kissed her fingers. It was an effort to focus on what he was saying.

"I told you this before you married me," she whispered, watching his mouth nibble on her flesh. "I told you that Edward was bribing you with an English bride. He will expect your complete loyalty now that you have taken The Wolfe's daughter as your wife."

Bhrodi turned her hand over and began depositing sweet, warm kisses on her wrist. "And I told you I liked the bribe," he said. "I will be truthful with you; I agreed to a peace alliance by marrying you so long as Edward remained peaceful as well. Did you know that it was part of the bargain? Edward swore he would remain peaceful in northern Wales if I agreed to this marriage. I knew better, however; I knew he would not. He was already well-entrenched here with his massive castles and I knew he would never stop his aggression."

Penelope was looking at him with some shock. "Yet you still agreed to the terms?"

His gaze was warm on her. "I agreed to *you*. It was worth the risk."

Penelope was surprised. "But... but why? You had never met me before the night the creature attacked. That was the first time we ever saw one another and even then, you did not know I was your intended bride. Why would you risk your life and the lives of your vassals for me?"

He smiled faintly. "Because once I discovered you were the prize, nothing else mattered," he said. "You asked me once before why I had agreed to this marriage, knowing what I do about Edward's intentions for Wales, and I told you that I made decisions that were always best for me. Know this now; there is something to be said in having the daughter of The Wolfe as my wife. Who do you think your father will fight for? Edward or his daughter's husband?"

Her surprise turned to shock. "You think by marrying me that my father will turn against his king?"

Bhrodi shrugged. "I knew this day was coming," he said. "I knew that someday, somehow, Edward would be knocking on my door. When he proposed a marriage for peace, I knew it was a lie. All of it was a lie. But when I found out he had proposed the daughter of his most powerful warlord to me, I thought to accept the marriage because it would mean that England's most respected knight, William de Wolfe, is now my father-in-law. That makes me family. Do you truly think your father will let Edward destroy my world and you along with it? Of course he will not. Your father will come and fight for me. Together, The Wolfe and The Serpent will destroy Edward once and for all."

Penelope sat there with her mouth hanging open. "But... but my father is sworn to Edward."

Bhrodi was too confident; that arrogance he displayed so easily was readily apparent. "Your father loves you more than he loves Edward," he said. "He will not let the man destroy you, and me along with you."

Penelope stared at him a very long time. She was thinking many things at that moment and not all of them good or complementary where Bhrodi was concerned. Yanking her hand out of his grip, she stood up from the bed.

"So that was what this was all about?" she asked somewhat heatedly. "You married me because you wanted William de Wolfe as your ally?"

He could see that she was growing increasingly upset and hastened to ease her. "That was true, at first," he said. "But the moment I saw you, I knew I had to have you no matter if your father became my ally or not."

She crossed her arms stubbornly. "And if my father does not side with you?"

Bhrodi lifted his big shoulders. "Then Edward will bring his army down around me and I will be executed," he said. "You, however, will be a very rich widow and the Countess of Coventry, which should make you an excellent prospect for a future husband."

He sounded so callous and matter of fact about it. Penelope stood there for several long moments, trying not to let his words hurt her, but somehow they did. It was all so easy for him to say these things; *you will be a very rich widow and an excellent prospect for a future husband.* Damn the man; he had hurt her feelings with such words. She didn't want to be a wealthy widow. But he had made it very clear that the entire marriage had been a calculated move on his part; he had wanted her, that was true, but his reasons were all his own. There had been no emotion involved, not true interest or feeling. She didn't know why she had expected differently. De Shera had only wanted her father and used her to get him.

She lost her stubborn stance and sat heavily on the bed, facing away from him. She was starting to feel very hollow and sad.

"Of course," she finally muttered. "I will be well taken care of in any case."

Bhrodi heard the sorrow in her tone and it made his heart beat a little faster; there was emotion in her tone, something he hadn't expected. Penelope had, since he'd known her, displayed an attitude that she truly didn't care about him one way or the other. There had been times when he thought she had warmed to him, that was true, but she had spent more time being distant and disinterested. Now he heard something from her that suggested she was, in fact, interested. He could only hope.

"Does the thought of my death distress you, then?" he asked, praying he didn't sound too hopeful.

She was still facing away from him but she nodded her head, unsteadily, as if she wasn't entirely sure. Or if she was sure but had no idea how to convey it.

"I have only just married you," she said. "I have heard that it is rare in any marriage for two people who have just met to actually... tolerate one another. But I am coming to tolerate you more and more every day."

He was so very glad to hear that. It made his heart sing. Reaching out, he pulled her to him again, embracing her against his broad, naked chest. She was stiff at first but quickly relaxed as their heat and flesh began to meld together. When their eyes met, he smiled sweetly at her.

"You have done something that I did not believe possible," he murmured. "You have made me feel something again, Penny. When Sian died... I was positive I had lost the ability to feel anything at all, but you have awoken things in me that I thought were long dead. When I first saw you, I wanted you because you were beautiful, but now that I have come to know you, I want you because you are intelligent and sweet, and you are trying very hard to be the kind of wife you think I want. You have no idea how much that touches me. Your efforts have nicked my heart and all of that emotion I thought to have died with Sian has come pouring through."

Because he was smiling, Penelope smiled. She was timid at first but as she began to realize what he meant, the smile turned genuine.

"You are arrogant and you are frustrating at times," she said, watching him laugh, "but you are also kind and generous and gentle. I think... I think my heart has been nicked, too. It has never been nicked before."

Of all of the words he had ever heard in his lifetime, those were about the sweetest. Leaning forward, he kissed her tenderly on her freckled nose.

"You have made me very happy," he whispered.

Penelope closed her eyes as his lips drifted across her cheek. "I am glad," she murmured. "But as happy as we are, there is still the trouble with Edward. What are you planning on doing?"

He stopped kissing her and looked at her. "You truly want to discuss that now?"

She was fairly naïve in lovemaking and had no real idea what he meant, so she nodded her head unsteadily. "Aye," she said, wondering why he suddenly looked perturbed. "Did you not wish to resolve this?

You have a serious problem, Bhrodi. What do you intend to do about it?"

He sighed sharply. "If I tell you, can I continue to kiss you without discussing the damn English king?"

She bit her lip to keep from grinning. "Aye."

"Will you support my decision no matter what it is?"

He was serious; therefore, she grew serious. "I will," she said. "I am your wife and that is my duty."

"Swear it?"

"I do."

He could see she meant it. Penelope understood what it meant to give one's word of honor. A knight's daughter, she was a knight herself. She understood a vow given. Taking a deep breath as he shifted his thoughts from her sweet flesh and back to Edward, he reached out and cupped her face with one hand, his thumb stroking her soft cheek.

"No matter what I do, Edward will come for me," he muttered. "He has come for Dafydd and he will come for me. Therefore, I must defend myself. I will not lay down and let the man destroy me."

Penelope had known his answer even before he said it and she was, in fact, in full support. Somehow, it didn't seem right to see Bhrodi paying homage to Edward, becoming the puppet of a greedy king. Bhrodi was a Welsh king himself, strong and proud, and it hurt her heart to think of him being subjected to English laws, governed by men who thought themselves better than him, and caged by an English monarch because of covetousness. Nay, it wasn't right at all.

"What will you do?" she asked.

Bhrodi continued to stroke her cheek. "My chieftains will be here on the morrow," he said. "I will discuss Dafydd's situation with them and ask for their support. Since I will be leading them into battle, they can no longer question my loyalty to Wales or my marriage to you. I will be risking my life on behalf of my country."

Penelope was thoughtful. "When do you suppose you will leave?"

"Immediately."

That struck her with disappointment but she didn't question him further. It seemed to her that all of her questions were answered but she truthfully didn't like the thought of him going into battle, not now when they were just coming to know each other. She knew that bad things happened in battle and there was every possibility that he would not return to her. Still, she understood, perhaps more than any other woman would have. Penelope understood a warrior's heart. But she also understood something else.

"Let me go with you," she begged softly. "I can fight as well as any man. Let me fight with you."

Bhrodi wasn't surprised by the request; he thought it would have come sooner than it had. He cupped her face with both big hands, looking into her eyes.

"As flattered as I am that you would risk your life for me, I must deny you," he said softly. "Were you to go to battle with me, my thoughts would be only of you and not on my duties. It would distract me so grievously that I would make an excellent target for the enemy. Distracted knights do not live very long."

She knew it would be his answer but she was disappointed just the same. "My father has taken me into battle with him before," she insisted. "I am...."

He cut her off, though it was gently. "You will remain here in command of Rhydilian," he told her. "I will leave you with a skeleton guard and it will be up to you to keep my castle safe. Will you do this for me?"

It was a compromise like the ones they had discussed earlier. She wanted to go to war with him, but he would not allow it. He didn't particularly want her in command of his fortress because, in his mind, she should be bottled up safely in the keep and not worrying over such things, but he suspected her military instincts were impeccable given her training and would therefore let her do something she was trained to do. He would let her command.

Penelope saw the request as the least desirable of all options but agreed to it anyway. "If you wish it," she said, resigned. "But I very much want a broadsword. I would feel naked in command without one."

He smiled faintly. "I will give you my father's broadsword until we can have one commissioned for you," he said. "I do not carry it because he had a special broadsword commissioned for me when I received my spurs. It is that broadsword I carry into battle, but I am sure my father would be very happy to permit you to use his."

That brightened Penelope up considerably. "Then I will be happy to remain in command of Rhydilian while you go to help Dafydd."

His smile broadened as he stroked her cheeks with both thumbs. "Good," he said. "Now that everything is settled, can we stop taking about Edward?"

She giggled and nodded. It was enough of a prompt for Bhrodi to lean forward and kiss her very sweetly. His lips suckled hers, gently at first, but with increasing ardor. His tongue licked at her lips, carefully pushing its way into her mouth as his hands left her face and his arms went tightly about her. Penelope gave herself over to him in every way.

Her shift came off swiftly and he tossed it to the floor, his naked flesh coming into contact with hers as he lay on top of her. His hands gently fondled her breasts, pinching the nipples and listening to her groan with excitement. His lust overwhelmed him as he pushed her legs apart, settling between them, and wasting no time in rubbing the tip of his phallus against her unfurled lips. She was wet, he could feel it, and he carefully thrust into her.

Penelope lay on her back, experiencing this second coupling with more excitement than she had the first. Each successive second seemed to bring more excitement, causing her body to arch against him as she met him thrust for thrust. Bhrodi held her tightly at first but released her, sitting back on his heels and holding her knees aloft as he thrust into her heated and slick body. Penelope opened her eyes to watch him, curious and aroused, and the sight of his powerful body as it joined with hers was enough to send her heart racing. Everything about the man sent her heart racing.

The bloom of heat in her loins, kindled by the friction of his manhood, grew into a fireball and exploded quite soon this time. As Penelope gasped with the thrill of her release, Bhrodi answered her with a powerful release of his own, spilling his seed deep. It was pleasure and passion and emotion all blended into one, and he hoped that a son with his strength and her sensibilities had been planted this night. He was going to war and it was quiet possible he would not return. If God was merciful, he had left something of himself behind. The Serpent would have a legacy.

Gathering Penelope into his arms, Bhrodi lay down beside her in silence. In truth, he didn't want to speak; words seemed so trivial at this point. Moreover, he wasn't sure he could verbalize what he was feeling.

Something had happened to him in the past several days, ever since he literally ran into the girl who had fought the great beast of the marsh. It was as if he couldn't remember his life before Penelope came, that dark and dreadful abyss where the days and nights seemed to run into one another in a great, horrible block of endless hours. Then Penelope entered that world and brought joy and light with her.

He never knew his heart could be so full but he was terrified to tell her, terrified he would overwhelm her with his happiness. So he kept his mouth shut and kept his feelings to himself. Perhaps someday, when he was a little braver, he might just tell her what he was thinking. Perhaps she would even respond. It was a little dream he had.

They slept.

⌘

CHAPTER SIXTEEN

The mist disguised the number of Welsh who had come to Rhydilian in the early morning hours the following day.

Bhrodi had sent Ianto and Yestin out into the crowd gathering at the base of Rhydilian's gatehouse so he could get a feel for who, and how many, had come to his *cyfarfod*. Before the sun had even risen, there were hordes of men and by the time the sun began to peak over the eastern horizon, there were gangs of Welshmen far down the hill, on the road that led up to the castle.

Ianto and Yestin returned to inform him that men as far as the Holy Isle on the extreme western end of Anglesey had come, all gathering to hear The Serpent speak, and they estimated there was somewhere between three and five thousand. It was a massive group.

They were also a very vocal group. They had been shouting up to the battlements well before sunrise, calling for de Shera, and Bhrodi showed himself just after sunrise. Bron had come with his men also, all one hundred and fourteen of them, and they crowded up by the enormous front gates. When Bhrodi saw them, he had his men admit them into the bailey. He knew Bron supported him unconditionally and should the group become unruly, he didn't want the man caught in the crossfire.

"Yn dod yn agosach a byddwch yn clywed mi!" he called. *Come closer and you shall hear me.* The group began to surge forward, crowding up around the gatehouse and walls as close as they could get. Surrounded by his *teulu* commanders upon the black-stoned battlements, Bhrodi surveyed his vassals with the aura of Caesar surveying all of Rome. There was an air of power about him that was inherent. He continued in Welsh.

"You have all heard by now that I have taken a wife," he bellowed to the crowd below. "You have also heard that my wife is Saesneg. Know now that it is true."

The crowd rumbled angrily and some began shouting insults. "Traitor!" Someone screamed at him. "You have betrayed us!"

"I have not betrayed you," Bhrodi replied steadily. "You know me well and you know I would never betray any of you."

That was true for the most part and the shouts of treachery died down somewhat, but not entirely. There was still dissension.

"Why did you not marry Welsh?" another man cried. "You could have strengthened ties with other Houses!"

Bhrodi wasn't going to get into a shouting match with one man in particular; what he had to say was directed at the entire group. "I had my reasons," he shouted "You must listen to them!"

The crowd was unwilling to give entirely. "Tudur and Lon resisted your reasons," someone else shouted. "You fed them to the beast!"

They were getting worked up again, shouting their anger and rejection of Bhrodi's actions. Bhrodi knew he had to gain control quickly or all would be lost. He needed something from them; he needed for these men, his vassals, to understand his reasons behind everything. It was imperative. He lifted hands to gain their attention.

"Tudur and Lon betrayed my friendship, my hospitality, and my trust," he told them. "Never did they come to me with their concerns. They tried to kill my wife's family at our wedding and this I would not tolerate. Tudur and Lon were punished for their actions against me and for no other reason!"

That gave the crowd something to think about. Betrayal, of course, was the ultimate sin and de Shera had never lied to them before. The man was supremely truthful in all things so they had no reason to believe he was lying about Tudur and Lon. Therefore, the agitation died down somewhat as the Welshmen began to rethink their anger. The grumbling lessened and Bhrodi took advantage of their confusion.

"As you love and respect me, then you must also trust me," he yelled. It took some time for them to die down enough for him to continue. "Edward himself proposed this marriage for the sake of peace and I accepted. But we all know that there is no peace with Edward. My wife is the daughter of the renowned English knight known as The Wolfe. You have all heard of this man. I married his daughter in order to ally myself with him in the face of Edward's conquest of Wales. When we fight Edward, and we will, it will now be with one of his own knights by my side!"

That seemed to throw the group into greater confusion. At least they weren't hurling insults. They seemed to be looking at each other, one man to another, looking for a consensus that what Bhrodi had done was an acceptable thing. Now, The Serpent's marriage was starting to make a little more sense but there were many who were still doubtful. It was to those men that Bhrodi's next word held impact for.

"We need this alliance," he called. "Edward has already established himself in Wales and I have just received word that the English king has captured Castell y Bere and that Dafydd ap Gruffydd has barely escaped him. Dafydd has asked me to send him support, which is what I intend to do. At dawn tomorrow, we will ride for Dolbadarn Castle where Dafydd is and save him from the English king. You will all ride with me, as my trusted brothers, and we shall defeat this man who covets our country. We shall crush him as he has tried to crush us and in this, we shall confirm our loyalty and love for Wales. I will risk my life for such freedom. I am an ap Gaerwen, the seed of Welsh royalty, and my love for this country runs deeper than yours. I will prove it. Will you join me?"

Bhrodi had a magnetism that was readily apparent and even though many of his vassals were still unhappy with his marriage to a Saesneg, his impassioned speech about crushing Edward had them rallying to his cause. The tide of favor was slowly turning because these men truly loved Bhrodi. He was their shining star, a man with a legendary reputation that they called one of their own.

Of course they wanted to trust him; rumors of his Saesneg marriage had filled them with outrage and disappointment. But his reasons behind the decision where sound, enough to sway their opinion for the most part. As the shouts of insult began to turn to shouts of support, Bhrodi caught movement out of the corner of his eye.

Penelope had mounted the battlements, now standing at the top of the stairwell that led up from the gatehouse. She was dressed in a long leather and fur tunic, leather breeches, and heavy boots. She was also wrapped up in a heavy woolen cloak, her long hair braided and draped over one shoulder. She was dressed more like a soldier than a fine lady, but it didn't matter; in the mist of the morning, she looked surreal and ethereal, like an angel emerging from the clouds. When their eyes met, she smiled timidly, and Bhrodi reached out a hand for her.

Taking her husband's hand, Penelope came to stand next to him on the battlements as he spoke to his vassals. She had heard him yelling but, not knowing Welsh, she had no idea what he had said. She could see a massive crowd below and the sight was rather startling.

"So many men," she whispered.

Bhrodi held her hand tightly. "It would seem that all of my vassals have come to hear me speak," he said. "I am pleased."

She tore her gaze away from the group below and looked at him. "What have you told them?"

He shrugged. "That my wife is an English tyrant and I fear her greatly." When Penelope shrieked with outrage, he laughed. "I told them that I married you to ally with your father. I also told them about Dafydd and asked for their support. That is what you hear them discussing."

She was still shaking her head reproachfully at him as she once again turned her attention to the crowds below. Even she could see that their angry shouts had become those of encouragement, but not entirely. One of the men who had been shouting loud insults at Bhrodi was standing directly below, hollering up at him.

"Bring Edward to these lands!" he shouted. "Let him come! Turn the beast of the marsh loose on him as you do all of your enemies! Even Edward cannot fight The Serpent!"

Penelope was hanging over the side of the wall, listening to the man shout in the harsh Welsh tongue. She looked at Bhrodi. "What did he say?"

Bhrodi had a half-grin on his face. "He says that I should allow Edward to come to Anglesey and turn the beast loose on him," he said, shrugging. "I have truthfully never thought of that. It might be worth considering."

She shrugged her shoulders in agreement. "You Welsh need all of the help you can get," she said. "Not even Edward can profess to have a beast to slay his enemies with."

Bhrodi's grin grew as he grasped her by the arm and pulled her against him, where he stood at the edge of the parapet. He lifted his hand again to get the attention of his vassals.

"This is my wife, daughter of The Wolfe," he yelled, introducing her to the crowd of men below. "She has his heart and his spirit, and you will respect her and love her as you do me. This I command."

The reaction was mixed for the most part but the men were very curious to see Penelope, who looked at Bhrodi with some uncertainty.

"What are they saying?" she asked.

Bhrodi paused before answering as he listened. "They are trying to decide whether or not to give you their loyalty," he said. "Tell them this: *Yr wyf yn tyngu i chi byddaf yn rhoi fy loyaty i Gymru.*"

Penelope looked at him in fear but dutifully struggled to repeat it. She leaned over the parapet and began to shout. "*Yr wyf yn tyngu...*"

He nodded encouragingly. "*I chi byddaf yn rhoi fy loyaty i Gymru.*"

She spit the rest out in one long sentence. "*I chi byddaf yn rhoi fy loyaty i Gymru!*" she said, looking to him for approval. "Did I say it right?"

"You said it beautifully."

"What did I just say?"

He was serious. "That you hate them all and you curse their families."

Penelope shrieked. "I said *what?*"

Bhrodi broke down into laughter, as did the *teulu* commanders; they had all been listening to the conversation, amused by her reaction to Bhrodi's tease. The man had been known to have a wicked sense of humor at times, as she was no doubt coming to discover. Bhrodi squeezed Penelope tightly around the shoulders, giving her a gentle hug.

"You told them that you swore your loyalty to Wales," he said, looking at the men below and trying to gauge their reactions. "They seem pleased by it."

Penelope still wasn't over his joke, shaking her head in exasperation. "You are a terrible man with your jesting," she told him. "You could have told me to repeat anything to them and I wouldn't have known what it was."

"Then I would suggest you learn Welsh very quickly."

Penelope could hardly disagree. "To be safe, I'd better," she said, watching Bhrodi as he listened to the crowd below. "What else are they saying? Are they agreeing with our marriage?"

He was leaning on his elbows over the parapet, listening to the rumblings. "It is difficult to tell," he said. "But they seem to be far less angry than they were even a few moments ago. Mayhap I can let them into the castle now and we can calmly discuss our plans to join Dafydd."

He turned to Ianto and Ivor, instructing them to begin letting the chieftains into the castle. Rhydilian wasn't big enough to hold thousands of men so those loyal to the chieftains needed to be kept outside the gates, an uncomfortable arrangement for men who were very aware of the beast that roamed the area. They felt vulnerable. Still, it couldn't be helped. Now that the initial animosity was over, Bhrodi was eager to get down to business and do what needed to be done.

He made Penelope go into the keep and lock it up tight before he opened the gates and allowed his chieftains admittance to the castle grounds, so she watched men pour in through the front gates from the safety of the chamber Thomas and Kevin shared. In fact, all three of them watched the bailey of Rhydilian fill up with Welshmen, a very strange sight indeed for the English. The only time they ever saw such numbers of Welsh were in battle, so it was an odd vision to Thomas and Kevin in particular.

With Penelope locked up tight in the keep, Bhrodi conducted business in the bailey, walking among his chieftains and reaffirming bonds. He discuss his marriage again and his reasons, and the second time around, almost all of them were willing to listen and also willing to agree. There were a few who were still uncertain but not in a violent way; they were men who had daughters of marriageable age and were offended Bhrodi hadn't considered their daughters first, but that insult soon passed into memory.

For now, they had a battle to plan because the last Welsh prince was in need of their help and with Bhrodi de Shera leading the army, they were apt to give it.

On the morrow, The Serpent would lead the way.

⌘

Corwen Castle
The Welsh Marches

At forty-four years of age, Edward the First of England was a tall man with curly dark blond hair that was starting to turn white. From years in combat, he was rather muscular but a poor diet had contributed to a rounded belly and an occasional bout with gout. Oddly enough, he was rather soft spoken but when he did speak, his persuasive tone was hindered with a hint of a lisp. Intelligent to a fault, he didn't need a great booming voice to get across his wishes; his well-spoken diatribes were filled with hazardous innuendos. There was no doubt in anyone's mind who was in control of the whole of England.

When Edward heard that William de Wolfe had entered his encampment, the king went out of his way to seek William out just as the man was dismounting his weary charger. Edward had grown up idolizing William, as the knight had been a great friend of his father's, so he promptly hugged William in greeting. It was an extreme break in royal protocol, but Edward showed no hints of embarrassment. He was thrilled to have The Wolfe in his camp and he took William and his men into his very large tent for conversation and refreshments. There was much to discuss.

"I received your missive last week regarding your daughter's betrothal to Bhrodi de Shera," Edward said as he handed William a pewter goblet of wine. "Has the wedding taken place?"

William sipped at the very fine wine. "It has," he said. "I sent the missive to you when we departed for Wales. She married de Shera probably about the same time you received the announcement."

Edward's pale eyes were alight. "I am extraordinarily pleased to hear that," he said. "I am more than pleased that de Shera accepted the contract."

William nodded. "He accepted it without much resistance," he said. "Therefore, the hereditary kings of Anglesey are now linked to the House of de Wolfe. I knew you would be pleased."

Edward was nodding eagerly, but it was clear that the wheels of his mind were turning. Edward's mind was always turning. "It is a fine day, indeed," he said. "It makes my life so much more... controlled."

"Why is that?" William asked.

Edward collected his own cup of wine. "Because de Shera is now allied with the English, of course," he said as if William was an idiot. "I have waited for this day, de Wolfe. I am so proud and happy that you have given this gift of peace to me."

William wasn't as joyful as Edward was, not in the least. He had no patience for not coming straight to the point of the matter. He'd spent three long days riding to Corwen and wasn't in the mood for idle chatter as Edward seemed to be. William was here for a purpose.

"We have heard that you captured Castell y Bere," he said, looking Edward in the eye. "We have also heard that Dafydd ap Gruffydd escaped the siege and is heading north, where you already have a heavy presence at Caernarfon, Rhuddlan, and Conwy. Where you do *not* have a heavy presence is Anglesey and it is my concern that Dafydd has sought refuge with de Shera."

Some of the joy drained from Edward's face. "Why do you worry?" he asked. "De Shera is now our ally."

William signed faintly and set down his wine. "It is not that simple and you know it," he said, his voice low. "Simply because de Shera married my daughter does not instantly make him your ally. He is still a Welshman and still deeply entrenched in his country's struggle against you. Did you truly believe something as simple as a marriage would remove all of his loyalty to his own people?"

Edward's good mood was completely vanished. He moved closer to William, a deadly gleam to his eye. "I offered a marriage contract between him and a daughter of your choosing for exactly that purpose," he said. "Never forget that de Shera is the Earl of Coventry. God's Blood, the man is half-English. It is time he shows some loyalty to that half. It is time he shows his loyalty to *me.*"

William could see that Edward was inflexible in the matter. It didn't surprise him necessarily, but it concerned him. He knew Paris and Kieran were in earshot; he could feel them. Having served with those men most of his life, he knew when they were close. It was a bond they shared. He could also sense their concern as well. But before William could reply, Edward turned away from him and focused on Paris.

"De Norville," he said amiably. "How do you find living at Castle Questing these days? It must be quite odd no longer serving as the captain of the guard for the Earl of Teviot."

Paris forced a smile; he didn't particularly like Edward and never had. There was something very untrustworthy and seedy about the man.

"I was very happy to turn the job over to my eldest son," he said. "Now I live at Questing with my wife and our younger children, and I force William to pay for my food and drink. It is an excellent arrangement."

Edward laughed, clapping Paris on the shoulder as he turned back to William. "William is a wealthy man," he said. "He can afford you. How is your wife?"

Paris' smile faded; he didn't like talking about his wife even on a good day, and he certainly didn't want to speak of her condition to a man he didn't like.

"She is well," he lied. "She sends her greetings, of course."

Edward nodded. "Of course," he said, moving on to Kieran, who was standing big and silent several feet away. Edward looked the man over. "And you, Hage? How is your family?"

Kieran didn't like him, either. "They are well," he said generically. "Thank you for asking, Your Grace."

Edward wasn't inclined to carry on any more of a conversation with Kieran than he already was; everything he'd said had only been pleasantries, anyway, mostly because he hadn't wanted to get into a heated discussion with William about de Shera's loyalties. Chatting with de Norville and Hage was a way of cooling his temper. As he reached for more wine, William spoke.

"What are your plans for seeking out Dafydd, Your Grace?" he asked. "Do you have any intelligence on where he may have gone?"

Edward poured himself more wine before answering. "We know he is north, in Snowdonia, but we do not know exactly where," he replied. "I have many men out searching for him as we speak and in two days, the entire encampment is moving out to aid in the search. I must be on-hand when Dafydd is found and flushed out, but now that I know de Shera is married to your daughter, I shall send men to Rhydilian Castle to see if Dafydd has gone there. I am sure your daughter will be truthful and tell us if the man has arrived even if de Shera's loyalties are not quite so clear."

William's jaw began to tick. "And what happens if de Shera chooses to side with Dafydd?"

Edward looked at him. "Then the man is in breach of the terms of his marital contract and I will treat him as I treat any other Welshman," he said coldly. "After I destroy Dafydd, I will destroy Bhrodi de Shera and you will help me. Am I making myself clear, de Wolfe?"

William met the king's gaze without flinching, even though it was a terrible and wicked gaze. God, there were so many things he wanted to say at that moment but just couldn't bring himself to. He had to get away from Edward and rethink his strategy. He also had to rethink his loyalties for if Edward went after Bhrodi, William wasn't entirely sure he would go with him. If he refused to fight for the king, that would bring up an entirely new set of issues. In fact, the prospect was quite horrifying.

Nay, he couldn't engage the king in any manner of argument. At least, not at the moment. Edward had to believe that The Wolfe was still loyal to England as he had always been. Fact was, William wasn't loyal to England at all. He was loyal to his daughter. After a moment, he forced a smile.

"Clear indeed, Your Grace," he said, rather lightly as he tried to throw the man off of his true thoughts. "But let us hope it does not come to that. For now, I would ask permission to rest. I'm too damn old to be riding day and night without sleep and if we are departing in two days, then I must ease my old bones for the difficult journey ahead."

Edward was back to being amiable; he had that ability in his personality to go from deadly to joyful in a split second, a trait that worried even his closest advisors.

"Go and rest, my friend," he said. "I will send for you when it is time to sup. You must tell me all about the wedding and all about de Shera. I've never met the man. I'd like to know what you think of him."

William nodded, set his wine down, and bowed out of the tent with Paris and Kieran on his heels. The three of them marched towards the southern end of the encampment where their men were gathered. All the while, William was struggling not to explode. His hands and jaw were working furiously.

"Breathe, William, breathe," Paris said quietly. "Be calm, man. We must think our way through this."

William was struggling. "There is nothing to think about," he said. "I have fought for England my entire life but at this moment, I will not fight for Edward if he goes after de Shera."

Paris put a big hand on William's shoulder. "Will you fight for de Shera, then?" he asked softly.

William came to an abrupt halt and looked at Paris. "My life, my love, and my loyalty are with my daughter," he said. "I will not let Edward destroy her. If it comes to that, I will fight for de Shera. I must. I cannot let the man destroy Penelope."

"It is what he has planned all along," Kieran said softly. When William and Paris looked at him, he met their gaze steadily. "We all know that Edward has always intended for complete domination of Wales. He will have it one way or the other. He was hoping that by marrying Penelope, de Shera would submit to English rule but I am equally sure that is not the case. De Shera may be half-English, but he is all Welsh – his heart and soul lie there. If Edward wants all of Wales, he is going to have to go through de Shera to get it. He has planned that all along. The marriage was just a ruse."

William put his hands on his hips angrily. "If you have known that, why didn't you tell me?"

Kieran shook his head. "Because it only became readily apparent right now. Edward never had any intention of honoring any manner of peaceful alliance with de Shera. He wants the man's submission or he wants his life."

He was absolutely right; it was shocking and terrible information but it was something they had all known from the beginning, or at least they should have. William sighed heavily, averting his gaze as he looked at his feet. His mind was in utter turmoil.

"Jordan told me that blood is stronger than a kingdom," he muttered. "She also told me I must side with Edward to keep control of him. I cannot do that if I am the opposition. She said the only way to protect Penelope is to undermine Edward."

"Jordan would make a fine battle commander."

William was feeling rather ill as he mulled over his conversation with the king. "Oh, God," he breathed. "I cannot fight with de Shera, can I? Jordan is correct; I must fight with Edward. It is the only way to help my daughter, mayhap even the only way to save her. I have to know every move Edward makes in order to do Penny, or de Shera, any good at all."

Paris sighed faintly. "You are walking a difficult path, my friend," he said softly. "This campaign with Edward could very well see your reputation tarnished if he discovers he does not have your completely loyalty."

William knew that. "I do not care about my reputation nearly so much as I care about my daughter," he said with some regret. "Who knew a serpent could destroy a Wolfe?"

No one had an answer for him; they all knew what was at stake. It was like a nightmare, one William had walked into with trust in his king and in an alliance with de Shera. Now, it was all falling apart. He should have been smarter about it and he cursed himself for his foolishness. He should have realized there would be no peace so long as Edward was determined to conquer Wales. In his old age, he had hoped for such things as peace.

The price of that foolishness might be his daughter's life.

⌘

CHAPTER SEVENTEEN

The Month of May, Rhydilian Castle

Penelope had never known loneliness like this.

Twenty-three days after Bhrodi's departure for Dolbadarn Castle, Penelope found herself up on the battlements of Rhydilian, watching the sun rise. In the forest that surrounded them, she could hear birds chirping and woodland creatures chattering. Everything was coming alive as the sun began to rise, signaling the start of a new day. Unlike the past several days, this morning was without the heavy mist and Penelope could see for miles. Rhydilian was perched in a perfect spot to survey the great and mysterious land.

It was beautiful, that was true. It wasn't quite like the land she came from, which had great hills and dales but no big mountains, but it was just as clean and lovely. To her left, to the northeast, was the marsh where the great beast roamed and she found herself studying the distant marsh for any signs of the creature. The Serpent of legend, Bhrodi had told her, a being that he was one and the same with although she didn't think that was quite true. The beast of the marsh killed without conscience and Bhrodi most definitely had a conscience. He had a heart and soul as well. As she watched the landscape, she felt his absence tremendously.

Penelope had spent a total of a week with the man and already she felt as if she had always been with him. He had marked her, as she had marked him, and his departure on that misty morning over three weeks ago had been a bittersweet one. He had kissed her and hugged her, and told her how much he would miss her, but he stopped short of declaring his love for her. He may as well have said it because his actions spoke far louder than words; his love for her was in his eyes, in his smile, and in his touch, and Penelope had reciprocated in kind. Still, she hadn't told him that she loved him, either, fearful that her statement would have met with indifference or, worse, rejection. So she had kissed and hugged him, too, and told him that she would miss him. She begged him to return safely to her.

But twenty-three days after his departure, she was coming to sorely regret not having told the man she loved him. Thinking back, she supposed that she had been falling in love with him all along but the morning he had spoken to his vassals about Dafydd's request for aid had been the morning she realized that she loved him very much. Bhrodi de Shera was a proud, arrogant, and powerful man, but he was also sweet and gentle and humorous. So many qualities she had fallen in love with because, in many ways, he reminded her of her father. She couldn't help but love him. And now he was gone and she had not told him of her feelings. Her regret was growing by the day.

As was her concern. Bhrodi had sent two messengers back to Rhydilian in the time he'd been away, men who had relayed the situation in and around Dolbadarn. Everything had been calm for the first week but after that, the English had been drawing close and there had been several skirmishes as a result. The castle was still intact but Dafydd, she was told, had long since fled and Bhrodi had gone with him. That was the last thing she had heard and that had been nine days ago. Her anxiety for more news was therefore growing.

As she stood on the battlements and pondered her thoughts, she heard movement off to the right and turned to see Kevin emerging from the stairwell. The man had recovered quite rapidly over the past three weeks thanks to the initial care he had received from Bhrodi's old surgeon. The puncture wound to his torso had not grown poisonous, which had been a miracle, so it was simply a matter of the man gaining back his strength. He was well on his way, very nearly back to normal. She smiled at Kevin as he approached, noting that Thomas was not far behind him. The two always seemed to travel in a pair. Her smile was meant for her brother as well.

"Good morn to you both," she said. "The day is half-over. Where have you been?"

Thomas yawned. "Sleeping," he said, eyeing Kevin. "That big bull keeps me up half the night with his snoring so I must catch sleep when I can."

218

Kevin gave him a wry expression. "Do not blame me," he said. "You are up late playing games with Lady Tacey or telling her stories. If you must blame anyone for your lack of sleep, blame her."

It was a sensitive subject with Thomas; over the past several weeks, he had become rather fond of Tacey, and she of him, and they spent a good deal of time together. At first, Penelope thought it was simply his brotherly instincts but now she wasn't so sure. Thomas was showing distinct signs of affection towards the girl, which she very much approved but she wondered if Bhrodi would. Therefore, the subject was treated very carefully.

"Tacey sleeps all day and is up all night these days," Penelope told Kevin what he already knew. "The baby will not let her sleep at night and Thomas is kind enough to sit up with her so she will not be alone."

Kevin grunted. He had things to say about that, thinking what Penelope thought about the situation, but he kept his mouth shut. He didn't want to get into an argument with Thomas, who was very touchy when it came to young Lady Tacey, so he changed the subject.

"It seems very odd to look over the Welsh countryside and not be at war in it," he said. "It seems very odd to be here in the first place."

Penelope's gaze moved out over the landscape. "I know you are well enough to return home," she said. "I appreciate that you have remained here with me to help me oversee Rhydilian."

Kevin braced his big arms against the parapet. "You do not need any help," he said. "We simply did not want to leave you alone in a strange land with strange men under your command."

Penelope shrugged. "There are only fifty of them," she said. "Bhrodi took his commanders with him and his entire *teulu* contingent. The men he left me with are rather old to fight. I suppose if I needed to, I could best every one of them so you really do not have to worry about leaving me alone with them."

Thomas reached out and yanked her braid in an affectionate gesture. "That is the thanks we get for remaining behind to protect you?" he asked in mock outrage. "If that is as much as you think of us, then we will leave today and good riddance to you."

Penelope giggled and took a swing at him, which he easily pushed away. As the siblings squabbled good-naturedly, Kevin caught sight of something on the road at the base of the mountain. From what he could see, it was a lone rider and on his current path it would take him straight to the castle.

"Look," he said, grasping at Penelope to pull her away from her brother. "A rider approaches."

Penelope's smile and good humor vanished as she hung over the parapet, her eyes straining to see what Kevin saw. It was very far in the distance but, gradually, she came to see the rider as well. Her heart leapt into her throat.

"Mayhap it is a messenger!" she gasped, filled with fear and excitement.

The knights didn't respond. They continued watching, as Penelope did, as the rider drew closer and closer. Within several minutes, they were able to make out small details and it was Thomas who spoke first.

"That is Edward," he hissed. "Penny, it's *Edward!*"

He meant their brother. Three years older than Thomas, Edward had ridden out with their father and now, for some reason, he was returning. Any scenario Penelope could come up with for his return was not a good one. She tried not to panic as she fled the battlements with Kevin and Thomas on her heels, flying down the narrow spiral staircase from the battlements until she reached the ground below. In the shadow of the great gatehouse, she shouted at the sentries to open the gate. Slowly, the ropes and chains choked back on their guides, creaking and groaning, and the old gates began to give way.

Penelope stood her ground as they moved, standing in the mud and cold as the panels yawned open and she could see Edward approaching. She couldn't stand it; she ran out of the gates and met Edward on the road.

"Edward!" she cried as he reined his frothing charger to a halt. "Why are you here? Has something happened?"

Edward de Wolfe was exhausted from his ride; he'd been awake for two straight days and then on the road since dawn when his father had sent him to Rhydilian with a missive. He didn't have the time or patience for his sister's demands.

"Inside," he boomed. "Get inside now!"

Startled, Penelope ran back inside the gates with Edward on her heels. It was Edward who gave the command to close the gates as Kevin and Thomas came forward to meet him. Thomas grabbed hold of his brother's horse as the man nearly fell off while dismounting. Penelope was at his side, holding on to him to keep him from pitching to his knees.

"What has happened, Edward?" she begged. "Is Papa well? Has something happened to him?"

Edward pulled off his helmet, facing his sister and brother and cousin. He was tall, like his namesake, William's father Edward, and he also had Edward's golden-hazel eyes. In fact, he was very much like his grandfather, well-spoken and politically savvy. That was why William had chosen him to ride for Rhydilian. Edward was the perfect messenger.

"Our father is well," he assured her. "But much has happened. Let us go someplace where we can speak in private."

It wasn't much of an answer, which frightened Penelope even more. Shaken, she led the way into the keep, calling for warmed drinks as they entered the small feasting hall. Together, the four of them sat around the scrubbed feasting table as Thomas helped Edward shed his weapons and pieces of plate. He was piling everything upon the table as Edward spoke.

"Have things been peaceful around here?" he asked.

Penelope nodded. "Very peaceful," she said. "Why do you ask?"

Edward looked around the table at Kevin and Thomas. "Dafydd ap Gruffydd has not come here, has he?"

Everyone shook their heads. "Not that we have seen," Kevin replied. "Why, Edward? What is this all about?"

Edward sighed heavily; where to start? His exhausted mind struggled to find a starting point to his complex message.

"When we were returning to England after leaving Penny's wedding, we came across English soldiers who told us of Edward's victory at Castell y Bere," he said. "They also told us that Dafydd ap Gruffydd was on the run and Father thought he might come here."

Penelope shook her head again. "He did not come here," she said, hesitating on how much she should tell him, afraid of putting Bhrodi in danger if she told him everything. "But... but he sent word to Bhrodi. He asked for Bhrodi to support him against Edward, and Bhrodi left over three weeks ago. Edward, what has happened? Why are you asking such questions?"

Edward could see that she was growing increasingly upset and hastened to ease her. "Father knew that Dafydd had fled and, suspecting he was heading for Rhydilian, he went in search of our king," he said. "Edward told Father that he was planning on destroying

Dafydd and when he was finished with the Welsh prince, his next target was Bhrodi."

It wasn't surprising news but Penelope was beginning to feel sick. "So why have you come?"

Edward put his hand on hers. "Because we engaged Dafydd about a week ago in Snowdonia," he said. "We saw Bhrodi's *teulu*, Penny, and so did Edward. De Shera was quite instrumental in preventing our king from getting ahold of Dafydd. Now Edward knows that Bhrodi is indeed fighting for Dafydd which makes him in breach of the marriage contract. Edward is furious to say the least and it is all Father can do to keep the man from riding to Anglesey and laying siege to Rhydilian."

Penelope's eyes were wide at the news. "So you've come to tell me to leave?" she asked. Then, she shook her head firmly. "I am *not* leaving, Edward. This is my home and my husband's home. He has left me in charge of it and I am not deserting. If Edward comes here, I am going to fight him until the death."

Edward sighed heavily, shutting down his answer as the serving women appeared and put food and drink on the table. He waited until they left the hall before speaking again.

"I am not telling you to leave," he said in a low voice. "But you must know what you will be facing; if Father cannot control the king, and it is quite possible he cannot, then Edward will come down around Rhydilian to punish Bhrodi for siding with Dafydd. How many men did your husband leave you?"

Penelope was ashen. "Fifty," she said, trying not to sound frightened. "But they are old. They could not fend off a siege by the king."

Edward took the cup of wine that Thomas handed him and drank deeply. "You should know that Father has given me permission to bind and gag you to remove you from this place," he said, glancing to Thomas and Kevin. "He commands you two to help me remove her should it come to that. He does not want her here if Edward comes."

Penelope looked around the table in shock. Her anger was roused. "You will *not* remove me," she said flatly. "I will fight you if you try."

Edward sighed. "Father knew that, too," he said. "Penny, I realize you are married to de Shera now and, rightfully, you are loyal to him, as his wife should be. But you must realize that the treaty he swore to uphold is now broken. There is no more treaty. "

"But there *is* my marriage," Penelope shot back firmly. "Simply because a treaty is dissolved does not mean my marriage is and I will not abandon my husband no matter what you say. If Edward comes, I will fight him off myself if I have to, so mayhap you and Thomas and Kevin should leave while there is still time. I must remain here but you three do not have to."

Edward looked at Thomas and the two of them shrugged their shoulders. Perhaps they had known what her answer would be all along and Thomas, more than any of them, was prepared with his reply.

"Well," Thomas finally said, "I cannot leave her. I have come to know de Shera and he is a fair and wise man. You do not know him like I do, Ed. If Penny stays to fight, I will, too. De Shera deserves some loyalty from us since he did not get it from Edward. He needs to see that not all English are treacherous. There are those of us with integrity."

"I am not leaving, either," Kevin said, his voice low and soft. "De Shera has been generous, that is true, but I do not stay for him. I stay for Penny. I will not leave her alone to face Edward's war machine."

Penelope was touched by their support but she was also very worried for them. To stay with her would be to side with the enemy and Edward would not take that lightly. She put her hand on Edward's arm.

"Is Bhrodi returning to Rhydilian?" she asked. "Have you seen him at all?"

Edward shook his head. "There has been some fairly nasty fighting over the past several days very close to here, in fact, near the village of Aber," he said. "It is said to be the hereditary seat of the Princes of Wales, and Edward is fairly confident that Dafydd is hiding there, somewhere. Edward's army is there as, I would imagine, is Bhrodi's."

Penelope could only think of Bhrodi in the midst of heavy fighting. "*How* close?"

Edward's weary eyes fixed on her. "Once you cross the channel, it is about an hour's ride," he said. "I am surprised you have not heard the screaming from here."

Edward's army is less than three hours away, Penelope thought but she did not speak those words aloud. To do so might convey the fear she was feeling and she would not do that. She was a knight, trained for battle, and she would do her best to hold Rhydilian should Edward decide to head their way. In truth, it was a terrifying thought.

"Then we must prepare for the potential threat of Edward's army," she said calmly. "I will go and tell the men now and we will plan what must be done. As long as I am alive, this fortress will not fall. I will not fail my husband."

She was resolute, which was very much like her. Penelope may have been a woman, but she had the heart and courage of a knight. She had displayed it before and would display it again. Thomas reached out and put a hand on her shoulder.

"I will help you," he assured her. "You are not alone."

Edward sighed heavily and raked his fingers through his dark hair. Now that he had delivered his message, his weary mind was growing more exhausted by the moment. His siblings were about to go against their father's recommendation and he hadn't the strength to fight them.

"I will not argue with you," he said. "I cannot. I am too exhausted. Penny, give me a place to sleep for a few hours. I cannot think straight."

Penelope called one of the serving women and had the old lady take Edward up to the second floor, to the chamber where Thomas and Kevin slept. Edward kissed her on the forehead before he went, staggering wearily after the old woman as he disappeared from the hall. Once he was gone, Penelope, Thomas and Kevin sat in silence for a few moments, each to their own thoughts. There was much to think about. Finally, Penelope broke the silence.

"If you two are going to help me hold the fortress, then we must go about our business," she said. "Kevin, find a man who can translate English to Welsh and then have the men gather in the bailey in one hour. I will speak to them at that time. Thomas, it will be your job to walk the perimeter of Rhydilian and look for any weaknesses. Since we will have so few forces, we will need to concentrate the men where there are obvious weaknesses. Go on about your duties and then join us in the bailey in an hour."

Thomas nodded and stood up, heading out of the hall, but Kevin was slower to move. His gaze lingered on Penelope as she stood up, her mind occupied, obviously thinking of what lay ahead. His heart, so soft when it came to her, was beginning to ache with sorrow.

"Penny," he said softly. "I will again ask you to run away with me and leave this all behind. You and de Shera have been married less than a week; it is not as if he has been your husband for many years and your lives and loyalties are intertwined. You have only known the man a few days. Surely you cannot feel such strong loyalty to him."

Penelope struggled with her patience; she didn't want to hear Kevin speak of such things. "I know you mean well, but it makes me feel so

224

very low and so very angry when you speak this way," she said. "You of all people understand honor. What I do, I do for my honor and for my father's honor. The Wolfe and his progeny do not run from anything and we do not break our bond, Kevin. You *know* this. I will not fail Bhrodi no matter how much you beg me to."

Kevin inhaled deeply, thoughtfully. "I am not begging you to fail him," he said. "I am begging you to spare your own life. Do you know what will happen if Edward captures you? Do you have any idea what the man will do?"

Penelope didn't want to hear him. She turned away, abruptly, but he was on her, grabbing her by the arms and forcing her to stop. Furious, she began to fight him.

"Let me go!" she demanded.

Kevin gave her a good shake to get her attention. "If Edward captures you, he will treat you as he would treat any enemy," he said. "You would be fortunate if you were only taken to London and bottled up in the Tower, but more than likely he would make an example of out of you. The executioner's axe, mayhap, or he might even purge you by fire. Do you have any idea how horrific that will be? Of course, your father would not allow it and he would go to war against Edward, but Edward's army is bigger and there is every chance your father would be defeated. Then he would be a prisoner, too, and have his lands and titles stripped. Your brothers would be fugitives more than likely and your mother... how do you think this will affect your mother, Penny?"

He had said too much. Tears formed in Penelope's eyes and, with a burst of anger, she reached up and slapped him across the face. Stung, Kevin loosened his grip enough for Penelope to pull away from him and run from the hall. Kevin stood there where she left him, with a stinging cheek and a hole where his heart used to be.

He couldn't make her understand; she was loyal to de Shera. In fact, she was *too* loyal and he was coming to think that perhaps it was more than just the marriage. Perhaps she had feeling for the man, which utterly broke his heart to think of. But it must have been the truth because she was behaving most irrationally. Women in love were irrational creatures.

Kevin was coming to curse the day he had ever heard the name Bhrodi de Shera. In silence, he quit the hall.

When the hall was dead and still, the wardrobe in the shadows began to rattle. It was only slight, not the usual banging that was normally witnessed. Very quietly, the wardrobe door opened and the tiny man appeared, only this time, it wasn't to fight the unseen enemy. In spite of what everyone had said about him and in spite of his usual routine for thirty years, the old man had very brief moments of lucidity and this one was one of them.

He had heard every word spoken.

⌘

CHAPTER EIGHTEEN

Three days later

It was near sunset, three days after Penelope had given a rather rousing speech to the old men who had remained behind at Rhydilian. She was much like her father in that she was charismatic and encouraging and, even though her words had been translated through an old soldier as well as through Tacey, the men of the old Welsh guard had listened to her. It was clear that she was fiercely supportive of de Shera and she wanted to protect Rhydilian from the English should they come.

The old men had come to know Lady de Shera somewhat since the departure of their lord and she had always been friendly and fair with them, which began to lay the foundation of trust. Moreover, Bhrodi had spoken with all of them before he left and assured them that she was trustworthy. She was William de Wolfe's daughter, after all, and by sheer reputation of the father did they even consider embracing the daughter. But as the days had passed, embrace they did, and the men started calling her *mae hi'n blaidd*. Now, she was known as the She Wolfe. It was a sign of respect.

They had also started showing some respect to the English knights who remained with her after Bhrodi had gone. They seemed to like Thomas in particular and after a productive day with the elderly guard of Rhydilian, Thomas was walking the wall with a few of the old men when they saw the approach of a party far off in the distance.

At first, Thomas thought it was a trick of the light but quite soon realized that it was, indeed, a group of riders on the road for Rhydilian. After watching the coming party for several minutes, he turned to the nearest sentry and sent the man for Penelope.

Kevin, who had been in Rhydilian's armory trying to organize what equipment was left after Bhrodi's departure, heard the calls of the sentries and joined Thomas on the battlements. He was still reeling from his conversation with Penelope three days prior so when she appeared on the wall to see about the incoming party, he tried not to look at her. He'd spent three days trying not to look or speak to her. He just couldn't. Therefore, he didn't notice that Penelope wouldn't look at him, either. There was tension between the two of them that wasn't normal as Penelope focused on the incoming group.

"Can you tell who they are yet?" she asked Thomas. "Are they flying any colors?"

Thomas shook his head. "Welsh do not fly colors," he said, "and it if was Edward, we would already know it."

Penelope knew all of that but she was still curious, now wrought with anxiety. Given Edward's visit and the news he bore, she was understandably apprehensive.

Edward soon joined them on the battlements to await the incoming group. The sun continued to set, streaking spectacular colors across the sky, as the party approaching Rhydilian continued to make its way towards the castle. Penelope and the others noticed that the group wasn't moving particularly fast and there were at least two wagons that they could see. But they were traveling so slowly that it would soon be dark and even though the moon was now a sliver in the sky, the beast of the marsh was always a fear once the sun went down. As they party approached the base of the mountain that Rhydilian was situated upon, a lone rider broke off from the group and thundered up the road.

Penelope, Thomas, Edward, and Kevin came off the wall and met the rider down at the gate. Slowly, the great panels cranked open and the rider, wearing the de Shera *teulu* tunic of deep red, galloped through the opening. The man was off his horse before it came to a complete halt and it took Penelope a moment to recognize the haggard and beard-covered face.

"Ianto!" she gasped in shock. "What is it? Why are you here?"

Ianto was beaten and weary as he moved for Penelope. "My lady," he said. "We are bringing Lord de Shera home."

Penelope didn't understand him at first. "You are bringing Bhrodi home?" she repeated. Then, her face lit up. "He has come with you?"

Ianto was the bearer of terrible news. He could see that she didn't comprehend his meaning and in an uncharacteristic breach of protocol, he reached out and grasped her arm as if to physically impart his news upon her. His eyes, big and sad, focused on her.

"He is with us," he said, his voice hoarse. "My lady, he was badly injured in the fighting at Aber two days ago. With the help of your father, we were able to break through the English lines in order to bring him home. He is… not well, my lady. Not well at all."

Ianto's words hit Penelope with the force of a lightning strike. She went from joyful to shattered all in a split second and, as the others watched, the color drained out of her face. She swayed, grasping at Ianto as if to keep from falling.

"What do you mean?" she breathed. "What are you telling me?"

Ianto was struggling. "My lady, he was…."

Panicked, Penelope cut him off. "Is he dead? Tell me now!"

Ianto could see the pain in her face; he had seen the same pain on Bhrodi's face before the man lost consciousness. It was tragic, truly; such emotion from a man and wife who, under normal circumstances, would have never been. Penelope would have been in her world and Bhrodi would have remained in his. Yet they had come together under impossible circumstances, and something fine was growing between them. Anyone could tell that simply by looking at them. Ianto hadn't seen Bhrodi so happy in over two years, and now this. He was greatly sorrowed, just like the rest of them.

"Nay, my lady, he is not dead," Ianto replied, grabbing her because she seemed to be collapsing somehow. She was difficult to hold on to, like water running through his fingers. "But he is badly injured. We had to bring him home."

The group had reached the top of the road by now and more horses began thundering in through the gates. The chaos of their swift arrival filled the bailey with dirt and noise. Penelope let go of Ianto and turned for the incoming party. She began to run, dodging men and horses, until she came to the first wagon that was just starting to enter the gates. Running up to the edge of the wagon bed, she was abruptly faced with her greatest fear.

Bhrodi lay in the bed of the wagon with the little old surgeon, the one who had tended Kevin and Thomas, hovering over him. He was lying on the wood slats; there weren't even any rushes or blankets beneath him. He simply lay on the wood, his arms and legs askew, like a poppet that had been thrown to the floor. He was unconscious, sporting several day's growth of beard, and as Penelope's gaze moved down his body to see where this horrific injury was, she could see that his entire pelvis was wrapped tightly. Bloodied stains marred the entire left side of wrappings and the breeches of his left thigh were stained and shredded.

Shocked, horrified, Penelope hoisted herself into the wagon bed. The first thing she did was lean over Bhrodi's face, her gentle hands on his head as she lifted first one eyelid and then the other. His eyes were bloodshot and the pupils were slow to react to the light. She looked at the surgeon.

"What is wrong with him?" she demanded. "What happened?"

The old surgeon didn't speak a lick of English. He simply shook his head. Frustrated, Penelope let out a yell of pure frustration.

"Ianto!" she bellowed. "Someone, *anyone*, help me translate to the surgeon!"

Ianto appeared at the side of the wagon; he murmured a few words to the surgeon, who muttered back at him. Penelope expression was frantic.

"Well?" she demanded. "What did he say? What happened to my husband?"

Ianto sighed heavily. "We were in close quarters fighting with some English knights who had cornered Dafydd in a church," he said softly. "Dafydd had lost most of his mail and protection in his flight from Edward and was dressed only in rags. Bhrodi gave him his own mail and weapons, my lady. He gave Dafydd everything except his sword. When a group of English knights invaded the church in search of Dafydd, we bought Dafydd enough time to help him escape by engaging the knights. We were outnumbered and heavily out-weaponed. Lord de Shera was without any mail or protection when he caught a morning star in his lower abdomen. It glanced off for the most part; had it hit him directly it would have killed him. Even so, it tore him to pieces."

Penelope clapped a hand over her mouth or she would have surely become sick. In fact, she did gag, a reflexive action to what she knew would be a devastating injury. Unable to recover, she gagged again and this time vomited over the side of the wagon, weeping as she did so. She couldn't help it; she was shattered and everything was spilling out, fueled by her horrible grief.

"Knights on foot do not use morning stars," she wept and gagged. "What business did they have bringing that type of weaponry into a church?"

Ianto had been joined by Yestin and Ivor, and they watched Lady de Shera become physically ill at the sight of her husband. It was a tragic sight to behold.

"Two knights were on horseback when they entered the church," Ianto tried to be gentle. "We had been fighting all around the town for most of the day, so each man was as heavily armed as he could manage. The men on horseback tore the church apart looking for Dafydd, but we held firm and fought them off. Lord de Shera was caught by the morning star after he had pushed a massive bank of candles down onto several knights, severely injuring them. After that, the other knights made a point of trying to kill him. They nearly succeeded and would have had your father not intervened."

Penelope wiped her mouth and returned to Bhrodi's side. She was trying so very hard not to openly sob but it was difficult for so many reasons; Bhrodi's injury and now evidence that her father had somehow saved him. She stroked Bhrodi's dirty hair tenderly.

"What did my father do?" she asked hoarsely.

"He entered the church just after Lord de Shera had been injured," Ianto replied. "He saw Lord de Shera sent to the floor by the first blow and he shouted at the English knights as they went in for the kill. The listened to your father and they left Lord de Shera alone, but the damage had already been done. Your father helped us remove Lord de Shera and smuggle him through the English lines dressed as an English knight. That is why he only wears breeches and a tunic; he made us take off the English armor as soon as we were clear. He said he couldn't stand the stench of it on him, not even for a moment, but he remained conscious long enough to thank your father. He thanked him for helping him return to the woman they both loved."

Penelope put a hand over her mouth to stifle the sobs but it was of little use; they broke through anyway as she wept her tears of anguish. Collapsing forward, she wept on Bhrodi's chest, so very broken in sorrow. God, if she had only told him she had loved him before he left, then that would have been of some comfort. At least he would have known. As it was, he had loved her, too, only he'd been too frightened or reluctant or shy to tell her. Maybe he had been afraid she hadn't shared those feelings. But he had told her father his feelings. That was something to hold on to.

But tears would not heal him. She was unused to weeping and struggled to stop the flow. She sat up, wiping furiously at her face as if embarrassed by her breakdown. She could see Kevin and Edward and Thomas standing by the edge of the wagon, their sorrowful gaze on Bhrodi.

"Help me," she pleaded. "Help me get him up into the keep."

Ianto, Ivor, Yestin, and Gwyllim were all on horseback, all exhausted men that were dismounting in an effort to aid their lord, but the English moved in more quickly; they were rested and strong, and between the three of them, lifted Bhrodi from the wagon bed and very carefully carried him towards the keep. As they cautiously moved him up the steps to the keep entry, Tacey emerged from the structure.

Lured by the sounds of men and horses, she had come out to see what all the commotion was about. One look at her brother, however, had her in hysterics.

"Bhrodi!" she cried. "What has happened to him?"

Penelope rushed up the stairs and put her arms around the girl. "Be calm, sweetheart," she said quietly. "Your brother has been injured. We will take very good care of him and he will be well again, I promise."

Tacey began sobbing, reaching out to touch Bhrodi as they carried him past her and on into the keep. "He looks dead!" she sobbed.

Penelope thought he did, too, but she didn't voice her thoughts. Her arm was around Tacey's shoulders as she escorted the young girl into the keep, following the men who were carrying her brother. It was like a funeral procession already, with grief and sadness filling the air they breathed. Rhydilian's keep was now full of it, bleeding sorrow from the very walls.

The spiral steps leading up to the third floor where the master's chamber was were narrow and steep, and it was difficult to maneuver Bhrodi up the stairs. Kevin had Bhrodi under the arms and was taking the steps backwards, moving the man very, very carefully so he would not hit his head, while Thomas and Edward supported his legs and torso. It made for extremely slow going but once they were to the third floor, they carried him swiftly into the master's chamber.

As Tacey stood by the door and wept, Penelope moved quickly into the room and helped the men settled Bhrodi on the bed. Keeping busy helped her focus on something other than her grief and she grabbed Ianto as the *teulu* filed exhausted into the room.

"Ask the surgeon what he needs," she said urgently.

Ianto spoke to the surgeon, who was already crawling onto the bed beside Bhrodi and fumbling with his bandages. When the little man murmured in return, Ianto turned to Penelope.

"Hot water," he replied. "He also needs his medicament bag, which I will go and retrieve. He also says to bring great quantities of wine."

It was an odd request but Penelope didn't argue. She ran downstairs and grabbed two of the old serving women, explaining what had happened. The old women ran off in a flurry to collect necessary items and Penelope raced back up the stairs and into the master chamber where Bhrodi was evidently starting to come around. She could hear his low, slow voice and she ran to the bed, a massive lump in her throat when she tried to speak.

Bhrodi, barely conscious, had been roused by all of the movement. His eyes were muddled and his entire body had an oddly numb feeling to hit, but the moment Penelope appeared in his line of sight, it was as if all else faded away. All he could see was her. He stared at her a moment before speaking.

"Are you real?" he whispered.

Penelope slapped a hand over her mouth to keep from sobbing as she nodded her head. "I am," she said tightly.

"I thought I may have dreamed you."

"You did not dream me. I am real."

Bhrodi lifted a weak hand in her direction and she collapsed on the bed beside him, taking his hand in hers. Bhrodi, seeing the tears streaming down her cheeks, shushed her softly.

"No tears," he muttered thickly. "Knights do not weep."

Penelope couldn't help it; his statement made her cry harder. "I am not a knight," she said. "You do not need another knight. I am your wife; you told me so."

He grinned ever so faintly. "Aye," he whispered. "You are my wife. In fact, there is something I must tell my wife."

Penelope wiped at her eyes. "What is it?"

His tone softened with emotion. "I must tell her that I love her very much," he breathed. "She must always remember that, for always."

Penelope broke down into sobs, laying her forehead against his chest. Bhrodi's arms went around her, weakly, holding her against him and relishing what he believed would be his last feel of her in this life. He knew he was badly injured; more than likely mortally injured. He'd never known anyone to recover from such a devastating wound and he thanked God that he was conscious at the moment and able to tell his wife what he wanted to. But he could feel his consciousness slipping away again and he hurried as much as he was able to tell her what he needed to. She had to know all of it.

"*Caria*, listen to me," he whispered. "I was foolish; so foolish. I should have told you of my love for you but I was afraid to, afraid you would not return the feelings. Forgive me for being a coward."

Penelope's head came up, her face very close to his. "If you are a coward, then I am one as well," she murmured. "I was afraid to tell you of my feelings also, knowing that you had once loved someone very much and that you had lost her. I was afraid you would not let yourself feel such things again. I love you deeply, Bhrodi. You are my husband and my heart and no matter what happens, know that you will be with me always."

He smiled at her and feebly touched her cheek. When she reached up to touch his face, he kissed her fingers gently. It was a warm and joyous moment in the midst of such anguish. As Penelope lay her head back on his chest, hearing his slow heartbeat, Bhrodi looked at the men surrounding his bed. He could hear Tacey crying in the background as his gaze fell on Kevin. He seemed to become a bit more lucid as he looked at the man, the dark green eyes wrought with both turmoil and hope. Thoughts began churning in his pain-hazed mind.

"You," he said weakly. "Come closer."

Puzzled, Kevin obediently moved around the bed and made his way next to Penelope. He stood there a moment, looking down at Bhrodi and, for a few long seconds, they simply stared at one another. It was no great secret between them that Kevin wanted what Bhrodi had; he wanted Penelope. But it was a secret only between the three of them. There was no shame of the entire castle knowing the details of confidential information. Therefore, as Penelope watched with some curiosity, Bhrodi lifted a hand to Kevin, who hesitantly took it. Bhrodi squeezed hard.

"You are the only knight in this room who is not related to Penelope by blood so I will therefore ask this of you," he said, grunting in pain because the old surgeon was beginning to unwrap his wound. "If I die, I want to die with the peace of knowing my beloved wife will be well taken care of. You have known her your entire life, have you not?"

Kevin's brow was slightly furrowed; he had a feeling what was coming. It was a deathbed request and one he could not refuse. If it was what he thought it was, he would not have refused it in any case.

"I have, my lord," he replied steadily.

Bhrodi gazed at the man a moment. "You know her well and she knows you," he said, his voice starting to fade a bit. "I would ask you to take care of my wife when I have gone. Love her as I would have and treat her as if she is the most important thing on this earth, because she is that to me and more. All I ask is that you worship her and be kind to her, *Saesneg*. Can you do this for me?"

Kevin was pale with the sorrow the request provoked. Surprisingly, he was starting to feel extremely guilty for having coveted another man's wife, even though he had coveted her well before Bhrodi had married her. Now, it seemed like such a dishonorable thing to do and Kevin was far from a dishonorable man. He was a man of great integrity but when it came to Penelope, his overwhelming love for her had twisted his common sense. Now, he couldn't escape the onslaught of remorse.

"Aye, my lord," he said, his voice hoarse. "I shall not fail you."

Bhrodi nodded faintly, his eyes glimmering, conveying with his gaze alone that he knew what Kevin was feeling. He knew the man loved Penelope and he knew the man would take great care of her. It was the last act of graciousness from a dying man, asking his competition to take care of the women they both loved. Then, and only then, did Kevin begin to understand that there was more to Bhrodi de Shera than simply a warlord; he was a man of forgiveness and benevolence, and it touched Kevin deeply.

"Then I am eased," Bhrodi finally muttered as he released Kevin's big hand. "I am only concerned with my wife and her comfort after I die. I know I leave her in good hands."

Penelope was looking at Kevin with big eyes, somewhere between shock and denial. Now he had permission to marry her should Bhrodi die and she was torn with grief and resentment. She turned to Bhrodi, gently touching his face.

"You will *not* die," she whispered firmly. "You and I will grow old together and have a dozen daughters. Isn't that what we agreed on?"

235

Bhrodi's gaze returned to her. He was growing increasingly weak and the urge to close his eyes was overwhelming. Collecting one of Penelope's hands, lingering near his chest, he kissed her flesh reverently.

"Sons only, you little vixen," he murmured.

Penelope smiled but the tears were on the surface. She could see he was having great difficulty keeping his eyes open and she reached up, gently closing his eyelids.

"Sleep now," she whispered, kissing each closed eye tenderly. "I will be here when you awaken and we will discuss the sex of our children further."

She thought she saw a faint smile tug at Bhrodi's lips and then he was unconscious again, fading off into a world he might never awaken from. Penelope struggled against the sobs that threatened, instead, turning to Ianto and the other *teulu* commanders standing next to the bed. They met her gaze with both sadness and defeat. Penelope didn't like it one bit; she didn't like seeing Bhrodi's men defeated. They thought he was as good as dead, too.

"Let the surgeon tend him now," she whispered, forcing herself to show courage. The men needed direction to help them function and she intended to give it. "You four will go get something to eat, and mayhap a bit of sleep, and meet me in the hall in a few hours. There is much to discuss."

Silently, they bowed out, shuffling from the room that was dark except for the fire in the hearth. The sun had set completely and shadows were cast upon the land. They were the shadows of death, some thought. Death that had come for Bhrodi.

Tacey was still standing by the doorway, weeping quietly. Penelope sighed faintly at the sight of the girl, so overwrought with grief. She turned to Thomas.

"Would you please remove Tacey?" she asked quietly. "She will need to eat something. Please see that she does and then put her to bed. She should not be so upset in her condition."

Thomas nodded silently and left the bedside, heading over to Tacey. He put his hands on the young woman's shoulders, gently, and turned her for the door. Penelope could still hear her crying as Thomas took her down to the hall below. When the sounds of weeping faded, she looked to Edward. She still couldn't bring herself to look at Kevin, at least not yet. There was great anger in her heart for him.

"Edward," she said. "Will you go down to the bailey and make sure the men that brought Bhrodi home are peacefully settled? And please make sure the castle is secure for the night."

Edward nodded and quit the room. When he was gone, the only people remaining in the room other than Bhrodi were the old surgeon, Penelope, and Kevin. A horrible, tense silence filled the air as the surgeon continued to cut away the wrappings from around Bhrodi's waist. Penelope continued to hold her husband's hand, looking at his sleeping face and murmuring prayers over and over. Surely God would hear her pleas; it would be purely tragic should Bhrodi leave her now, just when they had professed their love for one another. How cruel that would be. Kissing his hand, she happened to glance down at what the surgeon was doing and was met by the horrible sight of what the morning star had done to her husband.

The wound looked like raw meat. Slapping a hand over her mouth so she would not become ill again, she quickly stood up and moved away from the bed, her back to the scene. Even though she had seen her share of battle wounds, this time, it was different. Someone very close to her heart was injured and she simply couldn't watch.

Kevin, however, was closer; he had a clear sight of the wound and was not upset by the sight. He'd seen worse. It was, however, quiet terrible. When the surgeon pulled all of the bandages off and began pulling some of the dead flesh surrounding the wound, a pair of old serving women entered with steaming water and two big pitchers of wine.

The surgeon caught sight of the servants and indicated for them to set the things on the floor next to the bed. The water sloshed over as they set it on the floor and the old surgeon barked at the women in the harsh Welsh tongue, sending them scurrying out of the room. The surgeon took a rag, rinsed it in the hot water and then poured wine all over it, and began to clean Bhrodi's wound with it. Kevin watched it all closely as Penelope stood by the lancet window, letting the cold night breeze blow in her face.

"You finally have what you wanted," she said quietly. "Now you have his permission to marry me."

Kevin knew the accusations would be coming and it was an effort not to become emotional about it. "You are not being fair," he said. "Never did I wish for marriage under these circumstances. You know me well enough to know that I would not have hoped for your husband to be badly injured so that I could claim his bride."

He was right; Penelope knew him well and she knew he was not malicious or underhanded. Kevin Hage was a good man, a man to be trusted. He had been her good and close friend for many years, a friendship that had been very happy until her betrothal to Bhrodi. That was when things became complicated and Penelope was still trying to come to terms with all of it. She didn't like it when she and Kevin were at odds. After a moment, she sighed heavily.

"I apologize," she said softly. "I know you would not wish for such a thing. But what does this all mean now? Bhrodi is badly wounded and the last Prince of Wales is still running from Edward. God's Blood, if Dafydd ap Gruffydd was standing here I would kill him myself. It is all his fault."

Kevin turned to look at her. "You cannot blame the man when those loyal to him become injured or even die," he said. "If that was the case, then every monarch, lord, or battle commander would be responsible for every death in every war, ever. You know that you cannot cast blame like that."

Penelope turned away from the window, her eyes blazing as she looked at him. "I do not blame him because Bhrodi was loyal to him," she seethed. "I blame him because Bhrodi gave the man all of the protection that he was wearing. It left my husband defenseless!"

Her tears had turned to anger. Now, she was looking for someone to blame in all of this as Kevin remained calm.

"That was Bhrodi's choice," he reminded her softly. "Dafydd had nothing to do with that."

Penelope turned back to the window, still furious and still in anguish even though Kevin had been correct. She couldn't bring herself to acknowledge it. After a moment, she shook her head in frustration.

"The man is running from Edward," she grumbled. "He has been running for years. He is a rag-tag monarch of a kingdom that no longer exists. He should simply give himself over and be done with it but, instead, he continues to run and my husband, whilst defending this... this pauper, has been horribly injured. What if it is my father who is injured next? You heard what the *teulu* said; my father is in the middle of it, fighting with Edward again in Wales. He is too old to be fighting!"

Her agony was causing her to speak so; Kevin understood that. He went over her as she stood next to the window.

238

"Your father is doing what he has always done," he said quietly. "He is a knight, as is my father, and as is Uncle Paris. Fighting for England is in their blood, and I am equally sure he is not in the midst of the active fighting. I am sure he is simply commanding the active troops. Therefore, you mustn't worry about him. What I suppose we must worry about now is how Dafydd's resistance will be viewed now that Bhrodi is incapacitated. The Welsh have been known to be easily disheartened by bad fortune."

Penelope was in the midst of her anger when his words sank in. It was like water on a fire and she turned to him in confusion. "Why should you care?" she asked. "You are English, Kevin. I should think you would be happy should the Welsh be defeated once and for all."

He eyed her a moment before averting his gaze. "Under normal circumstances, that would be true," he said. "But these are not normal circumstances. If Dafydd is captured then, according to your brother, the king will come after Bhrodi next and, as we can see, the man is in no shape to defend his castle. That means the defenses will fall to you and since Edward, Thomas, and I will not allow you to defend Rhydilian alone, that means that all three of us will be caught up in the Welsh resistance."

Penelope considered his words, pondering them with a clearer head now that her anger had been suppressed for the moment. She turned her pensive gaze to the night beyond the window.

"I wonder if the Welsh even know that Bhrodi has been injured," she pondered.

Kevin leaned back against the wall, crossing his big arms thoughtfully. "According to your husband's *teulu*, Bhrodi was with Dafydd in a church and it would be my guess that it wasn't full of Welsh soldiers. There were probably very few. Even so, Ianto said that Bhrodi and the other *teulu* bought Dafydd time to escape the church by engaging the English, which leads me to believe that it was only Bhrodi and his men in the church, and his men and the English were the only ones that saw Bhrodi injured."

Penelope was following his train of thought. "But the English would not have known who he was," she said. "Unless my father told them, which I am sure he did not, they had no idea that Bhrodi de Shera was injured."

Kevin nodded. "Exactly," he said. "So it can only be assumed that no one other than Bhrodi's men know that he has been wounded. Why would you ask?"

Penelope sighed faintly, her mind, the one trained by her father, working furiously. "Because…," she said, then shook her head and turned from the window. "I must speak to Bhrodi's *teulu*. We must discuss what is to happen now."

Her gaze lingered on Bhrodi as the surgeon cleansed the wound and began to put some kind of herbal compound on it. Penelope really wasn't sure what the old man was doing because she refused to look, but she bent over and kissed her husband on the forehead before quitting the chamber.

Kevin followed her; he wanted to be there when she spoke to the *teulu* because he wasn't sure he liked the tone of her voice when she spoke of future plans. There was something decisive there, as if she had already made a decision about it.

He had to know what that decision was.

⌘

CHAPTER NINETEEN

"You *cannot* pose as Lord de Shera," Ianto said with some anger in his tone. "How would you propose to do this? Unlike English *marchogs* who wear full armor and mail, including a helm to obscure the face, Welsh do not fight like that. We fight without the heavy encumbrances. Lord de Shera was quite evident to all of his men and to all Welshmen most of the time. You cannot pretend to be him by covering yourself in mail and armor to obscure your identity!"

Penelope, sitting at the feasting table in the small hall, had listened to Bhrodi's *teulu* argue with her for the past fifteen minutes. They were unhappy with her suggestion that she should take Bhrodi's place in combat, and Kevin was even unhappier although he'd not said word about it. She could tell simply by the way the man was holding himself, standing off in the shadows with his big arms angrily crossed. He was resistant to the core.

But Penelope was tired of fighting about it. She had made up her mind and it was her intention to shut down the *teulu*'s argument once and for all.

"What do you mean most of the time?" she asked, fixed on a portion of Ianto's statement. "If he fought in clear view of the Welsh all of the time, why would you say he was only known most of the time?"

Ianto glanced at Ivor, at Gwyllim, before rolling his eyes in frustration. She had caught him on a technicality and he could not lie about it.

"There were times in heavy combat that he would wear pieces of his father's armor, including the man's helm," he said. "It is very distinctive and even though the Welsh could not see his face, they would know it was him. It was the trappings of the Earl of Coventry."

Penelope abruptly stood up, slamming the cup in her hand down onto the table. Wine splattered.

"Then that is what I shall wear," she snarled. "I am a trained knight and I know combat more than I know anything else. I was bred for this moment, don't you see? God knew that Bhrodi would need me in this capacity during this terrible time with Edward and that is why He sent me. Now I can fight for Bhrodi while the man is incapacitated. I will not allow men to know he has been wounded, do you hear? All will believe he is still as strong and capable as ever. The Serpent is immortal."

Ianto hissed and looked away while Gwyllim took up the battle against the very formidable Lady de Shera.

"If it is the illusion you wish to continue, then let one of us wear his armor and pose as Lord de Shera," he said. "You would not be convincing, my lady. You are far too small. Men would see you wearing his armor and know it was not him."

"But if I wore it, they would not know such a thing," Kevin said from the shadows. He came forward, struggling to resign himself to Penelope's outlandish idea because he knew, whatever happened, that she would go through with it. They could not stop her. "Lord de Shera and I are very close in size and the illusion would be better preserved. Listen to what Lady de Shera has told you; if King Edward knows that Lord de Shera is gravely injured, it will feed his confidence and Wales will fall beneath his hand faster than it already is. Moreover, if the Welsh know that Lord de Shera is injured and unable to fight, it will kill their fighting spirit. Dafydd will be the only Welsh prince left and, as we all know, the man is running for his life. Do you truly wish to see your country die so quickly? I have served with Lady Penelope in battle when she fought for her father and she had the mind and soul of a true knight. You will trust me when I tell you she is fully capable of commanding a battle."

Penelope was shocked that Kevin would actually come to her defense but she used it to her advantage. Like any good warrior, she acted on the *teulu*'s indecision. She went in for the kill.

"My husband is lying wounded because he believed in a free Wales," she said to the resistant Welshmen "I cannot let that sacrifice be in vain. I must help him fight against those who would seek to take away his legacy because it is now my legacy, too, and the legacy of our children. Tell me, Ianto; if the Welsh know that Bhrodi is badly wounded and unable to continue the fight, what will they do?"

Ianto looked at her with a guarded expression. After a moment, he sighed heavily. "It would not be good for their morale."

"Will they give up this fight?"

"It is possible."

"And what happens if they see Bhrodi returned to battle, leading the charge?"

Ianto glanced at the other *teulu*; he was having a difficult time fighting against Lady de Shera because he knew she was correct.

"They will be inspired."

Penelope pointed a finger at him. "Exactly," she said firmly. "They will be inspired and King Edward, who would celebrate my husband's death with great gladness, will understand that Wales is still standing. *Bhrodi* is still standing. Don't you see? We must keep up that charade if there is any hope of winning this fight."

The *teulu* began to look at each other, digesting her words, struggling to see things her way. She was correct, of course. But there was also something else.

"You are a *Saesneg*," Ianto finally said. "You would fight against your own king? Your own father?"

Penelope was knocked back a bit; although she knew, in theory, that she would be fighting her own father, the reality of it hit her hard when she heard the words spoken. It made her feel ill to think on it. After a moment, she simply nodded.

"I understand all of that," she said, "and to that regard, I will say only this - when we go into battle, we will leave my father's men alone if at all possible. When I go into battle, I am aiming for Edward."

"But he is your king."

"Not anymore." She looked around at the doubtful faces and it angered her. "I am Lady de Shera, wife of Bhrodi de Shera, hereditary King of Anglesey and Earl of Coventry. I will ride into battle by myself if I have to but I would prefer to do it with you behind me. Will you fight with me? For Bhrodi's sake, will you do it?"

It was a very hard sell. The *teulu* looked at each other, mulling over her words. They were men set in their ways and the thought of a woman riding into battle unsettled them. But times were changing; their liege had taken this woman as his wife and she was the daughter of The Wolfe. She was their own She Wolfe. If she was willing to fight for de Shera, then they should not resist her. They should support her. Ianto finally stood up and looked her in the eye.

"Lord de Shera thinks a great deal of you," he said, manner bordering between reluctance and sincerity. "Because I love and trust my lord, I will think a great deal of you, also, and I will trust you. If you want to ride into battle to create the illusion that Lord de Shera still leads the fight against the Saesneg king, then I will ride with you."

Penelope almost collapsed with relief; she was so sure they were going to deny her. She thought that, perhaps, she was going to have to do this all by herself. The realization that she had some support brought tears to her eyes.

"Thank you," she said softly, sitting heavily on the bench in relief. "Thank you very much."

"And I," Ivor said, looking at Gwyllim, who was nodding. "'Tis a brave woman who would ride into battle for her husband, I say. I will stand with you also."

As Penelope smiled at Ivor, Gwyllim spoke. "If Lord de Shera could speak, he would not let you go," he said, his dark eyes glimmering. "Mayhap we should not tell him."

Penelope grinned, noticing that Yestin, the arrogant one, had not said anything. He was staring at his cup of wine as if in deep thought. He must have felt the stares of everyone because he eventually looked up into the host of faces surrounding him. After a moment, he shook his head and stood up.

"*Ni allaf*," he said as he walked away from the table. "*Rhaid i mi feddwl.*"

Penelope watched him go, looking to Ianto. "What did he say?"

Ianto's gaze lingered on Yestin as the man disappeared from the hall. "He says he must think about it," he told her. "Give him time. Yestin believes women are best seen and not heard. He will come to terms with this, eventually."

Penelope nodded with some regret, thankful that she at least had most of the *teulu* on her side. Kevin came out of the shadows now that his anger at her suggestion had calmed and he sat down beside her.

"Where is the Earl of Coventry's armor?" he asked. "I did not see it in the armory when I was doing an inventory of weapons."

Ianto replied. "It is kept in a safe place," he said. "We do not keep *marchog* armor in a Welsh armory. It might invite those who hate the Saesneg to destroy it."

"Marchog?"

"English knights. Their armor does not get along well with our weapons. They cannot be in the same room together."

He said it with some humor and Kevin wriggled his eyebrows in agreement. He was prevented from saying anything further, however, because the old wardrobe in the shadows began to shake and rattle. The tiny old man who lived in the wardrobe was coming alive again, this time in the midst of a serious discussion. When the door to the wardrobe lurched open, however, the old man did not jump forth; instead, a broadsword came shooting out of the wardrobe and landed heavily on the floor.

Startled, Kevin was the first one to make his way over to it since he was the closest. He picked the broadsword up and as he curiously inspected it, Ianto spoke.

"That is Gareth de Shera's sword," he said.

Kevin looked up at him curiously. "Who is that?"

Ianto grinned. "Lord de Shera's father," he said, pointing to the wardrobe. "You wanted to know where his armor was? Now you know. We keep it in there with the old man to watch over it. No one would dare disturb his mad and troubled sleep."

Kevin grinned because Ianto was. "So that's where it is."

"Aye."

Kevin turned to look at the wardrobe, which was cracked open. "He is listening to us," he commented. "Mayhap he is not as mad as you think he is. He knew enough that we were speaking of Coventry's armor."

"I have often thought that myself," Ianto replied.

Penelope wasn't particularly concerned with the mad uncle and the fact that he was listening in on their conversation. She was more concerned with Kevin's intentions. She was looking at the man quite seriously.

"Why would you volunteer to wear his armor?" she asked. "You do not agree with any of what I am doing."

He cocked an eyebrow. "Mayhap I do not, but you are going to do it regardless of what I think. I cannot let you do it alone."

She eyed him doubtfully. "It will make you a target; you know that."

Kevin nodded. "Of course it will," he said. "But anyone who wears it will be a target. Who would you have more exposed? Me or one of the *teulu*?"

245

She frowned. "Not you," she said. "Kevin, this is not your fight. If you do this and you are caught...."

She couldn't finish because they all knew what the penalty was for a Welsh commander to be captured by the English, a penalty made worse if an English knight was caught fighting for the Welsh. Kevin met her gaze steadily.

"I will not be caught," he told her quietly. "As I said before, I will not let you go into battle alone. Neither will Edward or Thomas, I am guessing. If you go to fight, so do we."

Penelope shook her head. "But *why*?" she demanded. "You did not marry Bhrodi de Shera; I did. This is my fight."

"I do this because we are family," he said. "If you fight, I fight. It has always been that way."

Penelope didn't want to get into a squabble with him, not now. There was so much more to worry about. She looked at Ianto and Ivor and Gwyllim; they seemed to be gazing at her with some trust and perhaps some hope. She would settle for that, at least for now. She knew that full trust would have to be earned and she intended to do just that. For Bhrodi's sake, she would do her very best.

"When Bhrodi left for Dolbadarn Castle, he left with many of his vassals," she said. "He said it was around three thousand men. Where are they now?"

Ianto shrugged. "Those who were not killed in the battle at Dolbadarn fled into the hills with Dafydd," he said. "We were fighting for him, after all. Bhrodi sent most of his men into the mountains with Dafydd, including Bron Llwyd, Bhrodi's last important vassal."

Penelope listened carefully. "How many did he come home with? I am sorry that I did not notice. My attention was on my husband."

As Ianto thought on the numbers returning to Rhydilian, Kevin spoke. "It could not have been more than a couple of hundred," he said to her. "Edward is seeing to them, as you requested."

Penelope turned to look at him. "Is my brother still outside with them?"

"He is."

Penelope sighed faintly as she returned her attention to the *teulu*. It was clear she was pondering a great many things, including their lack of manpower. After a moment, she shook her head in resignation

"We cannot fight Edward with only two hundred men," she said. "He would massacre us. However, if we were to surprise the man or ambush him, we might be more successful."

Kevin leaned on the table to look her in the eye. "Ambush the king? You could never get close enough to do it."

Penelope began to chew her lip in thought. She was working on a tactic, a Scots tactic that she had heard her father discuss at times. *Move with stealth so that the enemy will not detect you until it is too late.* It was an often-used tactic when an army was outnumbered or outmanned. Covert movements worked better than a head-on assault. Aye, she was half-Scots. She could think like one. She had to try.

"Edward's army is all around Aber, is it not?" she asked Ianto.

The man nodded. "It is," he replied. "He has a massive encampment about three miles south of the village. He has reinforcements from Rhuddlan and Caernarfon."

"How many men does Edward have with him?"

"Thousands."

Penelope continued to think on that information, her mind working. "Kevin," she said, "when is an army the most vulnerable?"

Kevin considered her question. "When they are eating," he said. "Or sleeping."

She turned to look at him. "Exactly," she said firmly. "When they are sleeping. What... what if we infiltrate their camp before dawn and try to create as much chaos as we can, burning tents and destroying their corrals so their horses will bolt? If we do this, do you think it will give the Welsh enough time to secure their position against the English? Do you think it would give Dafydd more opportunity to escape Edward?"

Kevin looked at her, his brow furrowed in doubt. "Why would you do something like that?" he asked. "Why not simply find where the Welsh prince is hiding and join his men?"

She grew serious. "Because if we do, they will soon find out that Bhrodi is not among us," she said. "We must take opportunities to strike in Bhrodi's name, and mayhap leave some evidence of him, so that the Welsh and English will think he is still actively fighting for Dafydd. That is the whole point of this, isn't it? To give the illusion that The Serpent is still deadly?"

He was coming to see what she was suggesting, and why. He looked at the *teulu* commanders. "Will what she is suggesting work?" he asked. "Will it give your prince time to secure his position against Edward?"

Ianto looked to the others. It was clear they were mulling it over. "It is possible," Ianto finally said. "Dafydd is in the mountains. If nothing else, creating a diversion with the English would give him time to rest and prepare for the next round of battle."

"Would it be possible to coordinate our ambush on Edward's camp with an attack from Dafydd?" Kevin wanted to know. "We can attack Edward from two sides."

Ianto shook his head. "We do not know exactly where Dafydd is," he said. "It could take days or even weeks to contact him, and Edward will continue to hound him during that time. He may even capture Dafydd. If we infiltrate and burn Edward's camp as Lady de Shera suggests, it will disrupt the English and their momentum. Our only hope would be to do enough damage so it would delay them significantly or, even better, cause them to pull away from Aber."

"Then you are in favor of ambushing Edward's encampment with what men we have left?"

"Aye," Ianto said, sounding hopeful. "The sooner we do it, the better. Edward grows stronger by the hour. We must weaken him as much as we can."

Kevin looked at Penelope, who gazed back at him with a rather confident expression. "Then we must gather the men and prepare for our attack," she said, returning her attention to the *teulu* commanders. "Do we have enough horses for this purpose?"

Ianto was thoughtful. "We took most of them with us, but we can gather more horses from the villagers," he said. "It is possible we can collect what we need."

Penelope was seized with their future plans and what needed to be done. Already, she was thinking ahead and mentally preparing for the onslaught. She was preparing to take on the very man who had sent her to Wales in the first place, a man whom her father served. Edward had once been her king, but no longer. The moment he broke the treaty with the intention of killing Bhrodi was the moment he ceased to be her monarch. Now, she was Welsh. She was The Serpent's mate.

It was going to be a very long and very busy night.

"I want you and your commanders to send out men to collect more horses," she said to Ianto. "Then you will call a meeting of Bhrodi's remaining men for later on tonight. We will tell them of our plans and we must be prepared to ride out of here just after midnight. It is my intention to attack Edward's encampment at dawn and disrupt the man as much as I can. For Bhrodi, we must do this, and we must make sure that everyone knows this is Bhrodi's deed. Everyone must know that this is The Serpent's strike. On behalf of Wales and on behalf of the cause my husband has fought so hard for, we will make it so."

There wasn't much more to be said at that point. The *teulu* had their orders and they knew what needed to be done. As the men excused themselves from the table, Penelope waited until they had vacated the hall before turning to Kevin.

He was sitting in pensive silence, perhaps pondering what his future would bring. More than Penelope, he found himself in a peculiar situation. What he did, he did for her and no one else. As he was pondering his future as a Welsh rebel, Penelope interrupted his thoughts.

"I want you to leave," she told him, her voice low.

Kevin's eyebrows lifted. "What do you mean?"

Penelope crossed her arms stubbornly. "Exactly what I said," she told him. "You are no longer injured. There is no longer any reason for you to remain here. I want you to take Thomas and Edward, and I want you to all leave. Get out of here before I have you thrown out under guard."

Kevin wasn't offended by the command; in fact, he understood it well. He knew why she was doing it.

"You need not worry about us against Edward, Penny," he said, his voice soft. "We are fully aware of what will happen if we are caught."

Frightened for her loyal friend and family, Penelope lashed out. "I want you to go," she said angrily. "Get out, Hage. I do not want you here. I do not want *any* of you here. I will do this myself and without the three of you hanging over me, questioning my every move."

"We are not going anywhere."

"This is not your fight!"

"It is not, but I am fighting it anyway," he said, standing up from the table. "If you do not like it, then you can try to throw me out yourself but I promise I will not make it easy for you."

Kevin quit the hall before she could fight with him further, leaving Penelope frightened and fuming. She thought of the burden of command she had assumed, these men who were so loyal to her putting themselves at risk simply to help her. It was a terrible thing to be responsible for so many men's lives, but it was a burden she would be forced to carry. She felt very strongly that she needed to do this for

Bhrodi and for herself, to maintain his legacy, to help his cause, to fight for his country because he would have done the same for her. What was his was now hers, and the two blended seamlessly. Therefore, she would continue his fight. She was going to attack the King of England with her small band of Welsh rebels and she prayed they would all live through it. *God help us all,* she thought grimly.

She went upstairs to bid her unconscious husband a tender farewell. He wouldn't know that she was leaving, and that was the way she wanted it.

⌘

CHAPTER TWENTY

"I heard rumor that Bhrodi de Shera was injured in battle," Edward said, studying the cup of wine in his hand. "Would you know anything about that, de Wolfe?"

It was the just before dawn in Edward's red and yellow tent outside the village of Aber. Three days after Bhrodi's injury in the church near the edge of town, William was surprised it had taken Edward this long to ask him about it. It was just him, Paris, Kieran, and Edward in the tent. All of the rest of the king's advisors had gone to bed for the night, trying to catch some much-needed sleep before the onslaught on the morrow. Since he had been anticipating the question, he was ready with an answer.

"I have heard that also," he said neutrally.

Edward sipped at his wine. "And I was also told that you sent an English knight home two days ago," he said, turning to look at William. "You would not let anyone see who it was, however. Who was it?"

William met his gaze evenly. "My son."

"*Which* son?"

William stared at him a moment before breaking into a humorless smile. "So you are questioning me now, are you? You, who demanded I betroth one of my daughters to a Welsh warlord so you could undermine him? And now you are suspicious of *my* actions? I find this line of questioning astonishing."

"Maybe so, but you have not answered my question."

"And I am not going to if you have no more faith in me than that," William was growing increasingly agitated. "The only reason I am here is to give you more of a presence in Wales. You want me and my reputation fighting besides you, if for no other reason than to frighten the Welsh knowing that The Wolfe is in their midst. I can just as easily return home and let you fight the Welsh with the host of lesser border commanders you seem intent to surround yourself with. Not one of them is worthy of my attention much less my sword."

Extremely bold words spoken to the monarch. From anyone else, Edward would not have tolerated it, but coming from The Wolfe, he was apt to take what was dealt to him. Edward had very little respect for most men but he had a good deal of respect for William, like his father had, so he was more than willing to allow such insubordination. After a moment, he grinned and waved the man off as if to ease his anger.

"My apologies, then," he said, pouring wine into a cup and pushing it in William's direction. "I simply wanted to know if you'd heard of de Shera's injury."

"I told you I had."

"And I accept that," he said. "But the man is nowhere to be found and it is presumed he has escaped for home."

"If I was wounded, that is where I would go."

Edward nodded slowly, thoughtfully. "As would I," he agreed. "But if there is truth in the fact that de Shera is wounded, that gives me an idea. This could be the opportunity we have been looking for."

William didn't like the sound of that. "What do you mean?"

Edward took a long, deep drink of wine before speaking. "Dafydd is on the run," he said. "It is only a matter of time before we capture him. Already, my scouts are on his scent and soon we will capture him. With that confidence, I am able to focus my energies elsewhere."

William and Paris looked at each other. "Where?" William finally asked.

Edward looked at him. "De Shera, of course," he said. "With de Shera wounded, he will hardly be in a position to defend himself. Tomorrow, you will take a contingent of men to Rhydilian Castle and demand their surrender. Surely your daughter will obey you. If she does not, then you will lay siege to the castle and destroy it."

William stared at him a moment. Then, his eyebrows drew together in disbelief. "You can honestly give me that command in good conscience?" he asked, incredulous. "Do you really think I will do it?"

"You will do it if you value your life and your property," Edward said evenly. "I can quite easily strip you of everything."

"And I can quite easily kill you where you sit and say it was an accident," William fired back in a soft but deadly tone. "Your ten year old son, Alphonso, can assume the throne with all of your vicious advisors by his side and we can all watch as the country tears itself apart because of their greed. Is that truly what you wish?"

Edward stood up, eyeing William and Paris and Kieran; old men they may be but they were quite capable of carrying out the threat. After a moment, Edward simply shook his head.

"Then we are at quite an impasse," he said to William. "I want you to go to Wales and force Rhydilian to surrender, but you will not do it because your daughter is in residence there. You won't do anything I tell you to do. Therefore, since you have refused me, I will simply order another battle commander to ride to Rhydilian and force its surrender. I thought I was doing you a favor by having you accomplish this task, de Wolfe, but I can see that I was mistaken. If that is the case and you will not do what I tell you to do, then you can just take your men and go home. You are more of a hindrance than a help to me here. I do not need you."

William didn't have much more to say to that; he knew, one way or the other, that Edward was heading for Rhydilian and all he could think of was riding ahead of the man and warning them. He thought he might even stay and help them fight Edward off, but if he did, he knew that Castle Questing, and Jordan, would be in a great deal of danger. Edward was fully capable of laying siege to his castle and starving out his family. No, he didn't want that at all. He wasn't sure what more he could do but one thing was for certain; he didn't want another commander marching on Rhydilian. He forced down his pride and his anger, trying to present the picture of someone who was not verging on insubordination.

"You do not need to send another battle commander to Rhydilian," he said after a moment. "If anyone is going to lay siege to the castle, let it be me. My daughter might very well turn it over to me but I doubt she would to anyone else. You must let me try."

Edward eyed William as if he didn't believe him but, after a moment, he too relaxed. With a grin, he picked up the cup of wine he had poured for William and handed it to him.

"Of course I will let you try," he said. "I would like to have the castle intact and you are my best hope for that. Take de Shera alive if you can help it. I have plans for the man."

William sipped at the wine. "What plans?"

"The same plans I have for Dafydd when I capture him," Edward replied. "I have a special schedule for him."

William still wasn't following him. "What schedule is that?"

Edward went to collect his own cup of wine again. "Dafydd will be tried for high treason against the king," he said. "He will be hung, disemboweled, and drawn and quartered. There are too many rebels, William. I can no longer simply throw them in the Tower of London and hope others will not rebel as well. Nay; I must set an example with Dafydd. The man will be made an example of as a promise of what will happen to anyone who betrays me."

William tried not to look too horrified. "And you intend the same thing with de Shera?"

Edward nodded. "When I capture him, I do indeed," he said. He took a big gulp of wine. "When the time comes, keep your daughter away from London. You do not wish for her to see what we will do to her husband. It is a nasty business. Mayhap I will send a fine husband her way to make up for my lack of judgment in marrying her to a Welsh rebel. That will make things right with her, I am sure."

William just looked at him; then he glanced over at Paris and Kieran. Both men had varied degrees of disgust in their expressions. Aye, they were all thinking the same thing - that Edward often lived in a world without reality. He found it very easy to play with other people's lives. Now he was playing with William's. After a moment, William returned his focus to Edward.

"When do you want me to ride for Rhydilian?" he asked.

Edward shrugged. "Tomorrow, mayhap," he said. "Or the next day. Let us see how tomorrow fares with the Welsh. I would like to close in on Dafydd for certain by then. My scouts are fairly certain they know where he might be, so let us see what the day brings."

William simply nodded; he didn't have anything else to say. He was feeling ill and angry, his mind already racing ahead to Rhydilian and thinking of what he was going to do when he got there. One thing was for certain; he would not turn Bhrodi over to Edward. Therefore, he had some planning to do. He never thought he'd see the day when he would be the rebel in the bunch.

As William set down his wine and prepared to bid his king a good eve, a knight dressed in Edward's tunic of gold and yellow stuck his head in through the tent opening.

"Your Grace," he said breathlessly. "We have invaders in camp."

Edward set down his wine. "Where?" he demanded. "Who?"

The knight shook his head. "Sentries sounded the alarm on the western perimeter," he said. "I heard someone say de Shera is here."

Edward was seized with fury. "De Shera?" he shouted. "Send my squires in here! Send me my knights! I am going to catch that bastard, do you hear? Send them all in!"

The knight fled, and William, Paris, and Kieran ran from the tent before Edward could further monopolize them or, worse, put them into action. As they ran for William's encampment at the southeastern portion of Edward's spread, William suddenly came to a halt and grabbed Paris.

"It's impossible," he hissed. "Bhrodi could not possibly be launching a raid against the encampment. The man was on death's door!"

Paris was pale. "Mayhap he could not, but we both knew who could," he said grimly. "God help us all, if she sees this as her duty to avenge her wounded husband...."

William's good eye opened wide with horror. "She wouldn't...."

Paris grabbed him and, between him and Kieran, began shoving William in the direction of his camp.

"Get your weapons and your horse," Paris shouted. "We must find her before Edward does!"

⌘

Penelope, Kevin, Edward, Thomas, and one hundred and eighty-one of Bhrodi's men had ridden from Rhydilian sometime after midnight on the morning after Bhrodi's return home. They rode hard for the straits of Menai where they took a ferry across the fast-moving water. It had taken six ferry crossings to get everyone over and by that time, they had lost a great deal of time, so they had made haste towards Aber under the nearly-full moon. The horses were being pushed to the limit because they knew their attack would only be effective if they were to accomplish it before sunrise when Edward's camp would be unsuspecting. Time was ticking.

Ianto had taken them along the old Roman road that ran across north Wales. It was also the road that the party from Questing had traveled on to reach Rhydilian. The land was hilly and rocky, and they could smell the salt upon the sea breeze that blew steadily inland from the north.

It was a band of rebels filled with a purpose. Since Penelope's mother had denied her most of her armor and mail, and she was without her broadsword also, she wore a mail coat that was too big for her frame, borrowed from the Welsh armory. Her dark hair was braided and wound tightly around her head, covered by a woolen cap. But the sword she bore was Bhrodi's, having made it back with the man when they had returned him home. It had been in the wagon bed with him.

A massive thing with one serrated side and a hilt in the shape of a snake, it was a wicked-looking weapon that foretold Bhrodi's reputation. Any man would know simply to gaze upon it that it was The Serpent's blade. It was very heavy and unlike her own broadsword, but she carried it with pride and confidence. Even if Bhrodi could not continue the fight against the English, his sword would.

Kevin was at the head of the pack as they charged on in the darkness; he wore Coventry's armor, a breastplate that was too small for him and shoulder plate that barely covered his enormous shoulders. Bhrodi, too, had issue with the size of the armor his father had left him since he was quite a large man and his father had been big but not enormous. Still, Bhrodi had worn it on occasion just as Kevin was wearing it now, old and well-made armor that bore the crest of de Shera. He also wore the helm, which had oddly been modeled after Anglo-Saxony head protection. It was very distinctive.

The *teulu* commanders had acknowledged that Kevin looked very much as Bhrodi did when wearing the armor, an opinion that had been confirmed when the rest of Bhrodi's men saw Kevin emerge from the keep. Knowing they had brought a badly wounded Bhrodi back to Rhydilian, the sight of the man rising from his deathbed to ride back into battle had both their superstition and their awe fed. Even now, as they thundered towards the southern end of Aber where Edward's camp was located, they kept looking at Kevin as if the man was a phantom. The Serpent in all of his glory was indeed immortal and, as Penelope and Kevin and the *teulu* commanders had speculated, it was a boon for morale. With Bhrodi leading the rebels, they were riding high on patriotism and excitement.

For Penelope, it was an odd experience riding with the Welsh, but in the same breath, she was filled with determination to aid the cause her husband had fought so valiantly for. She couldn't think of the fact that they could very well engage her father shortly; she had to keep her focus on Edward and in the burning of his camp. This was all about Edward, after all. She found herself fervently hoping that her father had decided to go home although she knew that would not be the case. The Wolfe would stay, in any battle, until the bitter end.

Thomas and Edward, as she had known, were determined to come with her as she led the raid. At first, they'd shown the same reluctance that Kevin and the *teulu* commanders had, but they, too, realized she would go with or without them. With resignation, they began to help her plan out the details of the attack and they further assisted in helping the Welsh produce torches that would be used to create havoc. Working side by side with the Welsh in preparation for battle was, much like their sister had discovered, a very odd experience but they, too, had come to see one thing; the Welsh were very hard workers and very devoted to their cause.

Sometimes with the English, there wasn't passion behind their actions because they were often the ones doing the conquering. It wasn't as if they were defending their countries or the very lives of their families. But with the Welsh, that was exactly what they were doing - they were trying to preserve their very lives, and there was a fire in that determination that the English found admirable. When the Welsh party departed Rhydilian for Edward's camp, Thomas and Edward found they were quite proud to go along. There was a sense of accomplishment that they had never experienced before, misplaced as it was.

An hour and a half after crossing the Menai strait, they began to see the glow of campfires on the horizon as they neared Pen-y-Bren, a small town that had been built around the ancient road. Edward's camp was off to the northeast, near a cluster of hills, and they could see the spread plainly. If the sentries were vigilant, which Penelope suspected they were, their group may have already been sighted.

Quickly, she lifted her hand to Kevin, who in turn lifted his big arm and called the entire party to a halt. The men were watching Kevin more than they were watching her, so commands were funneled through him. Like wraiths, the group disappeared into a dark cluster of woods to prepare for the attack.

"Light the torches," Penelope ordered quietly.

Men began to rummage in their saddlebags for flint and stone while still others pulled forth pieces of wood and rags soaked in fat that they had brought with them from Rhydilian. They worked quickly, quietly, and efficiently. Soon enough, torches began to flare and the dark copse of trees began to fill with light.

It was light that could been seen from a distance and they were all well aware of that fact; therefore, the key was not to linger. The more they lingered, the better the chance of Edward's encampment being prepared for them or, worse, riding out to meet them. If that was the case, then they would surely fail, so as soon as the torches began to burn steadily, Penelope ordered everyone mounted. As men vaulted onto their horses and steadied their torches, she began to pace among the ranks.

"As we discussed earlier this evening, our purpose is to slow Edward's momentum against Dafydd," she said loudly, listening as Ianto, Ivor and Gwyllim translated her words into Welsh for those men who did not understand English. "We will burn all that we can and escape the camp. You will head back to Rhydilian without waiting to regroup, and you will not engage anyone in fighting if you can help it. We are outmanned by the English so our purpose is to create havoc and do as much damage as we can before retreating. Do you understand?"

As the words were translated, men began to yell in the affirmative. If the men seemed curious as to why de Shera hadn't said anything yet and why it was his wife relaying battle commands, they did not say so. For the past several hours, they had been riding high on their plans to attack the *Saesneg* encampment and the fact that de Shera rode with them was enough to bolster their courage. In fact, when Kevin spurred his charger out of the trees and thundered north towards Edward's camp, the men filtered out after him in firm support. Penelope scrambled to mount her charger and, collecting a torch handed to her by Edward, she and her brothers brought up the rear of the group.

Edward's camp before dawn had been surprisingly busy as the Welsh raiding party closed in on them. Near dawn, the sentries hadn't been as vigilant as they should have been because Kevin was nearly upon them when the cries of alarm finally when up. The first thing Kevin did was kick one of the sentries in the head as he rode past, throwing the man to the ground as Welsh spears, thrown by some of Bhrodi's men, took down three more sentries. Coming to the first tent,

Kevin threw the torch onto the top of it and the oiled fabric began to burn.

The Welsh poured into the eastern edge of the camp, throwing spears at the inhabitants and throwing torches at the tents. It was instant chaos as the camp came alive and men began to grab weapons, preparing to fight the onslaught. By the time Penelope, Thomas, and Edward entered the camp, there was a good amount of chaos with men running in their direction. Thomas and Edward were dressed much as their sister was, in the dark tunics and woolen caps of the Welsh to disguise them and they, too, were uncomfortable without their expensive plate armor, but it could not be helped. They had to travel, and fight, lightly in order to be convincing. Edward knew they were looking for the king's tent and, having spent the past few weeks with the man, knew it would be towards the center of the camp. He motioned to his siblings.

"Come this way!" he bellowed.

The three of them tore off, having no idea where Kevin or the *teulu* commanders had gone. There seemed to be men everywhere and several tents were already burning furiously. In the dark of night, with sparks soaring into the air, Penelope and her brothers thundered through the encampment. Penelope had tossed her torch onto a particularly large tent, knowing it must be someone of importance, and proceeded to draw Bhrodi's sword. She wanted everyone to see it, to know he was back in their midst. The Serpent had returned.

Just as the three of them drew around a corner, Edward brought them to an abrupt halt. He pointed off to the northeast where a massive tent and a corral with several excited horses were situated, set off from the rest of the encampment. There were also several soldiers around it and even more that were starting to mount the horses. They would soon be coming after them.

"That is Edward's tent," he said quickly. "If we are going to hit it, do it now while the men are still mounting. After you throw your torch, Thomas, ride as fast as you can out of here. We must get out now because Edward's men are arming themselves and mounting. We do not want them chasing and catching up to us."

Thomas nodded sharply and spurred his charger forward. Edward's guard saw him coming and rushed forward to meet him. Penelope and Edward were right behind him, however, and Penelope began swinging Bhrodi's massive sword, making contact on more than one occasion. It was such a heavy sword that even though she was adept at sword fighting, it wasn't long before she grew exhausted. But her intervention had helped Thomas; he had managed to launch the torch onto Edward's tent and the material had caught fire.

Seeing the king's tent begin to burn was all the confirmation Penelope needed to turn for home. The fire was spreading rapidly and there would be no opportunity for them to put it out before it did significant damage. Maybe the king was inside and it would damage him as well. She could only hope. Every lick of flame had Bhrodi's name on it and she took great delight in the destruction. But as she watched the fire burn, she failed to notice that two of Edward's guard had been able to mount and were now charging out after her. Startled by the sight of men nearly upon her, she dug her heels into her charger and launched herself off in the only direction that wasn't blocked. She headed south.

Separated from her brothers and from the rest of the Welsh, she thundered south where there were several smaller encampments spread out. She could hear the rush of horses behind her but she didn't dare turn around to look; if she could hear them, they must indeed be close. Off to her left was an open area and she thought to gain ground on them there because her charger was very fast; the horse had Spanish Jenette blood in it and had a good amount of speed.

But it wasn't fast enough. She realized one of the soldiers had managed to get up beside her and he took a swipe at her head with his sword. Penelope ducked, barely avoiding being beheaded, and she abruptly pulled her horse up so the pursuers ran past. Reining the horse to the left, and heading south again, she picked up a couple of more soldiers on her tail and she dodged between a pair of tents, emerging on the other side to a blockade of English soldiers. There were three of them and they had effectively cut her off. When she tried to turn around, four more men came up behind her.

She was boxed in. Greatly disappointed, and very frightened, Penelope held tightly to her excited horse as she eyed the English soldiers.

"You Welsh bastard," one man snarled. "We've got you now. You'll pay for what you've done."

Penelope still had Bhrodi's sword in her hand and she lifted it; there was no one around to help her, no one to save her. She knew that her life as a Welsh raider and her life in general was at an end. It had been a good life; she had no complaints. She was simply sorry that she would never be able to grow old with her husband, or see his face when she presented him with their first son. Aye, it was a terrible regret but she couldn't linger on any of that now. Death was approaching and she intended to meet it well.

Rather than embarrass her father with her capture or risk a horrible, tortuous death, she would die the only way she knew how. She would die like the knight she was trained to be, for the blood of The Wolfe flowed in her veins. She knew that her life would be coming to an end very shortly and she would not go down without a fight.

"Very well," she hissed. "Do what you must but know that I will not make an easy kill for you. If you want me, come and get me."

She wielded the sword defensively, spinning her horse around because of the knights behind her. She was positive one of them was going to sneak up behind her and gore her.

"Do it!" she yelled. "If you are going to kill me, then get on with it!"

It was not a Welshman who had yelled at them. It was, in fact, a woman who spoke flawless English. That moment of confusion cost them because as they looked at each other in bewilderment, great armored horses from the darkness swept upon them and, as Penelope watched, the seven English soldiers who had cornered her when down in a bloodied and loud collapse. Men fell, horses ran off, but nothing came close to touching her. She remained still as stone right in the center of the action. When she finally looked at the horses who had charged in from the darkness, she came face to face with her father.

"Papa!" Penelope gasped. "You have come!"

William was in battle armor from head to toe, every inch the mighty and formidable Wolfe. He looked at his daughter with something between great anger and great relief.

"Get out of here," he told her. "Ride back to Rhydilian and stay there. I will not be far behind."

"But... Papa!" she cried softly. "What do you mean? Why are you coming?"

Before William could answer, Kieran charged up beside her and gave her horse a shove. "You heard your father," Kieran boomed. "Go back to Rhydilian and wait for us!"

Penelope was terribly confused but she did as she was told. As she turned her horse around, Paris rode up, blocking her off.

"Did de Shera come with you?" he demanded.

Penelope shook her head. "He is badly wounded," she said. "But you already know that. Why did you ask?"

Paris was brittle with fear, with frustration. "Because men are shouting that they have captured de Shera," he snapped. "*Who* are they speaking of, Penny?"

Penelope's jaw dropped and her eyes immediately filled with tears. "Kevin is dressed in Bhrodi's armor," she was starting to weep. She spun her horse in the direction of her father. "If they think they have Bhrodi, then they have Kevin instead. Papa, you must save him!"

Filled with panic, Kieran was already racing for the center of the encampment. Paris, giving Penelope an expression of pure disbelief, tore off after him. Only William remained behind, his gaze on his youngest daughter.

He realized he couldn't become angry with her. She was doing what he would have done in the same situation, what any of them would have done, to avenge the person they loved. He would have done it for her a thousand times over, and she for him. She was a de Wolfe at heart, loyal to those she loved, and he simply couldn't become angry. But he was very frightened for her. He struggled to maintain his calm.

"You will head south across this field," he told her. "There is an old road at the end of the meadow that runs all the way to the coast. Follow it and it will lead you back to the ferry that crosses to Anglesey."

Penelope reined her animal towards him, reaching out to grasp his hand. "I love you, Papa," she said, tears on her cheeks. "Thank you... for saving me, thank you. And thank you for sending Bhrodi back to me."

It was no time for a family reunion. He squeezed her hand and let go. "Go home," he told her again. "I will be there as soon as I can."

"But why?"

"Just *go*, Penelope," he told her, reining his horse around to follow Paris and Kieran's paths. "Get out of here. I will see you later."

He started to take off and she yelled after him. "Thomas and Edward are here, too!" she cried. "Find them, Papa!"

She swore she heard the man groan as she, too, took off into the night.

⌘

CHAPTER TWENTY-ONE

Kevin was beginning to wonder if he hadn't been knocked off his charger by the same morning star that had injured Bhrodi. It had all happened fairly early in the raid and he didn't remember much other than the chain of the morning star wrapping around his arm and yanking him right off the horse. He'd fallen awkwardly and had landed on his forehead and face, which had knocked him unconscious. When he'd come to, he was being dragged by two of Edward's knights into a tent on the northern perimeter of the encampment that had not been burned in the raid.

The smell of smoke was heavy in the early morning sky as the knights tossed him into the tent. There were more men there, men with swords and armed with crossbows, and they had promptly beat him. He was wearing armor so the damage wasn't too bad until someone caught him in the mouth with a booted foot and knocked a couple of teeth loose. Blood poured and his mouth was full of it, but the beating didn't stop. It went on for several long minutes until they simply grew weary of kicking him.

So he lay on the ground and pretended to be injured. He was positive that if he sat up or tried to rise that they would start beating him again, so he simply remained on the cold, damp earth, smelling the acrid smoke and listening to the sounds of battle die away. He cursed himself for being stupid enough to have gotten caught.

Kevin wasn't entirely sure how long he lay there, listening, but he was suddenly pulled into a sitting position as someone yanked the helm off his head. Others were yanking at his plate protection, using dirks to slice through the leather straps and pull it off his body. He was roughed up by the stripping and more began to kick at him. On the breastplate that he had worn was the de Shera coat of arms and the motto, nicked and faded with age. The soldier who had pulled it off of him studied it closely.

"What's this?" the soldier demanded. "*Meam, legatum meum, quia Deus*. What does that mean?"

"That is Latin," a man said as he pushed into the tent. He yanked the armor out of the soldier's hand and looked at it closely. He read the passage over a couple of times. "My honor, my legacy, for God. That is what it says. And I have seen this crest before; it is the de Shera crest."

On his knees, Kevin was watching the man quite closely. He was very tall, with graying blond hair, and from the moment he had stepped into the tent, the atmosphere seemed to change. Men nearly cowered at his feet, which led Kevin to believe that the man standing before him was none other than Edward the First.

He had only met the man once, when he had been quite young, but had not seen him in at least twenty years. When the man finally looked at him, Kevin waited for the inevitable recognition but the man continued to gaze at him with no remembrance in his face. The eyes were dark and hollow.

"This is Coventry's coat of arms," the man pointed out, "and you were the only raider we saw that was wearing any armor."

"Welsh do not typically wear armor," Kevin replied.

"They do if their father was the Earl of Coventry. If *you* are, in fact, the Earl of Coventry."

Kevin gazed steadily at the man; he knew he was in grave danger with either path he chose – if he admitted he was de Shera or if he told the truth, that he was an English knight. He wasn't yet willing to provide all of the answers to their questions because he wasn't willing to hasten his demise. After a moment, he looked away.

"I borrowed the armor," he said. It was not a lie.

The man was not amused. "You may as well confess your identity," he said. "The armor and the name of de Shera inscribed on the broadsword tell me the entire story. It is unfortunate that you and I could not meet under better circumstances, de Shera."

Kevin could hear the hisses going up all around, like ripples in a pond, rippling out of the tent to the men beyond and spreading through the camp like wildfire. *De Shera*! They were saying. He, too, had noticed the name de Shera inscribed on the broadsword he had borrowed and it was like a calling card, announcing his identity. Or, at least, his stolen identity. He looked up at the tall man.

"I suppose it would not do any good to tell you that I am not Bhrodi de Shera, would it?" he asked rather drolly.

Edward lifted his eyebrows in feigned interest. "Who else could you possibly be?" he asked mockingly. "Another Welsh prince I do not know about yet?"

"There could be more who are in hiding," Kevin replied, "like Dafydd."

The man's expression tightened. "What do you know about Dafydd?"

Kevin shook his head. "I wish I knew more than I did," he said. "If I knew where he was, I would be with him now and not in the middle of an English camp."

The man regarded him closely. "You speak English extremely well," he said. "In fact, I cannot detect a Welsh accent at all. That is a surprise, de Shera. But, then again, you did foster in England so I suppose your mastery of the language would be impeccable."

"May I know who I am speaking with?"

The glimmer returned to the man's eyes. "I am called Edward," he said, somewhat casually. "I will soon be your king so I suppose introductions are in order. It was foolish to leave Anglesey, de Shera. You were safe there. Why did you leave?"

So his suspicions were correct; the King of England was standing before him. Kevin knew he could not have been in a worse position had he deliberately tried. Kneeling before Edward was like kneeling before a viper; it was only a matter of time before the man would strike. But he faced the question without fear.

"If your countrymen were in peril, would you not heed the call?" he asked.

Edward shrugged. "Mayhap," he replied, "but you have put yourself in grave danger. Mayhap it will be enough to pry Dafydd out of his hiding place in an attempt to rescue you. You have made a valuable prisoner, you know."

Kevin caught movement out of the corner of his eye, aiming for his head, and he lashed out a hand, grabbing a booted foot and twisting hard. Bones snapped and the man who had been kicking at Kevin's head screamed in pain as he went down in a heap. Kevin maintained his composure as he continued to face the king.

265

"All warfare has risks," he said as if nothing violent had just occurred. "I am equally sure Dafydd will not come out of hiding to attempt to rescue me. What will you do then?"

Edward had a hint of a smile on his lips. "What would *you* do?"

Kevin shrugged. "I suppose traitors cannot be tolerated, so I would kill the traitor. Is that what you intend to do?"

Edward stared at him; it was an appraising sort of stare, calculating, as if he was weighing his options. The man whose leg Kevin had broken was still lying on the ground groaning and Edward watched as a pair of men carried him out. After a moment, the king averted his gaze thoughtfully.

"You broke poor Hubert's leg," he commented.

"The man was going to kick me in the head."

"Your reflexes are impressive," Edward said as he pulled up a three-legged stool with an embroidered leather sling-like seat. He sat heavily. "You are a man of great breeding and skill, de Shera. I shouldn't like to kill you but you have left me little choice. I wed you to the daughter of England's greatest knight yet still you rebelled against me. What am I to do now?"

Kevin tried to put himself in Bhrodi's shoes. It was an odd experience, really, pretending to be a man who should have very well been his mortal enemy. Not only was the man Welsh, but he had married the only woman Kevin had ever loved. This entire fiasco was because of Penelope and still, Kevin found himself defending her, now with his life at risk. He was either very stupid of very loyal; he wasn't sure which.

"The marriage contract was for peace," Kevin said after a moment. "That goes both ways. That means you must be peaceful as well, and clearly you were not. Your presence in Wales demonstrates that."

Surprisingly, Edward didn't become angry. He actually appeared thoughtful. "Wales cannot rule itself, de Shera," he said after a moment. "There are several different kingdoms and many different princes, or at least there were, but there has never been one man able to bring them all together."

"So you intend to be that man?"

"Would you prefer that Wales tears itself apart from in-fighting?"

It was a good argument, but Kevin shook his head. "You are using that excuse to mask your greed," he said. "Wales does not need English rule."

"Wales cannot survive by Welsh rule."

Kevin was opening his mouth to reply when the tent flap snapped back and armored men were charging in. He turned around to see his father standing there, his face pale with shock, and Paris standing right behind him. Both men looked at Kevin with expressions of great astonishment and the ambiance in the air instantly changed; there was grief there as well. It became moody and heavy as Kevin regarded the pair. It was Edward who spoke first.

"Ah," he said, extending a hand at Kevin. "I believe you know Bhrodi de Shera. He married de Wolfe's daughter. Did you not tell him that he was no longer supposed to fight for Wales once he married her?"

Kieran was in no mood for jokes or cryptic statements. He looked at Kevin as if everyone in the tent had gone mad.

"De Shera?" he repeated, baffled.

Kevin couldn't have his father reveal the truth, not now when Edward believed him to be Bhrodi. To reveal that he was, in fact, a son of Hage would only convolute the issue. Moreover, it would embarrass his father greatly and perhaps even land him in trouble. In order to protect his father, and everyone else associated, Kevin had to make sure the man understood what was happening.

"My lord," he nodded at his father. "So we meet again but in not so festive an occasion as a wedding. Did your lady wife make it safely home to Castle Questing?"

Kieran was at a loss. He stared at Kevin, shaking his head in pure bewilderment. "What madness is this?" he hissed. "What are you doing here?"

"He led the raid tonight, of course," Edward said. "Someone should have really told him he was supposed to fight for me now. He has voided his marriage contract with his treacherous behavior."

Kevin's head snapped to Edward. "You voided that contract when you refused to cease your conquest of Wales," he said. "It was already broken when I took up arms to protect Wales so if anyone is to blame, it is you."

Harsh words against the king. Edward's amiability fled and he stood up, his expression harsh on Kevin. "If you think to...."

He was cut off when William burst into the tent. One look at Kevin on his knees in front of Edward and the man nearly lost his mind; or, at least it appeared that way. He swooped down on Kevin and grabbed the man by the neck.

"Get up," he snarled. "How dare you disgrace everything you have sworn to respect. What in the hell are you doing here?"

Kevin was roughly pulled to his feet. Now, his father was in on it and between him and William, they had Kevin around the neck and shoulders. Paris, not to be left out, reached in and grabbed him by the hair. Edward put up his hands.

"Wait," he stopped them. "You will not abuse him; not yet, anyway. De Wolfe, I realize you are angry with him, but I have more questions."

William's face was taut with rage. "Why? There is nothing more he can tell you that you probably haven't already figured out."

Edward shook his head firmly. "De Shera is a hereditary king," he said. "You will not treat him with such disrespect."

Now it was coming clear to William that Edward believed Kevin to be Bhrodi. Truthfully, when William had entered the tent, he hadn't been sure and that is why he had behaved as he had. Now, he wasn't sure if he was more relieved or more horrified to know that Edward believed Kevin to be the Welsh warlord. One thing was certain, however; he had to get Kevin out of here before someone, somehow, revealed the truth. The king would not act kindly to Kevin Hage posing as Bhrodi de Shera. It would more than likely see Kevin executed before the day was out. Therefore, William went into aggression mode; he yanked on Kevin's neck, pulling him in the direction of the tent flap.

"He is *my* son," William spat. "He has dishonored *my* daughter and *my* family. I will deal with him and you will not stop me. He is *mine*."

Truthfully, Edward had never seen William so furious. It was intimidating. Therefore, he backed off because he had little choice. He was afraid William would do him great bodily harm if he intervened in what William was viewing as a family matter. In a way, it was, because Bhrodi had tarnished the de Wolfe name with his rebellion. No, Edward didn't blame William in the least but he was surprised by the man's ferocity.

"Very well," he said. "Do what you must but I want him alive when you are done with him. Do you understand?"

William simply growled, pulling Kevin from the tent as Kieran slapped his son on the back of the skull. Paris still had him by the hair. Between the three of them, they dragged him from the tent.

The sun was rising now with shades of pink across the sky. It was surprisingly clear this morning except for the haze of smoke settled about the camp. Kevin was literally being dragged by his father and both uncles across the camp, all the while being mildly abused by them. He knew it was for show but their anger genuinely concerned him. He was too old to be spanked but he wasn't sure his father would remember that. William continued to drag and drag until they reached a clearing just south of the main encampment. William's camp was several hundred feet off to the left. Once they reached the clearing, William let him go, but only for the moment. A massive fist to Kevin's jaw sent the man to his knees.

"What in the hell were you thinking to pose as Bhrodi de Shera?" William growled. "Do you know the trouble you are in right now? Why did you do it, Kevin?"

Kevin was still on his knees, rubbing his jaw as he looked up at William. "You are not going to like my answer. "

"I already do not like it!"

Kevin sighed heavily as he moved his jaw around to make sure it wasn't broken. "Penelope was coming to raid Edward's camp," he said. "We could not dissuade her. I could not let her come alone."

William already knew the answer before Kevin confirmed it. Suddenly, he didn't feel quite so angry. He felt weak and overwhelmed. With a grunt, he wiped wearily at his eyes.

"She is avenging de Shera; I understand that," he said, his tone considerably less angry. "But why are you dressed as the man? I do not understand."

Kevin's manner softened. "She was not avenging him," he said quietly. "She was taking up arms in his stead. She is a knight, Uncle William; she must follow her instincts. I am wearing his armor because she was afraid the Welsh would not follow her unless they thought Bhrodi was riding at her side. She wanted the Welsh to see me, think it was Bhrodi, and be inspired. The man has been badly wounded doing what he believed in and she did not want his sacrifice to be in vain."

All three men were looking at Kevin with incredible sadness. William eventually put his hands to his face in disbelief, rubbing at his scratchy cheeks as if it would help him think. He was struggling to understand all of it but all he could see was death and heartache. Still, he understood it completely. He knew why Kevin did what he did and he utterly understood Penelope's actions. He was starting to feel sick.

"I did this," he muttered. "I made the decision to marry her to de Shera. I am a warrior; I know these wars in Wales have been going on longer than I have been alive but when James was killed, I was eager to stop the wars so that I would not lose anymore sons. Now I have placed my daughter on the front lines by marrying her to a Welsh warlord and it is quite possible I will lose her instead. I do not want to outlive my baby."

Kevin staggered to his feet. "Did you see her tonight?"

William had tears in his eyes. "Aye," he said hoarsely. "She was set upon by some English and we killed them in order to allow her to escape."

"What about Thomas and Edward? They rode with us."

William shook his head. He blinked and tears popped onto his cheeks. "I did not see them," he murmured. "Kevin, you must return to Rhydilian, do you hear? Edward wants it. You must head back now and prepare the defenses."

Kevin stared at him. "Edward wants Rhydilian?" he repeated, confused. "But... why? Wasn't that what de Shera's marriage to Penny was supposed to prevent?"

"I do not have time to explain," William snapped. "Do what I say and go back to Rhydilian. I will follow as soon as I can. But right now, I must search the camp and make sure Thomas and Edward have not been killed. I must find my boys."

It was a heartbreaking thought. The man had done all he could to prevent losing more children and now he was faced with just that prospect. As William staggered off, heading towards the encampment again, Kevin, Paris, and Kieran watched him go. When Kevin turned back to his father with some uncertainty, he was startled when Paris lashed out a big fist and hit Kieran squarely on the jaw. Kieran fell to one knee, seeing stars, and Paris grabbed Kevin by the arm.

"Get out of here," he told him, thrusting him away. "You attacked us both and escaped. Do what William told you to do and go back to Rhydilian, Kevin. Go *now!*"

Kevin ignored Paris' pushing and reached down to help his father up. "I did not attack either of you," he said. "If I...."

He was cut off when Kieran, regaining his balance, took a slug at Paris that sent the man flying onto his backside.

"Aye, you did," Kieran said, breathing heavily. "You attacked us both and escaped. If you do not get out of here, I am going to forget I am your father and pound you within an inch of your life."

Kieran jumped on top of Paris and they started throwing punches again. Kevin stood there, his mouth open at the sight of two old knights in hand to hand combat. In spite of their ages, they were landing some heavy blows, and he shook his head with exasperation.

"You are both mad!" he hissed. "What in the hell are you doing?"

Paris shoved Kieran's face into the mud. "Unless they see that we are bruised and bloodied, they will not believe that you attacked us," he spat. "Go now before we pull you into this fray!"

Kevin didn't need to be told again. He understood what they were doing and he found it extremely endearing. But he had expected no less. With a grin, he ran off into the breaking dawn, heading south towards the same road that Penelope had taken.

As the sun rose and a clear day loomed, Paris and Kieran beat each other to a pulp as Kevin escaped the clutches of the English king.

⌘

CHAPTER TWENTY-TWO

Rhydilian Castle

It was just after midday when Penelope came pounding up the road on her weary charger towards Rhydilian Castle. The few sentries she had left were on the walls and she could hear them shouting as she approached. By the time she reached the crest of the hill, the great iron gates were slowly creaking open.

The day was bright and cool as she entered the bailey and reined her frothing horse to a halt. She was exhausted and practically fell from the saddle, struggling to gain her footing. The flight from Aber before dawn and through damp fields until she reached the ferry had left her brittle and edgy. Only when she had crossed into Anglesey did she allow herself a measure of peace, but not completely until she reached Rhydilian. Now, she could finally relax somewhat. As she gained her balance and turned for the keep, the first familiar face she saw was Gwyllim's.

The man was practically running at her from across the muddied bailey. He had been on the walls when she had approached the gates and had nearly killed himself trying to get down into the bailey. Penelope moved towards him.

"Gwyllim!" she gasped. "You made it back. Who else has returned?"

Gwyllim reached out to steady the very weary lady. In truth, he was both surprised and glad to see her. As the morning had passed into afternoon and she hadn't appeared, he was increasingly worried that something had happened. Now, all he could feel was relief.

"Ianto is here," he told her, "but Ivor has not yet returned."

It was a grim statement. Penelope's fingers dug into his arm as she held on to him. "And my brothers?"

Gwyllim pointed to the keep. "Inside."

Her heart soared. "Both of them?"

"Aye."

"And Bhrodi?"

"He is awake," Gwyllim said, hesitance in his manner. "My lady, he was asking for you when he awoke and you were not here. Yestin had remained behind, as you recall, and he told him that you had left Rhydilian but he did not tell him why. Lord de Shera soon came to realize that most everyone had gone and when I returned, he made me tell him everything. I had little choice."

He seemed worried but Penelope couldn't muster the strength. All she knew was that she had to see her husband and that she would deal with his anger when the time came. It seemed like such a trivial thing, a little slip of anger, considering everything they'd been through. She broke off from Gwyllim, running those last few yards towards the keep. Her heart was pounding and in her exhaustion, her emotions were running wild. She slipped in the mud and landed on one knee but it did not deter her; with muddied hands, she scrambled up the steps that led into the keep, desperate to get inside.

The guts of the keep were cool and dark, lit only by what light managed to filter in through the lancet window. It was quiet and still. Bolting into the small feasting hall, she came into immediate contact with Thomas and Edward. They had heard her come in through the keep entry and were already moving towards her. Penelope threw her arms around Edward, the closest, and nearly strangled him.

"You are safe!" she exclaimed. "Praise God you are both safe."

Thomas moved to hug her when she was finished squeezing Edward. "We were nearly the first ones to return," Edward said. "We have been waiting frantically for any word of you and Kevin."

Penelope's excitement came to a halt with neck-breaking speed and she looked at her brothers with tears in her eyes.

"Kevin was captured," she said hoarsely. "I was nearly captured, too, but Papa and Uncle Kieran and Uncle Paris saved me. They had heard that Bhrodi had been captured in the raid but I told them that it was Kevin disguised as Bhrodi. They went to help him."

Edward was closer to Kevin than Thomas was; in fact, they were the best of friends. His features were particularly sorrowful.

"Damnation," he rumbled. "The English will kill him in any case; if they think he is Bhrodi or if he confesses to being an English knight fighting for the Welsh. Either way, the man is dead."

Bhrodi. Penelope's thoughts swiftly returned to her husband at the mention of his name and she could wait no longer to see him. She let go of her brothers and ran for the stairs that led to the upper levels.

"I must see to my husband," she said as she moved. "Remain here and keep an accounting of who returns. I will return after I've seen to Bhrodi."

"Be careful," Thomas called after her. "He was none too happy to find out you rode for battle!"

Penelope simply waved him off as she raced for the third floor of the keep where the master's chamber was situated. She was filthy, exhausted, sweaty and smelly, and in this form she burst into the chamber that smelled heavily of peppermint and vinegar. Her gaze immediately sought out her husband, who was lying flat on his back upon the big bed. He was conscious, however, and when their eyes met, Penelope raced to the bed and fell to her knees beside it. Her muddy fingers clutched at him.

"Bhrodi," she said breathlessly, "I...."

Bhrodi cut her off; he reached down and grabbed his smelly, filthy wife and pulled her up onto the bed with him. His arms, still strong in spite of his physical condition, wrapped tightly around her.

"You have returned," he murmured into her hair. "*Diolch i Dduw eich bod wedi dychwelyd.* Great thanks to God that you are back in my arms again."

Feeling the man warm and alive against her undid her already-taxed emotions and Penelope burst into tears. Arms around him, she buried her face in his neck.

"I am sorry if you are angry with me," she sobbed. "But I could not let your sacrifice be in vain. I had to help; I had to continue your cause whether or not you wanted me to. I know you do not want your wife to be a knight, but just this once I had to. I had to carry on your fight. Please do not be angry with me."

Bhrodi kissed her head, her cheek, finally pulling her back so he could look her in the face. Cupping her head between his two enormous palms, he gazed at her as he had never gazed at anyone in his life. There was such joy in his expression. When she had burst into the chamber, all he could feel was gratitude. He'd never felt anything like it so strongly in his life. But the gratitude gave way to peace and adoration, so much so that it was filling his chest to bursting. He kissed her salty eyes, easing her tears.

"*Caria*, I am not angry," he whispered. "I suppose I understand why you did what you did. When they first told me, I was terrified for you, I will admit it. I even tried to get out of bed to ride after you. But then I realized how fortunate I am to have a wife who would do such a thing for me. You are only doing what you have been trained to do and you understand honor in a way few women would. I do not have the words to express how humble and grateful I am that you would risk yourself so."

It was more than she could have hoped for and she searched his face for any hint that he might not be telling her the truth. Maybe there was anger that still lingered. But she only saw total, utter support.

"I would do anything for you," she whispered. "This was something I had to do."

He nodded. "I know," he murmured, looking her over and seeing how dirty and beat she was. "Are you sure you are well?"

Penelope nodded, sniffling as she struggled to calm her tears. "I am," she said. "My brothers are down in the hall."

"I know," he said softly. "I spoke to them at length about their stubborn sister."

That brought a weak smile to her lips. "Ivor has not yet returned," she said. "And Kevin... he wore your father's armor and the men thought he was you. It inspired them greatly, Bhrodi, and the raid was very disruptive to Edward, I believe. We burned a great many of the tents in his encampment. But Kevin was captured."

Bhrodi's pale face tightened with concern. "You know this for certain?"

She nodded, rubbing her cheek against his open palm in a sweet gesture. "Aye," she said quietly. "I was cornered by some English knights and surely would have been captured had my father not saved me. But there were rumors that you were captured in the raid but I told my father that Kevin had worn your father's armor. The English as well as the Welsh thought it was you. My father went off to save him but before he did, he told me to ride back to Rhydilian. He also said that he would be coming here shortly."

Bhrodi's mind was muddled from the slight fever he'd had most of the morning as well as the injury in general. Even now as he listened to

Penelope breathless assessment of the raid upon Edward's camp, he was struggling to process what she was telling him. It was a good deal of information and it took him a few moments to digest it.

"Your father saved me after the morning star struck," he muttered. "Now he has saved you also. We can only pray that he is successful with Hage. It would seem that your father is really a guardian angel masquerading as a knight."

Penelope nodded, her tears gone for the moment. "If anyone can save him, my father can," she said. "I did not even have the opportunity to thank him for what he did for you. I did, at least, thank him for returning you to me."

Bhrodi stroked her hair, pondering The Wolfe and all the man had done for them. So much had happened that it was almost beyond his comprehension at the moment. Lost to his thoughts, he heard Penelope's soft voice fill his ear.

"Papa said he would be here soon," she said. "I did not have the chance to ask him what he meant. Do you know?"

Bhrodi broke away from his thoughts and looked at her. "Nay," he said. "I cannot imagine why he would return here."

Penelope contemplated her own question. "Mayhap he is coming to see how you are faring," she said. "I am sure he is very concerned."

Bhrodi lifted his dark eyebrows in thought. "I never knew I could inspire such loyalty from the English," he said. "Your father, your brothers, and Hage... all of them rushing to assist me however they can. It is quite puzzling, actually. I was always under the impression that the English were selfish bastards."

Penelope smiled faintly. "No more so than the Welsh, I suppose," she said. "Mayhap someday you can return the favor."

He reached up and gently pinched her nose. "Gladly," he said, smiling. But the smile soon faded. "But I cannot do anything until the surgeon releases me from this damnable bed."

Penelope's smile grew; if he was complaining then he must be feeling better. At least, she hoped so. "What has he told you?" she asked. "How bad are your injuries?"

He made a face as the surgeon chose that moment to enter the room. He was carrying cups with him and one of them was steaming. Bhrodi watched the man warily.

"He says that the morning star dug holes into my body down by my hip and grazed the bone, taking a chunk out of it," he replied. "It miraculously missed anything terribly vital but it did nick my intestines, which someone had the foresight to seal up with honey until my own surgeon was able to get his hands on me somewhere near the ferry crossing. Gwyllim told me that Ianto found the surgeon back in Aber tending some of my men and brought him to me. So far, he's cleansed the wounds three times with wine and honey, and he's forced me to drink some horrible concoction that smells like rotted food but one that he swears will keep the poison away. He says he learnt it from his Irish cousin but I am not entire sure I want to drink anything the Irish have discovered. It might very well kill me."

Penelope laughed softly; he was speaking almost as if he felt well again but his voice was somewhat weak, reminding her of how sick he truly was. "But you must take it," she said firmly. "You must let him heal you. I must have you well again, husband."

He smiled faintly at her, reaching out to touch her dirty cheek. "And I must become well again if I am to keep you from running off and fighting the English," he murmured. "Promise me something, *caria*."

"What is that?"

His expression grew serious. "Promise me that you will not ride off to battle again, at least not without discussing it with me first," he said. "Will you swear?"

Penelope nodded contritely. "I swear."

"It would have destroyed me had something happened to you."

"It would?"

"Of course it would."

She smiled timidly. "Then... then the things you said to me yesterday," she said softly, "you really meant them? You did not say them simply because you thought you were dying?"

He frowned. "I never say anything I do not mean," he said, eyeing her. "Did *you* say them because you thought I was dying?"

She shook her head firmly. "I meant what I said."

He pushed. "Are you sure?" he asked. "After all, a dead man would not hold you to your word."

She scowled although it was lightly done. "That is a terrible thing to say!"

He laughed softly. "Then tell me again what you told me yesterday and I shall believe you."

She flushed a dull red, embarrassed because she was unused to expressing her feelings for him. Still, nothing had ever felt so right. She

277

would be quite happy to gush out her feelings for him daily for the rest of her life because she meant every word of it. She had risked her life for him. Her heart was full of the man and his beauty.

"I love you, husband," she murmured. "I love you very much."

His smile turned soft and sweet. "And I love you, my little knight," he whispered. "But no more riding into battle without my permission. Simply to think on it makes me feel faint."

She nodded patiently. "I swore that I would not. I will not go back on my word."

He stroked her dirty cheek again, smiling at her, not entirely sure she was being truthful with him. In discussions he'd had with her brothers earlier in the day when they had returned from the raid on Edward's camp, he was coming to realize his wife was no ordinary woman.

True, he'd known she had been raised as a knight and he knew she was having difficulty letting that part of her life go in order to become a wife and not a warrior, but he was coming to see that asking her to become something other than what she was had been a mistake. She was strong, fierce, and loyal. Aye, she was a fine wife. And she was a fine warrior, too.

As Bhrodi pondered that thought, Tacey entered the room. They didn't see her at first because she stood respectfully in the doorway in the shadows. When they didn't notice her right away, she thumped on the door jamb. When Bhrodi and Penelope finally looked over at her, she smiled timidly.

"May I come in?" she asked.

Penelope waved her over. "Come in, sweetheart," she said. "How are you feeling today?"

Tacey waddled into the room, her hand on her back. "Tight," she said, patting her stomach. "My belly feels very tight."

Penelope gave her a lop-sided grin. "I am sure that is because he is growing large and is nearly ready to come."

Tacey made her way to the bed, getting a look at Penelope close-up. "You are very dirty," she commented. "The serving women told me you left last night with my brother's men. Where did you go?"

Tacey had been confined to her room during the entire episode of gathering the men, planning for, and then riding to Edward's encampment. Therefore, she knew very little and it was probably best that way. In her condition, she didn't need to know about frightening situations that didn't concern her. Bhrodi cleared his throat softly.

"You should be worried about me and not where Penelope went during the night," he scolded lightly. "Moreover, if she had wanted you to know, she would have told you."

Tacey lowered her gaze remorsefully and Penelope took pity on her. "You were right," she said, changing the subject. "I am very dirty. Will you help me bathe?"

Tacey lifted her head and nodded eagerly. "I will tell the serving women to bring the tub," she said. "Where will you bathe?"

Penelope cast Bhrodi a glance. "Would it disturb you too much?"

He crooked a finger at her and when she leaned in, he grasped her gently by the neck to pull her close. "It will make me mad with desire," he whispered against her ear, "and I can do nothing about it."

Penelope was starting to flush red again. Unused to the sexual flirtations between men and women, she was unnerved, embarrassed, and excited all at the same time, but she was mostly embarrassed at the moment because Tacey was looking at her and was undoubtedly noting her reaction. Penelope didn't want to have to answer any curious questions.

"Let me bathe in your chamber," she told Tacey. "We must leave Bhrodi to rest."

Tacey nodded and fled the room as Penelope wearily rose to her feet. The surgeon, who had been busying himself at a table near the bed since entering the chamber, was now heading for Bhrodi with bowls in his hands. Bhrodi eyed the bowls.

"What black magic do you have in there?" he asked in English. "Do you think to cast a spell on me, you wicked sorcerer?"

The surgeon had no idea what he was saying but Penelope giggled. As the old man bent over him and began fussing with the bandages, Penelope blew him a kiss.

"Be brave, husband," she said. "I shall be upstairs should you need me."

Bhrodi lifted a hand to her. "Hurry back," he said. "I am not sure I can stand an over-amount of time away from you. Already I miss you."

It was a sweet thing to say. Penelope did indeed hurry with her bath but when she returned, warm and washed and clean, she found her husband sound asleep.

She fell asleep next to him.

⌘

As the sun rose steadily and approached the nooning hour, the encampment of Edward, King of England, was nearly a smoldering ruin. Hours after the Welsh rebels, led by Bhrodi de Shera, had tried to burn him out, there was still a great deal of confusion and reorganization going on because they had lost a great deal of material and stores in the fire. Now, they were pulling weapons, protection, gear, and other warfare items out of the rubble and hoping to salvage them. The hit by Bhrodi and his men had been sound, and Edward was currently picking up the pieces.

He was also in the process of deciding what to do about the fact that de Shera had escaped from de Wolfe's custody. He was absolutely furious but trying to keep his temper in check. It would do no good to scream at these men; they were old men, seasoned veterans, and they knew exactly how much trouble they were in. It would be of no use to shout it at them. What mattered now was what to do about it and as he stood in his tent, one of the only ones that had not been set completely ablaze, that was what Edward was trying to focus on – a solution. But it was a struggle.

"I trusted you, de Wolfe," he said, displeasure evident in his tone. "You and your minions are much better knights than what you are suggesting. How is it possible that de Shera bested all three of you and escaped? Well?"

William was standing a few feet away from Edward, legs braced apart and his big arms crossed. He was sporting a lovely black eye, courtesy of Kieran. When he had returned from his unfruitful search for Thomas and Edward, he had found Paris and Kieran battered and beaten. When they had explained why, he had understood completely and that was when Kieran had punched him in the face. There had to be evidence of a fight and William was the only man not showing nicks or bruises. In order to convince Edward, he needed at least one injury, and indeed he received one; a *good* one. The bruise spread across his entire right eye and onto his temple. But it wasn't enough to make the king sympathetic to the one-eyed knight who now had a damaged good eye.

"He caught me off guard," William replied, which was the truth; Kieran *had* caught him off guard. "It nearly knocked me out. I have no idea what he did to de Norville and Hage, but when I came around, the prisoner was gone."

Edward turned his furious gaze to Paris and Kieran. "And you two?" he growled. "Are you no better than weak squires letting that man beat you?"

Paris was sporting a black eye, a swollen nose, and a host of other injuries. "We fought," he said, which was also the truth; he and Kieran *had* fought. "It was a struggle but it was a struggle we lost. I cannot explain better than that, Your Grace. Hage and I fought but the prisoner escaped us."

Edward grunted in frustration and turned away. Angry as he was, he couldn't bring himself to punish these men, men he had grown up idolizing, but he certainly wanted to. De Wolfe in particular; there was something not right about this entire situation but he couldn't put his finger on it. De Wolfe seemed almost stoic about the entire thing when he had been insane with anger the moment he'd pulled de Shera from the tent. He'd cooled down inordinately fast. It was odd behavior from the man and something to watch, Edward thought. After a moment of chewing over the circumstances, he turned to William.

"You did not kill him and hide the body, did you?" he asked. "Are you afraid to tell me?"

William's brow furrowed. "I would not be afraid to tell you in any event, but I did not kill him."

"Swear it?"

"I do."

"Then you should have gone after him right away. Why didn't you?"

William gave him a rather droll expression. "Because someone had to tell you what had happened," he said. "If I had gone after him without telling you, you might have thought I had deserted you or, worse, aided him somehow. I cannot go after him in any case because you have kept me here since it happened. He is well away by now."

Edward was in no mood for de Wolfe's arrogance. His jaw began to tick. "It matters not," he said, "for you and I have an understanding, do we not? You are going to ride to Rhydilian this day and demand that de Shera and your daughter turn the castle over to me."

William was slow to concur. "That is what we agreed to."

Edward was increasingly interested in William's odd behavior, now adding reluctance to that list. He studied the man for a moment, pondering the march on Rhydilian. After a moment, he turned away. "I have changed my mind about it."

William was on his guard. "What do you mean?"

Edward's gaze was cold when he turned to look at him. "Since you are evidently no longer effective as a warrior, as evidenced by the fact that you let de Shera escape from your custody, I will be riding with you to Rhydilian and together we will lay siege. I cannot say my faith in you is strong, de Wolfe. Now I must go with you to ensure that you carry out my orders."

It was a great insult to William but he didn't flinch. He had expected worse and if this was as bad as it was going to get, he considered himself lucky. Even if Edward rode with him to Rhydilian, there were still a hundred ways in which he could either sabotage or deter the king's forces. Edward was correct not to trust him; he was, after all, The Wolfe and he was known for his cunning. He would put that cunning to good use, now against the man who was attempting to destroy his daughter and her husband. Blood was stronger than a kingdom. After a moment, he simply nodded his head.

"As you wish, Your Grace," he said evenly.

Edward didn't like the fact that William wasn't showing visible signs of distress. He hadn't been all afternoon and it made him more suspicious than ever. This wasn't the William he had known most of his life, the man who was full of fire and intelligence. This man seemed nearly apathetic. Eyes narrowed, he took a step towards the big knight.

"And know this," he hissed. "If you in any way fail or betray me, then I shall send an army to Castle Questing and burn it to the ground. I will destroy everything you have worked so hard for and I will cause your entire family to be destitute. You will be lucky if I do not throw them all in prison. Is this in any way unclear?"

All William could see was a grown man throwing a tantrum, although he knew that he meant what he said. It made his task just a bit more difficult. He found that he was increasingly anxious to get away from the man because had to think clearly about what was about to happen. He knew he would not aid the king in laying siege; that was a given fact. It therefore stood to reason that he had to either prevent him or deter him somehow, but he was at a loss as to what, exactly, to do. But it would come to him; he was resolute in what he needed to do.

"It is clear, Your Grace," he said. He very nearly sounded bored, unwilling to let himself be bullied. "When will we leave?"

Edward's gaze lingered on him for a moment as if to emphasize his threat before finally averting his gaze.

"At dawn on the morrow," he said. "You and your entire contingent will be ready."

"We will indeed, Your Grace."

"Good. Now, get out."

William quit the tent in silence with Paris and Kieran behind him. No one said a word until they were well out of ear shot and even then, the trio remained quiet. They were marching across the mashed grass, heading for William's encampment and his contingent of two hundred and fifty men. More were due in from Castle Questing and their ally, Northwood Castle, but they wouldn't arrive for at least ten days at best. William wished he had over a thousand men at the moment but it couldn't be helped. He had to utilize what he had.

Once they entered the perimeter of William's camp, they were finally able to speak freely but William pulled them into his tent before he said a word. Once inside the dark but comfortable quarters, he turned to his faithful friends.

"And so it comes," he muttered. "Edward intends to march on Rhydilian tomorrow and I must accompany him."

Paris was already reaching for the wine; he found he needed it. "What will you do?"

William sighed heavily. "I cannot let him destroy de Shera and Penny," he said. "I must do what I can in order to make it so that Edward is unsuccessful."

Kieran sat on the nearest folding chair, listening to it creak under his weight. "How are you going to do that?" he wanted to know. "Do you plan to turn against him in the heat of battle?"

William fell silent. Paris handed him a cup of wine and he drank the entire thing in two swallows. Slowly, he claimed his chair, the one that always came with him whenever he traveled. It was a big chair, made from sturdy oak, with a collapsible frame. Like a man with much on his mind, he plopped into the chair as if he had been thrown into it. He was weary and he was distressed, and it showed.

"Nay," he muttered. "I cannot do that. He would destroy us and then he would proceed to destroy Rhydilian. I think our best option might be the most distasteful one."

"What is that?" Kieran asked.

William glanced up at his old friend. "We ride to Rhydilian tonight under the cover of darkness and ask for them to abandon the castle," he said softly. "When Edward arrives tomorrow, he will find a vacant castle that he can claim if he wishes. We take de Shera and Penny and return to Questing. Edward will have what he wants even if means de Shera must flee his home. It is the only way for him, and for Penny, to survive."

"And if de Shera will not leave?" Paris asked the fatal question.

William turned to look at him. "What would you suggest?"

Paris sighed in a gesture that suggested remorse. "You will not like what I have to say."

"Say it and be done."

Paris nodded reluctantly. "Penny is your child, your flesh and blood, and she has only been married to de Shera for a week," he said. "If de Shera refuses to leave, then we take Penny and flee. Let the man face his fate alone; it is not her fate. It is his and his alone. Even if he is suicidal that does not mean she has to be. William, you cannot risk fifty years of a spotless reputation on an arrogant Welsh warlord who is nothing more to you than your daughter's husband of one week. He is not even family; he is simply married to your daughter, and look what he is risking – Kevin, Edward, Thomas, and most of all, Penelope. Will you let that man's arrogance cost your children their lives? If de Shera will not abandon Rhydilian in the face of Edward's onslaught, then you must think of yourself and your family first. Take Penny and leave as quickly as you can."

He had a point. William didn't like his advice but he knew, deep down, that the man was more than likely correct. "It is the coward's way," he muttered.

"So you would rather be a brave dead man that a living coward?" Paris shot back softly. "It is not cowardly; it is sensible. You are letting Bhrodi de Shera take away everything you have ever worked for, William. You are letting him take away your honor. Do not let him do it!"

He was right. William didn't have the strength to fight any longer. He simply wanted to get his daughter and go back to Questing where he belonged. He didn't belong in Wales fighting other men's wars; he wanted to go home to his wife and children and grandchildren. Aye, that was where he belonged. After several pensive moments, he looked at Kieran.

"Is that what you think, too?" he asked.

Kieran nodded faintly. "De Shera nearly cost me my son," he said. "I am not entirely sure I can forgive him. Paris is right; do not let that arrogant Welshman cost us everything."

William didn't intend to. Shortly after midnight, William's group silently slipped from Edward's encampment under the cover of darkness. He knew that Edward had spies about and he fully expected the king to be notified. Edward, thinking William was betraying him, would move swiftly to follow.

With that in mind, William and his men rode like the wind in their quest to reach Rhydilian before Edward caught up with them.

It was the most anxious ride of his life.

⌘

CHAPTER TWENTY-THREE

"Penny," came the hiss in her ear. "Penny, wake up!"

Penelope was so exhausted that it took two more hisses and a shake before she opened her eyes. When she did, the room was dark and a shadowy figure was looming over her. Startled out of a deep sleep, Penelope threw a fist up and caught the figure in the throat. He stumbled back, coughing.

"'Tis me!" Thomas hissed, louder. "Stop hitting!"

Penelope had rolled out of bed and was preparing to throw another punch but stopped short when her brother slapped her hand down. Shaken, she rubbed a weary hand over her eyes.

"I am sorry," she whispered. "I could not see who it was."

Thomas grabbed her by the wrist and began pulling her towards the chamber door. "An assassin would not have awoken you before finishing his task, little sister," he said flatly. "You must come with me now. It is important."

They were already through the chamber door and she pulled her wrist from his grip to shut the old wooden panel softly behind them. When the latch on the door clicked, she looked curiously at her brother. "What time is it?"

"Dawn is an hour or so away."

"Then what is the matter?" she asked.

Thomas' expression was grim. "Kevin has returned."

Penelope's eyes widened. Before Thomas could draw another breath, she was racing down the narrow stairs that led to the entry level. When she hit bottom, she could hear soft voices off to her left in the hall beyond and as she ran into the hall, she could see Kevin and Edward illuminated by the soft firelight. She could hardly believe her eyes.

"Kevin!" she gasped. "You have come back!"

Kevin, seated at the feasting table, turned in time to see Penelope rush up to him. In her excitement, she threw her arms around his neck and squeezed, just as she would have if it had been one of her brothers or any of her cousins. She was simply glad to see the man after everything that had happened and was demonstrating that relief.

But to Kevin, it was nothing short of heaven; he knew it was an innocent hug in a long line of many innocent hugs he had received from her during the course of their lives. He always wished the hugs had meant more than they did, and this one in particular. But that was his lot in love, in love with a woman who did not return that love. Still, he was very glad to see her, too.

"Aye, I have returned," he said as she released him. "I have much to tell."

Penelope sat down across the table from him, wide-eyed and apprehensive. She barely noticed that, behind Kevin, the door to the old wardrobe was open and the tiny old man was doing his dance of death back in the shadows. As the old man battled ghosts in the background, now a normal occurrence every time they were in the feasting hall, Penelope looked Kevin up and down.

"Is it true?" she asked. "Were you captured?"

"Aye."

"They did not hurt you, did they?"

He shook his head. "Nay."

"Did my father free you, then?"

Kevin nodded. "Your father, my father, and Uncle Paris found me in King Edward's tent in the midst of being interrogated," he said. Then, he shook his head with a smirk on his lips. "If you only could have seen them; Edward thought I was Bhrodi since I was wearing Coventry's armor. Your father charged in and started to beat me, trying to convince Edward that I was, in fact, de Shera and that I had shamed him by leading a raid. Edward let him remove me but then your father helped me to escape. I cannot even imagine how upset Edward is at your father at this moment, but that is not the worst of it."

Penelope was looking at him with horror. "What else has happened?"

Kevin looked at her, his expression grim. "Your father said that Edward wants Rhydilian," he said, his voice low so gossipy servants or soldiers would not hear him. "He told me to come back to Rhydilian and prepare. He further told me that he would be joining us shortly. Penny, when Edward comes to lay siege to Rhydilian, your father will be here to defend it. He is fighting against the king."

Penelope stared at him a moment, her disbelief evident. Her hands flew to her mouth as if to hold in the gasp of horror and over in the shadows, the crazy old man came to a complete halt and stood flush up against the wall as if to hide. No one even noticed that perhaps he was waiting for Coventry's armor to be returned to the wardrobe, or perhaps he was even listening to the conversation. It was difficult to know. Even so, no one paid attention to him, least of all Penelope. She was wracked with dread for her father.

"He *cannot*," she hissed. "If he does, everything he has ever achieved in his life will be finished. He will lose Questing and his titles. My family will become fugitives from the crown. Kevin, he cannot do this!"

Kevin sighed heavily; he was battered, bloodied, and exhausted but he was not beaten. He was fully prepared to defend those he loved until the death and that included siding with William de Wolfe who was now evidently a traitor. He still couldn't believe it.

"I know," he muttered. "But he is nonetheless and my father and Uncle Paris will be at his side. I suppose it is fitting; they have all fought together for so long that if one goes down, the others will go with him."

Penelope was in a panic. She stood up, motioning to the knights as she moved. "Come with me," she said. "Bhrodi must know what is happening."

She fled the hall and rushed up the stairs. She could hear the bootfalls of the knights behind her as she hit the landing on the third floor and opened the master chamber's door. She held out a hand to the men behind her to hold quiet as she awoke her husband, but as she bent down to rouse him she realized his eyes were open and he was looking at her.

"It sounds as if a herd of wild horses has run into this room," he said, his voice hoarse and sleepy. "What is happening?"

Penelope knelt down beside the bed as the others crowded close. "Kevin has returned," she said. "He has brought much news with him. You must hear it."

Bhrodi wasn't feeling particularly well; the slight fever he'd had for most of the day had grown worse and now his eyeballs hurt because they were so hot. The old surgeon was concerned about it and had him drinking his rotten brew every few hours to keep it under control. Still, his mind was also foggy with cobwebs and he struggled to clear it as he focused on Hage; the man looked as if he'd been in a row or two. Bhrodi was frankly surprised to see him.

"I was told you rode to battle in my father's armor," he said. "I am rather surprised to see that you are not Edward's prisoner. The entire English army must have been aiming for you."

Kevin lifted an eyebrow. "That is an understatement," he said. "I am sure you will not be shocked to know that I was Edward's prisoner for a time, but de Wolfe was able to help me escape."

Bhrodi nodded in understanding, studying the man for a moment. "How did Edward treat you?"

"Surprisingly well but, like most Englishmen, he was unhappy to see me... or you, as it were."

Bhrodi gave him a half-grin. "How was it to assume my identity, then?"

Kevin shook his head. "I did not like it," he said. "Too many people are out to kill you."

"Including Edward?"

"Especially Edward."

As Kevin and Bhrodi grinned at each other in an expected moment of levity, Penelope captured Bhrodi's attention.

"That is what we must speak to you about," she said. "My father told Kevin that Edward plans to lay siege to Rhydilian. Bhrodi, that is why my father told me he was coming here; he intends to help defend Rhydilian against Edward's onslaught. He intends to fight for you!"

Bhrodi could see how much it distressed her and he thought back to that time when they first met when he had told her of his reasons for marrying her. It had been because he wanted The Wolfe on his side. Now that it was about to become reality, he wasn't so sure he liked it. Like Penelope, he was well aware of the implications should de Wolfe side with him. William de Wolfe had done so much for them; he had saved Bhrodi's life as well as Penelope's and even Kevin's. Now, the man was about to lay his entire reputation on the line in his resistance to Edward's army. Bhrodi wasn't entirely sure he could let that happen. He sighed heavily.

"Do we know this for certain?" he asked. "Do we know that Edward is truly coming to lay siege to Rhydilian?"

Kevin nodded. "William said that he was," he replied. "As far as I am concerned, that is as good as Edward himself telling me of his plans."

Bhrodi accepted it as truth. He had always known at some point that Edward would come for him again after that disastrous attempt back in December. Now, he had more of an army behind him and although it would take time to ferry them across the strait, he was very capable of laying siege to Rhydilian. Only now there were no Welsh armies to stand between him and the rest of Anglesey; all of Bhrodi's vassals were either with Dafydd or dead. Hardly any remained in Anglesey. Aye, Bhrodi had been waiting for this moment most of his life. He knew what needed to be done.

"Get me up," he grunted, trying to sit up. "We have much work to do."

Penelope put her hands on his shoulders, pushing him down. "Are you mad?" she demanded. "You cannot get out of bed! You are badly injured!"

Bhrodi was trying to push her out of the way in his attempt to rise. "It does not matter," he said, his voice tight with pain. "Edward will not get my castle."

Penelope would not be shoved away; she thrust herself forward and pushed him down with her hands against his chest. Lacking even basic strength, Bhrodi went down easily. He looked up to see a very angry wife in his face.

"Listen to me," she hissed. "You cannot leave this bed and if I have to sit on you to ensure that you remain here, I most certainly will. You are too wounded to do any good with your sword but you are not too wounded to command. Your mind is sound. Therefore, you will tell us what needs to be done and we will do it. Do you understand? We will be your eyes and arms and legs, Bhrodi. Just tell us what you need for us to do and we will."

Bhrodi looked at his wife; she was hard with determination. *She's a warrior*, he reminded himself. She was very capable of following orders. He struggled with the alien concept of not being able to personally direct the defenses of Rhydilian but as he looked around his bed, he could see good men standing there - Kevin, who had already risked so much, Edward who was very seasoned and capable, and

Thomas, who was young and as strong as a bull. Aye, he had a powerful group of warriors. But the inactivity was surely going to kill him.

"Where are my *teulu*?" he asked Penelope.

She didn't seem to know and Thomas went in search of them. As the young knight quit the room, Bhrodi reached up and stroked her soft cheek.

"We will wait for my commanders," he said quietly. "I have much to say and they must hear it."

Penelope understood. "Gwyllim said that Ianto made it back from England but we do not know about Ivor," she said. "And Yestin... well, he did not come with us at all. He did not want to follow me, I suppose."

Bhrodi patted her arm. "Yestin is like a dog with only one master," he said. "He will more than likely only follow me, ever. You must not be discouraged by this. You were able to convince nearly every man in my command to follow you and that says something for your skill as a commander. Do you know how many men made it back to Rhydilian?"

Penelope looked at Edward, who had been assigned the task of accounting for the returning men. "We left the castle with one hundred and eighty-one men," Edward said. "As of an hour ago, ninety-seven have returned."

"Did Ivor return?"

Edward shook his head. "Nay."

That concerned Bhrodi greatly but he didn't dwell on it; he couldn't. He had too much on his mind. "If de Wolfe is on his way, how many men is he bringing?"

Again, Edward shook his head. "I have no way of knowing," he replied. "My father took over three hundred men with him when he went to find the king in Wales but that was before many battles that he participated in. There is truly no way of knowing how many he retains."

Bhrodi digested the information. "Rhydilian is extremely defensible by only a few good men," he said. "Its position atop the mountain and the sharp cliffs around it make it perfect. If Edward comes, his only manner of approach is the road that leads to Rhydilian; he cannot come at us from any other angle, and the gatehouse is nearly impenetrable."

Kevin had been listening to the boast. "He will bring men to build ladders with which to mount the walls, and Rhydilian's walls are not so tall that they cannot be mounted," he said. "If he has enough time, he will also build siege engines and there is plenty of lumber around here with which to build them. He'll have all the time in the world to mount his defense while we sit here and wait for him to capture us."

It was a grim assessment of the future. A sense of doom now hung in the air as well as the scent of futility. Bhrodi didn't like to hear such discouragement even if the man was correct.

"Then what would you suggest?" he asked Kevin. "You are an English knight so you think like one; what would you suggest to triumph over your king?"

Kevin looked at the faces surrounding him; Bhrodi, Edward, and finally Penelope. She was looking at him anxiously and he didn't like that expression, not in the least. She wouldn't even be in this peril had it not been for her marriage to de Shera. He was the cause of her fear, of the threat of her defeat. He struggled not to place all blame solely on de Shera.

But he was weary; *too* weary. He rubbed his eyes, so exhausted he could barely stand. That exhaustion was making him think mad and foolish thoughts.

"I do not know," he said. "I have not slept in nearly two days. Let me sleep a little and we will meet again to discuss what I think our options might be."

"Of course," Penelope said before Bhrodi could speak. "We will not meet to discuss battle strategies until you have had an opportunity to rest."

"We do not have much time," Bhrodi said as Kevin headed for the door. "If Edward's attack is imminent, then we must prepare."

Kevin merely nodded and quit the room. Now it was just Bhrodi, Penelope, and Edward in the chamber, a chamber that was filled with uneasiness for the future. So much had happened and so much was about to happen. It would have been easy to have become overwhelmed. Bhrodi turned to the two of them.

"Edward is a man who is fond of sieges and I am sure it would be his wish to starve us out," he told them. "The first order of business will be to make sure we have enough provisions to hold out as long as we can. Before we discuss defenses, will you both see to the state of our provisions? That will be most important in the long run."

He said it to give them something to do until everyone could be gathered in a complete group to discuss their plans for defense. Penelope and Edward nodded at his request and Penelope kissed him on the cheek as she stood up from her crouched position beside the bed. Bhrodi looked into her eyes, seeing such trust and adoration there. He wished he hadn't seen it because it was making him feel very guilty about the position she was in, all because of him.

In fact, all the English were in this position because of him. He thought briefly of asking Penelope to flee but he knew she wouldn't; she had already demonstrated how loyal she was to him. She would defend him until the death. God, he hoped it wouldn't come to that.

As Penelope and Edward were leaving, one of the old serving wenches appeared. She seemed a little flustered as she focused on Penelope.

"*Mae fy wraig,*" she said, twisting her hands. "*Y colli ifanc angen chi. Hi mewn ffordd wael.*"

In the entire group of women that Jordan had brought to Rhydilian, only two of them spoke English and this wasn't one of them, unfortunately. Penelope looked at Bhrodi.

"What did she say?" she asked.

Bhrodi's expression was tight with concern. "She says that something is wrong with Tacey," he said. "Go and see to her, Penny. Hurry."

Penelope and Edward both bolted up to the upper floors with the serving wench scurrying behind them. They burst into Tacey's big chamber only to find the girl writhing on the bed in pain. Penelope rushed to her side.

"Tacey?" she asked, fear in her voice. "What is wrong, sweetheart?"

Tacey was groaning and twisting. "I... I woke up to great pains in my belly," she grunted. "Something is wrong with my son!"

Penelope had been around her sisters when they had given birth to their children so she knew enough to know that Tacey was in labor. Terror surged through her and she struggled not to show it. She put her hands on the young woman's shoulders.

"Your baby is coming," she explained calmly. "It is his time to come into the world."

Tacey groaned. "It hurts!"

Penelope nodded and stroked her forehead. "I know," she said. "I am told it will hurt, but you must endure. We are all very anxious to meet your son."

Tacey started to cry and Penelope looked up at Edward. The man had two small children with his wife, Lady Cassiopeia de Norville, but he certainly hadn't been with her when she had birthed them. He'd been kept from his wife during the entire labor and delivery process, only to see her when she and the babies had been cleaned up. To see Tacey groaning on the bed was something entire different to him. He gazed at his sister with some trepidation.

"What do we do?" he hissed.

Penelope stood up and pushed him towards the door, away from Tacey so she wouldn't hear their conversation. Truth was, Penelope was very frightened. She had no idea what to do with a woman in labor. She'd never been near her sisters when they had delivered; that was left up to her mother and aunts. Now, she found herself in a situation she should have had some knowledge in but didn't. Knights didn't usually deliver children and for the first time in her life, she found herself wishing she'd learned something of womanly skills.

"I wish Uncle Paris was here," she whispered. "He used to be a Hospitaller. He would know what to do!"

Edward's expression was wry. "But he is not here," he whispered back. "What are we going to do? She cannot have this baby now! Edward is coming!"

Penelope rolled her eyes. "I do not think she planned it this way," she snapped softly, eyeing the young girl who was weeping softly on the bed. "Tell Bhrodi what is happening and send the surgeon up here. Mayhap he can help."

Edward nodded swiftly. "I'll see if the serving women can help also," he said decisively, rushing towards the chamber door and happy to be leaving the frightening scene. "You must say with her."

Penelope nodded as Edward fled the room. Fearfully, she turned in Tacey's direction, watching the young girl weep and squirm. The old serving wench that had come to tell them of the trouble was beside the girl, singing softly to her in Welsh. Timidly, Penelope approached the bed.

"Tacey?" she said softly.

Tacey twisted and grunted. "This hurts!" she gasped. "I am afraid!"

Penelope leaned forward and grasped the girl's hand. "Everything will be well, I promise," she assured her, though she wasn't sure if she believed it. "Ask this serving woman if she knows about birthing children. She does not speak any English."

Between grunts and sobs, Tacey asked the woman, who immediately nodded. Penelope nearly collapsed with relief. "Good," she sighed. "Then tell her she must prepare for the baby. Tell her that I will help her. As her what she needs."

Tacey relayed the information as she wept and the old woman, surprisingly, swept into action. The first thing she did was pull off the coverlet. Then, she tossed up Tacey's sleeping shift to expose the girl from the belly down. Penelope got a good look at Tacey's enormous belly, smooth and perfectly shaped, and her skinny little legs. As she watched, she could see the belly tightening with the contractions as the girl wept through them. It was both fascinating and frightening. The old serving woman put her hands on Tacey's belly as Penelope knelt beside the bed and held the girl's hand.

"Do not be afraid," she said softly. "We will help you. You do not need to fear."

Tacey held on to Penelope's hand tightly, so tightly that she was cutting off the circulation in Penelope's fingers.

"How long will this take?" she wept. "Will it be over soon?"

Penelope had no idea how to answer that. "It will be over soon enough," she said. Then she tried to distract her. "What names have you chosen for your son?"

Tacey was hit with a rather large contraction and she grunted and moaned until it was over. "I... I will name him after his father," she said. "His name was Perri."

Penelope smiled, stroking the girl's head. "I like that name," she said. "But what if it is a girl?"

Tacey frowned. "It will not be a girl," she said. "My son's name is Perri."

Penelope had to chuckle at the confidence. "Perri it is," she said. "Boy *or* girl."

As Tacey lay there and tried to recover from the last contraction, more serving women began to pour into the room, chattering excitedly in Welsh. They were pointing at the girl, discussing the situation, as another serving woman appeared with a bowl of water and a rag. She set it down on the nearest table, soaked the rag, and came over to the bed to wipe down Tacey's forehead and arms. It was really quite efficient, as if the woman knew exactly what she was doing. Penelope began to feel comforted; it seemed her mother had known what she was doing in hiring these women. They knew what Penelope did not.

Another serving woman entered the chamber and Penelope recognized her; it was Dilys from the kitchens. She spoke English and Penelope waved her over.

"Lady Tacey is having her baby," she said. "What more can we do for her? She is in pain."

Dilys looked at the young girl with kindness. "Your mother told us this day would come," she said to Penelope. "We are prepared."

"But what can you give her for the pain?"

Dilys shook her head. "She will have to suffer as all women have since the beginning of time," she replied. "She will know now what it means to be a true woman."

Penelope wasn't happy with the answer but she returned an encouraging smile to Tacey. As Penelope sat on the floor and held the girl's hand, the serving women were crowded around the bed, hands on Tacey's belly and discussing the situation in their native tongue. As she tried to whisper encouraging words to help the girl through a difficult contraction, she heard hissing at the door. Looking over her shoulder, she could see Edward motioning her to him.

She kissed Tacey before letting her hand go and moving to her brother. She couldn't help but notice that the man looked concerned.

"What is wrong?" she asked. "Why do you look so?"

Edward's face was grim. "The sentries have spotted an incoming army," he said. "They should be here in an hour or so. It is either Father or Edward; in any case, you must come with me."

Penelope felt a stab of fear as she gave one last glance to Tacey over on the bed. Surrounded by women, Penelope knew the girl was in good hands. She pushed her brother out of the chamber and quietly shut the door.

"Does Bhrodi know?" she asked.

"He is the one who told me to bring you."

Penelope sighed. "Then let us find out who approaches," she said, her tone suggesting caution. "I pray it is Papa because we are not nearly prepared enough to fight off Edward. God's Blood; why does everything have to happen all at once?"

Edward smirked. "Mayhap that is your lot in life, dear sister," he said. "You are not meant to have a moment's peace."

Penelope hoped he was wrong, but her apprehension was growing by the minute.

⌘

CHAPTER TWENTY-FOUR

"I feel as if we have only just been here," Paris said drolly as he looked at the walls of the great keep of Rhydilian.

Kieran, weary from the hard ride, sighed heavily. "That is because we have," he muttered. "I am coming to hate this place."

William came up behind them, removing his gauntlets as he pushed between the pair. "It hates you, too," he mumbled. "Shut your mouth and come with me. I am anxious to see my daughter."

Kieran and Paris followed, their exhaustion evident in their movements. Besides the three of them, they had also brought a little over two hundred men as well as the sons that had accompanied their fathers into Wales.

Taking command of the men and provisions wagons were Scott, Troy, and Patrick. While the other sons and cousins had escorted the women back to Questing and had remained there to protect the castle, all of the de Wolfe sons had gone with their father. They tended to travel in a bunch, anyway, and it was difficult to separate them so William no longer tried. It was a given fact that his sons went where he did, and they all went together. That bond only grew stronger after James was killed. Now, the de Wolfe sons settled the troops in the bailey of Rhydilian, telling the men to bed down and take a few hours of sleep while they could, as their father and uncles headed into the keep.

William had no sooner put his foot on the bottom step leading up to the keep when Penelope appeared at the top of the stairs. With a shriek, she flew down the steps and threw herself at her father, who nearly toppled over as she hit him squarely in the chest. Penelope's arms were around his neck, squeezing.

William coughed because she was strangling him. "Penny, lass," he hugged her tightly. "Loosen up on my neck a bit. You're about to make me lose consciousness."

Giggling, Penelope did as she was told. She kissed him loudly on the cheek and let him go long enough to hug Paris and Kieran.

"I'm so happy to see you all," she exclaimed. "We were afraid it was Edward."

William's smile faded. "Not yet," he said. "But soon. Come; let us go inside and discuss it. How is your husband?"

Penelope turned and headed up the steps with her father and uncles in tow. "He was very bad when he arrived the other night and now he has a fever," she said, trying not to sound as concerned as she felt. "We must go up and see him right away. He will want to speak with you."

William cast a long glance at Paris and Kieran. "And I will want to speak with him."

As they reached the keep entry, the big gaping door that led into the cool innards, Penelope came to a stop and faced them. Her expression was very serious.

"Are you really going to fight with Bhrodi, Papa?" she asked.

William put a hand on her shoulder and turned her for the keep. "We will be discussing one of many such options with your husband."

Penelope dug her heels in and ended up ramming her father in the gut with her elbow when he tried to push her along. As he grunted and rubbed his belly, she smiled contritely.

"Papa, of course I love you for wanting to help, but you cannot jeopardize everything you have worked for," she said firmly. "You are such a great man and you cannot damage what you have become."

William didn't say a word. He made it very clear he did not wish to discuss it with her. He turned her around for the second time and pushed her inside.

"Where is your husband?" he asked again.

Penelope pointed up the stairs just as Edward and Thomas were emerging from the hall. William smiled wearily at his two boys, men he had been worried about ever since he had been unable to locate them in the chaos of Penelope's raid at Edward's camp. He had held hope that they had escaped and as the men came towards him, he simply opened up his arms. Edward was hugged first and then Thomas.

William cupped Thomas' face with his big hands, staring at the man as if to reaffirm that he was indeed alive and well.

"I heard you both went along on your sister's assault into Edward's camp," he said, swallowing tears of joy. "I am very relieved to see you both unharmed. Thomas, how is your arm?"

Thomas moved it about gingerly. "The wound hurts but it is healing," he said. "I can hold a sword well enough."

William smiled at his youngest son. "It would take more than a simple scratch to keep you down," he said. Then he started looking around as if missing something. "Where is Kevin?"

"Sleeping," Penelope told him. "He was exhausted. He should be awake soon. Bhrodi wants to meet with everyone to discuss the defense for Edward's approach. Come; let us go up and see him before he attempts to climb out of bed and come down here."

The six of them headed up the stairs to the upper floor with the older knights dragging down the pace. They were weary and the steps were steep and near the top, Paris simply came to a halt and would have refused to go any further had Kieran not pushed him up the last few steps. Penelope was already in the doorway of the master's chamber.

"Bhrodi?" she called softly to make sure the man wasn't asleep. When he turned and looked at her, she smiled. "My father is here."

William entered the room, smiling weakly at Bhrodi, who immediately tried to sit up. Penelope rushed into the room to keep him from injuring himself further.

"Be still," she murmured. "You do not have to get up."

Bhrodi, wracked with fever, tried to push his wife aside. "I will greet the man in an upright position."

William could see that Bhrodi wasn't well. His face was pale, his eyes red-rimmed, and his dark hair was stuck to his head with sweat. He, too, pushed the man back to the bed. "If I was in your condition, I would not worry about sitting upright," he said. "Injuries such as yours can be deadly if you do take care. I would be focusing my energies on getting well again if I were you."

Ashen and perspiring, Bhrodi gazed up at the big knight. "What would you know about my condition?"

William pointed at his patched eye. "This," he said. "It nearly killed me. Had it not been for my wife, I would not have survived. Therefore, you must listen to your wife. She will take great care of you."

Bhrodi's gaze moved to Penelope, who was smiling down at him. He reached up, clutching her hand and bringing it to his lips for a sweet kiss.

"She had already taken great care of me," he murmured, looking into her eyes. "She has risked all for me. I owe her everything."

William's smile faded; in that brief statement, he could immediately see that this contract marriage was far more than that. He looked at his daughter's face and saw an expression he had never seen before; it was soft and gentle and, he thought, full of adoration. *God's Blood*, he thought. *She's in love with him!* The impact of the realization was enough to cause him to catch his breath.

Now, the scheme had changed; if Penelope was in love with de Shera, then removing her would not be a simple thing. She would not want to go – at least, she would not go willingly. She would want to remain with her husband. William suddenly felt very, very exhausted and discouraged. So much for taking his daughter and fleeing a man she had only been married to for a week. Somewhere over the past few days, the stakes had changed and he should have guessed all of this when she launched the raid into Edward's camp. Only a woman in love would have taken such a risk. He began to feel defeat already.

"Papa, how far behind you is Edward?" Penelope asked, breaking into his thoughts.

William looked at her, fighting down his sense of doom. "I am not entirely sure," he said. "We left under the cloak of darkness but if I know Edward, and I do, he had men watching me. If I could guess, I would say he is no more than three or four hours behind me. He has probably already amassed his men and is heading for the ferry at Menai."

"How many men do you believe he will be carrying?" Bhrodi asked quietly.

William shrugged. "He has thousands in Wales," he replied, "but he knows it will take time to cross the Menai Strait on a ferry, so it is my guess he will not bring more than a thousand if he can help it."

Bhrodi pondered that thought. "A thousand men can do a great deal of damage," he said softly. "Most of my men are in Wales with Dafydd. I barely have a hundred here."

William glanced at Paris and Kieran before continuing the conversation; if he was going to discuss his solution to the problem, then better to do it now. They needed time to escape so to delay the conversation that needed to take place, and the ensuing resistance to come, did not bode well in their favor. When Paris nodded faintly, as if to encourage him to go on, William took a deep breath and faced his daughter and her husband.

"I brought a little more than two hundred men with me," he said. "De Shera, I will be honest with you; there is no way to hold Edward off. I have spent all night trying to figure out how we could fend him off and the truth is that we cannot. He has more men and is better supplied than we are. Once he comes here, he will bottle Rhydilian up and wait for you to starve to death. He more than likely will not even launch an attack. He'll simply settle in around the castle and wait you out."

Bhrodi could sense something in de Wolfe's tone, something ominous. "You did not come here to fight with me, did you?"

William met his gaze steadily. "I came to remove you and my daughter and take you both away from here. If you will not go, I understand, but it is my intention to remove Penelope. I do not think you will resist my efforts. You want her safe just as much as I do."

Penelope, startled at the turn of the conversation, descended swiftly into denial. "I will *not* go with you," she said staunchly. "My place is with Bhrodi. If he stays to defend Rhydilian, then I stay."

William could already see that he was about to have a fight on his hands. He was prepared.

"Sweetheart, listen to me," he said steadily. "This is not your fight. Although I commend your loyalty to your husband, this marriage was to ensure peace. You were supposed to live a long and happy life. You were never supposed to endure a siege by Edward because the man will *win*. Do you understand me? I will take you and your husband back to Questing and make him a garrison commander for one of my outposts."

Penelope was on her feet, as furious as William had ever seen her. She had a lot of her mother's fire in her but it was never so evident as it was now.

"My husband is the hereditary King of Anglesey," she snarled. "What you are suggesting is... is cowardly and low. You are asking the man to flee his home!"

"I am offering to save his life."

"No!" Penelope bellowed "I am not going anywhere and neither is my husband. Did you really come here just to tell us to run?"

"I came here to save your lives."

Penelope wouldn't hear him. "Then get out of here, Papa. Go away and never come back. We do not need or want your help if all you are suggesting is that we run."

Bhrodi reached up and grasped her hand in an attempt to calm her. "Your father is trying to help us," he said softly. "If the situation was reversed, I cannot say that I would not suggest the same thing."

That lit a fire under Penelope. She pointed an accusing finger at her father. "Would *you* run if Edward was coming to Questing?" she demanded. "I do not believe you would. I believe you would stay and fight until the last man. Questing is your home and heritage and legacy; you would not leave it. You would defend it to the last stone!"

"And I may very well find myself in that position if you and your husband do not come with me," William said. "What do you think is going to happen to me when it is confirmed to Edward that I am taking up arms for de Shera? He will march on Questing. Penelope, if you do not leave this place with me, then we will not only lose your husband's heritage but mine as well."

Penelope threw her arms up in the air. "Who *are* you?" she cried. "My father would not speak of running. He is The Wolfe, the mightiest knight in England. He is not a coward who runs from danger!"

"You will not speak to your father like that," Paris said; he had remained silent as long as he could. "Your father is the greatest knight who has ever lived. If he is asking you to flee, then he has good reason. If you stay here, he will stay here, and if he remains with de Shera, then *you* will have caused your father to lose everything he has ever worked for. If anyone is foolish in all of this, it is you. Look at the entire situation with your head and not your heart. Your father is trying to help you."

Penelope had never heard her Uncle Paris speak to her that way. It was angry and, if she thought about it, threatening. But she didn't back down.

"Is that what you think?" she asked him. "That I am foolish? You have taught me loyalty above all and that is what I am; loyal to my husband. If he will not leave his home, then I will not leave it. I will not leave *him*."

Paris grunted in frustration. "Then you condemn your father."

Penelope nearly screamed. "I am not asking him to stay here!" she cried. "I have told him to leave; I want all of you to leave. If you are so concerned for your precious reputations and lives, then get out of here. I do not want you or need you. Go back to Questing where you are safe and respected. Go back and surround yourself with your grandchildren and die peacefully in your beds. But I will not go with you - I will stay here with my husband and fight for what became mine the moment I married him."

Paris turned away; he had to or he was going to say something he would regret. Bhrodi stepped in before things went out of control. When families fought, the situation was always very emotional and volatile, and he could see his wife throwing punches in the very near future if he didn't do something.

"Please," he said, holding up a hand as if to forcibly calm everyone. "Shouting will not solve anything. Penny, I want you to leave us. Please."

Penelope looked at him, shocked. "You are chasing me away?"

He smiled gently at her. "Nay, *caria*," he murmured. "But I wish to speak to your father alone. Will you please give us that privacy?"

Her face was one big scowl. "Are you going to talk him into leaving?"

"I am going to talk with him, yes. Now, please go. Please go and see to Tacey now."

Penelope was very unhappy with the request but she didn't dispute him. Perhaps it was better if she moved away from the old men who were throwing up blocks and frustrating her. She couldn't understand why they were asking her to run like a coward. These were not the honorable knights she had known all of her life. Angrily, she marched to the door but paused before leaving.

"Even if I agreed to leave, we can't," she said. "Bhrodi's sister is in labor. Her baby is coming and we cannot travel with a woman in labor."

Before Bhrodi could make a second request that she leave the room, she moved through the doorway and disappeared up the stairs. Now, it was just Bhrodi, William, Paris, Thomas, and Edward, only Thomas and Edward were standing on the opposite side of the room and seemed to be just as bewildered by their father's attitude as Penelope was. William wouldn't even look at them.

As they stood there in a room filled with tension, they began to hear shuffling and grunting coming from the landing outside the chamber. It was a curious sound and by the time they turned to look at the source of the noise, the tiny old man who lived in the wardrobe was making his way into the room, doing batting with his favorite unseen enemy.

Since everyone in the room had seen him before, they didn't give him more than a passing glance although Thomas moved out of his way because he knew the man could get violent if he came into contact with a living soul. The old warrior had become more bold as of late in venturing from his wardrobe, especially when there seemed to be an over amount of discussion pertaining to Edward. If Bhrodi hadn't known better, he would have thought the old man was just being nosy.

The tiny old knight lunged, parried, and sliced his way across the room until he came to a great tapestry that hung near the lancet window. It was actually a Nordic tapestry, having ended up at Rhydilian in the same raid that brought the tiny man's wardrobe. In fact, the little man danced around it, fought around it, and eventually wrapped himself up in it before coming to a stop. Hiding in the tapestry, he went largely ignored. They were all focused on William and his solution to Edward's siege.

Especially Bhrodi. He had not time to spare his mad uncle any semblance of attention. Sensing great dissention between William and his children, he realized there had to be a solution to all of this, something that wouldn't see de Wolfe stripped of everything and wouldn't see Bhrodi fleeing his home. In times of darkest need, when the House of ap Gaerwen and de Shera dealt with their most heinous enemies, it had always been the same – The Serpent protected Rhydilian. Only this time, Bhrodi was physically unable to meet the confrontation head-on. He was crippled. That mean that The Serpent was caged for the moment.

... or was he?

"I understand that you want your daughter safe from Edward's onslaught," Bhrodi finally said. "I want her safe, too, but I will not leave my home. I also do not want to see you betray your king, de Wolfe, by fighting for me. Once, I thought mayhap that was all I wanted out of this marriage – your alliance. But now I know I cannot ask you to ruin your reputation and put your entire family at risk. But your daughter will not leave me and because of that, I suspect you will not leave me, either. That creates a problem."

William sighed heavily. "Indeed it does."

Bhrodi studied the man, so battle scarred yet so ageless somehow. William de Wolfe was immortal in his eyes, a legend that would never die. But the Legend needed help; they *all* needed help. And Bhrodi had an idea.

"Would you be willing to do anything to save your daughter?" Bhrodi asked softly.

William looked at him. "Of course I would."

"Would you sacrifice your king to make it so?"

Now, William looked puzzled but he nodded. "Indeed I would."

Bhrodi lifted a dark eyebrow. "I have an idea that would save Rhydilian, save your daughter, and also save you as well," he said. "I am confident this will work. Will you hear me?"

William was intrigued; so was everyone else. But there was something decidedly smug in the question that made him shake his head.

"De Shera," he said, "I have said this before and I will say it again; you are one of the most arrogant men I have ever met but if you can truly come up with a plan that will save everything that is dear to me, I most certainly will hear you."

Bhrodi grinned. By the time he was finished relaying his scheme, William didn't think he was so arrogant anymore.

He thought he was bloody brilliant.

⌘

After having visited Tacey, who was in the throes of heavy labor and screaming every time a contraction rolled over her, Penelope very quickly realized that she did not want to remain in the room with her. Tacey was so overwhelmed with what was happening that she didn't even really acknowledge Penelope when she had entered the room. The serving women seemed to have everything well in hand so Penelope retreated, heading down to the feasting hall because no one seemed to want her around, including her husband and father. They were still discussing whatever it was that Bhrodi didn't want her to hear. Sad and distraught, she ended up down in the quiet and empty feasting hall.

Penelope sat at the feasting table with her head in her hands, never having felt more desolation in her entire life. Finally, she lay her head down on the table and the tears came, silent tears of an uncertain future. As she lay there and wept, the old wardrobe rattled and the door popped open. Sniffling, she turned around in time to see the tiny old man emerge from the darkness.

He began his standard leaping about, charging an unseen enemy and then being viciously beaten back. He fell down, rolled over, and writhed around on the ground. Penelope wiped at the tears on her face, watching the nasty battle take place.

"It is too bad you cannot really fight," she muttered. "We can use all the men we can get. It seems as if you may have been a very good swordsmen once."

The old man squirmed on the ground before leaping to his feet and continuing the fight. Penelope watched him as he suddenly clutched his belly and fell to his knees.

"Can you even understand me?" she muttered. "We could use your sword, do you hear? Can you fight real men as well as you seem to fight ghosts? We are in great trouble. Edward is coming and all my father seems to want to do is run."

"That is not true."

Penelope whirled around to see William standing in the hall entry. His expression was soft, his manner weary, as he made his way into the room. Penelope watched him warily as he sat down across the table from her. He caught sight of the old man back in the shadows, now evidently suffering a mortal wound from his attacker.

"Is he still around?" he asked, pointing to the tiny man. "I saw him the first day I arrived, you know. It made me think that Rhydilian was a rather bizarre place."

Penelope was in no mood for casual conversation or humor. She looked at her hands. "He is harmless if he is not bothered," she muttered.

William took his eyes off the dramatic old man and focused on his daughter's lowered head. "How is Lady Tacey?"

Penelope shrugged. "I do not know," she said. "She is in a good deal of pain. Mama never let me around women who were giving birth so I cannot say how she is doing."

William nodded as he pondered that, feeling the tension mount between them. There was so much that needed to be said, so much that needed to be clarified. He couldn't stand the fact that she thought he was turning cowardly. It was like a stab to his heart. After a moment, he sighed.

"Penny, I know that all of this is very confusing to you," he said. "I know that you think my suggestion to leave Rhydilian is cowardly, but I want to make something very clear to you – there is a difference between defending that which is defensible and utter suicide. Right now, defending Rhydilian with eight knights and three hundred men against an army of a thousand is suicide. You may as well throw yourself on your sword, sweetheart. It would be wiser to understand your limitations and live to fight another day."

Penelope lifted her head to look at her father. "I understand all of that," she said. "But if Bhrodi will not leave, then I will not, either. He is my husband, Papa. It is my duty to stay with him."

William nodded, studying her perhaps through new light. After a moment, he smiled. "You are a fiercely loyal and extremely intelligent woman," he said softly. "I would expect no less from you. You are very much like your mother in that respect. She is fiercely loyal as well. The woman has sacrificed much for me and I would be lost without her. I will tell you a secret; the older I get, the more terrified I become that she will die before me. I cannot face life without your mother, Penny. She is everything to me, much as you are becoming everything to Bhrodi."

Her tight expression seemed to relax. "Did he tell you that?"

William nodded. "It would seem the man loves you deeply," he said. "I cannot tell you how happy this makes me. I have only ever wished happiness for you, sweetheart. It seems that you have found it."

Penelope nodded. "I have," she said, her expression turning wistful. "That is why I cannot leave him, Papa."

William nodded, reaching out across the table to take her small hand in his. He looked at her hand a moment, studying the lines of her slender fingers and the callouses of her palms. He smiled.

"I remember this hand the day you were born," he said. "You were a very late baby, you know. Your mother was well past prime childbearing age when she became pregnant with you and on a cold February night, she delivered you in about two hours. It was very fast. I was the first person who held you, you know. You took your first breath in my arms and from that moment on, I have been determined to protect you from anything that would see you come to harm. That is why I suggested leaving Rhydilian, Penny. If Edward comes here and you remain, you will die. To lose you... it would destroy me. I would never be the same."

Penelope looked at him with tears in her eyes. "I know, Papa," she murmured. "But I cannot leave my husband."

308

He kissed her hand. "And you will not have to if everything goes according to plan," he said. "Did you know that de Shera has a very brilliant and devious mind?"

She cocked her head curiously. "What do you mean?"

William patted her hand and for the first time since his arrival at Rhydilian, she saw a spark of hope there. "He has devised a plan that should work," he said. "All I ask from you is that you not ask any questions, that you do what we tell you, and that you trust me. Will you do that?"

Penelope didn't like the sound of all of that but she agreed nonetheless. "I can," she said. "But won't you tell me what the plan is?"

William patted her hand. "Just... trust me," he said. "And go see to your husband, for in a few hours, I ride back to Edward and I want you upon the battlements."

Penelope's eyes widened. "You are going back to the king?" she gasped. "But... why?"

"I said no questions."

She nodded quickly as if very forgetful. "I am sorry," she said, fear in her eyes. "But... Edward?"

He nodded. "You and the other knights will mount the walls tonight," he said. "I will be riding to Edward and I want the rest of you on watch. "

Penelope couldn't stand it; she had never been very good with cryptic information. "Do you intend to fight with Edward, Papa?" she had to ask. "Is that why you are returning to him?"

He laughed softly. "I told you no questions and you have already asked six."

Penelope sighed miserably. "I am sorry, but... but I cannot help it. I am concerned."

"I know," he said softly "That is why I asked you to trust me. Will you do it?"

"Of course I will."

"Then everything should work out for the best," he said. "I must go speak to Scott and Troy and Patrick now. They must know what is to happen."

He kissed her hands once more before he stood up and left the table. Penelope watched the man go, thinking many different thoughts at that moment. So many unanswered questions. Was he going to fight with

Edward? Was he surrendering himself? She just didn't know and the not knowing was driving her mad with fear.

Leaving the hall, she ran up to see her husband, who was in the process of having his wound cleansed. Not surprisingly, he wouldn't initially tell her what the plan was, either, but eventually, her pleading broke him down and he confessed. It was an astonishing plan that would guarantee, without anyone lifting a finger and wielding a weapon, victory against the English king.

In a move that Edward could not have foretold when he had proposed that fateful marriage contract, his actions would ultimately cause the Welsh warlord and the English legend to unite against him.

The Serpent was about to strike, this time for good.

⌘

CHAPTER TWENTY-FIVE

As the full and silver moon began to rise in the sky, Edward and eleven hundred of his men were approximately three miles away from Rhydilian as the sun set. He could see the castle in the distance, silhouetted against the deep purple sky, and he knew that next morning at dawn would see the siege that would finally, once and for all, wrest control of Anglesey from de Shera. He could taste victory already.

It was the day after the raid upon his encampment as they made their way through the wooded vales of Anglesey. Edward had never gotten this far on the island; the closest he had come was last December when a bridge had been built over the straits but Bhrodi and his vassals had been waiting for the English once they crossed. It had been a disaster he still wasn't over and now, as his army kept a casual pace along the muddy road, he saw this as a redemption. Bhrodi may have won that first battle for Anglesey, but Edward intended to win the war.

Edward's mind was also on other things; the fact that de Wolfe had pulled out during the night and had fled to Rhydilian. He simply couldn't believe that the man would betray him but, then again, de Wolfe had behaved very strangely as of late. He knew the man's daughter was married to de Shera and he knew that was why William was so torn, but it really should have been no contest at all. Kingdom before blood. Once he caught up to William, he intended to pound that fact into the man's head.

As Edward pondered de Wolfe and his bizarre behavior, he began to hear his sentries taking up the call of alarm. Edward was riding somewhere back in the bulk of his army and once he heard the cries, he spurred his expensive Belgian charger forward through the lines. He ended up near the front of the column as one of his premier knights, a man who had traveled much with him and was solidly loyal, came to meet him.

Keir St. Hével, an enormous knight with a powerful sword, flipped up his three-point visor, of the latest fashion.

"Your Grace," he said in his deep voice. "We have spotted a rider coming from the castle."

Edward was mildly interested. "How soon will we intercept?"

St. Héver turned in the direction of the road, shrouded by the heavy canopy of trees. "Soon, Your Grace," he said. "If it is your pleasure, I shall ride out to meet him."

Edward shook his head. "Nay," he replied evenly. "Let him come to us."

"Very good, Your Grace," St. Héver responded.

St. Héver brought the column to a halt. He lifted his hand and gave the command to stop, and the order rippled back through the lines until everything came to a grinding halt. Most of the infantry was on foot but no one sought to rest; in the strange and mysterious land of Anglesey, the English soldiers were on their guard. As far as they were concerned, these were cursed lands.

The rider from the castle was swift, traveling with surprising speed through the dark trees. Even as the full moon rose, the ground beneath the heavy Welsh trees was very dark and shadowed. St. Héver was at the front of the column, waiting and watching as the rider approached at a distance. As the man drew closer, St. Héver could see that it was a very big man dressed in armor. In fact, he looked English. He was therefore not surprised when William de Wolfe drew his charger up and lifted his visor.

"St. Héver," he greeted, for he knew the man. "I have a message from de Shera for the king. I must speak with him."

St. Héver merely nodded, turning his charger down the center of the column as William followed. Men and horses parted out of their way until they came to the king. The man was where St. Héver had left him, surrounded by his personal guard. William lifted a hand in greeting.

"Your Grace," he said. "I come with a message from de Shera. I would deliver it privately."

Edward's gaze upon William was anything but understanding or kind. "What are you doing, de Wolfe?" he demanded. "You and your army left during the night and fled to Wales. I told you we were to assault Rhydilian together. You deserted me!"

William shook his head. "If deserted you, I would not be here at this moment, would I?" he asked a rather droll question. "I had a purpose, Your Grace. Will you hear me or will you let me spout your personal business so that every man may hear it?"

Edward was bordering on furious. "You do not make demands of me," he snarled. "I have already sent men to Castle Questing. If you betray me, I will send orders for them to lay siege and confiscate it. I may also have your wife brought to London and throw her in the Tower to punish you for your bad behavior. Well? What do you think about that?"

William would not let himself get caught up in Edward's anger. His expression didn't change. "I will ask you again," he said steadily. "Do you want me to relay de Shera's demands out here in the open for all to hear or will you grant me a private audience?"

Edward grunted in frustration and spurred his charger forward, knocking William aside as he proceeded to the front of the army. William followed the man until he came to a halt several dozen feet down the road. They were alone here, shadowed by the trees and the creatures of the night. Above them, a night owl hooted somewhere. William directed his charger up next to the king.

"I understand your frustration," he said to Edward, "but believe me when I tell you that I had to go. I wanted to give one last try to convince the man to submit. I had to do it before you arrived at Rhydilian and he grew defensive by your mere presence. I knew if that happened, there would be no negotiations. I had to speak to him without your threat looming. Do you understand?"

Edward was still frustrated but he was coming to see William's point. "Fine," he grumbled. "So you wanted to give it one last try before I swooped upon him and destroyed him. Well? What is his message?"

William voice was steady, calming. "De Shera has agreed that to hold out against you would be futile," he said. "He has authorized me to tell you that at dawn tomorrow, he will surrender Rhydilian to you."

Like water to a flame, Edward's frustration was instantly quenched. He had been so prepared for a verbal confrontation that to hear those words out of William's mouth actually caused him to choke. He coughed, harshly, choking on the words of argument and anger that had been preparing to spout forth. His eyes widened in surprise.

"Are you serious?" he demanded. "He will surrender to me on the morrow?"

William nodded. "Aye," he said. "He asks that you camp here for the night and in the morning, Rhydilian will be yours."

Edward was deeply pleased, feeling rather full of himself and his omnipotent power as king and conqueror. "That is shocking news, de Wolfe," he admitted. "Shocking but pleasing, I must say. But what about de Shera? I want him, too. The man is a rebel, you know. We cannot let him run free."

William sighed heavily. "That is something you and I will discuss," he said. "De Shera and my daughter are in love, which makes it very difficult for me to happily turn him over to you. It would make my daughter quite miserable. Would you be willing to let him return with me to Questing to be put under my management? I can guarantee he would not take up arms against you."

Edward was so happy about the fact that he would have Rhydilian on the morrow that he was willing to negotiate about de Shera's fate. Suddenly, William was in good standing with him again as a faithful knight who had once served his father with equal faith. All was well in the world once more.

"We will discuss it," he said, but his tone hinted that he would not be happy with such a compromise. "You will sup with me tonight and on the morrow, we will ride to Rhydilian together and claim it."

William shook his head. "You will understand if I respectfully decline, Your Grace," he said. "I would like to spend the evening with my daughter. She and I have much to discuss about her future. I am sure you understand."

Edward did, but he wasn't happy about it. "Always your daughter," he muttered. "This whole thing happened because of her. What about me? Where is your love and respect for me?"

William grinned. "I have demonstrated it all of your life," he said. Then, he pointed a big gloved hand off to the north. "There is a meadow up there bordering a marsh. The land is even and there is a lake bordering the marsh with fish in it. It should make for good eating for tonight."

Edward looked towards the north where the man was pointing. All he could see was glistening grass bordered by groves of trees, all silver and shadowed beneath the full moon. He nodded shortly.

"Very well," he said. "I will tell St. Héver to settle the men there."

William turned his steed for Rhydilian. "I will see you on the morrow, then."

"You will escort me to The Serpent's door."

William just looked at him. There was so much he wanted to say, as Edward's words could not have been more ironic. After a moment, he simply nodded.

"I believe you are already there."

As William rode off into the darkness, Edward gave little thought to the odd comment. Soon enough, his men were settling down in the meadow bordering the marsh, preparing a comfortable encampment beneath the brilliant silver moon.

⌘

"Is he camping in the marsh, Father?" Patrick asked as William rode in through the gates of Rhydilian. "Were you able to convince him?"

William dismounted his charger as his biggest son made demands. "Aye," he said. "He is camping in the marsh, in the same place that we camped when the beast attacked us."

Ianto and Gwyllim, having just come from the keep, joined the conversation. Ivor had never returned from the raid on Edward's encampment and was presumed dead, so the remaining *teulu* commanders were more diligent than ever with Ivor gone and Bhrodi injured. They were working side by side with the English, trusting them, to ensure this night saved them all. They listened to William's statement to Patrick with great interest as Kevin, Edward, Scott, and Troy also came to join their group.

The English knights had been on the wall, watching the exchange with Edward from a distance and they, too, had heard the last part of William's sentence. It was what they had all been waiting for. Now the die was cast and there was just one more element left in order to put their plan in motion. With everyone crowded around William, de Wolfe focused on the *teulu* commanders.

"De Shera told me that the beast comes out to feed on a full moon, just as there is a full moon tonight," he said, "but he also said that he has a horn that brings the creature forth?"

Ianto nodded. "The horn brings forth an angry beast," he replied. "I have sent Yestin for it."

William nodded firmly. "Excellent," he said. "Will it work if we blow the horn from the battlements?"

Ianto shook his head. "It will only work if we blow it from the swamp," he said. "The beast's hearing is not very good on land. Gwyllim and I will go. We know how to get in and how to get out without being seen, and we will bring the beast of the marsh down upon your king. Those who do not die will flee. They will never want to come back here again."

William sighed heavily, feeling excitement and regret as well as exhaustion. Regret that he was about to sacrifice many fellow English, but there was no going back. This had to be done or everything would be lost.

"That is the hope," he said. "It is the hope that Edward will forget all about Anglesey and leave Rhydilian well enough alone if he knows a beast protects it. The man will be fortunate to escape with his life."

The others agreed. "Where do you want us, Uncle William?" Kevin asked, indicating himself as well as the de Wolfe sons. "Would you have us remain on the walls?"

William nodded. "I believe that would be the best place for you," he said to them. "You will keep Edward's army in your sight at all times. You will witness what happens. We will leave nothing to chance. Patrick, you have command of the wall. All things will coordinate through you."

As Patrick nodded firmly, Kevin spoke again. "And if Edward breaks free and rides to Rhydilian for shelter?" he asked softly. "What then?"

William looked at him. His one-eyed gaze was deadly. "You will make sure he does not see anyone on the battlements," he said. "For all the king knows, everyone at Rhydilian is in the keep preparing for surrender. There will be no one to hear his cries. And you will not open the gates."

Kevin cocked an eyebrow. "Not even to our king?"

"Not even to our king."

Kevin nodded, his gaze lingering on William for a moment as he turned away and headed back for the battlements. He understood now what William already understood; blood over a kingdom. Family above all. Edward sought to destroy part of William's family and he would not tolerate it. Now, it was a fight for survival and William intended to win.

As Kevin moved away with the de Wolfe brothers in tow, Paris and Kieran emerged from the keep. Seeing that William had returned made them walk quickly in the man's direction.

"Well?" Paris demanded. "Is he setting up camp in the marsh?"

William nodded. "He is," he said, his gaze lingering on his oldest and dearest friend. "How is de Shera faring? Is his fever still raging?"

Paris shrugged. "It is not getting any worse," he said. "Penelope will not leave him, however, not even to see the beast make a meal out of Edward. She remains at his side."

William sighed, his gaze moving to the big, imposing keep silhouetted against the starry night. "I do not expect her to," he said. "She fears for her husband's life."

Paris had been a healer for many years and was more competent than most physics. William trusted his word on matters such as this.

"I do not believe the fever will claim him," Paris said. "It is bad, that is true, but de Shera's surgeon seems competent. He has taken good care of him. But the sister, however, is another issue."

William looked at him with some surprise. "What do you mean?"

Paris lifted his eyebrows. "She carries a very big baby and she is a very small girl," he said, somewhat quietly. "The baby is breech and I have tried twice to turn him around, but it is very tight. I will go in a little while and try again. She is so young, William. Her body is simply not prepared for this birth."

William was feeling some sadness at that prospect. "Is Thomas with her?"

Paris nodded. "He is."

"He is fond of her, you know. At least, that is what Penelope has told me."

Again, Paris nodded. "He is up there singing to her, very softly. It is sad, truly."

William was quite a moment. "If it looks as if she will not survive this birth, get him out of the chamber," he said softly. "I do not want him distressed by something he cannot help. He is still young, Paris. I do not want an experience like this affecting him for the rest of his life."

Paris nodded faintly. "If the girl does not survive the birth, it will be distressing to your wife and to Jemma. I believe they felt rather responsible for her while they were here."

William lifted his eyebrows, consigning young Lady Tacey to the grace of God. "Do what you can," he said. "You stay to the keep with de Shera and his sister. That is where you are needed most."

Paris turned and walked away, leaving William standing there with Kieran and the two *teulu* commanders. There was a lingering sadness over Tacey's state and Bhrodi's ill health. William glanced at the *teulu* commanders, seeing distress on their faces. Their entire world was changing, perhaps even about to shatter. But they were soldiers and soldiers had to endure. Clearing his throat, he changed the focus.

"This horn that calls the beast," he said, speaking on the first subject he could think of. "De Shera tells me that it is very old."

Ianto, still lingering over Tacey's situation, struggled to pull himself out of his gloom. "It is, my lord," he replied. "It belonged to the Northmen who brought the beast with them."

"And it will truly call this creature forth?"

"It will indeed, my lord."

"Have you had occasion to do that?"

Ianto could see that Bhrodi hadn't told de Wolfe why, exactly, they had the horn or what they did with it. The man's question told him that. He wondered how de Wolfe would react if he knew that de Shera used the creature to exact revenge on his enemies. But he supposed it didn't matter now; they were all in this together. After a moment, Ianto nodded.

"Indeed we have, my lord," he said. "The beast of the marsh has a taste for human flesh. Lord de Shera's father and forefathers summoned the creature to smite their enemies, just as we are doing tonight. What we do on this dark and clear night is something the lords of Rhydilian have done for generations. Your king will become the latest victim in a long line of many, all enemies of the House of de Shera."

William was listening to the man seriously. "Then that is why he suggested this," he said. "You have done this before."

Ianto nodded. "Many times, my lord."

It made perfect sense. De Shera was known as The Serpent but not merely because of his deadly battle tactics; there was something more to that reputation, something that blended into legend. As de Shera had once told him, the beast of the marsh and Bhrodi de Shera were one and the same. Perhaps that was really true. Now, the English enemies would fall victim to that legend as well.

As William pondered the many facets of Bhrodi de Shera, he noticed a figure emerging from the keep. But it wasn't any figure; it looked suspiciously like Bhrodi and when William realized that Penelope was emerging with him, hanging on to him, he was jolted into action. As he ran for the keep, he saw Paris at the top of the steps as well and he could hear the man's distressed voice. It was obvious that Paris was very unhappy. Still, Bhrodi, hunched over and moving like a cripple, seemed determined and Penelope right along with him. They were descending the steps but William ran up to meet them, an astonished expression on his face.

"What are you doing?" he demanded. "De Shera, you are going to put yourself into an early grave."

Bhrodi's arms were wrapped around his gut, his face pale and sweaty. But the look of determination on his features was powerful enough to move mountains.

"Edward is on my doorstep," he grunted. "Did you truly believe I would greet the man lying in my bed?"

William looked at Penelope; she had tears in her eyes but she was struggling very hard to be brave. A glance at Paris showed the man to be nearly as distressed as Penelope. As foolish as Bhrodi's actions were, unfortunately, William understood them completely. The man was a knight, and a very good one, and this night would either see his empire preserved or destroyed. Of course he could not have simply lain there and waited for Fate to strike. If his life was to be ended, then he wanted to meet it head-on and if he was to be saved, then he wanted to greet the fortunes of Fate for the same reason. William sighed heavily.

"Where do you intend to go?" he asked, his tone resigned.

Bhrodi looked around the bailey, to the walls of his mighty castle. His gaze lingered on the battlements. "Up there," he murmured, causing everyone to turn to see what he was looking at. "Upon the wall of the castle that has been in my family for almost two hundred years. I want to see Edward's destruction for myself. It is my right."

William could hardly disagree. "Bhrodi, you cannot make it," he muttered. "In your condition, you will be fortunate to make it across the bailey."

At Bhrodi's side, Penelope was trying very hard not to weep out loud. She wiped at the tears on her face. "I will help him, Papa," she said. "He has asked me to help him."

She was trying so hard to be brave and William's heart nearly broke for her. Bhrodi, damaged and ill, was doing what came naturally to him and Penelope understood that. Like William, she understood completely. William looked at Paris, standing behind the pair, and the two of them silently conveyed words of resignation. It would be of no use to try and stop the man. De Shera was determined to see the threat to his life, and his world, ended. Either that, or he would meet it head-on if the beast failed to complete its task. After a few moment's hesitation, William backed away and Bhrodi continued his hunched-over walk.

Penelope had a grip on her husband's left arm, struggling to assist the man who was quite a bit larger than she was. Paris walked behind them, holding out his hands to catch de Shera if the man faltered, and William ended up beside Paris doing much the same thing. Together, they followed Bhrodi and Penelope as they made their way very slowly across the bailey. It was a trek that was attracting attention.

Now, the de Wolfe brothers were watching from the battlements and Kevin went so far as to come down from the wall. He started to run towards the pair, to assist, but was intercepted by his father. Kieran had been watching it all from the gatehouse. When Kevin resisted his efforts, Kieran was firmer about it.

"Nay, lad," he muttered. "This is something they must do together. They do not need you."

Kevin was watching with great distress. "But he cannot make it alone," he pointed out. "She will need help."

Kieran had his hand on his son's chest. "It is time you learn that you cannot be there for Penny any longer," he murmured, making to meet Kevin's eye. "She is Bhrodi's wife and although I realize you have been very helpful to them during your stay here, you must think on it from Bhrodi's point of view – how would you feel if you were married to Penny and a man kept trying to interfere, no matter how altruistic his intentions?"

Kevin didn't like that question, mostly because he knew the answer. He started to say something but just couldn't find the words. His gaze followed Penelope as she struggled to assist Bhrodi across the muddy bailey. All the while, his heart was breaking; his father was right. He couldn't help her any longer. He could no longer interfere in her marriage.

Without another word, he turned away and headed back to the battlements. Kieran watched his son go, feeling heavy-hearted for him. It was difficult to accept that the woman he loved would never be his wife. It was difficult to accept that she belonged to another. He could have told Kevin that there would be other women and other loves for him, but that wasn't something he wanted to hear right now. Kevin would have to grieve the loss of Penelope before he would be able to move on. For Kevin, it was finally over.

Bhrodi and Penelope were now in the middle of the bailey, slowly making progress towards the gatehouse and the battlements. Penelope had a tight hold of him, now counting out the steps as he moved. *Step, step. Step, step. That's good. You are doing very well.* But it was a slow and painful journey. They were just entering the shadow of the gatehouse when behind them, Yestin emerged from the keep. The tall, lanky man ran down the stairs, nearly falling at the bottom, in his haste to reach his liege. As he ran across the ward, he began to shout.

"It is gone!" he cried. "The *tafod* is not in its place!"

Everyone seemed to come to a halt, particularly Bhrodi. Holding on to his guts, he looked over his shoulder as Yestin came running up. The man's eyes were wide with shock.

"Fy arglwydd," Yestin gasped. "Y tafod ar goll!

My lord, the horn is missing! Bhrodi's brow furrowed. "What do you mean?" he demanded, reaching out to grasp Yestin. "Did you look in my chamber?"

Yestin nodded furiously. "I did, my lord," he said, his English stilted and heavily accented. "I went to your chamber, to the chest near the tapestry, and it is not there. It is gone!"

Bhrodi tried not to get caught up in Yestin's panic. William and Paris came up to join the group, both men equally concerned. William looked to Bhrodi.

"Could someone have taken it?" he asked. "One of the servants, mayhap?"

Bhrodi was truly at a loss. "It is possible," he said, "but why? They would not know what it was. Only me and my *teulu* know what it is meant for."

William struggled not to become increasingly concerned. "Could it have been misplaced? Mayhap it was put elsewhere."

Bhrodi shook his head. "Never," he replied. "It is always in the same place. It has never been moved."

William wasn't sure what more to say; he turned to Paris, who looked back at him with some apprehension. *The horn was missing.* Would their night be over before it began? After a moment of indecision and confusion, William returned his attention to Bhrodi.

"You have said the beast emerges to feed on the full moon," he said, his voice quiet. "The moon is full tonight. The beast will come without the horn, will it not?"

Bhrodi sighed heavily, looking up to the brilliant moon and starry night. "Aye, it should," he replied, "unless it has already fed. If that is the case, then it will not feed again this night. That is why the horn is important... it is a sound that brings out the bloodlust in the creature. When the beast hears the horn, it knows that fear and blood and mayhem are expected. It comes forth because we summon it. We *must* rouse that bloodlust against Edward."

Now, everyone was starting to feel the same apprehension that Yestin and Bhrodi were feeling. The horn was somehow key to all of this, a crucial part of the plan that was now missing. If they couldn't find it, then it was very possible everything would fail; Edward would expect Rhydilian on the morrow and would be faced with three hundred Welsh and English socked in and prepared to fight. It would bring forth everything William and Bhrodi had been fearful of. It would bring about the end.

But Bhrodi was unwilling to give up. This was his plan and he would see it through to the bloody end; too many people were depending on it. His frustration began to get the better of him.

"It is always in that chest," he said, looking Penelope as if she could help him find the answers. "The only people who know it is there are me and my *teulu*. No one else would know its worth except...."

He trailed off and it was evident that a thought occurred to him. Penelope was nearly frantic. "What?" she demanded. "Who else would know its worth?"

Bhrodi was almost afraid to voice what he was thinking but the more he thought on it, the more it might be a viable possibility. He looked at William.

"When you came to me this morning and we discussed this plan," he said, "my uncle was in the room. Do you recall? He came upstairs and hid in the tapestry as we were discussing this very scheme."

William did indeed recall the tiny little man with the stringy white hair, fighting his way into the room and then wrapping himself up in the tapestry.

"Indeed I do," he said. "Why?"

Bhrodi's mind was moving quickly. "Because he has also been present nearly every time we have discussed Edward's want of Rhydilian," he said. "Even if the man is quite mad, he knows about the horn because he is my grandfather's brother. The man knows everything about Rhydilian. It is quite possible that somewhere in that insane and outlandish mind of his, he understood what we were speaking of. He understood our peril and he understood our plan. Is it possible that he actually took the horn and is now out wandering the marsh, preparing to unleash the beast?"

Penelope wasn't apt to believe it so quickly. "How is that possible?" she wanted to know. "He has been in the hall when we have discussed Edward but he never acknowledged that he understood anything. He fights his ghosts and returns to the wardrobe."

Bhrodi knew that. God help him, he knew that, but he just couldn't shake the possibility. He turned to Yestin. "Go see if my uncle is in his wardrobe," he ordered. "If he is, then we are right back where we started, but if he is not...."

Yestin nodded swiftly and began to run. But the moment he did so, a faint sound, like that of a mournful beastly cry, filled the air. The knights upon the battlements who had been watching the conversation with Bhrodi suddenly rushed to the parapets, straining to find the source of the sound. They were looking off towards the marsh, into that dark and cold night with the blanket of stars high above. Even William, Paris, and Kieran began to swiftly mount the ladders to the wall walk so they could see where the sound was coming from.

But Bhrodi knew; he knew the moment that heady, rough tone pierced the cold night air. He'd heard the sound a thousand times before. He looked at Penelope.

"That is the horn," he murmured hoarsely. "Someone is blowing it."

Yestin, who had momentarily paused when they heard the first few sounds of the horn, now ran for the keep and disappeared inside. Back in the bailey, however, Penelope was looking at Bhrodi with a mixture of disbelief and apprehension.

"Do you really think it is your uncle?" she whispered. "It is truly possible he understood everything we were saying and is now seeing the final element of your plan through?"

Bhrodi was gazing into her wide hazel eyes, seeing the woman he loved. But it was more than that; she was his strength, his heart, his soul, and the day he found her out in the marsh driving her broadsword into the eye of the beast was the day he had begun to live again. Only he didn't know it then; all he knew was that his life had been a dead thing, a terrible thing, and now it was pure joy. What Sian's death had taken out of him, Penelope had put back and then some. He was overflowing with the life and love she gave to him.

"It is not only possible, it is probable," he murmured.

Yestin suddenly appeared at the keep entry. "The old man is gone!" he shouted into the bailey. "Shall I look for him?"

Bhrodi called him off; there was no need. He knew where his uncle had gone. The horn sounded again and so did a host of distant cries; faint screams began to fill the air. As the English knights watched with amazement from their vantage point on the battlements of Rhydilian, the beast of the marsh, the serpent of legend, emerged from the murky depths to destroy more than half of Edward's army.

It was a brutal, bloody fight as men tried to fight off the creature with swords, only to see dozens upon dozens of men chopped to pieces by the beast's dagger-like teeth. The cries, the fight, went on into the night and Bhrodi, who had practically been lifted to the battlements by William and Paris, watched it all. On that dark and brilliant night, his legacy was saved at the jaws of the Serpent.

Edward managed to escape along with those fortunate enough to avoid the gnashing jaws, making all due haste back the way they had come. They had no choice, as the creature had virtually blocked their path to the castle, which would have offered quick shelter. They left everything behind – provisions wagons, equipment, and men, all of that as England's offering to Anglesey's angry beast, an apology for having come to Anglesey in the first place.

Terror followed Edward's men that night because when they reached the ferry over the Menai Strait and there wasn't enough room to shuttle everyone on the first crossing, many of them plunged into the frigid waters and tried to swim across. By the time Edward crossed the strait and headed back to his encampment at Aber, he had eighty-seven out of the nearly one thousand men he had traveled to Anglesey with. The creature's feast had been thorough.

Edward never spoke of that event again. It was hushed-up, a forbidden topic even in the most private of conversations. Even when he managed to conquer all of Wales in subsequent years, the topic of Rhydilian Castle and Bhrodi de Shera was strictly off limits, and the Pendraeth Forest was heavily avoided. No one really knew why, only that Edward had commanded it. He never ventured into that area again and de Shera never ventured out. At least, not that Edward was aware of. It was an unspoken arrangement that evidently made both of them happy. In truth, Edward didn't want the man badly enough to risk facing the creature of the marsh again.

Thoughts of that terrible night in the swamp gave the man nightmares up until his deathbed. Edward took the truth of that night, and the truth behind The Serpent, to his grave.

Nobody would have believed him, anyway.

CHAPTER TWENTY-SIX

Three weeks later

"Papa? Thomas?" Penelope called up the stairs. "Are you coming? Everyone is waiting!"

Penelope could hear hissing and fussing up on the third floor. Standing next to Bhrodi in the keep entry, they had been waiting for her father and brother for quite some time. Penelope looked at her husband who, in spite of his improving health, still appeared pale and drawn. And sad; he was most definitely sad. She put her arms around him.

"You do not have to do this," she murmured. "We can quite easily raise the child as our own."

Bhrodi sighed faintly as he planted a kiss on her forehead. "Nay," he said quietly. "This is the best thing for the child. Going to live with your father and mother and being raised far from Wales is the safest course of action. No one will ever think a full-blooded Welsh princess to be living with the greatest English knight in all of England. After what Edward did to Dafydd and his family, I am terrified for this child. We must spirit her out of Wales and away from Edward."

Penelope smiled sadly at him; she knew how hard it was. It had been very hard for all of them with Tacey's death after having given birth to a very large daughter. Paris had tried so hard to save the young woman but in the end, it had been too much for her immature body to handle. Thomas had been devastated.

But there were more threats to the Welsh now than ever before; even though Edward had been turned back from Rhydilian, Dafydd and his family had been captured. Edward had shown no mercy in sending Dafydd's children and wife to prisons all throughout England and in taking Dafydd himself to London to face execution. Fortunately, he seemed to have forgotten about Bhrodi altogether, which was as they had intended. No one would dare try to reach Rhydilian again with the threat of The Serpent lingering about. Still, Bhrodi didn't want his niece in Wales. He wanted her safe with The Wolfe where she could grow up without fear. He knew that was what Tacey would have wanted.

As Penelope clung contentedly to her husband, they could hear footsteps coming down the stairs. Thomas was first, carrying a chest of things for the baby, while Paris was next, fussing at William, who was coming down behind him carrying the infant in his arms.

"Paris, get out of my way," William told him. "You fuss and worry like an old fish wife. If I fall, it is because you tripped me."

Paris gave him a droll expression. "If you fall, it is because you are a one-eyed knight and have no business carrying an infant," he said flatly. "Give her to me."

William would not relinquish his prize and the baby slept peacefully through all of the scolding. Penelope shook her head at the two of them.

"Look at you two," she said reproachfully. "Fighting over a baby."

Paris scowled at her although it was good-naturedly. "You keep out of this," he told her. "This is between your father and me."

Penelope stuck her tongue out at him. "All of the arguing in the world is not going to force him to turn over the baby," she said. "You may as well stop begging."

William grinned as he came off the stairs with the tiny bundle in his big arms. He made his way over to Penelope and Bhrodi, who strained to get a look at the little girl with the perfect features.

"Is she a good baby, Papa?" Penelope asked. "I have never been around one long enough to have experience with them."

William was gazing down into the little face. "Aye," he said. "She is a good baby. Not like you were; you screamed all hours of the day or night. There were times that I was tempted to put you in a basket and send you out to sea."

Penelope scowled as Bhrodi grinned. "If she does not behave herself, I still may do that," he said.

Everyone chuckled at Penelope's expense. "I think you are all horrid," she said, reaching out to touch the tiny little hand that was exposed through the blankets. "Mama will love her, won't she? She will be so excited to have a baby around again."

William nodded. "She will indeed," he replied, glancing over at Paris. "We have the wet nurse, correct?"

Paris nodded patiently. "I have a wet nurse and two serving women to accompany us back to England," he said. "Trust me; Lady Tacey will have everything she needs. She will want for nothing."

William's gaze lingered on the baby before seeking out his daughter. For a moment, they simply gazed at one another with warmth and understanding until finally, he smiled weakly.

"I suppose this is appropriate," he said. "I brought my baby girl to Wales and now I leave with a baby girl to replace the one I have given away."

Penelope could sense his farewell coming and she fought off the lump in her throat. "You will spoil her as you spoiled me," she said softly. "You will be the best father in the world to her as you were to me."

William leaned over and kissed his daughter on the forehead. "I have done my job and now it is time for you to do yours," he said, trying not to notice the tears in her eyes because it would bring on his own. He looked at Bhrodi. "Your niece will be well tended and brought up to love and respect her Welsh heritage. You may come and visit her any time you wish."

Bhrodi nodded. "Mayhap someday," he said, his gaze lingering on the baby. "Thank you for taking her. I am at peace knowing she is out of Wales and out of Edward's reach."

William's gaze was on his daughter as Bhrodi spoke and he could see the tears beginning to trickle out of her eyes. That was his cue to leave before they both started weeping. He turned for the keep entry with Bhrodi and Penelope following.

"Once I have returned to Questing, I will discover what I can about Edward's current status and plans," he said. "Although I am sure he will leave you alone now, I am equally sure that his conquest of Wales is imminent. I am not entirely sure what he intends to do about Anglesey but I suppose time will tell. For now, you are safe."

They had reached the top of the steps leading down into the bailey where the de Wolfe party await. Penelope had already said her farewells to her brothers and she waved down at them as they wait impatient for their father. Edward, Thomas, and Patrick waved back while Scott yelled up at his father.

"We are already an hour late," he called. "Are you coming with us or not?"

William gave his eldest son a wry expression. "I am going to hand this baby over to Paris and come show you personally just how enthusiastic I am about your question."

As the knights snorted, Paris held out his hands. "Finally!" he exclaimed softly. "Give me the child so you can go teach your arrogant son a lesson."

William shielded the baby from the man's probing hands. "Never," he said. "My son will have to wait. For now, I plan to see this baby personally delivered to the nurse so we can depart. Go mount your horse and leave us alone."

Paris was unhappy but did as he was told. He kissed Penelope on the cheek before descending the steps and heading towards his charger. William, very carefully, began to take the steps as Penelope followed. Bhrodi, however, remained at the top; it was still difficult for him to take steps with ease. Besides, he had a feeling Penelope wanted a few moments alone with her father. She had been weepy about it all morning and now the time to say her goodbyes had come.

"De Wolfe," he called. When William paused and turned around, Bhrodi's gaze was warm. "For everything... I thank you. I owe my entire life to you and I will not forget it. Do you remember when we first met and I told you that I was raised on stories of your valor?"

William nodded. "I do."

Bhrodi smiled faintly. "I consider it an honor to now be part of those stories, however small."

It was the first humble thing William had ever heard the man say and he grinned. "I am flattered," he said, glancing to his daughter. "Now you will make your own stories with my daughter by your side. I will be proud to tell everyone that my daughter is married to The Serpent. It is the stuff legends are made of."

Penelope gazed at her father, unable to stop the tears. Wrapping her arms around his waist, she hugged him tightly.

"I miss you already, Papa," she whispered. "Safe travels."

William kissed the top of her head. "Thank you, sweetheart," he murmured. "And to you, I wish you only the best. Should you ever need me, you know I will come."

Penelope nodded, wiping at her eyes. "I know," she said. "And thank you."

He stepped off the last step, turning to look at her. "For what?"

She smiled faintly, glancing up at Bhrodi as she replied. "For making me come here," she said. "For giving me this future. You were right when you said this was an honor; I cannot think of anything more honorable than being the wife of Bhrodi de Shera."

William could hear the love in her voice and it touched him. "Love him well, Penny."

She turned to him, a smile of such warmth and joy on her face that it took William's breath away.

"I already do, Papa," she murmured. "I already do."

William's lingering recollection of that moment was of watching his daughter rush up the stairs and into the arms of the man she loved. For The Wolfe and The Serpent, their lives, their loves, and their legends were forever linked.

They were the Immortals.

⌘

The de Shera Dynasty

Children of Bhrodi and Penelope

William b1284
Perri b1287
Bowen b1289
Dai b1292
Catrin (g) b1294
Morgana (g) b1296
Maddock b1299
Anthea (g) b1303
Talan b1305

EPILOGUE

Present day, early June
Pendraeth Forest, Anglesey, Wales
Archaeological Dig for the University of California at San Marcos in
conjunction with the University of Aberystwyth

Eleven hundred and twenty one.

That was the number of broken and scattered skeletons the dig had managed to piece together under the direction of Dr. Becker, but there still wasn't one complete one. There were pieces missing from every single skeleton, small bones, broken bones, whatever... Becker was starting to believe he would never find everything.

But there was more now that had come to light over the past two weeks – weapons. Swords, shields, daggers and the like. They were strewn about near the broken bodies as if someone had thrown them all around without rhyme or reason. There was no logic to their locations, which made Becker think he wasn't witnessing a battle. More than that, these weapons could not do the amount of damage he was seeing. It was indeed baffling.

Because of this, both the University of California at San Marcos and University of Aberystwyth had allocated more funds to what was becoming a truly spectacular Medieval find, something never before found anywhere in the world. They'd called in Medieval scholars, paleontologists, anthropologists, cultural historians and the like. They had Welsh historians covering the place, searching out legends and myths, trying to determine what, exactly, they were dealing with but so

331

far they'd come up with very little. It was like one giant historical mystery that, naturally, made the historians foam at the mouth. Situations like this were rare and the small army of scholars was determined to solve the puzzle.

On this muggy day in early June, Dr. Becker was excavating an undisturbed section of the dig, uncovering more skeletons, while Dr. Paz was riveted to what they determined to be a nest of destroyed sauropod eggs near the skeleton of the creature. It seemed like a normal day, but things were about to change. It was mid-morning when a small Vauxhall sedan pulled up to the main section of tents and a woman emerged.

Dressed in a blouse, jeans, and Wellington boots, the woman was slender and very lovely with long dark hair pulled back into a ponytail. In her arms she carried a veritable mound of notebooks and file folders. She entered the first tent in her search for Dr. Becker but was told he was out in the field, so she headed into one of the tents where they were assembling the skeletons. They knew the woman here and she was greeted amiably. When she asked for Becker again, someone went off to fetch him.

The woman sat at one of the main plastic folding tables around the tent and, brushing the dirt off the surface, began to spread her papers out. She had a very specific order for them, as she had been sent out on this project by Dr. Becker. She was a Ph.D. candidate in Medieval Studies and had been loaned to Dr. Becker from the University of Pennsylvania because her advisor and Dr. Becker had been college buddies. Dr. Becker had needed a crack research assistant and Paige Wolfford had been recommended, but her first project with the famed Dr. Becker had been, in the truest sense of the vernacular, a doozy.

Paige spread her things out, organizing her thoughts, as she waited for Dr. Becker to make an appearance. He wasn't long in coming and he wasn't alone; there was a man with him, perhaps in his early thirties, and as he drew closer, Paige could see that he was a big man with dark hair and an extraordinarily handsome face. She had no way of knowing that she was looking at the man the rest of the women around the dig had been calling Lord McHotness since he had arrived two weeks earlier. As it was, she felt her heart leap a little as the man came near, his dark green eyes fixed on her. Dr. Becker spoiled the moment by putting himself between her and his Royal Hotness.

"Hello, Paige," he greeted pleasantly. "I didn't expect to see you here for at least another week or so."

Paige shook his outstretched hand. "Me, either, but I think I found something you'd be interested in so I didn't want to wait."

Becker nodded eagerly and then realized he hadn't introduced her to the big guy trailing after him. He indicated the future Mr. Paige Wolfford.

"Paige, this is Dr. Bodie Deshere," he said. "Bodie is from the University of Aberystwyth, well-versed on anything Welsh. He's been helping me try to piece this puzzle together."

Paige shook Bodie's hand. "Nice to meet you, Dr. Deshere," she said. "So you're the go-to guy for all things Welsh related?"

He grinned, a sexy gesture that Paige found captivating. "Maybe in a land of English people, I am," he said, his English spoken with a heavy Welsh accent that made it very difficult to understand. "But to the Welsh, I'm just a kicker."

Paige cocked her head. "What's a kicker?"

He shrugged. "Some smart kid who thinks he knows everything," he replied. "I have a doctorate and my father still thinks he knows more than I do."

Paige laughed. "I have a dad like that, too."

"Is your dad a scholar?"

She shook her head. "No," she replied. "He's with the United States Navy. In fact, both of my parents are. That's how they met; my mom is a nurse and dad came in with a busted up leg or something. I really don't know because he won't tell us the whole story. All we know is that my mom worked on my dad and it was love at first sight."

Bodie started to say something but Becker interrupted. "You kids can get more acquainted later," he said. "Right now, I want to know what you found out. Anything good?"

Paige nodded and turned back to her paperwork, disappointed she wasn't able to continue her conversation with Deshere. But her disappointment was forgotten as her attention shifted to the paper in front of her.

"Well," she began as she fingered through the sheets. "You know there wasn't a lot of information around here for some reason. We know Rhydilian Castle belonged to the de Shera family from about the conquest until the late fourteenth century when the family evidently abandoned it."

"Edward the First had conquered all of Wales at that point," Deshere said. "The de Sheras were the hereditary kings of Anglesey, but even they couldn't stand up to Edward's war machine."

Paige nodded. "That's what I thought, too," she said. "Edward the First is who I'm writing my thesis on so I know more about him, and his time period, than just about anything else in the High Middle Ages. So I started back-tracking in the de Shera family history thinking I might find something there that would help us understand what this site is all about, but they really didn't have any surviving records other than church records, and those only record marriages, deaths and births. Therefore, I started looking at all of the de Shera marriages moving back from 1394 A.D., which was when they abandoned the castle. I didn't find anything interesting until I came to 1283 A.D. when a lord by the name of Bhrodi de Shera married a bride from a very powerful English family. I thought that was kind of odd, you know, a Welsh warlord marrying an Englishwoman, so I began to trace the de Wolfe family. A really impressive history if you ever have the time to read about it."

Becker was nodding rather impatiently. "I know all about de Wolfe," he said. "But what did you find out pertaining to the de Sheras?"

Paige pulled out a sheet from a file folder and started reading. "The de Wolfe family was a heavy presence from late in the rule of Henry the Third and well into Edward's rule, so much in fact that I found evidence of a treaty brokered by Edward that betrothed a daughter of William de Wolfe, who was perhaps the greatest knight during that time period, to Bhrodi de Shera, who was the head of the family at that time. It was supposed to be a peace treaty for all of Northern Wales since the de Shera family had such influence there, but it didn't turn out that way at all. There was something really weird going on there because after the marriage, it was as if Edward made a conscious effort to stay away from the de Shera family and, specifically, this part of Wales, which isn't like him at all."

Becker was growing very interested. "What do you mean?"

Paige was still looking at a photocopy of something. "I was in London doing most of my research at the British Library and a colleague of mine, who has connections with Northumberland Heritage, made a call to see if I could get a look at the de Wolfe family papers. There are a ton of them, you know, from the time of the conquest up until the Georgian era. Their seat was Castle Questing,

334

which is now just a ruin. Sometime in the late sixteenth century they built a big manor house near Belford up on the Northumberland coast and abandoned the castle. Anyway, I was able to drive up to the manor and take a look at their papers."

Becker pulled up a chair, as did Deshere. The sat on opposite sides of her, straining to catch a glimpse at what she was looking at. Paige glanced up at the pair, seeing they were rather anxious.

"I know Dr. Paz is working on the skeleton of the creature," she said quietly. "Do you want to bring her in here to hear this?"

Becker sent one of the grad students on the run and Paige didn't say another word until several minutes later when Dr. Paz entered the tent. The woman was sweating profusely in the early June humidity, removing her gloves and ball cap as she approached.

"What's all the excitement?" she wanted to know, wiping at her forehead as her gaze fell on the young women with the stack of papers before her. "Hello, Paige. I thought Dr. Becker sent you to London."

Becker thrust a chair at her. "Sit down," he said. "Paige has discovered something about the site. She says you're going to want to hear this."

"Really?" Dr. Paz perked up. "What did you find?"

Paige looked up from the papers she had been reading. "Rhydilian Castle has connections to the House of de Wolfe, so I went to Northumberland to do some research and see if I could come up with some kind information about this sauropod and its history here by way of the de Wolfes. They had a daughter who married Bhrodi de Shera, a very big warlord during the late thirteenth century. I focused on William de Wolfe because it was his daughter who married de Shera, and it turns out that de Wolfe, in later life, ended up dictating a lot of his history to a local priest. It's all written in Latin, but there's a section that talks about his daughter's marriage to de Shera and how Edward betrayed the very treaty he had proposed. It says that one night, when Edward came to lay siege to Rhydilian, that The Serpent did smite its enemies and that Edward was turned back. According to William de Wolfe, Bhrodi de Shera was also known as The Serpent."

Becker's brow furrowed in confusion as he looked at Deshere. "Have you ever heard of that?" he asked. "You're the Welsh folklore expert."

Deshere sat back in his seat, pondering the question. After a moment, he cocked his head. "You know," he said thoughtfully, "I did a research paper once on the families of Anglesey and there was a

335

passage in one of the sources that described the de Shera family as having bred a beast. I didn't take it literally because they were known for their fierce warlords, but now that I think on it, it's quite possible that the source meant literally. If de Shera was known as The Serpent, the beast and The Serpent could have been one and the same, but there's a problem with that."

"Why?" Becker wanted to know.

Deshere shook his head. "Because the sources are very early, possibly eleventh century," he said. "Well before Bhrodi de Shera was born."

"Wait," Paige said, interrupting their conversation. "This gets better. I went back to the history of Edward the First during the time that Bhrodi de Shera married into the de Wolfe family somewhere around 1283 A.D. This was the same year that Dafydd ap Gruffydd was captured and executed as the last Welsh prince when, in fact, de Shera was really the last Welsh prince. He was a hereditary king, in fact, but Edward left the man completely alone, which I thought was really bizarre. I found all kinds of information about the battles Edward fought in northern Wales, including the battle of Moel-y-don, which was when Edward's men built a pontoon bridge over the Menai Strait and tried to invade Anglesey but were defeated. The only battles described between January and June of that year are, in fact, with Dafydd, but in cross-referencing those battles with other known sources, I came across an account of a knight who fought with Edward during those months. The knight's name was Keir St. Héver. It's St. Héver who describes Edward making an attempt to seize Rhydilian but was driven back by what he describes as a great and terrible serpent."

Becker digested the information, as did the others. "But you said de Shera was known as The Serpent," Becker said. "He could have meant de Shera."

Paige nodded. "Maybe," she said. "It seems pretty coincidental, don't you think? De Shera is known as The Serpent, yet you find this sauropod skeleton with bodies scattered all over the place. St. Héver stated that Edward lost nearly a thousand men. How many skeletons have you found?"

Becker was coming to understand that this entire situation was not so cut and dried. Now, it was starting to make some sense and that great mystery they had been trying to solve was slowly beginning to pull together.

"More than eleven hundred," he muttered, turning to look at the scene in the distance. Mind working furiously, he stood up, rubbing at his chin. "So... maybe what we're seeing here is an army and not a dumping ground for bodies. That would explain the weapons we've found."

Paige was startled by the information. "You have?"

Becker nodded. "Tons of them," he said. "The first big beautiful broadsword we found with the stones was only the beginning. Since then, we've found more swords, crossbows, spears... you name it. But those kinds of weapons don't make the injuries we've seen. Moreover, there are teeth marks all over the bones and we know those came from the beast. But now it's making some sense – this was Edward's army and that... that *skeleton* Dr. Paz is excavating annihilated them."

Paige nodded. "It makes a lot of sense," she said. "Interesting we had to find this out from English knights not local Welsh folklore, though. It's like the Welsh didn't want to acknowledge it."

Deshere held up a finger. "That might not be necessarily true," he said. "I seem to recall a nursery rhyme that most Welshmen know. It's very old but now that I recall it, it seems to fit this situation perfectly."

"How does it go?" Paige asked.

Bodie turned to look at her, his eyes glimmering. He began to recite in a soft, alluring voice.

"*...A knight, he traveled, lone and weary,*
Upon a road so high.
Upon this road, a wraith came leery,
And moved the knight to by.
'Behold,' said he, 'I clearly see,
Your heart is not content.'
'Be wise,' it replied, 'and know, forsooth,
That all is not as it seems.
Your road is long, and your path is wrong,
For you have entered the realm of the Serpent.'"

For a moment, no one spoke. Even Becker turned to look at him. "And you're just remembering that now?"

Deshere shrugged. "It's a common enough nursery rhyme," he said. "But I never made the connection until she said that de Shera was known as The Serpent. An ironic coincidence, I'd say."

Becker returned gaze to the archaeological dig in the near distance. After a moment, he sighed heavily.

"Well," he said, "I suppose what's left now is to start seeing if we can link the weapons we found to something Edward the First's army would carry. We'll need to call in some Medieval Military experts for that."

Deshere shook his head. "No need," he said. "I've got you covered on that. Medieval Warfare is one of my specialties."

Becker glanced at him. "Even for an English king?"

Deshere snorted. "*Especially* an English king," he said, looking rather peeved. "Those guys were always lusting after my country. Who was it that said 'know your enemy'?"

"Some Englishman," Paige muttered.

Everyone laughed as Becker and Paz trickled out into the site to begin re-examining the find, now with Paige's research attached. Deshere started to go but something made him hang back; he ended up back over by Paige's table as she neatly put her documents in order. He couldn't seem to move away from her, really; from the moment he saw her, there was something very magnetic about her. Familiar, even, as if he'd seen those wide hazel eyes before. *Maybe in my dreams*, he thought. In any case, he didn't want to walk away from her. He just couldn't seem to do it.

"Excellent job on your research," he said.

Paige looked up from her papers. "Thanks," she said, eyeing him as she put the sheets away. "So… how long have you been here with Becker?"

"Long enough."

She grinned. "Have you been up to the castle yet?" she asked. "I was thinking about heading up there. I've been reading so much about it lately that I feel as if I know it."

Deshere nodded. "I've been up there," he said, but he couldn't let the opportunity to learn more about her slip away. "I'd be happy to go up there with you. Maybe there are more clues up there about whatever this thing is. I'm all for a good mystery."

So was Paige. Once they arrived at the castle, she couldn't seem to explain why she felt so at home there, as if she knew it, or had at least visited there once even though she hadn't. As she wandered around in the ruined bailey struggling with a strong sense of déjà vu, she noticed that Bodie had climbed the steps to the keep and stood lingering in the keep entry.

She'd seen that before. As Paige stared at Bodie as the man ran his hands along the long-ruined doorway, she knew that she'd see him there before. Her heart began to pound. She didn't know how or why, but she knew she had envisioned that scene before. Something was telling her to run to him, to dash up the stairs and to make it to his side, although she had no idea what odd and impulsive sense was telling her that.

Still, she obeyed, and as she ran up the steps to the keep, it seemed like the most natural thing in the world to do. Instinctively, she knew he would be waiting for her there, and when he turned around and saw her, his arms opened up. Without explanation, without provocation. His arms opened up wide and Paige threw herself into them.

Six years and four kids later, she couldn't have explained that moment if she'd tried. And neither could he.

⌘

Kathryn Le Veque/SERPENT

AUTHOR'S NOTE

I hope you enjoyed Bhrodi and Penelope's story!
As you have discovered, this is a very involved and complex book. Lots
going on! First and foremost, what about that beast? Was it really a
dinosaur? My theory is this – every legend has a basis: dragons,
creatures, ever fairies or elves. Somewhere, somehow, there is a basis
of fact for all things. As for the creature, dinosaurs and other creatures
have survived into our modern times – crocodiles, for instance, and
ants. Yes, ants! They've been on the planet for fifty million years. And
over the past two thousand years, many species have become extinct,
so who's to say that some kind of sauropod didn't survive into
Medieval times as the last of its kind only to die out and become
extinct? That is certainly a question to ponder.
And let's think about this, shall we? Seriously... if you're Edward the
First and you get your ass kicked by a serpent, are you really going to
tell anyone? Of course not! Edward wasn't about to tell anyone he got
creamed by The Serpent. He was right – nobody would have believed
him, anyway.
This book was such a joy to write. William and Jordan are back! And
the camaraderie between William and Paris and Kieran is, I think, some
of the best in any of my books. They would do anything for each other
and their family, their loves, was so very important to them all. I tried
not to make this a "William" book and overshadow Bhrodi, but William
does figure very heavily in the novel and I'm not sorry about it one bit.
Bhrodi and Penelope were definitely left to shine but William had some
opportunity to shine once more as well. Love that guy.
And what about poor Kevin? Is he going to get his own story? You just
never know. I would say odds are that Kevin, too, will eventually have
his happy ending because that guy really grew on me. Now I have to
give him a good adventure!
Much in this book is historically accurate, by the way – Edward's
battles in Wales, the siege of Castell y Bere, the siege of Dolbadarn
Castle, and the eventual capture of Dafydd ap Gruffydd. The time frame
and the locations are accurate, except I added my own characters to the
mix. And did you notice Keir St. Héver making an appearance? Now

The Wolfe is linked to the Dragonblade series. This was pre-Chloe for Keir by about two years.

So, stay tuned for MORE of the Wolfe Pack. Perhaps Kevin's book will make it on to my 2015 release list. Visit my website at www.kathrynleveque.com for any and all updates on new releases. **And now, enjoy bonus chapters from William de Wolfe's novel, THE WOLFE, and Keir St. Hever's novel, FRAGMENTS OF GRACE.**

Bonus chapter #1

THE WOLFE

An Amazon #1 Best Seller in Medieval Historical Romance
145 five-star reviews
"The Best Medieval Romance I've ever read. Period."

§

There upon a midnight blue
The knights went riding two by two
Out upon the moonlit moors
Death consumed them, brought by war
Into their midst, a phantom came
Known by heart, this gentle rain
A lady's name...
A river, she was called
Loved and cherished, one and all
This lady known to knights so bold
This is now the story told.
       ~ Prelude to The Wolfe

CHAPTER ONE

The month of December
Year of our Lord 1231
Skirmish of Bog Wood near Blackadder Water, the England/Scotland
border

"By everything that is holy, I do hate a battle."
A soft female sigh filled the damp and cool air. The reply was harsh.
"So help me, Caladora, if ye faint again I shall take a stick to ye."
Five women stood high atop a hill, looking down upon a grisly scene
far below in what was once a peaceful and serene valley. Where

342

lavender heather used to wash amidst the lush green there were now broken, bloody corpses, the result of a fight that had lasted for a day and a night. Now, everything was eerily still with only the occasional cries of the dying. No more sounds of swords; only the sounds of death.

The sun was beginning to set over the distant hills, casting the valley in a shadowed light. To the women waiting on the high hill, it looked as if Hell itself was setting in to begin claiming its souls. It was ended, this battle; one battle in a mightier war that had been going on for as long as anyone could remember. The war for the Scots border.

The Lady Jordan Scott waited with her aunts and cousins, waiting for the signal from her father that would send them down into the valley to begin assessing their own wounded and making sure any enemy wounded were sent into the netherworld. She hated it; all of it. She hated seeing good men die, watching their life blood drain away and listening to their pleas for help. She hated the bloody English for causing all of this blessed pain and suffering because they believed themselves the superior race. All Scots were wild men in their eyes, unthinking and unfeeling, and somehow the English felt compelled to act as their cage-keeper.

But Jordan was anything but wild and unthinking. She had a heart and a mind and soul, sometimes softer than her clansmen would have liked. As the sun continued to set she pulled the hood of her woolen cloak closer, staving off the chill and the gloom. Just when the wait seemed excessive, a shout from one of her father's men released the dam of women who now poured down into the valley. . As the dusk deepened, the hunt began.

Jordan was one of the last one into the valley, dragging her feet even when her aunts cast her threatening glares. She ignored them. In fact, she moved away from them so they would not watch every move she made, removing her hood and picking her targets among the dead.

Her long, honey-colored hair hung loose about her as she bent over a young man and began to tug on a gold signet ring. It seemed to be securely stuck to his finger and she swallowed hard; her father would expect her to take out her dirk and cut off the finger, throwing the whole thing into her basket.

She wrinkled her nose at that prospect and let the dead hand fall back to the ground. She was not going to cut off the finger no matter what her father said. She didn't have the stomach for it. But the man at her feet suddenly groaned and Jordan startled with fear; without hesitation, she yanked her dirk from its sheath at her forearm plunged the blade deep into his soft neck. The man stilled, silenced forever by the cold steel of her knife.

Gasping with shock, Jordan stared down at the man and could scarcely believe what she had done. She didn't know why she had done it, only that she had been terrified and afraid if she didn't kill the man that he would rise up and kill her. Her breath came in short, horrified pants as she stared down at her kill. *Sweet Jesu'*, had she deteriorated to such a scared rabbit that she would kill before thinking?

In disgust she threw down her dirk and stumbled away from the dead man, wondering if indeed her father's warring ways were claiming her. Already, she had to get away from the destruction and clear her thoughts. She didn't care if her family thought she was weak. They had tried to toughen her up, to make her strong and fearless, but she didn't have it in her. She was sweet and nurturing, kind and gentle. There were those better suited to tend those on the battlefield and cut fingers off for the gold they wore; she was going to find a place to hide and wait until the hunting and killing was over.

Glancing over her shoulder to see if she was being watched, Jordan wandered away from the field of destruction and into a small valley. Nestled at the bottom among a few scrawny trees was a small stream, the water glistening silver in the moonlight.

It was peaceful and calm, and she could feel her composure returning. She knelt by the stream and washed her hands as if cleansing away the confusion and revulsion she felt. She knew she was a disappointment to her father on two accounts: not being born male, and not being able to sufficiently deal with the normal aspects of being a daughter of one of the fiercest war lords on the Scottish border. Although her father loved her dearly and never made her feel anything less, she knew deep down he wished she were stronger. Sometimes she wished it, too.

Her father did not pretend that he always understood his only child, especially where her loves for music and animals were concerned. Jordan could sing like an angel and could dance a Scottish jig like the devil himself, accomplishments for which he was enormously proud, but sometimes he just could not comprehend the female mind. He was a warrior, a baron by title, and his world was one of death and fighting, not the gentle world where his daughter dwelled.

Still, he would not be pleased if he found out she had run off like a scared goat and sought refuge this night. Jordan found a large boulder by the creek and sat on its icy surface, watching the water bubble in the moonlight and wondering why she wasn't like the rest of her female kin, bold and fearless. Above her, a nighthawk rode the drafts, crying out to its mate and she watched it for a moment before returning moodily to the stream.

"If you are thinking of drowning yourself, 'tis a bit shallow."

The voice came from the darkness behind her. Jordan leapt off the rock, terrified as she whirled to face her accoster. She could make out a form of a man lying at the base of one of the bushy trees but could not make out much more in the darkness.

Panic rose in her throat and she realized with deep regret that she had left her dirk back on the battle field. She could scream, but he appeared to be large and would most likely pounce and slit her throat before she could utter a sound. She froze, unsure of what to do next. She certainly did not want to provoke the man with the decidedly English accent.

"What...what do ye want?" she demanded shakily.

The moon emerged from behind the clouds, revealing the landscape in bright silver light. Jordan could see right away the man was gravely injured, as there was a great deal of dark blood covering his legs and the ground beneath him. It didn't take her long to figure out that he was unable to rise much less attack her. Her courage surged and she was sure she could run back and retrieve her dirk before he could move upon her, the damnable English devil. She would do to him exactly what he would do to her given half a chance.

But on the heels of that thought came another. Jordan's blood ran cold with abhorrence; she had just killed one man and punished herself endlessly for it. Now she was planning the death of another. More of her father's violent influence was a part of her than she cared to admit. Perhaps this wounded man was innocent of any killing at all, she thought naïvely. Mayhap he was a victim of the situation, forced to fight by the hated English king. Perhaps he didn't want to fight at all and then found himself a casualty.

Jordan forced herself to calm, realizing that the man could not hurt her. She took a step to get a better look at him yet still kept a healthy distance between them.

"Speak up," she told him, feeling braver. "What are ye doing here? What do ye want?"

She heard the man sigh. "What do I want?" he repeated wearily. "I want to return home. But what I want and what will be are two entirely different things all together. What do you intend to do with me?"

Jordan eyed him beneath the silver moonlight. "I intend to do nothing with ye," she replied softly. I dunna need to. From the looks of that wound, ye will be dead by morn."

The man laid his head back against the tree in a defeated gesture. "Mayhap," he said, eyeing her in the darkness just as she was eyeing him. "Will you tell me something?"

"What?"

"What is your name?"

She saw no harm in giving her name to a dying man. "Jordan."

His head came up from the trunk. "Jordan? A sound name. Yet it is usually a man's name."

Jordan moved a few steps closer. "My mother, being a pious woman, named me for the River Jordan," she replied. "Jordan Mary Joseph is my full name. Moreover, I was intended to be a male child."

The man's eyes grew intense and Jordan felt a shiver run down her spine. It struck her just how handsome he was, English or no, and her cheeks grew warm.

"You are most definitely not a male child, Jordan Mary Joseph," he said, almost seductively. "How old are you?"

"I have seen twenty years," she replied, flattered and disarmed by his statement.

"Then you are married with children," he stated. "Was your husband on the battlefield?"

"I have no husband," Jordan said flatly. At twenty, she was embarrassed that she had not yet wed; it was a sore subject and one she certainly did not wish to discuss with him.

"No husband?" he repeated, evidently shocked. "Why not?"

She frowned. "Ye ask too many questions, English."

He did not reply. He lay back against the tree again, closing his eyes. His strength was draining and Jordan guessed that he would be dead was swiftly approaching.

As she gazed at him, she began to feel pity for the knight. He was perhaps ten years older than her, still a young man. He was very big with enormous hands and big, muscular legs, and his facial features, although surrounded by mail and a helm, were chiseled and handsome. She was coming to feel sorry that his life would soon be over soon from a wound sustained in a senseless, meaningless skirmish.

A thought occurred to her; she knew that she could make his last hours more comfortable with what she carried in her satchel. The healing items were meant for her own people but she simply could not leave the knight and not help him. It was her soft heart tugging at her, concern for another. She hoped her Scot ancestors moldering in the ground would forgive her treasonous act.

"English," she said softly. "Would ye let me tend yer wound?"

One eye opened in mild surprise. She could see suspicion in the mysterious depths.

"Why?" he whispered. "So you may finish what your clansman started?"

"Nay," she answered, although she didn't blame his distrust. "So that I may make yer last hours a bit more bearable." When he did not reply, she frowned at him. "I promise I wunna intentionally hurt ye. Ye can bleed to death or ye can let me help ye; 'tis all the same to me."

After an eternal pause, he reached up with effort and tore the helmet from his head, revealing dark wet hair plastered to his pasty head. Clumsily, he began to remove his armor.

Jordan closed the distance between them with small, rapid steps and knelt beside him. His hands were heavy and unwieldy and she batted them away, finishing the job of the removal herself. She fumbled a bit with his cuisses, or thigh armor, because the wound was along the edge of the armor where it met his breeches. A vulnerable point, she noticed. She felt a little apprehensive being so close to an English warrior and deliberately avoided his gaze. She could feel his eyes on her, watching every move she made. Her palms began to sweat as she stripped off the remainder of the protective gear.

As Jordan bent over her work, her pink tongue between her teeth in concentration, the knight studied the fine porcelain features and the huge round eyes of the most amazing green color. He could see it even in the moonlight. Her eyebrows arched ever-so-delicately and her lashes were long and dense. She had stopped biting her tongue long enough for him to see that her lips were soft and sensuous.

Her hair licked at him as she moved and the scent of lavender was unmistakable. Her hair was dark blond, straight and silky. Every time she threw the satiny mass over her shoulder to keep it out of her way, he was greeted by the perfume of the purple buds and found it utterly captivating. Even as he stared at her, he could not believe this woman was a Scot; she embodied everything he had always believed they were not. In fact, it took him a moment to realize that she was physically perfect. If God himself had come to him and asked him to describe his perfect mate, he would have described Jordan feature for feature. It was an odd realization.

Unaware of the knight's thoughts, Jordan glanced up and met his gaze and was faced with the most fascinating shade of hazel she had ever seen. Yet for his size and his strength, and the fact that the man was obviously a seasoned knight, they were the kindest eyes she had ever encountered. Unnerved, she tore her eyes away and continued her good deed with draining concentration. The man intimidated her in too many ways to comprehend.

The armor off, Jordan could see the wound in his thigh was substantial. He had packed linen rags on it in an attempt to stop the bleeding, but he had quickly become too weak to do much more. It was a deep, long gash that ran nearly the entire length of his long thigh. She tore his breeches away in an attempt to have a clear field to tend the wound, noticing that his legs were as thick as tree trunks.

Jordan picked bits of material and mail from the wound, wiping at the clotted blood and dirt that had invaded the area. The further involved she became, the more she could see that the gash was all the way to the bone.

Jordan retrieved her bag and began to pull out her aids; whisky, silk thread and needle, and strips of boiled linen.

"Here," she said, thrusting the open whisky bottle at him and keeping her eyes on the wound. "Drink this."

He accepted the bottle from her and he took several long swallows. She took it back from him and set it beside her, pausing with a furrowed brow and thinking that even if he survived the wound, he would surely loose the leg. She did not know that he was still watching her face intently, marveling at the incredible beauty of it.

The knight, in fact, did not make it a habit of gawking at women. Outside of an occasional whore, he had never had a remotely serious relationship with a woman, although there had been many a female who had tried to woo him. He had a great deal of respect for the opposite sex, but Northwood Castle was his life and a wife did not fit into his plans.

"Will I live, Lady Jordan?" he asked after a moment. "Or should I prepare my greeting for St. Peter?"

She sighed and picked up the whisky bottle. Reluctantly, she met his eyes for a brief moment to convey a silent apology before dousing the entire length of the wound with the burning alcohol.

The knight's only reaction was to snap his head away from her so that she could not see his face. Not a sound was uttered nor a twitch of the muscle seen. *Remarkable*, she thought. She had never seen anyone take the pain of a whisky burn so well.

Some women preferred to wash the whisky away with water before closing the wound, but not Jordan. The liquor itself did incredibly well in helping heal wounds and preventing infection, so she left it on and took her threaded needle and began to sew up the laceration. She worked quickly, knowing the pain was unbearable and was continually amazed that the soldier had yet to utter one word. She had seen men scream and faint in similar situations.

When she was finally finished, she laid a strip of clean linen the length of the wound and bound him twice about the thigh to hold it in place, once at the top of his leg and once near the knee. She worked so fast that she knew she was not doing a very good job, just wanting to be done with her charitable act hurriedly lest she be discovered. She was increasingly concerned that her aunts and cousins would come looking for her. She knew that jostling him about must be excruciating, yet he had not so much as flinched.

Only when she had stopped completely did he turn his head back to look at her, and she swallowed at the agony she read in his eyes. She found new respect for this Englishman who bore his pain with stoic silence. She began to hope that he would live, although she did not know why. She furthermore wished she had done a better mending job on his leg, taking the time she took with her own wounded.

"I dunna know what good I have done for ye," she said quietly.

He grasped her soft hand tightly in his clammy one. Jordan stiffened, startled by the action and fighting the urge to yank her hand away.

"You are an angel of mercy," he whispered. "I thank you for your efforts, my lady. I shall do my best not to betray them."

His sincerity was gripping. Gently, she removed her hand and put her things away. The half-moon was high above and the scattered clouds had disappeared, bathing the land in a silver glow. Jordan felt as if she had done something good this night, albeit to the enemy and she felt better now than she had earlier when she first descended to the stream. Mayhap fate had led her to the stream purposely to find the soldier and tend him. She suddenly felt like returning to the battlefield to continue with her expected duties.

"I must return, English." She rose and gave him a long look. "I will forget that I saw ye here."

She turned to leave but he stopped her.

"My name is Sir William de Wolfe," he said with quiet authority. "Remember it, for I shall return one day to thank you properly and I do not wish to be cut down while bearing a gift."

It took a moment, but even in the moonlight he saw her face go white and her jaw slacken.

"*Sweet Jesu',*" she gasped. "Surely ye're not the English captain they call The Wolf?"

He looked at her, sensing her surge of fear. He sighed; he did not want her to fear him. This was the one time when he wished his reputation had not preceded him.

"I simply said my name was de Wolfe, not *The Wolf*," he murmured.

She looked extremely dubious. "But ye were in his command?"

He shrugged vaguely. "Now, back to what I said," he said, shifting the subject. "I will return with a proper reward for you. Will you accept it?"

She could not be sure that the knight wasn't, in fact, the hated Wolf, but it was truly of no matter now. It was done. Perhaps she did not want to believe he was the hated and feared devil, so she chose to believe as such. How could she live with herself if it was discovered that she had tended to the man that had killed more kinsmen that she could count? She knew she could not, so she forced herself to believe his words. Furthermore, her aunt had said The Wolf was dark and devilish. This man was uncannily beautiful in a masculine sense.

After a moment's pause, she finally spoke. "English, if ye survive this wound then I will gladly accept yer gift."

He smiled weakly, deep dimples in both cheeks and her heart fluttered strangely in her chest. He was indeed the most handsome man she had ever seen, even if he was English. But she had the most horrible lurking feeling that he was indeed who she feared he was. It made her want to run.

"Luck be with ye," she said as she abruptly turned and trudged back up the hill.

William watched the figure in the billowing cloak, his pain-clouded mind lingering on the silken hair and beautiful face. He had never seen such a fine woman. Angel was certainly an apt term. If she were to be the last person he saw on earth then he would die a contented man.

He suspected that she did not believe his evasive answer but, thankfully, had made no more mention of it. The thought that she feared and hated him brought a curious tightness in his stomach that he quickly attributed to his helpless state. He did not want to admit that it might be regret.

He was growing weaker with each breath. His strength was waning as he leaned back against the tree, wondering if he would again see the light of morning. He closed his eyes for he could not keep them open, and without realizing it, his mind drifted into unconsciousness, safe and warm and dark.

§

Bonus chapter #2

FRAGMENTS OF GRACE
Prequel to the DRAGONBLADE series
12 five-star reviews
"A beautifully written 13th Century romance"

(Make note that this book is classified as a tragedy but with a positive, bittersweet ending).

CHAPTER ONE

September 1294 A.D.
The siege of Exelby Castle

"You have your orders, St. Hèver," an older, much muddied warrior snapped at Keir. "Get moving."

Keir's jaw ticked but it was difficult to see beneath his wet and dirty hauberk. He said nothing in response, knowing his liege knew how he felt but disregarding his feelings completely. They had a job to do.

It had been raining heavily for three days, turning the ground in and around Exelby Castle into a quagmire of putrid muck. The army from Aysgarth Castle, seat of Baron Coverdale, was well acquainted with the mud and its detriment to a successful siege. The baron's powerful army could not move their five big siege engines into position because the mud was so thick, so the archers had taken to shooting heavily oiled projectiles over the wall in the hopes that they would burn long enough in the heavy rain to do some damage. This madness had gone on for two long days.

Keir had charge of the portcullis and the great iron and wooden grate had been heavily bombarded by flame, followed by the battering ram to twist the heated iron. Keir was methodical and skilled in his approach and made sure to keep the enemy soldiers on the battlements above the gate out of range by regular barrages from the archers. Over the course of the two days, wild wind and driving rain, Keir and his men were able to bend the portcullis enough so that two men at a time could squeeze through, and that was exactly what Baron Coverdale had in mind.

By dawn of the third day, the castle was finally breached. Now, Coverdale was shouting orders to Keir who was extremely reluctant to do as he was told. But Baron Coverdale, Lord Byron de Tiegh, was in no mood for disobedient knights. He was ready to be finished with this obligatory support of Exelby and return home to a warm fire and his young wife with her big, warm breasts.

"Take Pembury and de Velt with you," Coverdale barked again, scratching at his dirty, wet scalp before pulling his hauberk back on. "Get inside and get those women or Lord de Geld will lose his entire family. Of all people, surely you can understand what it means to face the loss of one's family, St. Hèver."

It was a tactless remark, one that had Keir's unusually cool temper rising. He felt disgusted and sick. Coverdale was a good commander but an insensitive man. Frustrated but driven by his sense of duty, Keir stormed off with Pembury and de Velt following, marching across the muck, puddles of urine and rivers of blood, until he came within range of the gatehouse. Keir's men were already gathered there, all one hundred and nine of them, awaiting direction from their liege.

Keir reached his men, standing beneath a pair of denuded oak trees, and bellowed orders to them, courtesy of Coverdale. They were to breach the keep and find Lord de Geld's wife and two daughters. De Geld was the lord of Exelby, his castle having been attacked and overrun in nearly the same situation that Pendragon had been those years ago. A neighboring war lord, covetous of de Geld's very rich castle and lands, had waited until the old man was away on business before laying siege and conquering. Coverdale, an old friend of de Geld's, had been tasked with regaining the fortress.

Infuriated and exhausted, St. Hèver was the first man through the twisted wreckage of the portcullis. He was immediately set upon by defenders but Keir had the advantage of tremendous size, strength and height. He was moderately tall, but the sheer breadth and circumference of his arms and chest made him a man above men. As he plowed his way through the gatehouse, he used his sword and fists to drive away attackers. Pembury and de Velt were right behind him, powerful and skilled men in their own right.

Miraculously, they made it through the gate house without injury. Considering those who held the castle were using the murder holes in the gatehouse entry to their advantage, it was something of a feat. Bursting into the cluttered and muddy bailey, which was oddly empty,

Keir directed more than half of his men to take the walls while he took another twenty men with him and headed towards the keep.

They fought their way through enemy soldiers, having suddenly appeared from the interior of the keep. The soldiers came rushing down at them from the keep entry, down the narrow wooden retractable stairs that were half-burned, and Keir found himself slugging men in the face and throwing them over the railing.

Because the stairs were so precarious, they could only mount them in single file and Keir was at the head, taking the brunt of the warriors coming at them. At one point, an enemy soldier managed to send him off-balance and he gripped the railing, almost falling fifteen or so feet down to the muddy bailey, but he managed to hold on to the broken railing even in the wet rain that was making everything dangerously slippery. Pembury, a mountain of a man with enormous fists, pushed forward and took the lead, throwing men aside with his enormous strength. De Velt pulled Keir away from the edge and steadied him and the three knights, along with their men at arms, continued up the stairs and eventually in to the keep.

As Keir slugged men with his big fists and fought off broadswords that were flying at him, he let his rage and frustration get the better of him. He didn't want to be here in the midst of this stupid skirmish and he certainly didn't want to be tasked with rescuing women. He didn't want to rescue anyone. He wanted to get out of this mess and return to Pendragon and resume his patrols for Coverdale. A siege is the last thing he wanted to participate in, much less be charged with. As he plowed his way into the keep and met with more violent resistance, he could only think one thing.

Damn Coverdale, he hissed to himself. *Damn the man to hell.*

***

She was waiting for them.

Braced in the large bed chamber at the top of Exelby's towering keep, she was waiting with an enormous piece of wood in her hands, the only weapon they could find in the room. It was her parents' chamber, a luxurious place with fine silks, furniture and under normal circumstances, a warm fire, but this day saw the chamber something of a gloomy and fearful place.

Chloë de Geld could hear men on the other side of the chamber door. They had been attempting to open it for the better part of two days but the panel was made from heavy oak reinforced with strips of iron, bolted together so that it formed a sort of net. The enemy had tried to burn away part of the door but it was so dense and old that it simply smoldered and glowed, falling away piece by piece and filling the chamber with a thin layer of smoke that hung near the ceiling. Yet even when the door burned away, the strips of iron would hold fast and would not allow the door to be opened. At least, that was at theory. Up until today, the theory had never been tested.

So Chloë stood against the wall near the door, club held at the ready and struggling to keep her sister calm. Cassandra was the skittish sort, like their father, whereas Chloë was calm and composed, like their mother. Even now, Lady Blanche de Geld sat in the corner and worked her needle and thread against an elaborately embroidered piece of linen, as cool as a lazy cat on a warm summer day.

Chloë stood near the door, preparing to beat to death anyone who entered the chamber and wondering if her mother even understood what was happening. There was calm composure and then there was pure apathy. Chloë had to shake her head at her mother, wondering which one it really was.

The door panel suddenly shook heavily, as if something had been thrown against it. Chloë and Cassandra shrieked with fear while their mother barely looked up from her needlework. . The door rattled again and a huge chunk of it fell away, revealing those on both sides of the door. Gloves fingers began to poke through the iron grate, moving for the lock, and Chloë began clubbing the fingers with wild abandon.

Someone on the opposite side of the door grunted with pain as his fingers were smacked. He tried to thrust his fingers through again and Chloë bashed his fingers furiously.

"Nay!" she shrieked, punctuating each word with a smack from the club. "Nay, nay, *nay*!"

"Lady!" the knight on the other side of the door roared. "Cease! I am here to rescue you!"

Chloë didn't believe him for a moment. More fingers were coming through the grate and she smashed at them as if killing ugly spiders on the wall. *Smack, smack, smack*!

"Nay!" she barked. "Go away!"

As Chloë bashed at the grate with her club, convinced that she was the only thing that stood between her family and complete obliteration, Keir was tired of getting his fingers smashed so he shoved de Velt forward.

"Open the door," he growled.

Lucan looked at him as if he was mad. "Nay, *you* open the door. I do not want my fingers broken."

Frustrated, Keir grabbed him by the neck as Pembury charged at the door, shoving them both out of the way. He grabbed at the iron grate and got his fingers smashed for his trouble. He drew his hands back, shaking out his bashed fingers.

"Foolish wench," he yelled at Chloë. "That bloody well hurt."

On the other side of the blackened iron, Chloë was unrepentant. "Touch this door again and I will pound your fingers into dust."

Michael stared at her in disbelief; he could see a portion of her face through the grate and long, shimmering sheets of deep red hair. One big brown eye was gazing back at him.

"Do you not understand that we are trying to save you?" he asked, incredulous.

On the opposite side of the door, Chloë shook her head, gripping the club with white knuckles. "You are attempting to coerce me into opening this door," she spat. "I am not so idiotic that I would believe you."

"But it is true."

"Liar!"

Michael put his hands on his hips, looking to Keir. "Well?" he lifted a frustrated hand at the half-demolished door. "What do you want to do?"

Keir's frustration was driven beyond endurance. He was struggling to accomplish an unwanted assignment and meeting with great resistance. It would have been extremely easy to walk away and tell Coverdale that the women were beyond recovery. But he gave it one last try. He'd come this far. Moreover, he wasn't accustomed to failure and to walk away would mean surrender. He moved to the grate, shoving Michael aside.

"Listen to me and listen well," he growled to the brown eye staring back at him. "My name is Keir St. Hèver and I have been battling to free Exelby for the better part of two days. We have chased off, killed or captured most of the fools who invaded your castle and the last thing I need is a foolish wench resisting my efforts to help her. I can just as easily walk away and leave you here to rot if that is your wish."

"Walk away, then! We do not need or want your help!"

Keir clenched his teeth, struggling with his temper. "You are behaving most ungratefully towards men who have risked their lives to save you."

As Keir spoke, Lucan moved up on his right side and, with stealth, reached for the iron grate. As Keir held the frightened lady's attention, Lucan managed to get his fingers through the grate with great care and carefully lift the bolt. Keir was barely finished with what he had to say when Lucan suddenly threw his big shoulder into the door and the panel popped open.

Cassandra screamed as Chloë began swinging the club with all her might. She caught Lucan on the back of the head, sending the man to the ground.

Keir charged in and made a swipe for the weapon, but Chloë was fast and she darted out of his range, jumping on the fluffy bed in the middle of the chamber and swinging the club with all her might. Keir put up an arm to deflect the blow but she still managed to clip not only his elbow but his head.

Furious, Keir grabbed the club from her hand and tossed it away, hitting Pembury in the process. As Michael grunted from the blow to his chest, Keir leapt onto the bed as Chloë tried to jump to the floor and he caught her around the waist, a wisp of a woman with a head full of intense red hair that tumbled to her knees. The straight, silky strands were over them both as he lost his balance and fell back onto the straw-stuffed bed. In fact, there was hair in his mouth and all over his face as he struggled to get hold of Chloë as she fought for her life.

"Lady," he grunted as she twisted and fought. "Cease your struggles. I swear that you will come to no harm. We serve Lord Coverdale and have come to rescue you."

Chloë was in a world of panic. The knight that had her was easily three times her size and she managed to turn in his arms, throwing a hand up into the open faceplate of his visor. Hit in the face by her fists, Keir did nothing more than grunt. He tried to stand up with the snarling wildcat in his grip but he ended up tripping on her surcoat and they both fell to the floor.

Keir fell on top of Chloë, who ended up on her back. It was a hard fall that momentarily stunned her. Moreover, Keir was an enormous man and his full weight came down on her, armor and all. Suddenly, they were in a very intimate position and when Chloë regained her senses, she went mad, beating at his head and shoulders with her little fists.

"Get off me!" she howled. "You foul beast, get *off*!"

Keir was trying to capture the fifty slapping hands that were flying at his face from all directions. He managed to capture one only to be struck by another. Chloë began gouging at his eyes and he closed them both, pressing his face into her chest as he grabbed for that one final hand in the darkness. Beneath him, the lady's body was soft and supple, but he wasn't thinking about that. He was thinking about trying not to go blind from her frantic fingers.

"Cease!" he finally roared as he captured the last errant hand. He pinned her arms on either side of her slender body, daring to open his eyes and gaze down into her hair-covered face. "Did you not understand me? We are here to rescue you. We are not here to harm you in any way but from the way you are fighting, it will more than likely be me who ends up injured."

Chloë wasn't ready to surrender to the strange knight with the smooth, deep voice. "Get *off*," she commanded.

"Not until you stop fighting me. I have no desire to be maimed by a foolish girl."

"I am not foolish," she grunted as she tried to dislodge him.

He watched her face contort with effort. "You are indeed foolish when you fight against someone who is attempting to help you."

She looked at him, barring her straight white teeth. "I do not know you. You could be lying for all I know, an enemy with the devil's tongue."

"Yet I am not," he said as he cocked an eyebrow at her. "I told you who I am – I am Keir St. Hèver, a much decorated warrior who has served Edward Longshanks in the wars in Wales. I am an honorable knight from a long line of honorable knights and your refusal to believe my word is a direct insult. I do not lie and I certainly would not lie to a lady. In any case, you are trapped by a man who is a good deal larger and stronger than you are so if I were you, I would no longer resist. It is futile."

Chloë's struggle ground to a halt and she gazed up at Keir with baleful eyes. He could only see two big brown orbs through the mess of long red hair that was all over them both. Keir could see the turmoil in the brown depths, swirling like a maelstrom, but in that same thought, it occurred to him that they were the most beautiful eyes he had ever seen. The thought startled him.

"Do you understand what I have told you?" he asked again, somewhat less hostile, wondering why he was so mesmerized by those eyes.

Chloë nodded unsteadily. "Are you going to strike me again?" he asked.

She shook her head. Keir immediately let go of her arms and, out of necessity, began pulling strands of long red hair out of his mail so he could stand up and not pull hair from her scalp. Chloë watched him with some fear as he pushed himself off of her. Then he took her by the wrist and pulled her to her feet.

Now that the atmosphere was somewhat calmer and the women realized that the enemy had not captured them after two days of hell, Chloë seemed rather weak and unsteady. It was as if the fight had taken everything out of her. He slumped against the wall, exhaling heavily as she pushed her hair from her face and tried to smooth it down. The long, luxurious red hair was her pride and joy, something she was almost as well known for in the shire as her beauty. To those in West Yorkshire, Chloë de Geld's radiance was the stuff of legends.

It was something that had not escaped Keir's notice, try as he might. He was still frustrated, angry and exhausted, but somewhere in the mix, he realized that he had interest in the lady's fine looks. Rescuing a hag would have been a duty but rescuing an angel was something entirely different. He should have had the same opinion for either, but the truth was most men would prefer to associate with a lovely young lady to an old haggard one. It was beastly but true.

The lady in front of him was average in height but slender in build, with large soft breasts that he had felt against him when he had fallen on top of her. Even through the mail and layers of tunics, he had felt them. Her skin was pale, like cream, and she had a perfectly formed face with porcelain skin and full pink lips. But the eyes that gazed back at him had his attention, a shade of brown that was as deep and brilliant as a gemstone. They were big and beautiful. Keir watched the woman as she struggled to recover her composure.

"What is your name?" he finally asked.

She looked up at him. "I am the Lady Chloë de Geld," she murmured in a sweet, silky voice. "My father is Anton de Geld, Baron Kirklington.

This is my mother, the Lady Blanche, and my sister, the Lady Cassandra."

Chloë. It was all Keir heard. The rest sounded like mumble after that - *I am the Lady Chloë blah, blah, blah.* He snapped his fingers at Pembury and de Velt, indicating that each man take a lady in hand, and the two of them rushed to see who would be the one to escort the Lady Cassandra, a pretty blond with her sister's big brown eyes. Michael was a shade faster than Lucan, collecting the lady by the elbow and sneering at Lucan over the top of her head.

Truth was, Pembury was a massive man of great power and even Lucan de Velt, a man of considering strength and skill himself, would not voluntarily tangle with him. So he grudgingly took charge of the mother, an older woman who had sat in the corner doing her needlework while a battle raged on around her. During the entire time Chloë and Keir had scuffled, the woman hadn't moved.

Quietly, Lucan helped the old woman to stand, even helped her with her sewing, which he found a rather ridiculous hobby in the midst of a battle, and followed Pembury from the chamber. He even smacked the man in the back of the head when no one was looking.

With everyone gone and the noise from the fighting faded into nothingness, the chamber was suddenly very still. Chloë was still leaning against the wall, feeling weak and weary as Keir moved to the door, adjusting the helm on his head that she had so furiously smacked. As he fumbled with the hauberk beneath it, adjusting it, he turned to Chloë.

"Come along, my lady," he said quietly.

She looked up from where she had been staring the floor. "Where are you taking us?"

"That is for Lord Coverdale and your father to decide."

She sighed faintly and pushed herself up off the wall, looking around the room as if searching for something. "My father was in Darlington when all of this started," she murmured. "Is the castle badly damaged?"

Keir finished fiddling with his mail. "Badly enough," he told her. "It is not safe as it stands."

She looked at him and he noted the sad brown eyes. They were such lovely eyes, he thought, but just as quickly jolted himself from that line of thought. He'd thought it once before and that was forgivable, a natural reaction. But to think it twice was unnerving. It was too shocking and painful to even consider. He hadn't thought on a lovely woman since....

"Who attacked us?" Chloë asked.

Keir realized he was struggling not to feel something soft or compassionate for the woman. It was purely based on her beauty, he knew that, but he was feeling something warm nonetheless. He was furious at himself, sick to his stomach, realizing he was weak and foolish to think such things. It was ridiculous. Taking a deep breath, he labored to shake off both the foolishness and fatigue.

"They came from Sandhutton," he told her. "We believe Ingilby is involved."

Chloë's big brown eyes widened. "Baron Ingilby from Ripon?"

"The same."

Her pretty, shapely mouth popped open in both outrage and surprise. Then she closed her mouth and turned away, returning with distraction to her search of the room. Keir stood by the door, watching her, as she came across what she had apparently been searching for.

She shook out the cloak that had been wedged in behind her mother's sewing chair, silently moving for the door as she swung it around her slender shoulders. Keir didn't touch her as he preceded her from the room; not an elbow to take or an arm to hold. He was afraid of what would happen to his exhaustion-fed thoughts if he touched her again.

Just as they were passing through the doorway, past the twisted charred wreckage of the chamber door, Chloë suddenly came to a halt and looked at him.

"Did I hurt your fingers?" she asked.

She seemed rather dull and somber, not at all like the firebrand who had given him a fight moments before. He gazed steadily at her.

"Nay, lady, you did not."

She simply nodded, looking rather contrite. "I am sorry... well, if I hurt you," she turned around and headed towards the stairs. "You must understand that strange and violent men have been attempting to get into the chamber for the better part of two days."

He watched her luscious red head as it began to descend the stairs. "I would imagine you would not have made it easy for them if they had managed to breach the door."

In spite of her fatigue, Chloë smiled faintly. "A piece of wood is no match for a man with a sword."

Keir grunted in disagreement. "You under estimate yourself, lady," he said as they came to the landing on the third floor. "You are a formidable foe. My fingers can attest to that."

Her grin broadened and she turned to look at him. "You still managed to capture me."

Keir's heart beat strangely at the sight of her smile, as beautiful and shapely as the rest of her. He shrugged, fighting down the confusing feelings brewing. "Perhaps," he muttered. "But I almost lost an eye doing it."

That comment made her peer more closely at him, noting his ice blue eyes, so pale they were nearly white. "One of them is rather red," she admitted. "I am sorry if I injured your eyes."

Keir almost took a step back as she leaned in to get a better look at his eyes, a natural reaction when something perfect and awe-inspiring makes its presence known. Already, he was fearful of the woman, one who could stir feelings in his chest without even trying. He didn't want to have anything to do with her but on the other hand, in the few minutes he had known her, she had captured his attention no matter how resistant he was. It was an odd amalgamation of curiosity and fear.

"I am fine," he reiterated.

He directed her towards the next flight of stone spiral stairs, this one leading down to the entry level of the dark and smoky keep. Chloë took the lead once again, followed by Keir who was trying very hard not to look at her or touch her in any way.

"I have not seen you before," she made conversation with him, perhaps out of guilt for having nearly blinded the man. "My father and Lord Coverdale have been allies for years. Lord Coverdale visits often and I thought I had seen all of his knights."

Keir had to pick up the hem of her cloak so he wouldn't step on it. "I am a garrison commander for Coverdale," he told her. "Usually, I am at my post. I do not make Aysgarth Castle my home."

"Where is your post?" she looked at him, an innocent question.

He held up the edge of her cloak as he took the stairs. "Coverdale's garrison in Cumbria."

She nodded in understanding. "I see," she said as they reached the entry level. "Did he recall you to help regain my father's castle?"

Keir let go of the cloak, allowing himself to look her in the face. He could feel his palms start to sweat and his heart beat pick up again at the sight.

363

"I was at Aysgarth already when one of your father's men came with the request to bear arms," he told her. "My presence here is purely by chance."

Chloë smiled. "Then we are most fortunate for your assistance, Sir Keir," she said. "I am sorry we had to meet under such strenuous circumstances but it was very nice to make your acquaintance. I hope that you do not hold the first few violent moments of our association against me."

Keir stared at her. She was sweet, intelligent and well spoken, something he found deeply attractive. She had such a sweet little voice, like the tinkle of tiny silver bells, and he swore he could have listened to that voice forever. As he opened his mouth to reply, he heard a roar off to his left and he turned to see a soldier he did not recognize charge from a shadowed alcove, a heavy broadsword leveled.

Keir grabbed Chloë and pulled her away from the door, shoving her back behind him as he unsheathed his sword. He brought the weapon up just as the soldier brought his blade down, and sparks flew as metal upon metal met in the darkness of the entry hall.

He was at a disadvantage with a lady to protect in a small space, but he made the best of it. Lashing out a massive boot, he kicked the man in the legs, sending him backwards, and went on the attack. Keir brought his blade down twice in heavy succession, eventually knocking the weapon from the hands of his weaker opponent. Then he grabbed the man by the head, pointing the tip of his razor-sharp blade at the man's neck.

"Mercy, milord, mercy," the soldier threw up his hands, begging. "Don't kill me!"

Keir was emotionless and professional. Simply from the man's rough pattern of speech, he realized that he wasn't an educated or particularly intelligent warrior. He was simply a servant, doing as he was told. A more experienced man would have given him a better fight. Keir tossed him to the floor and put an enormous boot on the man's neck.

"Who do you serve?" he asked.

The man could barely breathe. "I... I...."

The boot pressure grew stronger. "Answer me or I will end your life now."

The man was struggling. "In...gilby...."

Although they already knew as much, it was confirmation. Keir never took his eyes off his captive.

"What were your orders?"

The man was squirming, his face turning shades of red. "I.... don't...."

Keir put more pressure on the man's neck. "Your orders or you die."

"The... *goddess!*" the man croaked.

Keir cocked his head. "The goddess?" he repeated, confused. "Who is the goddess?"

Out of the shadows, they both heard the response.

"The goddess is me."

δ

Read the rest of FRAGMENTS OF GRACE and THE WOLFE on Amazon in Kindle format and in paperback.

29296637R00204

Made in the USA
San Bernardino, CA
20 January 2016